The Best is yet to
Come! Love Ya both.
Norma Jean

Promises to Keep

Norma J. Singleton

Copyright © 2011 Norma J. Singleton
All rights reserved.

Barringer Publishing, Naples, Florida
www.barringerpublishing.com
Cover, graphics, layout design by Lisa Camp
Editing by Carole Greene

ISBN: 978-0-9833088-5-0

Library of Congress Cataloging-in-Publication Data
Promises to Keep / Norma J. Singleton

Printed in U.S.A.

IN GOD WE TRUST

Dedication

It is with honor, I dedicate this book to the wonderful friends who inspired me to write this story. It is their wish to remain unknown. To Joyce McDonald, a talented writer and dear friend, who helped me through my frustrations and urged me to keep writing. She is an angel sent by God. Most of all, to my love, Lloyd Hamilton who with his endless patience put up with the long hours I spent writing this novel.

Chapter 1

Eric Adams was going to bag a moose today, for his friend Jim, or die trying. If he'd known how close to the truth that promise would become, he might have changed his mind. But Jim knew him as self confident, persistent, and proud—almost to the point of egoism. Eric could do anything he set his mind to.

Perched in a tree, near where moose come to feed, his eyes scanned the area. *What a beautiful place,* he thought, even here in the slough, with the birch trees and the pines, like the one he was sitting in to await the coming of a magnificent moose. It boosted his ego to have Jim ask him to help bag the yearly moose he needed to get his family through the Alaskan winter. Eric had already secured the winter stores for his family, so now he needed to come through for Jim. The winter chill was already in the air, and soon the snows would come.

He checked everything again to be sure he was in position to have a good clean shot. However, he wasn't happy where he was sitting. Seeing a nearby birch tree with a perfect landing spot as well as a clear view of the slough, he prepared to make a leap. He sailed through the air with confidence, as he had done many times before. As his feet hit the landing spot, the horrifying sound of dead timber breaking beneath his weight signaled he was in trouble! As he fell limbs whipped at his body. He frantically grabbed for anything to break his fall. Smaller limbs slashed at his face and head. He bounced off larger limbs until he landed at the base of the tree with a hard thud. His head whipped backward, his neck and shoulders smacking against a leaf-covered stump. Sudden pain in his spine wrenched his body. Stars exploded in his head. The trees above were spiraling as blackness threatened. Fighting to stay conscious, with blood running down his face, he called out, "Jim! Help!"

Hearing the cracking noise and thinking it could be a moose charging through the slough, Jim turned in time to see Eric fall. Practically leaping from his tree, he rushed over to help him. "Eric, my God. What happened? You're bleeding! Are you hurt?"

"Don't move me," whimpered Eric, "I'm hurt bad. I tried wiping the blood off my face, but I couldn't move my arms! Then I tried to push myself up against the tree with my feet. I couldn't move my legs! Go! Go now! Call Medivac to come and get me out!"

"Okay, I'm on my way!" Jim wiped the blood from Eric's face, checked his gun, laid it beside him and then took off running, shouting as he ran. "We'll get you out of here and to a hospital. Don't worry. Stay alert. I'll be back shortly, with help."

To keep awake, Eric began to think, trying to keep his mind occupied and off the pain in his neck. It was an unusual Alaskan September, with temperatures spiking from bitter cold to warm, as the early morning sun helped take the previous night's chill from the air. He thought, *What a way to spend the day, here in God's country doing what I love to do best, helping a friend hunt his yearly moose. But now this! I didn't even ask Laura if she needed me to do anything at home. I just up and yelled to her that I was going hunting with Jim. Oh well, she never minded, at least she never said anything; it didn't matter anyway, I'm here now. Yeah! Boy! Just look at me now! I'll bet she'll say plenty. Why didn't I say no to Jim and stay home? Wonder what time it is? I can't even move to see my watch.*

A slight breeze wafted leaves over and around him. He felt himself losing control; the pain in his spine was so severe he hyperventilated. His thoughts came in earnest now. *I've got to keep control... been in bad spots in Vietnam and kept control. Can't get overly excited... got to stay calm and breathe slowly. But what if they can't find me? What if Jim has trouble getting back? He's from Kansas and used to hunting only pheasant and rabbits, and not quite used to our Alaskan terrain.*

As thoughts raced around his mind, his breathing quickened again. *Stop it! Stop! Breathe slowly! Just the way Laura and I learned as a way to ease the pain when she was having our babies.*

Oh, Lord! Laura and the girls! How will I care for them if I can't move? They really are the most important things in my life. Why'd I come today? Why didn't I stay around the house and cut that extra wood for winter? Why was hunting and fishing so important? Laura and the girls never held me back from it. They've never kept me from doing what I loved. I guess I was selfish in that respect. I love them so. Why didn't I tell them that more often? Guess I was always putting me first.

The pain was becoming more intense now. Fear nipped at the corners of his mind. *Will I be this way the rest of my life?* His body was beginning to tingle now. He began to feel drowsy. *Must stay awake!* He thought of Vietnam and his best buddy Carl who had been shot during a 'recon' mission. Carl reacted much the same way. He remembered how he kept shouting to him, "Stay with me, Carl! Stay with me!" *Carl kept saying he felt tingly and cold and he began to shake violently. Soon he was gone.*

He'd held Carl close to him as he rocked his lifeless body and he whispered to him, *I'll keep the promise we made to each other and go to Alaska when I get out.* He did keep that promise, but was it to end here? Eric felt he was beginning to shake a little despite the fact that the sun was warm. His only thought was he must stay awake.

He lay there thinking about earlier that morning, *Laura and I talking about how summer had come and gone; how the wood was cut and laid up for the long winter ahead; the garden that yielded such a fruitful bounty was stripped of its prized production, which was safely canned or in the freezer. He thought of how he'd bagged and prepared their yearly quota of moose and put it away in their winter stores, as well as the salmon that Laura had canned and put in the pantry. The lupines and wild roses were long past the bloom stage, the fireweed had already gone to seed, and the sound of the wind hinted of winter. They were ready. It was the first time since they had moved to Alaska six years ago that they were completely ready and felt comfortable about the long winter that was fast approaching.*

He also thought of how Laura had fixed them a hearty breakfast and then fired up the stove again to set about making bread for the week, all the while she had a bear stew simmering. *It was so like her, always being the dutiful wife, so good about being there for people. She never had to face the hardships she went through when we moved to Alaska. I never thought once about how she'd get along when I'd go off on my jaunts. What'll she do now? How will she handle this news if I can't move or be able to take care of things? How will she manage with two babies, so young, so young, just two and four?*

When Jim came along and asked me to go with him, I called to her saying I was going hunting and left. Why didn't I tell Jim no? I could have told him where to go to find moose.

The leaves were blowing harder now and beginning to cover him completely. He tried to shake free of them but couldn't move.... He could not move!

Jim was still breathless from his three mile run to the jeep when he pulled up in front of the Adams' cabin. He drove up so fast that Laura came running out to see what the commotion was about. Seeing Jim alone, with worry written all over his face, her heart jumped into her throat. She sensed something was terribly wrong, "Jim, where's Eric? What's happened?"

Jumping out of the jeep, Jim grabbed her by the shoulders and held her, "Now stay calm; you have to keep your head about you!" He felt her body tense up as his words came pouring out. "Eric fell from a tree and is badly injured. He can't move his arms or legs; we must get Medivac to him right away!"

Even though Laura was a nurse, her first reaction was to cry out a barrage of questions. "Oh no! Where's he now? How is he? Is he conscious? Is he bleeding?" Tears welled up in her eyes, as fear set in. She knew she must immediately call the state troopers to transport Eric out of the woods. Her years of training as a nurse returned and she took charge. "Come in. I'll call Medivac and tell them to come here to get you; you'll need to show the pilot where Eric is, in the woods. Warm yourself with some coffee while I call."

After knowing that help was on the way, she nervously set about to get a sitter for their two girls. She called Mary and Patty to her, hugged them, and then dialed her nearest neighbor and friend, Connie. After a short, tearful conversation she hung up, wiped her eyes, blew her nose, and stood wringing her hands. She didn't know what to do next.

She stooped to the girls and spoke softly to them. "Your daddy has been hurt and I must go to him. Connie or Sam will come and take you home with them. I'll call Connie after I see your daddy, to let you know how he's doing." She gave them their dolls to hug. "Here, hold onto your dollies and don't worry. Daddy will be okay and so will we. Connie will be here soon." She turned to look out the window, so the girls wouldn't see her cry.

Clearing her throat, Laura turned to Jim. "Connie said that she'd come over to get them and take them home with her. Since we don't know what's going to happen next, it would be better to have them with her and Sam."

Jim wiped away Laura's tears now falling in a constant stream, even though she appeared to be calm. "It's okay to cry; no one can blame you for that, but I know you don't want to upset the girls more."

Laura nodded and a tiny smile thanked Jim for his comfort. "When Connie comes, I'll go to the hospital and wait. I know the hospital in Soldotna is equipped and staffed to handle a serious injury. Make sure Eric goes there."

Jim, knowing she was worried about what she'd do if something happened to Eric, spoke softly to her, "Laura, let's ask God to give each of us the strength and courage needed to get through the next few hours and days to come."

"Oh, yes, I'd like that." She called the girls to her. They gathered close and prayed for guidance, strength, and care when they heard the sounds of the helicopter landing outside the cabin. At the same time, Connie was driving up. Help had arrived.

The leaves of the birch trees had nearly covered Eric. Between that and the rust colored plaid shirt he had on, he was well camouflaged, making it very difficult for the rescue team to spot him. When he first heard the helicopter, he was relieved. *But they aren't landing? Can't they see me? Panic* began to creep back into his mind. *What if they can't find me before dark? Jim knows where I am. Is Jim with them? Surely they could see our tracks in the snow, but wait; there isn't any snow. What is the matter with me? Is my mind going? Am I losing touch with reality?* He was unable to move to signal them. They circled the area above him for nearly two hours.

As he lay knowing how badly he was injured and hearing them circle, his thoughts went to his family again. *What will they do if I'm not found in time?* All his life he'd had a deep faith in God, but he sort of lost it in Nam. He was never a people person, but he would never pass up helping anyone if it was needed. Now here were people, who he didn't even know, looking for him. *God must still be with me. He hasn't given up on me.* It was nearly sundown when they spotted him. As he heard the helicopter hovering above the trees, he thanked God that they found him before dark. There were wolves in this area!

Chapter 2

The trees were too close together for the helicopter to set down, so the medical team repelled to Eric. They evaluated his condition and the extent of his injuries, while the helicopter hovered above them. "What's your name? Do you know what day this is? Can you hear me? How many fingers do you see?" Questions flew as they eased him onto a rigid backboard, covered him, and strapped him securely into the basket to elevate him into the helicopter.

"Eric," the paramedic shouted over the roar of the blades, "you've been lying here for hours. We're taking you directly to Providence Hospital in Anchorage. Their staff will stabilize you. Understood?"

"Got it. Whatever you say." Eric barely got it out.

Jim shouted to the pilot, "Can someone call his wife? She went to Soldotna to wait."

"Sure, we can do that!" the pilot shouted back, "I'll radio the hospital and have them tell her we're taking Eric to the best possible facility to handle this sort of injury. What's her first name?"

"Laura!" Eric muttered... the pain now so severe he was close to passing out.

"Keep him awake!" The medic shouted over the noise of the chopper engine. "He could have a concussion and we don't want him to slip into a coma!"

Laura made it to Soldotna, a town with a population of about five thousand people and a small hospital with twenty-eight beds. She remembered so well when she'd been employed at this hospital, before she started working for a doctor at the clinic in Sterling. For four hours she paced the floor, anticipating the arrival of the Medivac helicopter. When not up and moving about, she would find a chair, fall into it and stare out the window, watching, waiting for some word. Her heartbeat raced, tears welled up in her eyes and ran down her cheeks. She sat and prayed to God not to take Eric. He was the love of her life and he meant the world to her...and the girls. Many questions swirled in her head. *Why hasn't the helicopter come? Are they having trouble-finding Eric? Jim knows where he is! Wait, don't panic, you have to keep your head. Eric's going to need you to be strong.*

She tried to rest, for she knew there was going to be a long night ahead. She thought of Mary and Patty, and wondered how they all would make it, if something should happen, and they lost Eric. *No! No! Everything will be all right, but how could I manage with the girls here in Alaska, if something should happen? Stop thinking that way! Eric is going to be fine! I won't worry until I find out what is really wrong. I must think of what I'd tell a patient's relatives in a situation like this."*

Suddenly a nurse rushed into the waiting room calling her name. "Mrs. Adams, Laura Adams? We've just received a call from Medivac. They found your husband, but they aren't bringing him here; they're taking him to Anchorage. When they told him of his possible condition, he agreed to go to Providence Hospital, where he can get the treatment he needs."

"Please, can you tell me anymore?" Laura pleaded with the nurse.

"I'm sorry, that's all I know, but I think you should pull yourself together. Your husband is going to need all your strength and support."

Hearing this, Laura went to phone Connie and Sam. When Sam finally answered, Laura informed him of the change of plans. "Oh, Sam, Eric is worse than we thought; they're flying him into Anchorage! How can I get a plane to Anchorage?"

Sam remained cool and collected, "Stay calm, I'll call and get you a seat on the commuter flight out of Sterling. Drive home and I'll meet you there and take you to the airport. The girls will be fine here with Connie and me until you can get things straightened out with Eric. Try not to worry. Just be careful driving back."

"Thank God for friends like you. I'll be there soon!" As she hung up the phone, she broke down and cried. Then, finding her strength, she pulled herself together and headed for Sterling.

As promised, Sam had a seat for her on the commuter plane to Anchorage. As she boarded the plane, Sam took her hand and pressed some money into it. "You may need some extra cash while you're there. Stay strong, Eric needs you!"

She hugged him and was on her way. It was a scant thirty-minute flight to Anchorage. Once there, she grabbed a cab and headed for the hospital.

Entering through the emergency room, she inquired at the desk. "I'm here to see about Mr. Adams, who was flown in by Medivac from Sterling."

"Oh, yes! Are you his wife? Could you give us some information on his insurance and any allergies he may have to meds?"

"I'm a nurse," Laura said as she fished a list out of her wallet. "I carry this everywhere."

"When can I see him? It's been six or seven hours since I first heard of the accident. Can't anyone tell me something about him?"

"They're running some tests now. We can't tell you anything. You'll have to see the doctor in charge. Sorry, we don't know anymore at this time."

How cold, thought Laura. She wondered if her bedside manner was as abrupt with patients' relatives. *I certainly hope I don't come across that way.* Finding a coffee machine, she sat down in the waiting room. Would her nerves hold out?

After what seemed like an eternity, one of the emergency room nurses called her. "Mrs. Adams, please follow me. I'll take you to see your husband." The nurse's face was grim, "Don't be too shocked when you see him. This is how we had to start treatment." Her voice trailed as they neared a cubicle surrounded by a curtain. She pointed toward it and turned away from Laura.

Laura's nursing experience should have prepared her for what she might see, but this was Eric, not just a stranger she was to take care of for a short while. She was taken aback when she pulled the curtain aside and saw Eric lying there naked, in traction, connected to several tubes. She went to him, trying to be calm so her precious Eric would not see the anguish she was surging through every cell of her being.

Eric opened his eyes and croaked out some words. "Hey you, when did you get here?" She reached for his hand. He asked her, "What are you doing?"

"I'm just holding your hand!"

"I can't feel you. The doctor told me I would never move again." His voice sounded cold, remote.

Laura knew him inside and out; Eric was a very matter-of-fact person. He took life on its terms and made no bones about the situation, so the next few words out of his mouth did not come as a surprise to her.

"You can turn and walk out of here right now. I'll understand. No emotion, no tears, no remorse. Just accept this condition now or leave and not look back."

"Eric," she kept her voice quiet, yet firm. "I can accept the fact that you have an injured back, but I'll not accept that there is no hope whatsoever and that you will never move again." She leaned over and kissed him and gently touched his lips with her fingers. "I made a promise to you; to love you in sickness and in health, for better or for worse, 'til death do us part. And I will keep that promise. You are my life!" As the tears rolled down her cheeks, she gently wiped away the tears now appearing in Eric's eyes. "We can't know what or how extensive the injuries are until the doctors run more tests, so we won't be foolish saying things we can't be sure of at this time." She kissed him, then again took his hand in hers.

They remained in silence together. She was still holding his hand in hers when a doctor peered in and motioned for her to step outside with him. She leaned over and said to Eric, "I'll be right back, hon."

As she stepped outside the curtain, the doctor dropped his head toward hers. "Mrs. Adams, I'm Dr. Goodman. I understand you're a nurse?"

"Yes, and Dr. Goodman, I have seen this type of injury before, during my training in New York. While working in the hospital at Soldotna, I heard that you are the best neurosurgeon around, so I'm grateful to have you caring for Eric."

"Your husband has numerous fractures of the vertebrae in his neck. We don't know yet how extensive the nerve damage is. I want to operate tomorrow. We'll know more if he stabilizes and regains any functions. He may regain some use of his hands. I'm going to call in an orthopedic surgeon to join me. In the meantime, we'll try to make him as comfortable as possible. You may stay with him if you'd like." He patted her on the arm, "Try not to worry too much. He needs to see you being strong."

Laura returned to Eric's side and again placed his hand in hers. She gazed upon his strong body. *Would he ever be the same as he was before the accident? He took such pride in being fit.* She looked at him, seeing his concern, and wondered if they were thinking the same thoughts. We'll have to take one day at a time. *We'll just have to wait to see what tomorrow might bring.*

"Where are our girls?"

"With Connie and Sam, I called Connie when Jim came to tell me of the accident. The girls were afraid; they didn't realize what was happening. I explained to them that you were injured, and that Connie and Sam would take care of them, so I could be with you. They'll keep a good eye on them, and on the house. Now you try to relax and get some rest."

"Do you suppose they could cover me with a sheet or something?" he whispered.

"No honey, not yet, they want to keep everything free and open, so they can see if there is any body movement at all. They will cover you when they put you in a room. It shouldn't be long." She rubbed his arm, leaned down and kissed him again. "Now try to rest."

At 3:30 AM they transferred Eric to a room in the neurology ward. It was almost eighteen hours since the accident and he was still in pain above the nipple line, even though the doctor had put him on IV pain medication. The nurses checked him every fifteen to thirty minutes to make sure all was okay with the medication and the traction. Then, as if things weren't bad enough, the electricity went out. In an instant it was back on again. A nurse came in. "There was a power failure, but the backup generators kicked in and we'll be fine. It happens periodically here. Not to worry! We must check on all the patients, so could you keep a sharp eye on Eric for us? The doctor said you were a nurse and could handle it."

17

"Sure, I've been watching it all anyway; old habits."

Laura felt her confidence come back. Dr. Goodman must have felt she was very capable if he told the other nurses about her. They were treating her as one of them, even though they just met her. She breathed deeply and let out a sigh. Still holding Eric's hand, she leaned close. "Now big guy, since they will not be popping in and out, why not try to sleep. I'll keep a good eye out for you."

"I can't, the pain is so bad. Why don't you just talk to me, Laura? Get my mind on other things. What are we going to do? How can I support you and the girls, the way I am? How can I work?"

"Eric, we can't worry about that right now. We have to get you through this! We'll have to take one step at a time. Remember when we first got married and how we planned to come to Alaska? We knew that we couldn't do it all at once. We'd have to take it step by step, and we did. I know you are strong-willed and intelligent and we'll figure out a way. You just wait and see. We'll be fine." The words just poured out of her. "But for now, try to relax and remember, I'm here and I love you." The pain medication started to kick in; his eyes grew heavy. Laura continued to talk. She spoke to him of anything and everything she could think of until he finally drifted off. She settled down in the chair beside the bed and tried to rest.

The next morning after Dr. Goodman and Dr. Miller, the orthopedic surgeon, conferred and looked at the results of Eric's myelogram, they decided to operate. The myelogram showed the fracture was where they expected. They scheduled him for surgery early that afternoon.

While Eric was being prepared for surgery, Laura waited in his room. A doctor in green scrubs soon came in to see her.

"Hello, Mrs. Adams? My name is Dr. Greene. I'm the anesthesiologist. I need to speak with you about what I need to do. They told me you were a nurse, so you'd understand all the medical terms. As you know, Mrs.

Adams, I'll not be able to tilt Eric's head back far enough to get an endotracheal tube down for the anesthesia. If I tilt it too much, it could kill him." He paused, seeing the fear on Laura's face. "I'm sorry, that was cruel and abrupt of me. Of course there is another option. I can spray cocaine in his throat and force the tube down. Do you understand the risk?"

Choking back the urge to cry, Laura cleared her throat. "Yes, I understand it very well. Eric could die if his head is tilted back too far to insert the tube. This would put pressure on the vertebrae and cut the nerves. I agree with you about using the cocaine spray. If you don't get the tube down correctly, he could stop breathing when he is turned over. I understand completely, but it must be done!"

He gave her the thumbs up sign. "Just leave him in my hands. I'll be right there for the both of you! Try not to worry."

Somehow, sitting in Eric's room looking at the empty bed made Laura uneasy. She had already called the clinic where she worked, explained to them what was happening. She'd keep them informed as things progressed. It was one o' clock in the afternoon, and she chose to wait in the waiting room outside surgery during the operation rather than in Eric's room. She'd rather be where there were people around. Staring out the picture window she saw a light snow starting. It made her think of how she and Eric met almost eleven years ago.

Chapter 3

She was a student nurse in college, home for Christmas to visit her family on their dairy farm in upstate New York. It was a modest dairy farm and supported their family of five comfortably. Her father, a quiet man, went about his business in a good, honest way. Her mother kept busy with chores and raising their three children: Ruth the older sister, a teacher; and brother Tom, who was an engineer; and Laura, the youngest, studying to be a nurse.

A light shower of huge soft feathery snowflakes fell between spells of bright sunshine that day. She was walking by the barn when she heard someone cursing. The only time anyone in the family did that was when there was trouble or something was extremely wrong. She opened the barn door and went inside to investigate, thinking someone might be hurt. She stood at the door letting her eyes become accustomed to the dark interior of the barn. She drew in the odors of the barn that she remembered as a little girl; the hay that her father threw down out of the haymow for the cows to eat, the manure that needed to be cleaned out, and the bleach that was used to keep the barn completely clean, to meet the dairy standards. She turned to the left and felt her way to the milking stanchions ready for the cows to march into like soldiers lined up for inspection. It was automatic for the cows—they did it day in and day out—entering their spot for the routine milking.

Soon her eyes adjusted and she saw a young man, built like a body builder, with the bluest eyes she had ever seen peeking through the lock of blonde hair that he kept blowing out of his eyes. He was struggling to give a cow an injection and hold her tail at the same time. As she approached him, her pulse quickened and suddenly she was short of breath.

Hearing her steps, the young man looked up to take in her slim body and her blonde hair that bounced as she walked. He also noticed, she had a smile to die for, and after looking at her for what seemed a very long time, he said, "You must be the daughter home from college?"

"Why yes and you must be the person dad hired to help with the milking." She answered nervously, thinking how young, strong, and good looking he was as he struggled with the cow.

"Here, hold this!" he ordered, as he shoved a dirty, smelly cow's tail into her hand. "Then maybe, just maybe, I can get this antibiotic injected!"

She held the cow's tail thinking, *He's certainly bossy. I wonder if he is like this all the time.*

When the task was finished he stood up and proceeded to introduce himself. "I'm Eric and your father hired me to help with the chores. I just got out of the Marines and the job I had before the war was no longer available. My folks wanted me to go to Seminary school, but I said no and so here I am working for your dad. What's your name?"

She blushed at his intense stare. "I'm Laura, and I'm in nursing school and just home for Christmas vacation."

"Well, welcome home and Merry Christmas, Laura. Thanks for helping with that stubborn cow. She kept swatting me in the face with that dirty old tail and I guess I lost my temper. I apologize for my misuse of the English language." Before Laura could answer him, he took a quick breath and continued. "Hey, I'm going skating later tonight. Would you like to go along? There's not much to do around here at Christmas. Ah…er…ah…you won't hurt my feelings if you say no, since we just met."

"I'd love to go, Eric, what time?"

"How about seven o'clock? I'll be at your door on time, so be ready."

"Okay! But now I've got to run. Dad will be wondering where I am. See you tonight!" She turned and left the barn.

As she returned to the house, her face felt red hot even though the air was quite crisp and chilly. Were her hands sweating? All she could think about was the young man she'd just met in the barn. She never really dated in school. Her association with the opposite sex had been in-group outings. Now she could only think about being with this blonde, blue eyed, guy. Why did she accept him so readily? She hardly knew him, yet her heart was still pounding. She liked him right off. He must be an all right guy; after all, her father had hired him. She hurried to the house to help her mother with supper. She needed time to look just right for tonight.

At seven sharp—not one minute before or one minute after—there came a knock on the front door and Laura's father went to answer it. He invited Eric in, letting him know that Laura was ready and would be down directly.

"So, the two of you are going skating?" he inquired, knowing that was their plan.

"Yes sir, we are, and I hope that Laura can skate as well as she looks," he answered, winking at her father.

Mr. Morgan smiled. "She will give you a run for your money, she will."

"What will I give him a run for his money for, Dad?" Laura asked as she entered the room, carrying her skates.

"Skating, of course, my dear. What else?" He handed Laura's coat to

Eric. "Now be off with the two of you and have fun, but be careful."

Eric helped Laura with her coat and they were out the door to the truck. He held the door for her and put her skates in back of the seat.

Eric pointed to the bag Laura held. "What have you there?"

"Some hot chocolate and cookies that Mom and I baked today. I thought they might taste pretty good after skating for awhile."

"Are you always so happy and smiling?" He reached over and gave her hand a squeeze. "Somehow I just know you are, and yes, I bet those cookies will taste good. I know your mom is an excellent cook, and if you are half the cook she is, then I have found a gem!"

She blushed as they pulled up to the millpond and put on their skates. "You know Eric, I really like you. I like you a lot, but Dad said you may not stay around too long because you have some other plans about working in the oil fields of Alaska."

"Well yes, I did tell him that when he hired me, but that was before I met you. You see, when I was over in Vietnam I had this buddy, Carl. We were very close. We met when we both were first inducted into the service. Carl was a down-to-earth, honest guy from a small town in New York State too." He paused as they sat on a bench by the pond to put on their skates. As they did, Eric continued, "Carl was someone you could really depend upon. His parents died in a car accident when he was ten years old, and his dad's brother, who was an avid outdoor sportsman, raised him. So it came natural for Carl to love hunting and fishing, as I did. We spent many a night telling stories to each other. We both worked for the phone company before entering the service, so they put us into communications. I was glad I decided to go into that type of career. At first I thought I might like to be a minister. I knew my Bible inside and out, but then I went to work for the phone company and got drafted. Glad I did too. Carl and I got to carry the radios and go on most of the recons together."

As Laura tied her skates, she asked, "So how did Alaska get in there?"

"On missions, we talked about what we were going to do when we got out of the service. We both loved hunting and fishing and heard about the jobs in the oil fields in Alaska, we promised we'd look each other up after the war and go to Alaska to work."

She prodded him to go on, as he suddenly stopped talking and became very quiet.

"Well, why didn't you two get together and do it? What stopped you from following your plans and keeping your promise to each other?"

All she could hear was the sound of the ice cracking under the cold that was settling in on this bright, crisp, moonlit night. The wind blew gently and the tall pines surrounding the pond seemed to whisper a sad song. Laura turned to Eric and in the intense moonlight saw tears in his eyes. She touched his cheek with her mitten.

"Eric, I'm so sorry. I didn't mean to pry!"

"It's okay, Laura, it has been awhile, but I still remember him so vividly. I came home, but he didn't." He paused, looked off into the distance. "I'm still going to keep my promise to him though. Come on… let's skate, so we can get at those cookies and hot chocolate!" He pulled her off the bench with such strength that she fell against him. He hugged her tightly for a second, kissed her on the cheek, grabbed her hand and pulled her out onto the ice.

Later that night as she snuggled down in bed, in her mind she retraced the evening. Everything was perfect, right down to the moon being so bright that there was no need for a lantern to light the pond. The crisp, cold air flushed their cheeks so that Eric couldn't notice how much she blushed when he kissed her on the cheek and later on, when he brought her home and walked her to the door, pulled her close and kissed her again. This time he kissed her on the mouth, a warm, gentle kiss that conveyed he liked her and wanted to see her again, before she went back to school. It was still tingling on her lips as she pulled up the eiderdown comforter. She gently touched her lips with her fingertips; just to be sure they were still there. He awakened a passion in her she never felt before, and she wanted very much to see him again. She could still feel the strength of his arms when he held her to kiss her. She wanted to feel it again. How could she manage that? *I know, she thought, I can invite him to the house for supper tomorrow night. I can ask him when I take more cookies down to the barn.* Feeling proud of her plan, she rolled over and blissfully fell asleep with the moon streaming into the room on her smiling face.

"Hey! Sleepyhead, are you going to hug that pillow of yours all day or are you going to get up and help your mother with Christmas dinner?" Her father was calling from the foot of the stairs. After a long stretch, putting her warm toes to the very foot of the bed where the sheet was cold and stretching her head to the headboard, she jumped out of bed and ran to the window. She heard the grandfather clock in the downstairs hall strike one o' clock. *My, I did sleep late,* she thought as she started scratching away some of the frost on the windowpane. She anxiously peered through the hole she made to see if she could see any movement around the barn. Seeing none, she hurriedly dressed and ran down the stairs.

She entered the kitchen where her mother was cooking up a storm. The smell of gingerbread cookies filled the air; along with the aroma of yeast... homemade bread was also in the making. The enticing smell of the turkey was beginning to fill the kitchen as well as that of the homemade pies. Oh, it was good to be alive and home on this Christmas holiday. She slipped up behind her mother, put her arms around her waist, and snuggled her chin on her mother's shoulder.

"Mom?" she asked in a pleading voice, "do you suppose that I might ask Eric to join us for Christmas dinner? He's been working so hard for Dad, and I'm sure he'd love to come."

"You know, of course, that Ruth and Tom will be arriving later this afternoon." Her mother searched Laura's face for a hint of her feelings. "Sure, why not. The more the merrier at Christmas; after all it is a time of sharing. Besides, I think it's a good idea!" She let a small grin come onto her face, turning to catch a glimpse of Laura as she headed out the door to the barn with a plate of cookies.

The snow squeaked beneath Laura's steps as she approached the barn door. The sun was doing its job, starting to melt it and pack it down. She knew Eric wouldn't be in the milking section of the barn at this time of day so she headed to the haymow area and called, "Eric," No answer. She called again. No reply. She turned so she could see the barn easier when suddenly a big clump of hay came plummeting down on her head. "Hey! Watch it! A person could get hurt!"

"Oh! Excuse me; I didn't realize you were down there! Did I get the cookies dirty?" Eric laughed after he saw she was all right. "What brings you out here at this time of day?"

"I was going to invite you for dinner tonight, but after treatment like that, I'm not so sure," she chided, picking the hay from her hair. "Ruth and Tom will be here soon. Mom and I are cooking a big dinner, and after we eat, we'll open our gifts. I thought you might want to join us. Do you have any other plans?"

"Well, as a matter of fact, I don't, so you can tell your mother I accept her kind invitation to join the Morgan family for Christmas dinner. What time?" He smiled at her and winked.

"Seven o'clock and don't be late. See you tonight; now I have to go and help Mother." She put the plate of cookies down and turned to make a hasty retreat to the house, trailing a call back to him, "Don't forget! Seven o'clock, seven sharp!"

Chapter 4

"Mrs. Adams, wake up, it's seven o'clock! Where were you just now? Are you okay?" It was Dr. Goodman, tapping on her shoulder. "You must have been dreaming. I know it's been a long wait."

He dropped into the chair beside her, still in his scrubs, with his surgical mask hanging loosely around his neck. Gently he took her hand in his. "The surgery went well. We took a portion of Eric's right hip and put it in his neck to stabilize the neck fracture, and then wired it in place. I'm sure you know he'll have to wear a halo; we'll put that on in about ten days. There will be braces coming up each side of his head from both of his shoulders, which will anchor into his skull to immobilize him. There was some nerve damage and there will be quadriplegia—motor and sensory paralyses of the entire lower half of the body, from the neck down. Of course, with intense physical therapy Eric could and should be able to get some hand movement back, enough that he can hold a fork to eat, and he should be able to hold a large pen to write. It will be more like a painting movement, not quite the dexterity he had before. If this happens then he would be classified as a paraplegic."

He paused to clear his throat and search Laura's face for a reaction, then continued, feeling she was stronger than most wives would be upon hearing such news. "Perhaps he'll regain some bicep muscle control, to raise his arms. What we'll try to do to strengthen the biceps is to place a sling-like device on him, which will enable him to get a swinging movement to point food, to be lifted to his mouth. However coming down, he'll have no control at all over his triceps movement, so the arm will just drop."

Laura asked, "Any possibility he will gain triceps control?"

"We'll do everything we possibly can to help. Only time will tell. We feel fortunate that we accomplished as much as we did with the procedure."

"I'm grateful for what you did, thank you."

"He is in recovery now and will be asleep for a while yet, but you can go in to be with him. We'll start the therapy as soon as we can." Squeezing her hand, he changed his tone. "Do try to get some rest. You were mumbling something about seven o'clock when I came up to you. Are you psychic? I'll talk with you later as Eric progresses." Wearily, he rose from his chair and walked away to get some much needed rest of his own.

Laura sat and digested all Dr. Goodman told her. He was matter of fact about the prognosis of Eric's injuries, but he was reassuring about the therapy. This made her feel a little better, but she knew they were in for a rough road ahead. She also knew that everyone must be positive with Eric. They must give him the love and support he would need, far and above their normal love for him. She knew about the type of therapy they would be giving for this kind of injury, and it wasn't going to be easy!

Then she laughed to herself, thinking that Dr. Goodman must think she was going a bit loony, talking in her sleep. *When I tell Eric, he'll be tickled and probably confirm the thought.* She made her way back to the recovery room. Eric was very still and that was good. He needed to stay as quiet as possible, at least until he regained consciousness. She curled up in the chair beside his bed and tried to stay out of the way of the recovery nurses as they went about their business of caring for Eric, constantly checking his vital signs.

As she sat watching him in deep sleep, her thoughts went back again to when they first met and how she felt about him. She still got the same tingling feeling, even now, when she looked at him. She did love him so. Her prayers went up to thank God for His blessings. She let her thoughts drift back again to that Christmas Eve when Eric came to dinner. She recaptured every moment and word. It was all so vivid.

Chapter 5

She remembered Eric had said, "When I walked up your neatly shoveled walkway that night, I felt a warm feeling inside, it was like going to a place where I was part of it all. I hadn't experienced this since I was a boy. I stopped on the walk and looked in the window at you, your sister Ruth, and your mother bustling about to put the last minute touches on the dinner table. I saw the candles giving a warm glow to the faces within their light. Through to the living room, I saw your dad and Tom, tending a warm, inviting fire in the fireplace next to the seven-foot spruce tree accented with many twinkling lights.

"My last Christmas was spent in Vietnam. A far cry from what this Christmas was going to be. Carl and I shared a cold can of Spam in a muddy rice paddy. Then a few rough-talking soldiers played cards by an emergency candle.

"There was love in this house and you were willing to share it with me."

Eric continued, "I pulled the gifts I brought for the family closer to me, said a little prayer of thanks, and rang the bell.

"You answered the door, took my hand and led me to the table and seated me next to you. (Even now as Eric lay so still before her, she found herself slipping her hand into his and holding it with love, ever so gently.) When everyone settled, your dad gave thanks for all of our blessings, and I looked at you and said, 'Amen!'

"After dinner everyone sang carols and exchanged gifts. I brought wine and rum cake for everyone to share and a small gift for you, a book on Alaska, and in turn you gave me an address and phone book with your address and phone number at school written inside.

"We each opened our gifts and hugged each other and you said, 'I do hope you will write me or call, and I promise to read the book on Alaska.'

"Everyone chatted and sang away the evening until it was time for me to leave. I thanked your parents for a lovely evening, and you walked me to the door. You helped me with my coat, and I turned and pulled you close and kissed you, whispering, 'I want to see more of you before you go back to school.'"

She remembered how she felt that warm tingly feeling course through her body again, and whispered back, "Oh yes, me too!"

Even now, as she looked at him lying there so still, she whispered, "I still feel that way. I love you so Eric."

Suddenly Eric whimpered, "Are you still here?"

"Always!" she whispered as she rubbed his hand and arm with love and caring.

Three days later Dr. Goodman gave the okay to take out the tubes. Eric was resting relatively easy in spite of the pain. Laura was happy the tubes were coming out, so she told Eric, "I need to go home to tell my employers of the situation and see about an extended leave of absence. Then I'll return and bring the girls back with me. I've called Connie and

Sam daily since your surgery and Connie says the girls keep asking about us: they are worried about you and keep asking when we'll be home."

"But where will you stay with them?" he asked. "You know they've let you stay here in the hospital with me, just because you're a nurse. We can't afford for you and the girls to stay in a hotel."

"No worry, Reverend Brown who comes in to see you every day, told me that he and his family live near the hospital and they've been kind enough to invite us to stay with them. They have an extra room and Mrs. Brown said her girls would be glad to watch ours. Besides, Mary and Patty miss you very much."

Eric replied with reservation in his voice, "That'll be great but don't you think they'll be afraid of me with the halo? You do know I'll have that on when you get back. Will they understand the whole contraption?"

"It'll be fine! They love you and miss you very much. Besides that, I'll tell them because you are an angel to all of us you must wear that here in the hospital for awhile." Laura wiped a tear from her eye.

Eric's eyes were moist too. "I'm not much looking forward to wearing it either. Thank God the people here in Alaska are so quick to help each other. Be sure and thank the Brown family for both of us!"

"You can count on me to do that, but I would think you could thank Reverend Brown yourself, when he drops by to see you while I am gone. I'll leave here in about a week or so. I want to get things settled at the Brown's before I get the girls."

It took a week for Eric to get leveled out when they put the halo on. He would soon start his therapy. After the first day of his therapy Laura told him, "I'll leave tomorrow to get the girls. You're in good hands here, and we'll be back soon! Work at your therapy. I love you!" She leaned over to kiss him good-by.

Sam bought Laura an open-end round trip ticket for the commuter plane. She quickly caught a cab to the airport and was home in no time.

She called Connie to let her know of her plans to return home, to get the girls and drive back to Anchorage. Connie and Sam met her at the airport with the girls. As soon as the girls saw Laura, they ran to her, yelling, "Mommy! Mommy!" Laura cried when she saw them and hugged them tightly. She thought, *How would they handle seeing their daddy?* She kissed them repeatedly. "Mommy's here now. Let's go home."

Connie and Sam took Laura home so she could gather some things for herself, Eric, and the girls. After Mary and Patty were in bed she filled Connie and Sam in on Eric's condition. "Eric's doing as well as can be expected for now, but he's got a big job ahead of him in therapy, and adjusting to his new condition."

She crossed and uncrossed her legs. "I need to put some things in order here at home and to make arrangements for an extended leave of absence from work. So I'll wait a day or so before going back to Anchorage with the girls. I'll let you know when we'll be leaving, so I can get an early start that morning for the three-hour drive back. You both were so wonderful to help as you did, and Eric and I will never be able to thank you enough."

Connie spoke up, "There's no need to thank us…the girls were no bother. They were just worried about their daddy, which is understandable. You and Eric would do the same for us if we needed help."

Sam stood and laid another log in the fireplace. "There, that should get you through the rest of the night. I'll come over in the morning and check the truck before you and the girls return to Anchorage. We don't want you three having a problem on the road. Come on, Connie, let's go home now and give this lady some rest. I bet her bed will feel good to her tonight. Sitting in a hospital room is a far cry from being home in your own bed."

"You're right Sam, let's go. Laura, call us if you need us, you hear? I'll come over with Sam in the morning and take you to see your boss while he checks over the truck." Connie hugged Laura tightly and whispered in her ear, "Trust in God and try to get some rest."

When the family finally returned to Anchorage Eric had the halo in place and had made a good start on his therapy.

"How's the therapy going?" Laura asked.

"I'm determined to do it and work extremely hard. I want to get movement back and am motivated to do better." He answered.

Laura explained to her daughters, in words they would understand, "The goal of the therapy is to move his arms as much as possible and to keep from getting contractures."

She defined that term for them. "Because he doesn't have much energy yet, it's a full-time job for your daddy to keep his arms from getting smaller."

The aides and therapist worked with Eric for two or two and half-hours, every day. It was necessary to maintain his range of motion with his arms and to keep him loose and maintain muscle function. Many different stretches were done with Eric lying supine and prone, and also while in the wheelchair. As he had some bicep function returning, he was able to use pulleys on a machine, while seated in his wheelchair. The therapy helped decrease the spasms, which would likely occur when he was moved and transferred from a bed to a chair or a chair to a wheelchair.

The day Laura brought the girls in to see their dad he looked a little scary to them, with the braces, the halo and the apparatus around his head and neck. He was still their daddy though and they were happy to see him. They laughed when he said hello to them and Mary said, "Daddy, you look like a robot!"

"Well, how about giving this robot a kiss?" Laura held each of them up, being careful not to bump him, as Laura had told them that he must wear the halo for a while. After the kisses, they each had something they brought for him. Mary gave him some shaving lotion and Patty handed him a box of candy.

"That was very thoughtful of you. I love you both. This shaving lotion will make me smell good and all the nurses will be extra good to me so they can have some candy." Eric said, and they all laughed.

Laura didn't realize it, but Eric was putting on a happy face for them. He was really very despondent about his condition. He was making progress, but he wanted to be back to normal, if he would ever be normal again. When he was alone, he would lie in his bed and think of all he used to do and would never be able to do again. *What of the plans he had for their future? Just to be able to walk, to sit, and to cut wood. Would he ever be able to play with his daughters? Could they run, ski, and sled together? Even the chores. Will I ever be able to do them again? And then there's hunting and fishing. They were a huge part of my life, and they're gone forever.*

But these thoughts did not dampen his persistence to keep up with his therapy. The doctors said that it was unusual to see anyone as positive about doing the exercises as Eric. But, Eric reminded them, "That's the kind of person I am, a very strong-willed individual. Once I decide to do something, I don't give up easily."

Laura watched Eric go through his prescribed routines. "You seem to have the same fortitude and tenacity as when we were first married. Way back in August 1973. Remember? In September I returned to my junior year of college and was doing my clinical work at a hospital in Rochester. We lived with my parents from August until March."

"I remember," said Eric. "During that time, I remodeled my grandmother's house I was given when I got home from Vietnam. When my grandfather died in 1963, grandmother went to live with my parents. The house had been empty for ten years and it needed a great deal of work. There was no running water or indoor plumbing, and the roof was giving away. When I took you to see the house, you almost fell through the kitchen floor. My uncle said to burn it, but grandmother said if I fixed it up, we could have it. So I set about doing that, and with the help of family and friends, it was in livable condition again by 1974."

Laura jumped in, "Yes, it became our first home in New York. You continued to work on it, while we lived there, until we moved to Alaska in June 1978. You were then, and still are today, a determined man!"

Her thoughts switched to what they would do now? *How would they make ends meet and survive life here in Alaska? Would that decisiveness still be in him? Or would there be declension of all his plans for their lives? She felt somehow, they would make it, that there would be a way.* "As you know, we already have our moose for winter, and all the vegetables harvested. We also have a good supply of wood for the stove. It's our sixth winter here in Alaska and the first one for which we're really prepared."

Finally she said, "God is watching over us for sure, Eric!"

When Eric was returned to his room after therapy, he asked her, "While you're here in Anchorage with me, who is looking after the house? It's getting to be the end of October! You know how quickly the water pipes can freeze without a fire in the house."

"Jim is watching it but has to leave soon, so the girls and I will have to go home to make sure everything is okay." Laura patted his hand. "Since you're being transferred from Providence Hospital to Humana Hospital here in Anchorage for at least three months to receive a different type of therapy, it is just as well that we go home. I was hoping you could come home by Christmas and stay."

"I'm afraid that won't be possible," Eric said moving his hand toward hers, "but you really must be home to keep those pipes from freezing." He rubbed her hand and squeezed it slightly, as much as he could. "I don't want you to leave, but you must go."

"I'll bring the girls by, early in the morning, to say good-bye and then we'll be on our way. It's a long drive and we could be getting our first deep snow anytime now. We must get home before it gets too late."

The next day when Mary and Patty came, they gave him pictures they drew of him, looking like a robot. They also brought him a teddy bear to keep him company. "Look Daddy, what we made for you. You can put these on your wall, and here's Mr. Bear for you to love while we're gone," said Mary. They were so excited to give their gifts to him.

"I sure will and I'll miss you both, but I'm sure Mr. Bear will be a lot of company to me," he said as they hugged him and he kissed them both. "I love you very much. For being almost three and five, you are really growing up fast."

They all kissed him and wheeled him down the hall to his therapy on their way out of the hospital. Laura was thinking as they left the hospital, *this is the hardest thing for me to do, to go home and leave Eric here.*

Once outside the hospital, they rushed to the truck. Laura wanted to get home before evening set in. She thought the girls might be asleep before they got too far along, but they surprised her. They sat quietly until she got out of Anchorage and onto the open road. Then Mary spoke up. "Momma, will Daddy have to wear his robot thing for the rest of his life? Will he still be able to ski with us? I don't like to see him like that! It hurts me and I want to cry."

"Me too!" said Patty; "do those pins hurt? I want Daddy to ski me down the drive."

"I know it hurts you, honey, but we must be extra careful of Daddy's feelings now. He needs us to be positive for him. We must tell him that everything will be all right and that he can do things like he used to do." Laura spoke softly to them. "We must tell him like we told you, when you both learned to walk and talk. You can do it! Sure, you'll have some bumps, but you can do it! We have faith in you. Do you think that you two can do that?"

"Yes, Daddy can do it, if we did," said Mary. "We love him and know he can!" After agreeing emphatically, they were quiet the rest of the way home.

Chapter 6

October came and went. Laura took Mary and Patty trick or treating, but it was not the same without Eric there to share it with them. They kept busy with the everyday chores and keeping the house warm to protect the water pipes. Laura repeatedly told Mary and Patty how proud she was of them and grateful for their help. Then one day at breakfast, she mentioned to them. "Girls, your daddy will turn thirty-five on November 3, and will be alone in the hospital. Why don't we drive up and surprise him!"

"Yea, Mommy! Yeah, let's do it! We'll make him a present and you can make him a cake! It will be exciting to have a party with him," Mary said, jumping up and down.

Laura called Sam and asked him to keep an eye on the cabin while they were gone. He agreed, and once more checked the truck to see that it was safe for the trip to Anchorage. It was only 130 miles to Anchorage from Sterling, so they could make it up and back in one day.

Eric got tears in his eyes, when they walked in saying, "Surprise, Happy Birthday!" Even the nurses came in to join in singing happy birthday...

and eating birthday cake.

"You shouldn't have come this far with the girls alone," Eric told her, "but I 'm glad you did. Mr. Bear and I have missed you all so much. It's good to see you!"

It was good to be together again. The girls had brought him a bracelet made from string beads, wrapped up in a small package. Laura bought him a robe to wear in the hospital. There was much that they all wanted to tell him.

Eric was eager to hear about how they were doing at home alone. "Tell me... really... are you and the girls doing fine without me?"

Pulling the girls closer to her, Laura replied, "Look at us! Do we look like we're struggling? We do our chores and keep busy; it helps to keep our minds off of missing you so much. We sure do want you home!"

"So tell me what's new at home? Did you go trick or treating?"

Mary, the oldest, spoke up, "Uh huh," shaking her head yes at the same time. "But we had to wear our costumes over our winter coats, because of the snow. We even had to wear boots!"

Laura added, "We only went to a few of the neighbors. I really didn't want to change the girl's routines."

He reached for her hand. "Of course, you know best. We have to try to stay normal. But since when have you and I ever been normal? You know, lying here, I think how crazy we were to move away from our families and come to Alaska. Just how many newlyweds do that?"

He gave her that silly little smile she loved. She leaned over and kissed him. "Well, crazy man, we did it. Remember how we felt after our first visit here? I think it was back in 1976. We camped out for three months; it was in June, July, and August. George, a childhood friend, came with us because you wanted to do a little hunting while we were here. You wanted to see if you two could bag a mountain goat. We asked an old-timer and found out where to go to see some, and we hiked up the mountainside. We camped at the snow line near a small stream. We didn't know much about anything; we all just fell in love with the land. The mountains were beautiful and pristine. The air was so fresh and invigorating, we were hooked. Somehow, Alaska just gets into your blood. It's really hard to explain, but it does."

Eric jumped in to continue the story, "Yes, I do remember George and I asked an old-timer we saw there in town, where we should go. He told us that we should hike up this mountain and we might get lucky and get a ram. So what did we do, but hike up that mountain. What a trek! You were right. How green we were. You kept saying that the bushes were moving all the way up the mountain, but there was no breeze. I finally had to tell you that it was the bears in the bushes making them move. And we just kept hiking. I didn't want you to be scared." Eric was grinning now too, caught up in the story.

Laura picked it up. "Yes, and then we camped for the night. The next morning you two went on up the mountain, and I stayed behind, I was tired from hiking. You were gone all day, and I got worried. I came out of the tent, looked up the mountain and saw something in the distance standing and I thought it was you, waving to me. I waved back, but it wasn't you; it was a bear! I hurried back into the tent and got into the sleeping bag and was very quiet. The next noise I heard, I thought was the bear, and I was scared to death. I didn't have a gun or anything. Luckily, it was you and George.

"Both of you were bloody, so I immediately asked, 'What happened?' I thought you might have run into that bear.

"You said you got a ram, but it was too late to bring him down, so you butchered him up there and brought part of the meat down with you. You were going back for more in the morning."

"We did eat well that night!"

Eric took her hand, "What a trooper you were. I think you were bitten by the bug to stay in Alaska right then."

"Yes, you're right; it does get into your blood. I was into it from the first; it was my form of heaven, next to you, of course."

He lightly squeezed her hand. "I think I was meant for you and Alaska!"

"Even though I loved it, I do remember how extremely home sick I was. Other than being at school for nursing, I was never away from home for very long. You know how close our family has always been. It was a feeling deep inside that would not let up for a long time." Laura put her cake plate on the tray table. "I have that same feeling now… now that you're here in the hospital and the girls and I are at home. But I know it won't be long before you can be home with us again. I do love you so, and miss you not being with us."

She looked at her watch. "Sorry, honey, it's time to head back." She leaned over and kissed him good-bye.

"We have to get going!" she said and kissed him again. "Hey, girls, we better head for home before it gets much later. They are predicting more snow late tonight. Besides, we need to keep the home fires going! Kiss Daddy good-bye and wish him a Happy Birthday!"

Chapter 7

❧

It wasn't long until Thanksgiving and Laura called Eric on the phone, trying to sound as cheerful as she could. "I wish you could come home. I don't want to prepare a big Thanksgiving dinner for just the girls and me!"

He answered her very quickly, "Oh no, go ahead and fix it, with all the trimmings! You should keep our routines the same as always for the girls. Do it for me, then call me and let me know how it tasted!"

"Oh, you!" she answered. "How can I refuse a request like that? I'll do it."

Unknown to Laura, Eric and his lifelong friend George, who had come to Alaska with them when they moved from New York, had planned that he and Sam would drive the 130 miles to Anchorage to pick Eric up and bring him home for Thanksgiving weekend.

Connie called Laura and asked, "Could we spend Thanksgiving with you? I know you and the girls will be alone, so the kids, Sam and I would like to come over and spend it with you."

Laura quickly jumped at the chance for company. "Sure, that would be great! Eric wanted me to go ahead and cook Thanksgiving dinner anyway; he said we should keep things normal for the girls, as much as possible. I would love to have you all come over." Before hanging up they both discussed what each would fix for the feast.

Thanksgiving Day arrived with all the holiday smells coming from the Adams' kitchen. The aroma of fresh baked bread and pies permeated the cabin. The enticing smell of the moose roast mingled with the others, signifying that the meal was ready. Laura looked at her watch and thought, *Connie, Sam, and the boys should be arriving soon.* She took a fast check of the table setting to be sure all was ready. As she was lighting candles and checking last minute things, she heard the sound of someone pulling up to the house. She took off her apron and went to the door to greet them. She saw Sam and George… with Eric.

Letting out a cry of surprise she ran to the truck. She pulled the truck door open and leapt onto the running board, hugging and kissing Eric. All she could do was cry and ask a million questions. "How did you arrange this? How long can you stay? Are you home for good? Are you hungry? Are you all right? Oh, hurry; let's get him in the house!" She was beside herself.

She called to the girls inside, "Girls, look who's here? It's Daddy! Wait until we get him in, to hug him. Stand back!"

The house was built in the side of a hill, and they didn't have a ramp built yet for Eric's wheelchair, so Sam and George carried him up a full flight of basement stairs to the living room. Laura was so surprised she could hardly speak. All she could do was cry. "This is truly a Thanksgiving to end all Thanksgivings, to have Eric back in the house again."

She could hardly keep her eyes off Eric and her mind on being a good hostess. Every once in awhile she had to walk away into a corner and wipe the tears from her eyes. After coming so close to losing him in the fall, she was really overwhelmed. Mary and Patty were sticking close to their daddy too. They didn't want to let him get away. Soon Connie and the children came; they finished dinner preparations and everyone sat down to enjoy the meal. Eric returned thanks and the festivities began. Everyone was grinning and happy. It was truly the best Thanksgiving ever.

When the evening ended and everyone left, Laura was preparing to put Eric into bed when he said to her, "That was a wonderful Thanksgiving dinner. I wanted to be home with you and the girls more than anything in the whole world. But you know my emotions were mixed all day."

"Why do you say that? What's wrong?" Laura asked.

"Honey, do you realize that here I have all my things around me? In the hospital I was in a controlled environment, a real controlled environment. But here I see my bow and arrows in the corner of our bedroom, my guns right there where I can see them, my hunting boots there on the floor, where I always kept them, by the bed. Do you realize what it's doing to me to see everything here? Today when I came back to the life I had lived, it was a reality shock to me. I saw our skis in the corner and remembered how we used to enjoy cross-country skiing, but now I can barely move my arms and hands. I saw my canoe paddles; would I ever be able to paddle a canoe? I don't need my legs for that! Oh Lord, even my everyday chores... how am I going to do them? This has always been on my mind and now just seeing everything around me, how could I not think of these things?" His eyes filled with tears.

She went to him and held him. "I know, it's going to be different, but we'll manage. As long as we have each other, that's all that matters."

"I know we'll manage! We have wonderful friends, two beautiful girls, and I've the best wife ever. Just hold me and thrill me like only you can." Then he gave that little sly grin he always gave her when they were alone together.

Laura didn't realize the depth of the hurt he felt. It was an emotional, physical, mental hurt that he never showed her. Even though he enjoyed being home, the hardest part would be going back to the hospital for another month of rehabilitation.

The staff and Dr. Goodman were anxious for Eric to return. He was so determined to work at his therapy, they were eager to see how the home visit had gone.

Dr. Goodman came in to see Eric the first morning he was back, "Well, Eric how was your Thanksgiving? Tell me about your visit."

"Dr. Goodman, it was good to be physically home with Laura and the girls. All my friends were there too. There was lots of talk and we had fun. The visit was wonderful; I didn't mind the trip at all because I knew I was going home. You can't believe how much I wanted to be there for Thanksgiving. We have so much to be thankful for, you know, even with the accident and all; I'm blessed with a beautiful family and friends.

"But I do have to be honest with you and with myself. It was hard for me to see all my sporting equipment there... and my tools. Many thoughts were going through my mind. I know we've been working on the therapy full force. But just how much will I be able to do? There are millions of questions rolling around in my mind. I've always been independent in my thinking and my life. I've never depended on anyone for anything. How will I learn to adjust to that now?" Eric gave a deep sigh. "Will I ever be what I must be, from this chair? Will I ever meet my own expectations?"

Dr. Goodman took Eric's hands in his. "Your future will depend on these hands, your mind, and your heart. You must learn to use them all. It will be difficult at best, but I've faith in you. You're a bright, independent, individual who will eventually find his way. It'll not come easy, but you'll work it out. Just keep the faith. You have a good family and good support from everyone. You'll be okay." He stood and picked up

Eric's chart, making a couple notes.

"We'll talk more later. For now, let's concentrate on your physical therapy. You'll see, it'll come."

Dr. Goodman rubbed his chin as if deep in thought. "Let's see, you had surgery on September 15 and we put the halo on almost a week later. You should be able to shed that monster around the 20th of December. Just before we let you go home for Christmas. Until then, I do want you to transfer to Humana Hospital to be in therapy. You can be an inspiration to those patients there, while you finish your needed therapy. We're going to put 'quad pegs' on your wheel chair rims. With the therapy you are receiving, it will enable you to move yourself about on very smooth floors, no plush carpet or anything like that, but it'll be your goal before you go home. You'll need to wear leather bicycle gloves to protect your hands until you get good at handling the motion, and then you can get rid of the gloves and the quad pegs, if you work at it."

Eric nodded. "What good news! Laura will be happy to hear that. I'm looking forward to going home for good. I promise you I'll work hard at my therapy, so I can."

Eric was not the only one who was thinking about his Thanksgiving home visit and his permanent return. Laura, too, reflected on everything that had happened. She was filled with many feelings. Never a day went by that she didn't wonder just how she was going to handle Eric's incapacity, and hold down her job at the clinic so she could keep a cash flow coming into the house. *How am I going to handle his emotions?*

The clinic and doctor's office where she worked had given her time off while Eric was in the hospital and she needed to be in Anchorage with him. At that time, Dr. Goodman talked with her, "You should be thinking about getting a full time caregiver for Eric, when he gets home. There are counseling classes you and Eric could attend, to help cope with problems that might arise"

Laura answered, "Eric feels that since I'm a nurse, I could handle his needs once he's home."

Dr. Goodman looked thoughtful. "Consider it and think about it for a while."

Even now, her workplace was willing to extend her leave of absence for an additional two weeks, to enable her to get Eric settled into a routine once he was home. She wanted things to be as normal as possible, but it was going to be difficult.

Many thoughts swirled through her mind. *Should I put away Eric's hunting and fishing gear? He might be angry if they weren't there when he came home. Should I leave them where they are and let him be the one to tell me what to do with them?* Then too, there was Eric's physical care. She thought at length and decided, *I'll have to leave my job in order to be home to change and clean Eric's catheter every four hours, as well as move him about from chair to bed, bed to chair, and do his daily routines of exercise and such. It would be much easier if we could get a caregiver, but it was Eric's decision not to.*

She managed to get work, cleaning houses, to provide a little extra income. She also picked up an occasional home health care. It all helped financially. Connie and Sam, their closest neighbors, were also a big help. It was like having a brother and sister next door. Before Eric's accident, he and Sam would cut firewood together. Sam, a master mechanic, also helped Eric do mechanical repairs on the vehicles. Laura and Connie would process and freeze vegetables together; they'd go into the woods and pick Golden Delicious mushrooms and low bush cranberries. Connie was great at sewing, crocheting, knitting and doing crafts. They helped make life a little easier and not so lonely. Sam worked up on the North Slope, in the oil fields, and sometimes he would be gone from home for two to three weeks at a stretch. But when he was home, he made it a point to come over and check to see if Laura needed any help around the house. What a blessing they were.

Eric finally was transferred to Humana Hospital for additional therapy until Christmas, and to motivate other quadriplegic patients. The therapy was not easy for him, but he was set on doing it so he could get back some of his motor skills. One type of therapy involved a kind of push up to strengthen his biceps. He would lie flat on his stomach on the floor, bring his arms up and under his chest above the nipple line, and push upward from the elbow to his fingertips, raising his upper body off the floor. It was very difficult to do, but his determination to do it was strong. He used to do gymnastics with the girls on the floor before the accident and he felt that once he mastered this, he could have them sit on his shoulders and he could raise them up and down. In this way, he could still play with them, one-on-one.

Each and every day his thoughts nagged him. *How will I cope? Will we be able to manage? How much will I have to depend on someone else to do what I should be doing as head of the household?* The therapy was hard work, but the time was fast approaching when he would be discharged. *He had to do it!*

Chapter 8

It was the week before Christmas when Eric was discharged from Humana Hospital. Sam was to bring him home in his new extended cab truck, with the equipment in the back, under cover. Eric would ride in the front seat with Sam and Laura in the back seat. Mary and Patty would stay home with Connie.

When Laura and Sam stepped into the room to get Eric, Laura noticed two big, black garbage bags sitting on the floor. As she hugged Eric she asked him, "What are these? Surely it is not more equipment for you, is it?"

"The nurses from Providence Hospital brought them over for us to take home," Eric replied. "They said they were for our family!"

"Okay!" She didn't question anymore and took the bags to put in the back of the truck. "I'm just happy to be leaving the hospital with you, Eric."

The three-hour drive seemed to pass quickly. When they got home, Sam helped Laura get Eric situated and unloaded the truck, then went to get the girls.

Once the girls were home and Sam left, they opened the two large bags.

Inside they found wrapped gifts for the whole family, along with a note from the staff on the orthopedic floor, who voted them as the family they wanted to help for Christmas, and they bought gifts for all of them. Laura with moist eyes, said, "Here I was thinking how much a gift it was just to be together again. Now here are all these gifts to put under the Christmas tree. The girls are going to have a Christmas after all!"

"Yes!" Eric said. "We're reminded again of the spirit of the people in Alaska. Most of them had family members in other parts of the world, so they banded together to do this for us. It's wonderful how people help each other as a family would, how they all depend on each other. Where would we be, if not for that spirit?"

It was the best Christmas the girls ever had.

Laura went to Eric and hugged him. "You know, Eric, when I told our girls you had been in an accident, and you might never walk again, it didn't matter. They knew you were still their same daddy. You still loved them and cared for them. Even when you had the halo device anchored into your skull with four screws, and you looked so frightening, when you kissed them, it was okay. They knew you just couldn't walk."

Eric looked at Laura with a cold, defiant stare. "That's right, Laura! I can't walk and I don't think I'll ever walk again. So what are we going to do? You know when the lady from financial aid visited me in the hospital to set me up to get on Social Security or veterans disability, I told her I didn't want it. I refused it! See what being a very independent and proud person gets you? Nothing!"

Surprised at his outburst, Laura tried to soothe him. "I know Eric, and I'll find a way to work to support us. I have quite a few cleaning jobs and I'm picking up some home health care jobs, along with other odd jobs, which will help. We can't give up now; we've come too far to do that.

"As far as food and supplies, we should be all right this year. We have a good supply of moose meat, salmon, and garden veggies. As for household expenses, we should be okay. The only big thing we need worry about is the fact that we're still paying on our land. I'll try to double up on our payments. As long as we keep the payments up to date, we won't lose it." Laura hoped this would calm him for the time. "We can talk more about this later. It's Christmas and you're home. Let's just enjoy the moment."

That evening after the girls were in bed, Eric and Laura retired too, and talked about the situation and what they were going to do. He became a little despondent. "The first time I came home from the hospital at Thanksgiving, and saw all my things here in the bedroom, it was hard because I realized I was never going to be able to do those things again."

"We could modify the equipment so you can use them."

"But it would never be the same, once I've done them the other way. You should just leave me. Take the girls and go back to New York."

Tears welled up in Laura's eyes. She sat up in bed and looked straight at him. "When we met and decided to get married, we made a promise to each other that we would always be together, no matter what, good or bad! You haven't gone back on a promise yet, and I am not going to let you do so now! Remember when you gave me the book on Alaska? I first read it or I should say, I tried to read it on the bus going back to school after Christmas, but I had a hard time keeping my mind on the book because you kept popping into my mind." She started to reminisce with him, hoping to bring him out of his depression.

"Eric, I know how hard it must have been for you to leave and go back to the hospital after Thanksgiving. It was hard for me too. I remember how hard it was for me to return to school after we had met at Christmas that first year. The only thing that sustained me was the thought that we would be together again and hoping we could face whatever might come our way together. I know it's hard for you to see any future ahead for us right now, but it'll come. I promise you that. We *will* make it through this!" She started to chuckle.

"What's so funny?"

"Oh, I just remembered thinking while I was on the bus back to school, why did you tell me about wanting to keep your promise to Carl, about going to Alaska? Why did you give me a book on Alaska for Christmas? What must have been in the back of your mind? I was hoping you felt the same way I felt when we met. There was something between us that would not be forgotten. We only had a few days together before I was on my way back to school. But you know, I could still feel the warmth of your kiss on my lips and your arms around me as you hugged me good-bye. I remember picking up my gloves after sitting down on the bus and holding them to my nose, smelling the scent of your cologne where I had rubbed your face with my hand as we said good-bye." Laura's eyes misted as she pictured this in her mind.

"You really must have had it bad for me! Come over closer to me now and kiss me. Let me see if I can smell your cologne."

She moved closer to him, gave him a loving kiss and snuggled close to his body, being very careful not to jostle him too much to bring him any discomfort. After the kiss, she asked him: "There, now can you smell the scent of my cologne?"

"No," he said, "but I can smell the scent of the soft fragrant soap you use. Tell me more of how you were entranced by our first meeting. I want to hear it."

Snuggling closer to him, she slipped her hand into his. "Well, as usual at school we all gathered around together and each told our holiday stories.

Finally someone said, 'Hey Laura, how about you?' They were all expecting me to say that it was just like every other Christmas at home, so they all were surprised to hear me say, 'Oh, it was wonderful! I met the nicest guy who works for my father!' I guess I said it with so much enthusiasm that they all crowded around me and urged me to tell them more about you. I told them about our meeting and my friends seemed to be so happy for me. They had never seen me react like that to meeting someone. I couldn't wait to hear from you again.

"Time seemed to drag by with the exception of mail calls; I looked forward to getting a letter from you. It made me feel on top of the world when you too spoke of never meeting anyone who made you feel the way you felt about me.

"Remember writing me of your promise to your buddy from Vietnam and asking me if I had been reading my Christmas gift, the book on Alaska? Then you spoke of an area south of Anchorage called the Kenai Peninsula. You asked me to look up what I could find on the area and we would talk about it when we saw each other again."

"Yes, I do," Eric said, "and you wrote back saying you would try to come home for a weekend in March. We even made plans to meet when you got home. I remember as much as you do, because I fell in love with you the first time I saw you and knew that I wanted you to be my wife, for the rest of my life." He choked back the next words and Laura wiped a tear from his eyes.

Not wanting him to get depressed again, she continued telling him her story. "After that letter, I got deep into my studies, but you never left my mind. Even the patients I was caring for in my student nursing time noticed a difference in me. They asked me where I might be going to do nursing after graduation. I would smile at them and say, 'Wherever I went, I would be happy about the placement.'"

She was getting excited. "Then, darling, eventually the winter gave way to the small buds on the trees. Spring was around the corner. Even the glimpse of a robin or two made me begin to notice the time, and I began counting the days until I would leave for home on spring break in March.

"In my spare time, I read up on the area that you indicated, and this made the time go faster. There was so much to learn about Alaska. There were so many questions, but the main thought was just to see you again. I could hardly wait. Finally, the day came when I bought my bus ticket. I packed only a few clothes, as I would only be home for a long weekend. But I did take care to put the book on Alaska in my carry-on bag."

Eric grinned at her. "Was it me or Alaska that excited you so much?"

Laura winked. "You figure it out. It seemed as if the bus was crawling that day as it headed toward home. I could hardly wait to see your handsome face under that blonde crop of hair, smiling at me as I stepped down from the bus."

"Your parents knew you were coming and they arranged for me to meet you at the bus station. I think they knew we would want to be alone." He paused a long time.

"Hey!" she whispered to him, "are you still awake?"

"Yes, yes, I was just lying here picturing this story in my mind, just like a movie. You tell a beautiful story!" He paused then went on. "You know, I had already talked to your father about my intentions and he said nothing would make him happier than to see us get married. But he also told me that the final decision was up to you. But go on with your story. You have my undivided attention now." He chuckled to himself. He felt good hearing how much this girl loved him.

"Soon the big, old, lumbering bus pulled into the bus station and I looked anxiously out of the window. There you were, beaming from ear to ear, shifting your weight from leg to leg and peering into each window of the bus. Finally you saw me and broke into a huge smile and started toward the door of the bus. It seemed as if the bus driver would never open the door to release the passengers, but when he did, I burst from the door into your arms. You hugged and kissed me, with those wonderful kisses, then grabbed my bag and we sped off in the pickup.

"As we drove home, you told me, 'I'm planning to go to Alaska and inquire about a job in the oil fields and if I can get work, I want to move there.'

"You stopped the truck along the road and looked into my eyes, and asked me, 'How do you feel about me? I love you and want you to be with me! I know we haven't known each other very long, but I couldn't think of anything but my promise to Carl...and you. So I decided to combine the two thoughts into one major question!'

"You confused me Eric, so I asked, 'Question to what?'

Eric jumped in with a memory of his own. "I pulled a ring box from my pocket and held it out to you and pleaded, 'Laura Morgan, will you marry me and go to Alaska with me to live happily ever after?'"

Laura quickly said, "I squealed with delight, threw my arms around you and nodded till I thought my head would fall off. 'Oh yes, Eric, yes, yes, and yes!'"

By now, Eric was smiling readily, and all signs of his depression were gone. "You were a little excited, if I remember right! Then I slipped the ring on your finger and told you there were a lot of things we had to consider before making the move to Alaska. There was your graduation; you must finish school; your job placement after school; where we would live; what we would need, etc. You know, I mulled this over in my mind a million times. That is why I told you we needed to come up here first and see about jobs and inquire about living conditions."

"Yes, was my answer, and we did have many serious talks about the future alone, together, and with our families. We researched everything we thought we should know. I'm so glad I finished my nursing, as it has come in handy here. There were many obstacles ahead of us, but we did make it. And we made it work because we loved each other, and stuck by our promises to each other. So let's not hear any more talk about me going back to New York."

She turned out the light, kissed him, slid her body closer to him, and moved his hand over her body. "Just love me."

Chapter 9

❧

The next morning Laura was awake early. She glanced over at Eric and saw that he was resting easily. She slipped quietly out of bed and into the bath to get ready to interview for a home care job not far away. She was thankful for the opportunity to work jobs that were close, so she could slip home and check on Eric and the girls. When she emerged from the bath, Eric was awake and ready to be transferred to his wheelchair.

She was attending to his needs when he said to her, "You know I laid awake a long time last night, thinking of our conversation. I'm a very lucky guy to find you for my wife. Just look at what we have come through to this point in our lives. I know we have always scrambled to make a go of it. But you were always there. Why, even our honeymoon was a comedy of errors, do you remember?"

"You bet I do. I was so angry with my brother and his friends. You told me to pack my bag and hide it because we were going to leave as soon as we got married. We wanted to be married outdoors but decided on the church because of the predicted storm coming. I was so worried that you had stood me up because you were late getting to the church by almost a half-hour; you and my brother were still milking cows. Our reception was a simple one, held in the church basement with cake and ice cream, punch and coffee. We wanted to leave there and head to my brother's cottage in Canada to spend a few nights for our honeymoon."

"Yeah, some honeymoon it was too. When I went to get the truck, your brother had loaded the back end of it with bales of straw, so I hurried to unload it, and threw my back out. We didn't even make it into Canada. My back hurt so badly we had to stop at a motel in Buffalo. When you opened your suitcase, they had filled it with straw, so you had to shake the straw out of your nightgown. It was a sexy one, too. So you slept in the bed alone, in a negligee with straw in it, and I lay flat on my back on the floor all night. Some wedding night! It's a wonder you didn't leave me then."

"I would never do that. You have to take things that happen in your stride; people in love do that. They are there for each other." She started to chuckle. "Do you remember what happened when we got to the cottage?"

"Do I!" He started to laugh too. "We thought we would have the cottage to ourselves and there were your parents and five other couples from their card club. Your brother had a boat so we decided to water ski and I had never done it before."

"You did pretty well too," said Laura, smiling, "until you decided to jump the wake. Good thing you had on that life belt. And that borrowed bathing suit, for awhile... anyway." Now she was laughing.

"You're laughing! It wasn't funny! I got up all right, but when I fell my right arm went through the tow handle and the rope wrapped around my arm. It pulled me under and completely took the skin off my hand to the fingertips. Finally I popped up and you asked if I wanted in the boat, I told you 'no' and for good reason. I hurt so badly. I had to kick off the skis and the life belt that was down around my ankles before I could come up. You towed me in the water to the dock. When I got out, my swimsuit was gone too. And there were your parents and all their friends, watching and laughing."

"Yes and when we went to bed early that night we had to sleep in a twin bed. We put ointment on your hand, your back was killing you, and you were in so much pain you couldn't get comfortable. Besides, we heard cowbells all night long because there was a pasture out back of the cottage." Laura went on, "Next morning, I asked if anyone heard the cows out back." They all started laughing because they knew my brother had tied cowbells under our bed. 'Believe me,' I said, 'it wasn't what you guys are thinking about. It was due to lots of pain from skiing.'

Eric added, "But the topper was when we drove to Algonquin Park and rented a canoe. We paddled forty miles in one day, got caught in the rapids, and I yelled to jump out and hold onto the canoe. You jumped into a hole and finally we got to shore. We camped for the night and picked stones out of each other's feet. We did finally get to sleep together, in peace… and it was wonderful, I might add. Next day, we headed back, returned the canoe and there on the truck window was a sign, 'Kilroy Was Here!'"

Eric was grinning now too. "Your parents struck again. But the kicker was when we crossed the border and the guard asked what was in the bag you were holding and you said 'Pots.' We had to get out and they searched us thoroughly because the guard thought you said 'Pot.' He didn't know you meant cooking pots. We finally made it home. Yes sir, I would call that, 'The Honeymoon from Hell.'"

"It seemed like Heaven to me," said Laura, and she reached over and kissed him ever so softly. "We had a rough start, but we made it, didn't we?"

"I know, but just look. Our first home was a fallen down old house and you and I made it into something to live in until we came here in June of 1978. And what did I bring you to, a new house? No, we rented a ram-shackled, run down, old house outside of Soldotna for three months until we could build on the land we bought."

Quickly she added, "But, honey, wasn't that the plan? To build on the land?"

"Yes, it was." He was beginning to sound despondent now. "But did I build you a new home? No! We lived in that old rented place three months while I built us a basement home, finished just enough so we could move into it."

"Eric! It was the first home we owned in Alaska; to me it was beautiful!"

"Yeah, oh sure, some home. Love must have really blinded you! Some home!"

Eric was quick to remind her that it was a basement, 24 feet by 24 feet. "Cement block walls built into a hillside with the front looking out onto the grandiose mountains. It was wide open and everything we owned was in it. In the middle of the back wall we stacked boxes of things we brought to separate George, in one corner and in the other corner was our bed. The kitchen table with a kerosene lamp on it for light and a propane gas stove to use for cooking we placed in one of the front corners and a tall bookshelf separated our bed from a sleeper sofa in the other front corner. There was a wood stove in the middle of the basement and we always kept a huge pot of water on the top of it. No electricity or plumbing. We had an outhouse, and we had to haul our water in five-gallon jugs from an artesian spring five miles away. That first winter in the basement house, the snow came so fast we barely had time to put on a makeshift ceiling. We covered it with plywood and tarpaper and put dirt over it and let the snow cover it. It wasn't the warmest place that we could have built, but we braved it through."

Laura was adamant by now. "But it was our home in Alaska!" She chuckled. "And besides we had to snuggle a lot at night to keep warm. That wasn't all bad."

Eric sighed. "Don't you remember that when we heated the basement the heat went up and the ceiling got warm enough to melt the snow and we had leaks all over the ceiling? Then we did a real dumb thing and put plastic up on the inside of the ceiling. The water made puddles and drooped in big bubbles, so we put four oil drums in the center of the room and poked holes in the plastic so the water would run into the barrels."

By now Laura was shaking her head yes, and laughing.

Eric looked at her in disbelief. "You must have been awfully courageous or awfully crazy. I didn't really know which at the time because we were pretty green and stupid then."

She hugged him. "Crazy! Crazy about you! In my eyes you were not an average person. You were strong willed and had a very strong inner spirit, and it's still in there somewhere. You were meant for Alaska... and me!"

Kissing her softly on her hair he whispered, "I think you were too; it just took you awhile to adjust. You were pretty homesick, missed our families and friends. But we decided we could survive. After all, we were the 'Moles from New York!'"

She flushed a bit. "Oh my yes, I had almost forgotten about that. That's why the natives called us, cheeckapos."

He asked her if she remembered their first impression of Alaska.

"Of course, who could forget that? When we arrived here in June, it was gorgeous! Twenty-two hours of daylight each day and beautiful purple lupines in bloom all over. By the middle of June the wild roses started blooming, followed by the stunning fireweed. And when it storms here, there is very little lightning and hardly any thunder, which is very strange. The temperature was in the 60s and mid 70s here on Kenai Peninsula, and when the end of August rolled around and the fireweed went to seed; people told us that frost could come anytime. Snow fell a few days before mid-October. It was heavenly."

Eric began to laugh. "Boy, you are really some gal, always looking at things in a positive way. Remember the first winter? You said the winter seemed milder than in western New York, because we didn't get the 'damp cold' or the wind blowing the snow into 'blizzard conditions.'" Eric looked at her sitting beside him with wide open eyes and a grin on her face. "It was 20 degrees Fahrenheit outside and you'd run outside to use the outhouse with only a sweater on because it was a dry cold."

She stood up. "Yes, I remember it all. But for now, I best get you settled down here with the girls and get off to my work appointment. The daylight is getting longer every day, but I don't want to lose it."

She settled him in, fixed the sandwiches for their lunch so they could handle it if she ran late getting home. She instructed Mary to feed Patty, Daddy, and herself, if she wasn't home by lunchtime. Laura knew this was a lot to ask of one so young, but she knew Mary could do it. She was very grown up for her age.

"I'll see you soon. If you need help, call Connie. She knows I'll be out for a little while, so she is staying close to the phone." Laura kissed Eric. "I promise I won't be long. I love you… and you still make me tingle."

She drove to the store where people posted help wanted ads on a community bulletin board. She took a pad and wrote down phone numbers and gave a few calls to people looking for help with cleaning. There also was an ad for someone needing a caregiver with a phone number. She took that and decided to call that one at home and set up an appointment.

She had no trouble getting the cleaning jobs, as most people in the area knew of their situation and when she called, they said yes, they could use her once a week. After several calls she picked up their mail and returned home.

"I'm back!" She called as she opened the door. Everything was quiet and it worried her a bit. She went into the bedroom and there was Mary, holding a book so Eric could see it and he was reading a story to the girls. "Well, look at you three. What a nice picture to come home to. And here I was worried. Carry on with your reading; I'll go get lunch."

After lunch, the girls took a nap and Laura told Eric that she had have been hired to do about four cleaning jobs a week. At $10 an hour, each job should take about three or four hours, so that should bring in roughly one hundred and sixty dollars a week or about five hundred dollars a month. She also had a number to call about Home Care. Maybe it would be nearby, so she could be close, if she was needed at home. "If I'm lucky it'll just be going for groceries, meds, mail, errands etc. No big health problem. We'll see! Maybe I can pick up a baby-sitting job here or there. There could be some nurses at the hospital that might need someone to watch their children, while they work. I'll call there tomorrow."

Eric patted her hand. "You did a great job, honey. I'm proud of you!"

"See, I told you we would be OK; we just have to have faith!" However, privately she wondered if the work she had found would make enough money to sustain them. "As I mentioned before, I would like to make enough to double up on our land payments; we sure don't want to lose our land. Do you remember how we scrambled to get the down payment for it?"

"I sure do," said Eric. "When we found out that Agnes was going to sell off some of her land after Charley died, we asked her what she wanted for ten acres. I saw this piece and knew it was what we needed. She told me there was another couple that wanted it also and, to be fair, she decided that whoever came up with the down payment of two thousand dollars first was going to be the new landowner. I remember how we worked and scrambled to get that money, and when we got it I ran it over to Agnes's and just got there about one half hour before the other couple. I guess the good Lord has been with us all along."

"Did she tell you we got there one-half hour before the other couple?" Laura looked puzzled.

"She sure did, and it made me happy, I can tell you, for sure. This was prime property then and still is!"

"Yes, it is." Laura grinned. "Agnes told me the other couple was there first, but she told them we had given her earnest money, and you were coming with the rest soon." Laura hugged him. "She said old Charley would like it that way because we had no land and the other couple was already settled. She fudged a little, but she maintains it was fair and square. She really is a good woman!"

"She sure enough is and spunky too!" He smiled that shy smile. "She told me she remembered how she and Charley had struggled and we reminded her of them. More than she cared to remember. I wish I could've met Charley. She said he was a lot like me: determined and proud."

"So you see, she liked us; she is a good woman. I can make the payments, double, or give more when I can, and we'll be fine." Laura rambled on before he could speak. "So quit worrying. I can feed you a good breakfast every morning, go out and get my work done, be home every three or four hours to check on you, and be home in the evening to fix us all a good meal. Now that's a promise!" She said it with conviction. She knew she could do it because people were so good about helping out. "It's a great thing when people help each other in times of stress. It's very humbling to learn what people will do to help one another."

That first year seemed to go pretty much as Laura believed it would. Everything did go well. She had her jobs and a few extras now and then. She made the land payments on time. Their food was ample. There was just one thing she hadn't noticed.

During all this time Eric was depressed and angry. He didn't show it to Laura and she didn't realize how much he was holding back. One day, while the girls napped and Laura was working, he wheeled himself into their bedroom and over to the chest of drawers. The top drawer was a little difficult to reach so he put pillows on the floor, leaned the skis on them, and rolled up on the skis. With much difficulty, he pulled the drawer open, reached in and felt around for his gun. After finding the gun, he struggled to see if he could get it to his head. For a long time, he sat alone in the quiet house with the gun to his head. Then he reversed the motion and returned the gun to the drawer, got the skis back in the corner and picked up the pillows. It was done. He knew he could do it, when and if he couldn't stand being depressed anymore.

He brightened up when she came home. It wasn't until later on, that she found out he'd considered suicide, many times. Jim had come over one day to spend the day with him. It was then that Eric told him of his feelings.

When Jim asked how he was doing, Eric shook his head. "Jim, to tell the truth, I've considered suicide many times. I think the only thing that keeps me from it is Laura and the girls. Laura is working so hard to make ends meet. Even Mary and Patty are acting older than they are, to help care for me. If they can be strong, then I have to let my faith come through somehow."

Jim sat silent for a bit, then answered Eric, "The Lord will never let you down. He is giving you the strength not to end your life."

"But Jim, I keep praying to God to change things and make it better, and when it doesn't happen I become very bitter." Eric touched his heart with his hand. "Why can others have miracles happen to them and not me?"

"I don't know their situations, so I don't have all the answers." Jim whispered, "I just know that we have our faith and hope, and that keeps us going. Look how far you've come since September. Miracles don't happen overnight. I think He is with you a lot. Look how long your old 1973 Chevy pickup has lasted you. Then you got an even older pickup, which was a good truck. He provided for you there. I just feel He is with you every day and you have to get those thoughts of suicide out of your mind. You need to start looking at your everyday miracles happening around you. He is providing."

Eric was still for a long time. "Yes, you're right. I am looking for too much to happen all at once. My miracles are whenever Laura needs to take me anyplace; neighbors and friends are there to help carry me down the basement steps and to the truck. And that isn't easy in the winter with the snow and ice. I have been foolish."

Later, when Laura came home, Jim told her of their conversation. "I spoke to him at length and told him he was looking for miracles to happen that were already there, the everyday miracles."

Laura grabbed Jim by the hand. "Jim! What are you saying to me? I had no idea Eric was having these dreadful thoughts. Do you think he is just pacifying you? Will I be able to leave him alone, with the girls?"

Jim looked her straight in the eye. "No Laura, I strongly feel that after our conversation, he is back on the right track. He just needed to be reminded of just how much the Lord is watching over this family."

Laura hugged Jim and thanked him. He left and she never mentioned their conversation to Eric.

But she did move the gun.

Chapter 10

The winter of 1985 passed, and soon signs of spring began to show, bringing moderate weather to the Kenai Peninsula. *Spring Break Up* was starting to show on the roads. Laura dreaded that annual event when the dirt roads turn to the consistency of muddy jell-o until they dry down. Spring on the peninsula was beautiful, the birch, willow and popular trees budding their leaves. The cottonwood buds smelled wonderful, as usual. Everyone knew the summer would be full of wild lupines, roses, and fireweed and the temperature would be around 60 to 70 degrees. Absolutely balmy.

Because of the difficulty during the winter months of getting Eric down the basement steps, and to the pickup, Sam and George suggested to Laura and Eric if they bought material for a ramp, they'd get people together to build it for them. So that spring, some of the neighbors and friends got together and built the ramp and a new porch on the upper level of their log home. Again Laura thought, *how can we ever repay them for all they are doing?*

While the ramp and the new porch were being built, George brought a Doberman along with him and asked the girls to keep her occupied so she wouldn't get in the way of the work.

Mary stooped down to pet the dog. "What's your dog's name, Uncle George?"

"I just call her dog. She doesn't have one yet. She's still a puppy. Why don't you two name her for me?"

This tickled the girls and after they talked it over and decided, Mary said, "We chose the name Ruby, because she is a reddish color, like a ruby. Is that okay?"

"Whatever suits you two is fine by me. She seems to like being here with you. Maybe your mom and dad would let you keep her. With your mom being gone from time to time at work, she would let you and your dad know when someone was around. I have her house trained already. Ask your folks if you can keep her."

"Can we, Mom?" Patty pleaded.

"Yeah, Mom, we'll let her sleep in our room." Mary added.

"Well, I don't know… what do you think, Daddy?"

"Sure, why not. We should have a dog for protection around here, especially with me in this chair. I say yes."

This pleased the girls very much. By the time the work was finished on the ramp and porch, the whole family had become attached to the dog and the dog to them.

Laura and the girls could push Eric out on the porch to see the mountains and the coming of spring and summer. Then one day Eric voiced an idea: "Why don't we have a huge garden this year? It's nearing Memorial Day. I'll ask Jim, Sam and George to build a greenhouse for us."

So they did, and it was a beautiful greenhouse that lasted for a couple of years. It had rounded metal arches covered with plastic with side plastic windows that would open. It was great for them. Eric loved being out in the greenhouse, working with the plants. One day he called to Laura. "Why don't you plant some potatoes in the garden, while the girls and I get the vegetable plants started here in the greenhouse?"

"OK, sir, that I will."

I will show him I can do it. I know he thinks I can't, she thought to herself, so she planted a lot of potatoes. In fact she planted about a quarter of an acre to garden.

"Isn't it great being able to work outside all summer, with the long hours of daylight?" she said to Eric. "We can work outside until midnight."

Of course, the girls had a lot of watering to do. While Laura was at work during the day, they would carry full watering cans to irrigate the plants. It was a great experience for them, and it gave them a real work ethic.

One day when Laura came home, she found Eric and the girls laughing and having a good time. The girls were so tickled.

"What's so funny in here?" she asked as she entered the house.

Eric stopped giggling. "Oh, I was just telling the girls how you all looked more like beekeepers than gardeners. What with the long sleeves and long pants and the mosquito netting over your hats and tucked into your shirts. You all look as scary as I did with the halo on my head when I was in the hospital. And the girls thought that was funny! And so did I. Don't you?"

"Yeah," she said and started chuckling too, "When you get a mental picture. It is funny! But it's so necessary with the mosquitoes being so bad!" Then they all laughed.

It seemed like they were finally in a routine. Life was pretty close to normal. Laura was working at her odd jobs, Eric and the girls were happy working in the garden. One day after they had eaten their lunch, Eric was still sitting at the table, the girls playing outside. Mary had just stepped in for a minute. Laura was doing the dishes and happened to look out the window. "Oh! My holy mother of God! Eric!" she screamed wildly.

"What is it, Laura!" he yelled at her, as she suddenly ran for the door. She opened the door and Ruby, their trusted Doberman, sped past her running toward the garden. There in the garden was a cow moose and her baby. And between the huge cow moose and her baby was Patty. Mother moose was pawing the ground and snorting. The hair was standing up on her neck. Ruby ran between Patty and the cow, barking loudly and frantically. The fear Laura felt for her baby had the adrenaline flowing. She seemed to have extra speed and strength coming from somewhere. Not thinking of anything but saving Patty, Laura ran, scooped her up, and rushed back into the house. Then she turned and loudly called Ruby back also, holding the door open for the dog. They were out and back before anyone had time to even think. As soon as Laura grabbed Patty and ran toward the house, calling Ruby to follow, the mother moose ran to her calf, and they both moved toward the woods.

By then Mary, who was now six years old, was trying to push Eric to the door, crying for Daddy to help. Eric was agitated. "Laura, do you know the danger you and Patty were in? Thank God, Ruby kept the cow at bay! That mother moose would not have stopped until she stomped you and Patty to death; they will do anything to protect their offspring."

"Well, Eric, as a mother, so did I. You saw! I didn't stop to think. I just ran to get Patty!" Laura was out of breath and breathing very fast. Tears were welling up in her eyes. Only now did the full impact hit her. "We must really reward Ruby; she is the real heroine here." They all embraced each other and Ruby too. Finally, Laura put Patty down. "Sweetie, tell me whatever possessed you to go out into the garden alone? I know you are four years old now, but you must always have someone with you in the garden."

"But Mama, I wanted to see the pony!" she said, not realizing the danger she had been in at the time.

"Well, I guess the baby moose does look like a pony to a little girl. Let's all settle down now. I've got dishes to finish." Laura looked at Eric and winked as she sat Patty on his lap.

As Laura returned to her dishes she was still shaking and crying softly to herself. Eric took the cue of the wink she gave and called Mary over to him and Patty. "You know, there is no better time than the present, to tell you two all about the animal that was out there in our garden. We call them moose. They have families just like ours. There is a daddy moose called a bull moose, and then the mommy moose called a cow. And then of course the babies are called calves. The daddy moose can grow to weigh as much as 1200 to 1600 pounds. Now that is real big, real big! And the mommy moose can weigh as much as 800 to 1300 pounds; she is big too, but not as big as the daddy moose. The little calves when born only weigh thirty pounds. The one you saw today wasn't too old, as he was just born this spring. They are nice to look at, but only from a long way away. Never! Never! Do you understand? Never ever, do you run out to see one up close! They are very dangerous, especially when they have a young one, as today. Thanks to Ruby, our trusted Doberman, and your Mom, Patty was saved from being stomped to death; so don't ever go up to any moose again. Big or little, stay away and look from a safe distance. Do you understand?"

They both shook their heads yes and gave Ruby big hugs and lots of love.

Eric looked at Laura. "Boy, I hope they remember what they were just told. That was a close one!"

As summer wore on, the garden grew, and they harvested the produce. As the neighbors caught salmon, they always seemed to have a little more than they needed, so they'd stop by and give them to the family, and Laura added them to their stock of canned salmon.

Fall was just coming on when Eric said one morning, "I am so proud of you and the girls, and what a good job you've done with the garden.

By the way, did you notice we had a light frost last night? And Laura, did you also notice the leaves turning color? Fall is hunting and harvesting season, so it always seems so busy. I've already asked Jim and George to try to bag a moose for us."

Laura looked up from her breakfast with a startled look on her face. "Oh my gosh! Help! How am I going to get all those potatoes dug before a deep frost comes? Oh, Eric what am I going to do?"

Eric chuckled. "I'm sure you'll find a way to get your spuds dug!"

Then one day several of the neighbor children were over and Laura asked, "Would you children like to help me dig the potatoes? And when we get them all done, we'll have a 'Potato Party.'"

Of course this intrigued the children. "What's a potato party?" one child ventured.

So she thought about it, and after they'd dug fifteen hundred pounds of potatoes, she set a date for the party. She would have to come up with every way she could find to fixing potatoes. They had the party after school and before dark. For the party, she made potato pancakes, mashed potatoes, French fries, hash browns, and curly fries. The house was potato control central. All the kids had a ball. The kids worked hard and enjoyed the party, plus they all went home with one hundred pounds of potatoes.

This was two years after Eric's accident, and he enjoyed watching all this progress and fun happening before him. To top it off, they had enough potatoes for a year.

Chapter 11

The winter passed and along with it the thought of suicide that Eric harbored the year before when he was so depressed. It seemed Jim's talk to him sunk in, and he was thinking of what he could do, instead of what he couldn't. Now his thoughts were on planning the garden again. He seemed to enjoy working with the plants in the greenhouse, instructing the girls with the watering, and being outside to instruct the tilling of the ground and planting. The garden kept Eric busy during the summer. He could move around pretty well in his wheelchair now. The intense therapy at the Humana hospital had gained him enough muscle control in his arms to control it well enough that he no longer needed the Quad pegs on the wheels. Because of his paralysis from mid-chest down, and the onset of the fall and winter months, it was necessary to take him into Soldotna for Peninsula physical therapy. It was needed to help from getting contractures. If he didn't have the therapy, he would have shortening or shrinkage of a tendon or the resulting persistent flexion or distortion at a joint. Laura took him twice a week, on Tuesday, and

Thursday, to keep his muscles stretched.

It was a chore to get him down the ramp and into the vehicle to make the trip and one day he said to Laura. "Why are you putting me, yourself and the girls through all this? Can't you do the hand passive methods at home? It would be easier on me not to be jostled around so much."

"Yes, I could," she replied, "but they have pulleys you need to work with while seated in your wheelchair and tables to lay you on prone and supine to do the necessary movements. They are much better methods than I can do here at home, and besides they have equipment to use we don't have at home."

"Okay, you're right. I do need the therapy, and it does help me," he said reluctantly. "I just hate to have another thing piled onto your shoulders... and another expense."

"Susan Archer is your therapist, and a very good friend of mine. All we have to pay for is the use of the equipment and the facility. She wanted to do this for you and me, so she's not turning in her fees," Laura explained to him. "We are fortunate to have such friends. If you had accepted help, with some disability income from the VA, it would be a lot easier."

Eric had been too proud to accept the help when it was offered to him in the hospital, and knowing this, he did work hard in therapy. Laura and the girls would watch him while they waited. Then Susan said to them, "You know, you and the girls don't need to sit here with Eric. He is, and will be, fine. Why don't you take the girls and do something for these two hours?"

Laura and the girls did begin to plan other activities on Tuesday and Thursday afternoons. They would go window-shopping or, on nice days, to the park. This way, Laura got a break and a chance to spend some one-on-one time with the girls. When they returned one day from their shopping tour to pick up Eric, Susan said to her, "I just want you to know what a strong willed person Eric is. He has an intense inner spirit that drives him."

"Yes, I know, and I'm thankful for that," Laura answered, "and I don't think he could've survived out in the woods after his fall if it hadn't been for that spirit. He's not your average person. He's very special to me, and I want to thank you for all you're doing to help us during this difficult time." Laura and Susan hugged each other and went in to get Eric ready to go home.

During the time Eric needed to be going to Soldotna for his therapy, the pick-up truck needed some repairs. Whenever Sam would come home from working on the slope, sometimes two weeks at a time, he would come over and give the vehicle a good going over to keep it in good running condition for Laura and Eric. Sam was a wonderful mechanic and an even better neighbor.

One weekend when Sam came over he seemed to be troubled. When they went out to work on the pickup, Eric asked him, "Sam, is something wrong? You don't seem to be yourself today."

Sam stopped his work under the hood, and looked at Eric. "I think that Connie may be disillusioned with me, working up on the slope, and may be thinking of leaving me. She has always complained that I'm never home enough and when I am, I'm always sleeping or doing other things and not paying enough attention to her."

"Do you know for sure? How did you find out?" Eric quizzed him. "It isn't because you spend so much time over here helping us, is it? Because if that's the case, even though it is a big help to Laura and me, we would want you to spend more time at home with Connie. Lord knows we wouldn't want to be the cause of a rift between you two."

"No, don't you worry about you two being the cause of our problem." Sam turned away to check the truck over. "We both think the world and all of you two, and besides, any more when I am home, she's gone most of the time. So it doesn't matter how much I come over here."

"Well, what are you going to do about it? Have you talked to her? Can you work things out between the two of you? Is there anything we can do to help?" Eric wheeled up to Sam and touched his back. "If you ever need to vent, always remember it will go no further than me. You can always talk to Laura or me. I truly am sorry to hear this."

"I appreciate it, Eric. You two, without a doubt, are our truest friends. And I want you to know I'll always be there for you and Laura, whenever you need me. I promise you that." Sam grabbed Eric's hand and gave him a pat on the shoulder. "But for right now, I should be going home."

Sam returned Eric to the house, said a few words to Laura and then left for home. Laura looked at Eric with a question on her face. "What's the matter with Sam? Did you two have words out there working on the truck?"

"No we didn't, heaven sakes no. Sam would be the last man I would have words with over mechanics; after all, he's the expert. I'll bet there isn't anything he can't fix." He paused for a moment and then quietly said, "Unless it's trouble between him and Connie. He told me today that he thinks she may leave him. He knew I would tell you, but don't let it get any farther than us, for now."

"Oh, Eric, I sure hate to hear that! Connie and Sam have been our good friends for a long time. I remember the first time I met Connie; Agnes brought her over to see, as only Agnes could put it, 'the new neighbor's baby.' That's really how we became friends. It was almost eight years ago, as Mary will be eight in March." Laura sat down at the kitchen table and putting her hands over her eyes, cried softly. "I'm sorry, Eric, but this shocked me so, I can hardly believe it. Did he tell you why she would do such a thing?"

"No nothing, other than the fact that he's gone from home most of the time. You know how word travels, especially here in Sterling. People make a mountain out of a molehill. What with only one furniture store, one gas station, one laundromat, a Mom and Pop grocery and several churches, news spreads fast among only 1500 people. Why, we only have an elementary school; the kids are bussed eighteen miles to Soldotna for middle and high school. I wouldn't be surprised if it wasn't known over in Soldotna too." Pausing only a moment to digest the idea, he continued, "We just have to try not to spread anything at all. We must respect Sam's wishes. He's a good man; you know Sam works up on the slope for two weeks at a whack before he gets to come home sometimes. He's gone quite a bit and maybe Connie goes out and talks to other people, and you know how gossip starts. Some busybody could just be starting something nasty. I sure hope that's all it is."

"I do too, Eric; after all, Connie sews, crochets, knits and does crafts to keep herself busy. I imagine it does get lonely, but I hardly think she would really leave Sam. We'll just have to wait and see. All we can do now is be supportive of Sam… and Connie too, if this is not true." She got up from the table. "But for now, I have to go and clean a house. Things are ready for supper and I have some sandwiches in the fridge for you and the girls, should you get hungry. Take care now; I'll see you in a little while."

As Laura drove to her cleaning job, she could not help but think about Sam and Connie splitting up. They had been so close for years. They had never seemed to have any problems. Maybe they were private about their dissentions. She sent up a little prayer for them, and thanked God for the good marriage she and Eric had, in spite of all their problems. *Maybe all the obstacles we've endured made us closer*, she thought.

She remembered when she and Eric found out she was pregnant with Mary. It was mid June of 1979, while they still lived in the basement house. It was then they decided to go ahead with building the top part of the house. They had heard from a friend about the permit area to cut logs, in the latter part of 1978, and they decided to see if they could get a permit from the government to cut in a certain area off of Swanson

River Road. They wouldn't have to pay for the trees, but they had to stay within a certain area and be able to get the logs out themselves and leave the area clean.

During the two years they lived in the basement, they cut and peeled the logs for the house and set them in place. After the trees were cut, Eric hired a log skidder and they were put on a fifth wheel trailer and hauled the fifteen miles to the property. Eric even showed her how to peel the logs, how to use a "draw-knife"—a knife blade with a handle at each end at a 90-degree angle so you can get the blade under the cambium layer of the tree bark. Then you pull it back toward your body and "peel" the bark off the logs.

If the logs were freshly cut they peeled easier. How long it would take varied. She chuckled to herself, remembering how they first started out "peeling" the logs. All three of them had screwdrivers and were trying to get the bark off using the screwdrivers. Had it not been for a seasoned old-timer passing by the day they started, they would still be peeling. He asked them what they were doing with those screwdrivers and hammers. They answered, "Peeling logs."

"Haven't you ever heard of a draw-knife?" he asked. "Go to the hardware and buy a few, and the job will go much faster."

So they did.

Eric and their friend George were faster than she was. She would take about one and a quarter hour per log, depending on the weather conditions. She remembered how she told Eric that she was slower because she was pregnant.

After all the logs were peeled, Eric would scribe each log, then cut the cups in them with the chain saw, chunk the pieces, and use an adz to make the cupping smooth. They put sill-seal insulation between the logs and the logs fit on top of each other well enough that you didn't have to chink between them. In this manner, the logs showed on both the inside and the outside. It was rough work, but they made it. They even took time out to plant their first garden in 1979. They were on their way.

Laura remembered how she had to quit helping because Eric was worried that she would hurt the baby. But Mary arrived as healthy as any baby could be. She didn't have a crib or basket; she slept in a dresser drawer with a pillow in it.

It was then that little, tiny, spunky Agnes brought Connie over to meet us. We hit it off right away and became fast friends. Sam came whenever he could to help with the finishing of the upper house. No one could ask for better friends than those two.

Connie watched Mary while Laura worked in the hospital from May to November in 1980. After that, Laura worked in the clinics, the doctor's office and the home health care units until Patty was born in 1982. By then, Laura had her hands full at home and had a fairly good nest egg, so they could even afford to buy a crib for Patty.

Her thoughts ended as she pulled up in front of the Mitchell family home. Mrs. Mitchell had been in the hospital for quite some time and would be coming home soon. HMMMMM, maybe she will need some home care when she returns. Turning off the engine, she gathered her cleaning supplies and went inside.

Chapter 12

❦

Things were finally down to a routine for Eric, Laura, and the girls. Mary, almost eight, and Patty, almost six, both attended school in Sterling. Laura had cleaning jobs to go to routinely, and a few Health Care rounds to check on. Every Tuesday and Thursday she took Eric to Soldotna for his physical therapy with Sue.

It was then she and the girls had a break to go Christmas shopping while the girls were on Christmas vacation. This pleased Patty to no end, to see the Christmas decorations in the town and to visit the stores. Laura picked up a few little things for the girls for Christmas and bought some cards to send. The weather had become quite a bit colder and the snow heavier. The five hours of daylight each day were starting to lengthen. One could tell that Christmas was right around the corner.

One day after they dropped Eric off at therapy, Laura asked the girls, "How would you like to go back home and decorate the house for Christmas while Daddy is doing his therapy? We could surprise him, when we get back home, after his treatment. Would you like to do that?"

They were very excited at the idea and Laura cautioned: "Now don't tell Daddy what we're going to do. Mary has been making paper chains out of red and green paper and Sam has cut us a Christmas tree, which is hidden in the greenhouse. We can put it up and decorate it this evening."

So when they left Eric with Sue, Laura kissed him and said, "We're going to be back for you in about two or three hours; you should be finished by then. I have some errands to run for Home Health Care."

"OK, don't rush. The roads are not in the best condition, and neither is the truck, so be careful. We don't need you to have an accident. I'll be all right here with Sue. She takes excellent care of me while you are gone." He looked at Sue for confirmation. "Don't you, Sue?"

"You bet I do, so come on big guy, let's start our torture exercises," she said. "And, Laura, don't worry if you run a little late. Eric will be fine here, no problem."

So they were off for home. The roads were snow covered with a light dusting of new snow, but the snowplows had been out and spread dirt to keep them from becoming slippery. When they reached home, Laura noticed some truck tracks in their drive. They looked like Sam's. They had come in and out. She thought, *I bet he's been here and put the tree up in the corner we talked about.* Connie and Sam knew where they kept the extra keys in case they had to let themselves in to help Eric.

When she opened the door to the cabin, sure enough, Sam had been there and set the tree in the corner. He also strung some evergreen boughs around the room. It smelled so good, just like being outdoors in the woods. She and the girls decorated the house with Christmas things: candles, nativity scene, ribbons, everything festive they could find. As soon as they finished, they hopped in the truck and drove back to Soldotna to pick up Eric.

When they got there Eric was ready to go. When he got in, he said, looking at the girls, "Hey, Laura, where did you find these two angels?

Were they in here with us the first trip?"

Mary was quick enough to say, "Of course, Daddy, don't be silly. We were just quiet." She wanted to giggle, but she kept a straight face. They all loved surprises.

"Well, I am sure glad you were. I was worried about you being at home alone after school. I wondered if Mom made arrangements for you since she was running errands. I guess I underestimated your mom. She's pretty good about taking care of things. After all, she takes good care of all of us, doesn't she?"

"You bet! But you didn't need to worry 'cause we're on Christmas vacation, remember?" was the reply from the girls together.

The ride home was a continuous line of chatter about what happened that day running errands, how Eric's therapy went, and just about everything in general. It made the time go by quickly, and they were home before they knew it. When they got there, Laura said, "Let me get the packages and the girls in first and I'll be back to get you, love."

"Okay, whatever is the easiest for you, honey."

Laura got the packages and girls inside the house, helped them off with their boots and coats, and instructed them to be ready to open the door for her when she got there with Eric. They were both so excited to be able to surprise their daddy, they could hardly wait. Laura lit the candles then went out to get Eric.

When the girls opened the door for them, Eric was really surprised. "Oh, my gosh! Who did this? Do we have Christmas elves in this neck of the woods? This is like a Christmas special. Did you guys do this?"

The girls could hardly contain themselves. They were all smiles and giggles, and they ran to Eric and gave him hugs and kisses. "Gee, Daddy, your nose is cold! Are you surprised?"

"You bet I am. No one could ever ask for a better family than I have. Look at what you all do… to make me happy!" He choked a little on his words, thinking how selfish he had been at times, putting himself before them. "Christmas holds a very special place in my heart, you know. I met your mother at Christmas time. She was probably the best gift anyone could ever get for Christmas." He looked at Laura and gave her that special little shy grin that she loved. And she knew he was pleased. "Hey, I'm hungry, let's eat and then we can decorate the Christmas tree, okay?"

After they finished the job Laura put the girls to bed. Then, as she started getting Eric ready for the night, they heard a truck pull up outside. Laura went to the deck to peer out. Getting out of his truck and heading for the house was Sam. She quickly stepped out onto the deck and motioned him to come upstairs. She let Sam in. "Sam, what on earth is the matter? You pulled in here like you were in a powerful hurry!"

"Connie told me she wanted a divorce," he blurted out. "My God, we've been married for sixteen years; the boys, David and Danny, are fourteen and twelve. She said she wanted out; she couldn't stand being alone all the time! She said that I'm never home. She's moving into an apartment in Soldotna. I just can't believe it! What did I do wrong? She even accused me of seeing you, Laura, while Eric is having his therapy treatments in Soldotna! What is wrong with her? Why does she have to drag you into this mess?"

"Here, Sam, sit down. I'll fix some coffee. You, Eric, and I will talk about this." Laura went to the kitchen to fix the coffee.

"What's the matter, Laura?" Eric called to her, "What's wrong with Sam? He sounds distraught. Come get me out there."

Laura went into the bedroom, teary eyed. "Oh Eric, Connie asked Sam for a divorce! She's moving to an apartment in Soldotna. You must go talk to him. He's really upset."

She finished with Eric's preparations for the night, and then pushed him into the kitchen and up to the table with Sam. She pulled a chair up too. Eric said quietly, "Sam, we're so sorry. Can't we do something to help?

What about the boys? Is she taking them too?"

Sam looked up from staring into his coffee cup. "I don't know. When she told me, I left the house immediately; I just had to get away and think."

"Well, let's just talk it over, Sam. You have to ask her why. You have to ask her what's made her so unhappy that she would want this. You have to think of your boys too. What about when you are on the slope? Could the boys be trusted to stay alone in the house without her there?"

"Oh yeah, the boys would be fine at home. They're very responsible. I've seen to that in their up-bringing," Sam said proudly. "You know, I came here to Alaska when I was thirteen or fourteen. I heard my uncle talking of Alaska, and the oil fields, and it intrigued me so that I left for school one morning and never returned home again. I got in with my uncle, when he was leaving, and told him my parents said it was okay, and here I am. Of course, when we got here, I told him what I did, and we called my parents so they wouldn't worry over me. I lied about my age, got a job on the slope, and have been working there ever since. I lived in a room with my uncle for awhile, and then I got a room of my own, when I started getting paychecks under my belt.

"I've taught David and Danny about mechanics and carpenter work, and they're very knowledgeable. They'll be okay. And as far as knowing right from wrong, there is no doubt in my mind they are God-fearing children. They know all about the Bible. They have studied it well." Sam looked at Laura and held out his coffee cup. "Laura, is there any more coffee back there?"

As Laura got up to get more coffee, Eric said, "Well, Sam, the only thing you have to decide is your feelings about Connie. I know the boys love her, and so do you. What now?"

"I guess that's up to Connie. I can't force her to stay. Where would the love be then? If we were meant to be together, she'll come back to me. As for the boys, we'll have to decide that too. I can't hold her if she doesn't want to stay." Sam held his cup out to Laura as she poured more coffee. "I wanted you two to know first. You're like a brother to me, Eric. And Laura, not a sweeter person do I know, so I need to tell you this; Connie drove past here today after I was here to put your Christmas tree in the house. She saw my truck tracks and she accused me of coming over here to see you while Eric was in therapy in Soldotna. You weren't even here when I came over to set up the tree. That is how her mind is working right now. She isn't using common sense."

Sam finished his coffee and got up. "You are two of my best friends, and the last thing I would ever do is hurt you. I won't stand for Connie thinking the way she is. It's up to me to straighten her out on that issue. I have to get my life in order. I know, you know the truth, so wish me luck." He patted Eric on the back and waved to Laura, got into his truck and was gone.

"Oh, Eric," said Laura, wringing her hands, "I feel so bad. Do you think I should call Connie and explain to her why Sam was here today or go to see her?"

"I wouldn't now. Sam came to us and I think we should let Connie do the same. We really don't want to take sides in this. We love both of them. We should just be here if they need us." Eric looked at her and extended his hand toward her as best he could. "I am so lucky to have you. Where would I be without you? Let's say a prayer for Connie and Sam, then go to bed and enjoy what we have with each other. Maybe tomorrow will be brighter for them."

Christmas came and went, with Eric and Laura just having a quiet Christmas with the girls. They had heard little from either Connie or Sam, although they did send an invitation through Sam for them to join them for Christmas dinner.

Then one day Laura came home from cleaning in Soldotna and told

Eric she ran into Connie. "Connie rented a furnished apartment. She asked me about the day Sam came over to our house and set up our Christmas tree and I told her Mary, Patty and I were not even home. Sam had cut the tree for us, to help surprise you, at Christmas. She apologized to me for even thinking that there was something going on between Sam and me. She said that the boys stay with her awhile and then awhile with Sam, when he's home. The split did not seem to bother them; they adjusted well."

The divorce took place in early January of 1988. After that, Laura saw Connie pretty regularly when she took Eric for his treatments. And they would see Sam whenever he came down from the slope to spend a little time at home. He would come over and help with any repairs that Eric or Laura might need, and to help with the big things that Laura couldn't handle. Periodically, Eric would invite the boys over and he would talk to them about hunting and fishing. He even gave them some of his fishing equipment.

They in turn helped catch the salmon that Laura canned for the following winter. She canned some for Sam, too. It was neighbor helping neighbor in times of stress and adversity.

The year was slipping by pretty fast, and the end of summer was approaching. Sam came over one weekend on his time away from the slope and said to Eric and Laura, "You are not going to believe this… but Connie came over and talked to me at length and told me she had made a big mistake and she wanted to be married again."

Eric was very surprised. "I can't believe it! You mean you are going to take her back? Why?"

Sam looked down and said, "She told me her parents were finally coming to visit us and they didn't know we were divorced, so she thought it would be great to get remarried. She said there was no one else for her and that one was a lonely number. So I agreed. We would like to have you and Laura stand up with us."

"How are the boys taking the news?" Laura asked.

"They think it's a great idea. It will be the first time Connie's parents have come here to see us, and the boys are excited. They want to show their grandparents around." Sam continued, "Connie doesn't want to hurt her parents, so she thinks we should be married when they come. They have both just retired, have the time to come, and they want to see where and how we live in Alaska."

Both Laura and Eric were stunned by the news, so Laura quickly asked Sam, "Hey, why don't you stay for supper with us. It will give us a chance to digest all of this and talk some more. Just one thing, my wood is running low and I need some more for the stove. Would you mind getting some in for me?"

"Sure, no problem, and yes I'd like to talk some more. This has taken me back a bit too," Sam answered as he went out the door.

As Sam closed the door behind him, Eric said, "I still can't believe it! They have only been divorced a little over six months and Sam agreed to take her back. Do you really think it will work? Has Connie said anything to you about this whole thing?"

"No, but we must not interfere. If he wants to take her back, it's not our place to say any different. We don't really know how he feels about her. He never comes right out and answers your question when you ask. As you said before, we have to stay neutral; we can't pick sides on this."

By this time, Sam came back into the house with an armload of wood. Laura already had supper going. Sam was happy for the invitation and during supper they discussed when and where he and Connie would be remarried.

It was a cool July evening when they all stood in front of the minister of the church and Sam and Connie took their vows of marriage again. It was a simple ceremony, just the four of them and the children, David, Danny, Mary and Patty. After the ceremony, they all returned to Laura and Eric's home for cake and coffee. They sat and visited for a while and Sam and Connie talked of her parents' visit and what they planned to do while they were here. Connie said, "One thing I do want them to do is to meet both of you and your girls. We have talked so much about the two of you."

"Sure, we want to meet them, too. We could just have a good old-fashioned neighborhood get together with all of our friends. Don't you think that would be a good idea?" Eric suggested.

"That's a real good idea. We can have it at our place. It will give them a chance to meet all of our friends. They can finally put faces to all the names we've talked about since we've been here," said Sam, grinning.

They all laughed and enjoyed the evening talking about what they were going to discuss with Connie's parents. "They're going to see a different way of life here than what they have in Illinois. It might even be a little bit of a cultural shock to them." Laura excused herself and put the girls to bed, and then Connie and Sam said they should be going home too. After all, they had to honeymoon. The boys blushed and said, "Oh Dad, don't tell us that!" They all laughed again and said their good-byes.

Within two weeks, Connie's folks came and spent their two weeks with them, and they seemed to enjoy themselves immensely. But never once did Connie or Sam mention that they had separated and then remarried. They took Mr. and Mrs. Cooper to see all the sights. Mrs. Cooper could not get over how beautiful it was in Alaska in the summer. She was happy with their visit, but she was ready to return to Illinois when their time was up. After they left, Connie and Sam seemed to get along with each other, *but Sam is so easy going, anyone could get along with him,* Laura thought. He would come over as he always did and work on the truck when it needed repair. He'd help with the garden chores and anything else that needed to be done.

Things were going along fairly well for Eric and Laura, but each year they seemed to fall a little further behind financially than the year before. Laura had finally gotten the land paid off, but it was almost more than she could keep up, with only her part-time cleaning and Home Health Care jobs for income.

One Tuesday, as she was canning salmon that Sam's boys had brought her, she heard a truck pull up outside. It was Sam. He called to her and she went to the door. "Laura," he said, "do you mind if I come in? I know that Eric is away at therapy and you and the girls are here alone, but I need to talk with you."

"Why of course. You know you are always welcome here. Eric would be the first to tell you that." Looking at the expression on Sam's face, she asked: "What is it? What's the matter, Sam? There is something wrong, I can tell."

"I wanted to tell you first and you can tell Eric. I am really ashamed to tell Eric myself." Sam dropped into the first chair and put his head in his hands. "Connie is filing for divorce again. She only wanted to be married while her parents were here. She was ashamed to let them know she was through with me. The Coopers and I always got along. They like me. Well, this is the last time she will ever trick me. She has moved back into the apartment she had before; she didn't let it go. She had a friend stay in it until her folks left."

"Oh, Sam, what a horrible thing to do to you." Laura knelt down and took his hands in hers. "You are a fine man. You were too good to her. Are you keeping the boys? You have every right to keep them, you know."

"How could I have been so blind, not to see what she was doing?" Sam rambled on.

"Laura, when we were first married I loved her so much I would have moved the world for her. I trusted her and I thought she loved me. I know that I have spent a lot of our married life up on the slope, working for the Oil Company. But that was where the money was to be made. Connie is a high maintenance woman. When she left me the first time, I was hurt deeply; so were the boys. It tarnished the love we had, so when she came back, I was willing to try again. I thought we could rekindle that love. I was willing, but she wasn't. Life isn't fair! But you of all people should know that. I wish I had your strength. You and Eric have been through a lot and look, you are still able to make a go of it. You are some kind of woman! Eric is really a lucky man. Should there ever be anything you need or I can help you two with, I promise you, I'll be there for you. Now I better go. Please tell Eric for me because I don't want to hear him say, 'I told you so!'"

"Sam, you know he wouldn't do that. You're like a brother to him. We both want you to know if we can help with the boys while you are on the slope, we will. They help us a lot too." As Sam got up to leave, Laura gave him a hug. "You are welcome here anytime. You know that. We love you!"

Sam pulled back from her hug and looked her straight in the eye. "I know that. I love you too!" He kissed her lightly on the cheek and left.

After Sam left, Laura got ready to pick up Eric. It seemed like a long drive to Soldotna. She couldn't think of anything but Connie leaving Sam. Arriving at the clinic, she went in, spoke to Sue, and got Eric into the truck. They said their good-byes and started home.

"You are unusually quiet," Eric said. "What's up?"

Laura turned to him with tears in her eyes. "Sam came by today and asked me to tell you that Connie has left him again, and is filing for divorce. She moved back to the apartment in Soldotna. He felt so ashamed he didn't want to tell you himself. He feels so betrayed."

Eric sighed deeply. "She's crazy!"

They rode home in silence.

Chapter 13

✙

It was almost a year before Eric and Laura saw Sam again. It was as though he pulled himself into a shell to heal. He went back to the slope and only came down to check on the boys once or twice a month. When he came home, toward the end of the year, he came over to check on the truck for Eric. Otherwise, life was pretty much routine. Every Tuesday and Thursday, Laura took Eric to therapy. On one particular Thursday, Sue asked Laura if she could speak to her for a moment. "Sure, as soon as I get Eric situated for you to do his therapy, I'll be right out," replied Laura, wondering what could be wrong now, if anything.

Sue was sitting at her desk when Laura came out from the therapy room, and she motioned for her to sit down. "You know probably as well as I do Laura that this is as far as I can go with this type of therapy. It just keeps Eric from having contractures. I think he should go to the Veterans Hospital in Seattle for further treatment; after all, it's been over six years since the accident. They could help him so much more there. All we're doing here is just maintenance."

"Oh, Sue, if only he would, but you know he didn't want any aid, when the accident first happened. He's so proud and independent he refuses their help. I have tried to get him to accept the benefits he has coming from them. Lord knows, it sure would help."

Sue reached over to take Laura's hand. "How much more of this work schedule can you take? I see you working so hard to keep your head above water and yet you never complain at all. Surely, Eric can see the toll this is taking on you! Have you talked to him about taking help lately?"

"No, I'd never do anything to take away his control of the household. That is so important to him. He does help as much as he can." By now Laura was wringing her hands.

"Look at you," Sue prompted. "You are on the verge of a nervous breakdown yourself. How much longer do you think you can keep this up? I am going to suggest to Eric today that he look into the financial aid he could get from the Veterans Administration. He surely is entitled to it. Would you be terribly upset with me if I talked to him about it?"

"Well, I guess it wouldn't hurt if someone who isn't related to him would say something. You are surely close enough to the situation to have the right to do so." Laura seemed relieved that someone was taking an interest in her side of the problem. "I'm going to go home and dig potatoes before the first big frost, so do what you can do." She stood up, hugged Sue, and went in to tell Eric that she was going home, and she would be back to get him in three hours. She kissed him and was gone.

Sue walked back to the therapy room and turned to her patient. "Well Eric, you know the routine, let's get at it. You know not many wives would leave a good-looking chap like you alone with me for two to three hours twice a week."

Eric laughed. "You know I would never hurt you, Sue. You keep me functioning."

Sue took the opportunity to jump right in with the subject on her mind.

"Have you seriously given any thought to allowing the Veterans Administration to help you? You could go to Seattle for a complete physical and advanced therapy, a lot more than I am giving you here. They could help you with a lot of things." She paused for a second or two and noticed Eric's expression change. Maybe she was starting to make him think.

He said, "Do you think they could help me more than you?"

"Yes, I do. They can help you in many ways. The biggest one is financial. Have you looked at Laura lately and seen how tired she is from doing what she's been doing? And what about your girls? They're spending time inside, caring for you, when they should be outside playing and just being kids. You know Social Services and Home Health Care could be doing that instead."

Eric said almost nothing while Sue put him through his paces. Then: "You know, Sue, you're right. I've been very selfish and foolish. I've let my need for independence and my pride blind me to a lot of things. Here I thought we were doing so well on our own, but really we aren't. After all, each year, I depend on my friends to get us our moose for the winter. People have brought us salmon for Laura to can or smoke for the winter stores. Sam has been keeping our vehicle going. And Lord knows, it's so old by now, it's a wonder it can still run. We've put a lot of short miles on it, coming here twice a week. It doesn't seem like much, but it all adds up. And you're right about the girls. They are just little kids, but bless them, they are good helpers. It just seemed like they were all grown up. Yes, it's time to put aside my sense of independence and think about the Veterans Administration."

"Eric, I know you're right to think about it. Things can be so much easier for all of you. It's good that you have made a decision to call them." Sue thought, *Good, I made it seem like the whole thing was Eric's idea. In this way, his pride is still intact and he is making an independent decision.* She could hardly wait to tell Laura when she returned.

When Laura came back, Sue said to her, "Things are set in motion on what we talked about earlier. All you have to do now is to make a few suggestions that you could use some help and let Eric pick up the ball and run with it. In this way, you let him maintain his independence and his pride. He still is in control and will seem like his idea. Okay?" She hugged Laura and went with her to get Eric into the truck, telling him. "See you next Tuesday!"

The ride home was light and airy, with the girls talking about what they did at school that day. Eric said, "Boy am I ever a lucky guy. Gorgeous women surround me. Well, one grown and two half-pints." The girls giggled at that. "I can't tell you how much you're appreciated, all of you. I love you so much. You are the best family a man could ever have." This made the girls laugh as they took turns hugging him around the neck from over the seat. Eric continued, "Mom, how about getting some ice cream to take home for a treat after supper? All those in favor say Aye." The response was unanimous.

When they arrived home, they busied themselves with the evening chores, supper, dishes, homework, and finally a dish of ice cream. Then Eric told the girls their story and they were off to bed. They loved to hear stories about the moose, the salmon, and the bears. It was Eric's way of teaching them what he could not show them.

"That ice cream sure was good," said Laura. "But it was a little extravagant. We could have made some here at home and saved a little money."

"No, I've been thinking," said Eric. "You have been working so hard, watching our food, tending the garden, working extra jobs. You hardly have any time to spend with the girls, like I do. I think it's about time we put a call in to the Veterans Administration and see what they could do to help us out financially. You know the truck isn't getting any newer. The girls are growing so fast that each year they need new clothes. School expenses aren't cheap either. The ice cream was just a little celebration, because tomorrow I'm going to call the Veterans Administration to see if we can get some financial aid. I think it's time I put my pride behind me and kept up with the times. After all, there's talk of the Berlin Wall coming down. If that can be accomplished, then I can bend and get some help for us from the Social Security and/or the VA. 1989 and 1990 will be dates to remember for the Adams family too."

When Laura got up the next day, she put more wood in the stove to take the chill and dampness out of the cabin. It was cozy, just right for sleeping, but to get up, bathe, and get dressed it was a bit chilly, although sometimes it aided in getting the girls ready to go to school on time. The chill made them dress faster. She came back into the bedroom to awaken Eric; he seemed to have slept soundly last night. Maybe it was because he had decided to get some help, taking a load off his mind.

She leaned over the bed and kissed him softly on the lips and then placed her cheek against his and whispered in his ear. "Hey you, it's time we got our act together this morning. I have to take the girls to school and then go clean a house. It won't take me long to do the house so I should be back in two hours and then I can help you call the V. A. office."

He opened his eyes and gave her that sly smile she loved. "Okay love, let's get at it!" She then lifted him out of bed, bathed and dressed him, and then wheeled him out to the kitchen for breakfast. She had already made coffee, so she gave him a cup and started cooking oatmeal. She then called to the girls, "Get up and get moving girls. Its Friday, last day for school this week, tomorrow you can sleep in. This bus will be leaving soon, and you better be ready to be in it."

"Coming, Mom. Is breakfast ready?" called Mary. "Patty is just now getting up."

Mary was first out every morning, all neat as a pin. She came over to kiss and hug Eric. "Morning, Daddy, are you okay?" Then she moved to

Laura. "Patty is almost ready." Then she kissed and hugged her Mom. Just then Patty came out, smoothing her dress, and copied Mary's actions.

Eric said, "What's with all this love stuff? What do you two want now?" and he chuckled as they headed for Laura.

"Okay now, sit down and eat your breakfast." Laura was stern. "We don't have time to dawdle today. Your dad and I have lots to do." They soon finished eating and cleared the dishes. Laura put them to soak and told Eric she would be back in two hours. She hustled the girls out the door, into the truck, and they were on their way.

Dropping them off at school, she then went on to clean the house, as she wanted to get home to help Eric with the call, before he changed his mind.

After Laura and the girls left, Eric sat and ran everything through in his mind that he was going to say to the Veteran's Administrator. "I'll need the phone number and her name, I can get that I know where it is, it's in the desk over here," he said out loud, as he rolled over to the desk. "Yep, here it is, Mrs. Madeline Parker, she had been very nice to me in the hospital. I hope she doesn't remember how short I was with her, when she suggested we get help." Resting after getting out her name, he thought, *how selfish he had been, thinking only of his pride as a man. Somehow I couldn't give up my independence and my right to make my decisions. It was not being able to do anything and having to rely on Laura for everything. That's why I worked so hard on my therapy in the hospital. I felt somehow, maybe a miracle would happen and I would just get up one day and be like I was before the accident.*

He also remembered all the times he thought of committing suicide. *What a foolish thing to do; that would have just laid more hardship on Laura and the girls. It was a good thing that Jim had come to visit me and I talked to him about the suicide. Jim was right; I was looking for miracles in all the wrong places. The miracles were the little things that happened every day. How I got the movement back into my biceps. The neighbors helping Laura get me up and down the steps before they all pitched in and helped build the ramp and the porch to the upstairs. And Sue, doing her therapy on me every Tuesday and Thursday, and not charging for her services, only the use of the facility, and Sam keeping the truck going. I have been selfish, thinking only of myself. Things are different here in Alaska, people don't sweat the small things, they accept you for what you are, and they have a laid back attitude. They are willing to lend a hand, but they want to remain anonymous. You can just feel the love they have in their hearts.*

With those thoughts in his mind, Eric sent a silent prayer of thanks to God. And then he said aloud, "Lord, I promise to carry your word and to live my life in your service. You have been in my life all this time, even if I didn't see it."

He felt a peace come over him, a feeling he hadn't felt in a long time. He knew everything was going to be all right. "Maybe I know now what I must do." He continued to sit, looking out the window at the mountains, with the sun shining brightly on them, and thought. *It's good to be alive.*

Laura finished her cleaning and talked awhile with Mrs. Mitchell. She had recovered nicely from her trip to the hospital and thanked Laura for coming to clean her house and do the laundry while she was recuperating. "No problem, I'm just glad you're better." She headed for the truck to go home to Eric.

As she pulled up in front of their cabin, she could see Eric looking out the window at the mountains. She thought, *if only Eric could get back to normal like Mrs. Mitchell.* She jumped out of the truck, waved to Eric, and headed into the cabin. "Hey, I'm back, that didn't take long, did it? "She took off her coat and hung it up. "Are you ready to make some telephone calls now?"

"You bet your best potato, I am." He chuckled. "I'm sorry, potato lady;

I just can't forget the look on your face during your last potato party. You had 1500 pounds of potatoes to take care of and you did it. I was so proud of you. I was thinking today how determined you were to do that, and I told myself I could be determined to make this call."

"You seem in pretty good spirits today. What's up? Do you know something I don't know?"

"No, I've just been thinking while you were gone, and I know now what I want to do with this life of mine. I think that starting today there will be a lot of changes around here. Get me a cup of coffee and the phone, let's give Mrs. Parker a call and see if we can't get the ball rolling on some of those changes." He said as he rolled himself to the table.

"I'll get her number, hon," said Laura.

"I already have it, you dial."

Laura dialed the phone for him and he got Mrs. Parker on the line. "Mrs. Parker, this is Eric Adams. I don't know if you remember me or not, but back in September 1984, I had a hunting accident and was paralyzed from the neck down. I went through therapy in Anchorage, both in Providence Hospital and Humana Hospital, before I was released in December of 1984. As you may or may not remember you talked to me about getting on Social Security or Disability from the Veteran's Administration. Then I told you I didn't want it, I refused it. I know you may not remember, as that was six years ago."

"Oh no, Mr. Adams," she replied, "I most certainly do remember you. If fact, I still have your papers here in my desk.

"I knew you were a proud, independent, person, but the odds were, you would eventually call me. Six years, has it been that long? You and your wife are hardy people. I thought you would be calling long before this. Do you want me to put the wheels in motion and see what we can do to help you and your family?"

"Yes Ma'am, we do," he answered. "What do Laura and I have to do?"

"I can send you the necessary papers for the application. Then once you get the application sent in, someone should contact you within a few days." Mrs. Parker's confidence sounded in her voice." I really don't think you will have any problem getting assistance."

Eric hung up. For the first time in a long while, he felt like they were really going to be okay.

"That sounds good, Eric." Laura sighed. She too, felt a sense of some burden being lifted off of her shoulders. Maybe she could be home more, keep track of things in the garden and spend time with Eric and the girls.

Just as Mrs. Parker had said, Eric soon received the papers to fill out and return to the V. A. The forms never seemed to end; there were many questions to answer. After looking at the forms, Eric said to Laura, "Boy, they want to know everything. When we get these all filled out they will know me from the time I was born. They really get personal."

"I guess it's really necessary, Eric." Laura sat beside him at the table. "I would imagine there are many who are just looking for a way to get out of caring for themselves. Here, I'll read each question to you and you tell me what to write and I'll fill it out for you. We'll get through in no time."

They zipped through the first questions with no problem. Then when they got to the question of what type of work he did for a living, there was a long pause.

"Now, how can I really answer that?" questioned Eric. "You know what my background has been!"

"Of course I do, and I also know you are a very knowledgeable, driven man. There is nothing you can't do when you put your mind to it."

"Except move like I used to. Did you forget about that?" Eric almost shouted to her.

"Of course not!" She kept her voice calm, soft, hoping not to get him too excited. "They know that only too well, hence the questionnaire. They are hoping to seek out a possible line of work you could do even though you are paraplegic."

"I'm sorry, you are so right. I was smart to have taken up with you. You are so cool, calm and collected." He smiled and winked at her. "No wonder I love you, girl." He caressed her hand with his and worked his way up her arm, touching her breast lightly and down again.

"Laura giggled and pulled her hand away. "I know you do, but there is no time to dwell on that! Let's answer their questions."

Eric thought awhile and then started, "Let's see, when I got out of school, I got a job with the telephone company. I installed and repaired telephones, as an apprentice, until I was nineteen. Then when I went into the service during the Vietnam War, because of my training with the phone company, I was put into communications. I got more schooling in basic training and during my time in Nam, I was almost always on 'Recon' carrying a radio pack and broadcasting." Eric stopped, looked at Laura writing furiously and asked, "Am I going too fast for you?"

"No," she said, "I'm fine. I have my own type of shorthand so I'm okay. I will rewrite all this later."

Eric went on, "When I got out, I went to work for your father. And as you know, met you and got married at age twenty-three and a half. I spent from 1973 to 1978 fixing up and repairing grandmother's old house, along with doing other carpentry and electrical work on the side. And then, of course, I helped your father on the dairy farm that first year.

"In 1978, you, George, and I moved to Alaska and built our house from scratch on the ten acres we bought from Agnes. I also did barter and trade work with friends to get it done. Then I did some guide work on the side. I did all this until September 15, 1984." He paused, looked down at himself and said. "And you know it all from there!"

Laura finished catching up with him, put her pencil down and said, "And so do they! Let's hope it will be enough. Mrs. Parker said she was going to get the medical records from Providence and Humana Hospital in Anchorage. Sue said would send all of her therapy reports too. We can only pray. It will be in God's hands once we send this."

Laying all the paper aside she said, "There, that's done; the girls will be home soon on the bus. Now, I have to get things ready, because I have a surprise for you! It'll be here soon. We set the time for five o'clock. I'd best hustle with the food."

Soon the bus pulled up at the end of the drive with the girls. They came into the house and greeted their parents as usual and Laura told them to get freshened up for supper as they were having guests.

It didn't take her long to fix the fish and chips she had planned. She had made a salad and baked a cake for dessert. "Now girls, help me set the table for seven." She pulled Eric away from the table momentarily.

"Who is coming? Tell me! Don't keep secrets from me!"

As he was speaking, there was a knock at the door. Laura said, "There, go see for yourself!" Laura rolled him over to open the door and called, "Come in!"

The door opened and there were Sam and his boys, David and Danny.

"Sam! David! Danny! Laura, look who's here!" said Eric with surprise, "I had no inkling that you guys were going to be here for supper, but how glad I am to see you."

"I thought you would be," said Laura. "I ran into Sam in town, when I went to clean Mrs. Mitchell's house, so I invited him and the boys for supper."

"Boy, I'm sure glad you did." Eric's voice and lopsided smile still showed his surprise. "Come and sit down. Tell me all about what's been happening with you. We thought you fell off the map!"

Laura interrupted, "Why not just sit at the table for supper. We can talk while we eat."

They began a nonstop conversation that lasted all during supper and on into the evening. Laura, their girls, and Sam's sons cleared the table and washed the dishes. The children then went off to play some games.

100

"Now that the children are out of earshot, tell me what's up with you and Connie." Eric asked Sam. "Has she had the boys while you were on the slope?"

"Yes and no," Sam answered. "She had them for awhile after our second divorce, but they didn't like her boyfriend. They said they wanted to stay at home with me. They asked me to trust them; after all, they were thirteen and fifteen. I told them no, they should stay with her and her boyfriend in town in the apartment, for one more year; then they could stay at home.

Eric asked, "Did she go along with that?"

Sam answered him, "No, she and her friend wanted to get married but waited until after the boys came back to live with me. That's why I started to come home on the weekends, at least every two weeks. I've only been doing it for about two months now."

"But could you do that? I know how hard it is for you to come home sometimes. Connie used to tell me that," Laura said. "You know you could have asked us to help you out."

"No, no, you and Eric had too much to care for as it was, but I appreciate the thought." Sam reached over and patted her hand. "If I couldn't make it home, I would call Connie in Soldotna, to look in on them: after all, she is their mother."

"But what about cooking, cleaning, and going to school?" Laura was concerned.

Sam answered, "No worry there. Connie taught them to cook basics. She wanted all of us to be able to fend for ourselves. It made the boys grow up fast. It runs in the family, I guess. Besides, Alaska makes you grow up pretty fast, right?

"How about you two, are you making it all right? I hear you are going to go for disability aid. Is that right? It sure would help you out a lot!" He looked at Laura, and then quickly looked back to Eric for some reaction to his question.

"We just filled out the application papers today," Eric said. "You might know it would be spread all over Sterling, and Soldotna too, for that matter. Word spreads here quicker than a fire in dry timber."

"How's the truck running, Laura?" Sam asked, as if to change the subject.

"Okay!" she said quietly, "Thanks to you and God's hand!"

Sam rose and called to his boys. "David, Danny, we best get on home, it's getting late. Thank Laura for the supper, you two. I'll swing by tomorrow and check on the pickup. Good seeing the both of you again. Next time shouldn't be so long. I may be transferred off the slope to the Soldotna Branch office."

Sam came over to pat Eric on the back and shake his hand. "Thanks again for supper. See you tomorrow!"

Eric nodded. "I'm sure the truck needs some attention. It's getting pretty old."

After Sam and his boys left, Eric said to Laura, "There goes a really great guy. He is a good man. Promise me, Laura, if something should ever happen to me, you would call on Sam for help. I can guarantee you he would be there for you and the girls. He has never let us down."

"Don't talk like that." Laura put her fingertips to Eric's lips to shush him, "Nothing's going to happen to you. Now that we're going to get your disability help, we'll be fine; you just wait and see!"

"Maybe we will and maybe we won't." He came right back to her. "It all remains to be seen. I just want you to promise me you will call Sam, should you ever need help. Hear me out; he'll be the one you can count on."

Eric seemed so insistent and determined for her to promise him that Laura nodded acceptance of his request. "Okay! All right! I promise you, if ever the girls and I need help, I'll call Sam."

Chapter 14

ﬁ

After sending in the questionnaire to Mrs. Parker, it wasn't long before a representative from the Veterans Administration set up an appointment to see Eric.

"Mrs. Adams, my name is Todd Duran. I'm with the Veterans Administration and I'm calling to see when it would be convenient for me to come to see Mr. Adams. I'll be coming to assess the home and the situation there. We've received an application for disability aid, and if everything meets with my expectations, Mr. Adams can sign the necessary papers, which will immediately set the wheels in motion."

"Mr. Duran, my husband is right here. I have the speakerphone on, and he's heard everything you've just told me."

"Mr. Duran, this is Eric Adams. Anytime you can make it would be convenient for us. You're the one who has to travel to Sterling. So it's up to you."

"That is very kind of you," he answered. "How about next Tuesday?"

"That will be fine. Laura usually takes me to Soldotna for therapy on

Tuesday, but we can change that."

"Oh, no, don't change it. I'll be there early so I can go with you to the therapy session," he quickly offered. "In that way, it will give me a chance to speak with your therapist. That'll be good! What time does she take you?"

This surprised Eric, so he answered slowly, "Usually, right after lunch. We go to therapy and then we pick up our daughters from school before coming home."

"Good, I'll be at your home early Tuesday. We can get my assessment out of the way before we go to your therapy." Mr. Duran seemed pleased. "That would work out great! See you early Tuesday morning, and thank you."

After ending the call, Eric sighed deeply. "Well, the date is set for him to come; I suppose you and I will be walking a tightrope until then."

Many thoughts went through Eric's mind. *I wonder if he'll be able to see how much work Laura's had to do. Getting me back and forth to therapy is no easy task. Then there are the children. She must keep life as normal as possible for them. I have to give her a lot of credit. Not many people could stand up under that kind of strain. If it bothers her, she doesn't let it show.*

Laura sat with her hands folded in her lap for a few seconds. "Eric, finally we're going to get some assistance for you to get some extensive physical care. Mr. Duran will surely recommend the VA Hospital in Seattle for a complete physical exam. There you'll get the therapy Sue couldn't do here. Oh Eric, I'm so happy!"

"You're right again, sweetheart!" Eric said, as he reached out for her. "Come over here and hug me. I just hope they'll be able teach me to be more independent, so I can take some burdens off of your shoulders."

"Eric, you are my love, and things will be just fine again… you just wait and see." Laura sat on his lap in the wheelchair and kissed him deeply, caressing him as she whispered softly in his ear. "Now, since we're home alone, let's proceed with what you wanted when we were filling out the application. That'll make us both feel fine."

Eric thought, Y*es love, things will be fine again someday, and that I can promise you.* Returning her kisses, he ran his fingers gently up her arm, caressed her breast, and he wheeled them into the bedroom.

On Tuesday morning Laura greeted Mr. Duran. He was on time, just as he had promised. He talked with Eric for a long time and then discussed some things with Laura. This took most of the morning so Laura fixed some lunch. They ate, and looking at the clock, Laura said, "We best be getting ready to leave for Soldotna."

"I'll drive my car, Mrs. Adams. That way we'll have room to pick up the girls too." Mr. Duran replied. "I want to see them, also. So far, you both seem to be handling the situation with great style. I give you a lot of credit for that."

"If it hadn't been for our friends and neighbors, I don't know what we would have done," said Eric. "Living up here in Alaska is wonderful, but it does try one's mind and heart, believe me! Now, if you would help me out to the car, we can leave." Eric thought it would be good to have Mr. Duran see that it wasn't easy getting him out of the house and into a vehicle alone. He wanted him to have a taste of what Laura endured every day.

When they arrived at therapy, Mr. Duran spoke with Sue about Eric's therapy. Sue began, "I am so glad to speak with you and have this opportunity to tell I've done about all I can do with his therapy here. I suggest sending him to the VA hospital in Seattle for more extended therapy. He would find he could do so much more and maybe ease some of the work load off of Laura."

Mr. Duran agreed with her on the idea and thanked her. As soon as they finished their conversation he suggested they pick up the girls. As usual, the girls were happy to see their parents; but this time, they were in a car. They hadn't ridden in a car very often, always in pickup trucks.

Trucks seemed to be the best mode of transportation in Alaska. They hugged and kissed their mom and dad and were very polite when Laura introduced them to Mr. Duran. On the way home, Mr. Duran asked a lot of questions of the girls. When they arrived home, the girls were out of the car and into the house like a shot. Laura and Mr. Duran, together, helped Eric out of the car and into the house.

"How about a cup of coffee?" asked Laura. "It's a bit chilly out and it should warm us."

"Sure, that would be nice." Mr. Duran said. "Then I need to get Eric to sign some papers, and I'll be off. I want to tell you that I am impressed by what I've seen here today. I can see that you have gone as far as you can with helping Eric. Now it is up to us to see what we can do."

Laura served the coffee, and Mr. Duran gave Eric the papers to sign. "All we need is your signature and then Laura can sign under yours."

Eric pulled up to the table and struggled to sign them all.

"You should start getting checks on a monthly basis, beginning in December. But it'll be about a year after your first check arrives before we can arrange for you to go to Seattle for further rehabilitation and personal care training. I'm sorry to have to tell you that, but you know how the government moves: not very fast. But you didn't hear that from me." Mr. Duran chuckled. "Well, good people, it's time I got out of your way. Good luck to you both, and God bless."

Laura walked him to the door and shook his hand. Watching him drive away, she turned to Eric. "What welcome news!"

"Yes! I want you to start being around here more. Let some of those cleaning jobs go. We'll manage somehow on the money from the VA. We have managed before on very little, and we can do it again. I want to spend as much time with you as I can. I love you, Laura."

Fall came and went quickly. It seemed as if even the seasons were trying to hurry by, to ease the workload on Laura and bring Eric closer to an income. It would help Eric's morale to once again be the one responsible for providing an income for his family. Laura still kept some of her cleaning jobs but was home more for Eric and the girls.

Early one day, Jim knocked on their front door. Laura invited him in and offered to share breakfast with him. She had already fed the girls, and they were off to school.

"Sure, I'd love to have some breakfast with you two," he quickly replied, "but first I'd like to put this moose meat in your freezer. I just finished dressing it out yesterday."

Eric was excited to see his buddy. "Hey Jim, you're getting pretty good at getting two moose a year. You're not getting any flack from the conservation people, are you? I thought maybe they'd say something to you about it."

"Oh, no, I went directly to them and explained what I was doing, and that it was for your family. They issued me a special tag to put on my license. They were glad to be of help. No problem! None! After all, who taught me the tricks to moose hunting?"

"Well, you were pretty green when you first started, but you were sure a quick learner," chuckled Eric.

Laura broke in, "Let me help you get the meat into the freezer, and then we'll have breakfast." She brought Eric out onto the porch where he could see what they were doing. She thought it would help him to feel more a part of the procuring of the meat.

Instead, as he sat there with the autumn sun shining on him, listening to the wind through the birch trees and seeing Jim decked out in his outdoor gear, it made him feel a little despondent. Of course, he would never tell Laura. He put on his charade, as he had many times before.

It didn't take long to put the meat in the freezer, and Laura again thanked Jim.

"Now if you'll excuse me, I'll get breakfast."

Jim sat on the porch with Eric and the two of them shared the story of how Jim bagged this moose. Eric wanted to know every detail. "Where did you get him? How big was he? Did you go alone?"

Jim answered all his questions and even talked about some incidents he had heard from other hunters. He then asked Eric, "Hey, are you okay with this talk? It doesn't bother you? I know you told me one time about how you felt when you thought you couldn't hunt or fish anymore."

"Sometimes it really gets to me and I feel those pangs of depression, but then I remember your talk to me, about the everyday miracles." Eric drew a little closer to Jim. "Jim, I've decided what I must do to pay back for all the miracles that God has given this family. I promised Him that I would dedicate my life to spread His word. Does that sound crazy to you?"

"No, no," was Jim's ready reply. "We should all live our lives like that. The world would be a better place if we did."

Eric nodded. "I hope this help, from the government, will bring our lives a little more back to normal. Laura is continuously urging me to get their help, to go to Seattle, and get more extensive therapy. I should be using my knowledge and determination to make our life better. I only hope this will help as much as she is counting on it to help."

From inside they heard Laura call, "Breakfast is ready. Come in and eat while it's still warm."

"Sure sounds good to me, Eric. Let's hit it," said Jim as they went inside.

"Hope this suits you, Jim," said Laura. "Would you like coffee with your breakfast or later?"

"Now is fine," he replied. "How about you, Eric? Want a refill?" He grabbed Eric's cup and held them both out for a fill-up.

As she poured the coffee, Laura said, "Jim, how can we ever repay you for what you have done for this family? You and so many others have rallied to our needs and never once have we ever had to come right out and ask. We might make a mere statement or suggestion of needing something and it's there. You never take any compensation for it either."

Jim looked at Eric and then to her. "Laura, you two would have done the same for me or anyone else who needed help. That's what friends are for; besides, it is God's way of giving us "ole" Alaskans something to do with our lives." Then he chuckled and held up his cup for a toast. "Here's to all of us 'ole' tough Alaskans."

They all laughed and enjoyed the moment. It was good to have come to Alaska, to meet each other, and share the hardships along with the good times.

Chapter 15

Eric's checks started coming, just as Mr. Duran promised, the first part of December. They had a rather quiet Christmas and enjoyed attending the girls' Christmas programs. They still continued the Tuesday and Thursday trips to Soldotna for therapy with Sue. The daylight hours were short and the nights were long.

Sam was transferred to the recently established branch office in Soldotna for the oil company so he could be closer to his boys. He still came over periodically and checked on any repairs needed on the truck, as well as any odd jobs that needed to be done.

One morning in March, at breakfast, Laura said of out the blue, "You know Eric, around Memorial Day this year, when it comes time to plant the garden, let's have a Garden Party! I'll invite everyone who usually helps with the tilling of the ground and planting, and while the guys work, I'll fix a cookout with bear stew and sandwiches. We'll make ice cream and desserts. We can have a real party. Maybe even a dance afterwards. In that way, we can show our appreciation to everyone for what they've done for us."

"That sounds like a great idea," said Eric. "Want me to help with the invitations?"

"Sure, you can speak with the guys, and I'll get with their wives about not bringing anything. We want to put on the feed!" Laura was getting excited about it.

"I'm sure Mary and Patty can arrange to have some of the games they play at school. Oh Eric, this will be fun! We can invite Sam and his boys, Jim, Nadine and their two children, George, Sue, and of course, Agnes, dear sweet Agnes. How could I forget her? And also Reverend Buck's family. That should make about eighteen people. We can handle that!"

"Laura, this is only March. Don't you think it's a little early to be thinking of a May Garden Party?" Eric asked.

"Oh, no, Eric, I must plan what to serve. I can make a big pot of bear stew and freeze it. Make up some moose burgers and a lot of other big dishes ahead, and freeze them. Bake some pies and cakes, and freeze them too. There is a lot to do ahead of time." She paused. "I can't wait to tell the girls. They'll be so excited! They'll love to start planning, too."

When the girls got home from school and Laura told them they were to have a party on Memorial Day, they too, became very excited and anxious to start planning. Eric just sat at the table taking in all of their excitement. He looked at them and wondered what had happened to their babies. They had grown so much! Mary was turning eleven, and Patty, nine. Mary was starting to shoot upward. She was beginning to lose her little girl look and take on one of a teenager: long, straight, auburn hair parted in the middle, sometimes in a pony tail or sometimes up in the back. He didn't even know if she was interested in boys yet. He certainly hoped not. They had enough problems. She was losing some of her freckles, and even some of her baby fat.

Patty still had a little girl look to her. She wore ribbons in her hair, when it was down. Occasionally, she wore it braided in a long French braid that hung down her back. Her hair was a dusty blonde. Her face was almost like that of a porcelain doll.

They were both sturdy, athletic kids. They'd been cross-country skiing since they were big enough to handle the skis. Eric smiled when he thought back to when he first started them on skis. *Mary was only eighteen months old when he got her a pair of small skis and put them on her. Her snowsuit had a belt around it and he got on his skis, grabbed her by the backside of the belt and they skied down the small hill in the driveway together. It wasn't long before she was skiing like a pro. When Patty turned eighteen months old, she had the same routine. They were Alaskan born and bred. They knew the ropes of living in Alaska, for as young as they were. They had been taught the dangers of hypothermia, and how to dress right for the outdoors. Teaching them cross country skiing kept them outside and busy during the winter months, and in this way they didn't get "Cabin Fever."* Eric was so proud of them.

He thought to himself, *Have I been so wrapped up in my physical problems, that I didn't even notice my family and how much they have been giving to me? I didn't even see the changes in them.* The laughter and squeal of the girls and Laura interrupted his thoughts. They were talking of the party plans. He could only watch and look at the happiness in their faces. *I haven't heard or seen this in a very long time. This all had been taken away with the accident. It wasn't fair.* He knew now, more than anything, that his decision to give his life to the Lord was the right thing to do.

The days came and went, with Laura and the girls busy with their daily chores, planning the garden party, and taking Eric to therapy twice a week. They didn't even notice that Eric seemed always to be deep in thought. He said to Laura one day on their way home from therapy, "Laura, I've been thinking that we can't really afford for me to go to Seattle for rehabilitation and personal training. We're still just barely making it, even with the disability money."

"Eric, I won't hear of it," she snapped quickly. "You have to go! It'll help you so much. You can't deny yourself this chance for better therapy. Look at the movement you've regained, just from your initial therapy here. Wouldn't you like to gain more mobility and control?"

"I guess you're right, as usual." He knew she was. "Maybe I could call Mrs. Parker and see if we could get an increase in my disability income, since to go to Seattle will be an added expense. I guess I've just been worried whether we could both afford to go."

"We can't afford for you not to go!" She kept her eyes on the road and at the same time reached for his hand to hold. As she drove home, nothing more was said about not going to Seattle for treatments.

Then he changed topics and asked, "How are the party plans coming? I see signs now of 'Spring Break-Up,' the dirt roads are starting to look like muddy Jell-O. Yep, May and planting time for the garden will be here before we know it."

"We pretty much have things under control except for the last minute food and preparations," she answered. "The girls are quite excited, and so am I! It seems like we're getting back to doing things we did before your accident, and that's good! Are you looking forward to the party?"

"You bet I am!" was his quick reply. They were silent the rest of the way home.

The next day Laura had some houses to clean while the girls were in school, so she got everyone up and off, then said to Eric, "I know you wanted to call Mrs. Parker. I've three houses to clean. Can you wait until this afternoon to call, so I can be here?"

Eric replied, "No, that's okay. George is coming over today to visit. He can help me. He'll be here all day, so don't worry about coming home between houses to get my lunch. George can do it. He knows how!"

"All right then, I 'm off to work." She kissed him good-bye and left.

It wasn't long before George arrived. After coffee, and chatting awhile, Eric asked him to get Mrs. Parker on the phone.

"Sure thing, where's her number?"

"It's right there on the table."

George dialed the number, turned on the speakerphone so Eric could hear, and when someone answered, asked for Mrs. Parker.

"Please wait while I put you through," said the voice on the other end of the line.

"I'll take over now, George," said Eric.

When Mrs. Parker answered, Eric identified himself and explained to her about the extra costs for him to go to Seattle, and so on. He told her he felt an increase in his disability check would help him with the trip and asked if it would be possible to get more.

Mrs. Parker replied, "Well, Mr. Adams, we're giving you what a married veteran is allowed on your disability. A single veteran would get more. I guess they figure as you have a mate, who can be working, that constitutes a two-income family. I'm sorry, but that is how the government sees it. If you weren't married, you would get more money per month."

"That hardly seems fair to give more to a single man than a married man. There is no way I would ever give up my wife, Laura! We've been married for eighteen years, and she has stood by me through some very rough times. I love her because of her strength and courage to face all we had to face. I love her more than life itself, and I would never do that to her. We made a promise to love, honor, and cherish each other eighteen years ago, and I won't break that promise and neither would she!"

Mrs. Parker waited in silence before answering him. "But Mr. Adams, sometimes you love someone so much the best thing you can do is to give up something for that love. You two will probably always love each other. I've seen you together. Dissolution just ends the legal end of the marriage, not the love. You think about it. Dissolution has to be your idea."

"I'll talk it over with Laura. Thanks for all your help, Mrs. Parker." Eric hung up the phone.

He sat for a minute, looking at George. "What am I to do? I guess we'll just have to make do. Laura insists I go. We can't afford for both of us to go and I can't go alone. Lord only knows that. What can I do?"

George spoke up. "Look man, you and I have been friends forever. I came here to Alaska with you and Laura; we helped each other build our log homes, so the least I can do is to go to Seattle with you. In that way you can cut out the expense it would be for Laura to go, as well as save getting someone to stay with the girls and watch your place for you. I've never been to Seattle and I'd love to escort you. I'll be there for you and Laura! You know that!"

"Would you do that for us?" Eric said. "I need to know for sure, as they are getting me set up to go in February of this coming year."

"Sure thing. I have enough time accumulated at work that I can take off for a year or more if I wanted. So don't fret. You can count on me. I'll make arrangements right away to be off. I promise. That is for sure!"

George's reassuring manner made Eric feel better telling Laura what Mrs. Parker had said, and that George was going to Seattle with him, which solved the problem of extra expenses. Then he thought, maybe I won't even mention what Mrs. Parker said about a single veteran getting more money than a married veteran. No sense in upsetting her with thoughts of dissolution.

George was still there when Laura came home with the girls. When they came in, George picked them up and swung them in a circle. "Hey, you two Aleuts. My, you're sure growing. It won't be long before I won't be able to do this anymore."

The girls were laughing and squealing at George's antics. "Put us down. We're getting dizzy," then quickly added, "Uncle George, we're having a garden party when we plant the garden this year. We want you to come. Please!"

"Hey, wouldn't miss it!" George grinned at them slyly, "but for now, I've got to go. See you guys later."

"Don't forget the party. Mark it down somewhere," they urged him as they followed him out the door.

"Yes, don't forget George, we want you to be here." Laura added, "Would you stay for supper?"

"Nope, got to go. See you later!" And he was gone.

Laura asked Eric, "Did you get in touch with Mrs. Parker?"

"Sure did. She told me I was getting as much as possible right now, for a veteran with a family." Eric continued without pausing, "but to save us some cost on the trip, George said he'd go and stay with me. In that way, we could save the expense of your traveling with me. He said he could take off work, that he has time coming."

She paused a moment, then replied, "But Eric, won't I need to be with you to learn the new therapy?" She paused again, digesting the situation. "But if George can take off, it will be great. I won't have to have someone look after the girls or come in to keep the fire going so the plumbing won't freeze. They can send me written instructions for what to do when you come home. They know I'm a nurse. It is on your records. Yes, that may be the best thing to do."

She came over to him and hugged him, "But you do know, the girls and I will miss you being away again. Did Mrs. Parker have any idea how long you'll be gone?"

He grabbed her hand and held it tightly. "No, but there are times when a separation is the only answer." He kissed her hand. "You go on now and get supper, and I know you and the girls will handle being here without me. You've done it before."

Chapter 16

Spring soon arrived and with it Memorial Day. The day of the party the household was bursting with excitement. The girls were up early so that Laura could fix breakfast, get Eric started for the day, and still have time to get herself ready. The big coffeepot was on, and drinks were on ice for all the guests. George, Sam, and his boys saw to that. They set up benches around outside for eating, and they constructed a big table for all the food.

Soon people started to arrive, and they all checked with Eric for what needed to be done. By lunchtime the garden plot was pretty well in shape to be planted. They all washed up in the outside water trough, and were soon ready to start filling their plates and stomachs. Laura and the girls grinned widely all morning. The girls' games were going over in a big way with all the children. The ground had been plowed, dragged, and was ready for planting. Laura could do that later. All the heavy work was done. The women helped Laura get the food on the table, just in time to ring the dinner bell.

Eric clanged the bell to get everyone's attention. "I certainly want to thank you all for your help, not only at this garden party, but also for everything you have done for this family since my accident. I don't think we would have made it without your help, and God's everyday miracles. So now I would like Reverend Buck to return thanks for us. Laura and I certainly do thank you all."

Reverend Buck offered up a prayer, and then the fun began. Everyone feasted, the children played games, and laughter surrounded them all.

Laura went to Eric and hugged him. "Thank you, for you. I am so glad you came into my life, even with all the hardships we have had to face. We are making it with God's help, and that of our friends. We are so lucky."

Eric kissed her. "I'm the lucky one, to have you in my life when I needed someone the most. But now, I promise you, I'm going to Seattle and work at this therapy to help myself become more independent, and then I can help you more. I know I can do this. I will return to God all he has given to us, and no matter what happens, I will always love you. I want you to know that."

"I love you too, Eric." She squeezed him. "Now I best go mingle and thank all our friends."

She left his side, and he watched her with their friends. They all hugged her and she laughed with them. His glance went to the girls. They, too, were enjoying this party. It was a good thing to do. It opened his eyes to see what it took, to care for him. It was then he decided definitely the path his life must take from that point on.

After some time, the crowd started to thin out. Their guests thanked Eric and Laura for the fun gathering, a treat they all looked forward to after the long winter. It seemed to brighten everyone in some way. Soon they were all gone except George, Sam, and his boys. The guys gathered up the tables and benches and put them away. The girls helped Laura clean up the food that was left. Almost everything was gone. The party was a success.

When all was cleared and put away, Laura pushed Eric into the house and extended an invitation to George and Sam. "Come in and sit for a little. I'll make some fresh coffee. You two deserve a break. It was a lot of work, but it was sure a lot of fun."

Eric, George, Sam and the boys sat around the table and discussed the day while Laura and the girls finished the dishes. By then the fresh coffee was ready and everyone enjoyed a cup along with some blueberry cobbler.

"Oh my!" George said. "There goes my Paul Bunyan physique." They all laughed and enjoyed the cobbler.

"Sam!" Eric said to get his attention, "Sam, when I get my appointment set in Seattle, George is going to go with me, so that Laura and the girls won't have to be uprooted too. I don't know how long it will take with the personal therapy and such. Would you look in on them, while we're gone? I would feel much better if you would."

"Sure I will," said Sam. "George, how about your place? I'll keep an eye on it too. It would be no problem to do that."

"Hey, that would be super." George replied gratefully. "Thanks a lot. Then I won't have to worry about it. I can give all my attention to Eric."

Laura, taking all this in, felt things were finally falling together in a positive way. She put her arm around Eric's neck from behind his chair. "See, I told you everything would be all right."

That night when they got into bed, Eric whispered, "Laura, you awake?"

"Uh huh," she answered sleepily.

"There is something I want to discuss with you," he said in a non-emotional, matter-of-fact tone. "You know I told you about Mrs. Parker saying we were getting what a married veteran with a family was allowed per month on my disability. What I didn't tell you was that she also said I could get more if I was a single veteran and your income was separate from mine."

Laura turned quickly and faced him. "What did you just say? Did I hear you right?"

He went on in his monotone voice. "Now hear me out. In Seattle, I may have unknown expenses, so I feel we are going to need more money than we have now."

"So what are you saying? What's in your mind? What are you thinking?"

"I think with dissolution of our marriage, I'd get a larger disability check every month. We could still live together. We just wouldn't be legally married."

"Oh, but Eric," she gasped, "would that seem right in the eyes of God and everyone… our parents and friends? What about the girls?" She was almost in tears. It was a real shock to her. "What have I done to have you want to divorce the girls and me? Don't you love us anymore?"

"Of course, I love you!" He reached over and touched her. "Come here, lay close to me. You know I've loved you from the first day I saw you in your Dad's barn. I will never, ever, stop loving you. But sometimes life throws us queer turns and we can't have the Utopian life we are all looking for, even though we were pretty darn close. Sometimes we have to let go of the things that mean the most to us. But don't worry; I'll still be the girls' Daddy. I'll still be loving you, and I hope you will always be loving me, no matter whether we have that paper that says we are married or not. Am I not right?"

She protested, "That piece of paper has meant everything to me since the day I signed it. It meant that I would be yours and you mine until death do us part. It didn't say that we should be together only during the good and easy times. But always, always! Understand?"

Eric kissed her gently, "Sweetheart, it meant the same to me too. I've thought over what Mrs. Parker said about us, that she'd seen us together and we'd be loving each other forever. And that not having that piece of paper could never make us love each other less. If anything, we would love each other more. It's a sacrifice we can make outwardly to gain the financial uplift we need now. I could never love you less. It's because I love you so much, that I feel it's necessary to do this."

He kissed her again. "Think about it. Am I not right? This can be our secret; we don't need to tell anyone else that we filed for dissolution of our marriage."

She was silent for a long time, and then she kissed him. "I guess so." She snuggled closer to him. "You are right about one thing, though. I will always love you, too."

"Okay, then let's do it. Let's file for a dissolution. Don't worry; we'll still be here in our home, together." He reassured her.

All night they lay close to one another. Neither said another word, but the thoughts were going through both their minds on whether this was the right thing to do.

Eric's mind was working. *Was this sacrifice worth what he had planned to do with his life after Seattle? Could he really be able to tell her that he was leaving her and the girls, so they could have a different life? That he wanted them to be able to live without having to care for him forever? He knew that he thought this through and planned it step by step, but when the day would come to go away, would he be able to do it?*

Laura was asking herself questions too. *What is going to happen to the girls and me because of this sacrifice? Was there more to his plan than just to gain more financially? He has been saying strange things and making people promise to do certain things for him. What's really on his mind?* Many questions popped into her mind. It was a sleepless night for both of them and a crushing end to a perfect day.

The next day he called to see what they had to do to set the wheels of the law in motion. Then when they got the dissolution papers, he would send them to Mrs. Parker. It was a hard thing for him to do, probably the hardest ever in his life. But in his mind, he knew his plan was started and he would survive it. After all, it was the best thing to do.

Chapter 17

From the time they had decided to dissolve their marriage, Laura had a constant gnawing sensation in her stomach, even though they had decided not to let anyone know about the dissolution, as they were still living together. Was Eric planning on doing something she didn't know about? He said it would mean more money and it was the reason for doing it. The extra income could help build up the money they would need when he went to Seattle. She still felt uneasy about it all.

The gardening went well during the summer. Jim got their moose and Laura put the meat up in the freezer. Sam's boys, David and Danny, saw to it that she had plenty of salmon to can. She continued to bake and put things in the freezer. Danny and David also cut wood for their winter needs. Things were running close to normal.

Laura took Eric, every Tuesday and Thursday to Soldotna for his therapy. It was good to talk girl-talk with Sue, when they had the chance. One day Sue put Eric in the spa and she had time to speak to Laura alone. "Laura, Eric says you feel hurt that George is taking him to Seattle.

Is this true?"

"No, not exactly," Laura replied gingerly. "It's just the being away from him again, I guess. I know how lonely I felt when he was in the hospital before."

"Don't worry!" Sue went on to say. "You are a strong, courageous woman. I know you and you can handle anything that comes your way, but don't let a good thing pass you by if the opportunity should come. Things have been hard enough, but you've handled it, because Eric was there." Sue did not stop there, "Besides it is good to have George learn to care for Eric too! Do you understand what I am saying? Sometimes we have to bend with life the way it comes to us, learn to accept it. That is what Eric has learned finally. He is looking forward and you should too! You have always been there for him, but now you have to learn that he must help himself too. Let him broaden his life's circle. Help him to do this without worry."

"I think I see what you are saying to me now. I think I've been living with this overwhelming sense of sadness over me, and I wonder if I've ever really come to terms with what happened. I guess in that one moment, both our lives changed forever. I see now it took a very long time for both of us to understand and accept that. Is that what you're trying to say to me?" Laura put her head in her hands and wept softly.

"Yes, now you are starting to see it." Sue patted at tears in her own eyes. "You have to loosen up a bit and start to let Eric do his own thing. I truly love you, Laura, and hope you don't hate me for saying these things to you. But I see what it is doing to you both. Now let's go get Eric. Remember; start to treat him like you would one of your patients in the hospital, not the love of your life. Make him do things for himself; they will when he gets to Seattle. Be tough on him. They will be!"

Sue got Eric out of the spa and ready to go. She and Laura got him into the truck, and they were off for home. On the way, Laura said to Eric, "It will soon be time for the girls to go back to school. We should be thinking of getting them registered. And of course, they will need to have their physicals. That's going to take some time. Do you think George could come over on the days I'll be gone? I never know how long we'll be shopping, or at the school, or even at the doctors, for that matter. Do you think he might do that favor for me?"

"Sure, I'll ask him." Eric looked at her in a surprised way. She had never suggested that before. She had always taken care of those matters with no problem. Could this be Laura? Asking for help? "It should be no problem for George. Let's stop by the post office and see if we have any mail. We should be hearing soon about my Seattle appointments."

"OK," she said and pulled up to the post office. "I'll be right back hon; don't leave me."

Soon she came bursting out of the post office, waving the mail. "It's here! What a blessing. Oh Eric, I am so excited! It'll be so good for you to go. Here open it while I drive."

He tore open the envelope with difficulty, held the paper, and read it aloud to her. "They're even going to pay my travel expenses, but then I figured they would. They say here that my escort will have to arrange for housing at night. He can be with me during the day. There is a cafeteria where he can eat. This is great! George can wander at night if he wants. They say there are rooms to be had close by for the escort at a reduced rate. Great! Great! Oh, Laura, this is going to be good. I'm looking forward to going. Maybe I'll be able to help you more, when I'm through with therapy."

"Yes, I believe you will. We may have had tough times, but our faith brought us through it." She looked at him quickly and winked.

When they got home they found a note the girls left saying that David had taken them hiking. Eric suggested that they assess the home situation, to be sure she and the girls would be fine while he was gone.

They made a fast check… food, fuel for the wood stove, freezer full of berries, veggies, moose, and some bear meat. What more could they want?

David returned with the girls to find Laura and Eric checking everything. "What's up? Anything wrong?" Mary asked.

"No." Eric told them. "I got my letter to go to Seattle in February, so your mom and I were checking to see what you guys might need, in case I'm gone a long time. So David took you hiking? What did you see and where did you go?"

David by now was almost seventeen, and had offered to bring the girls home from school while Laura had Eric at therapy. He was a tall, muscular-looking boy with dark wavy hair. He had grown a Van Dyke beard to make him look older, so he could work on the slope. He was pleasant and practical, kind and gentle. He was protective of those he cared for and would do anything for them. He was a good young man. He had worked to buy himself a truck and was allowed to drive the girls into Sterling. So when Eric inquired of the girls where they went to hike and what they saw, David politely waited for them to answer their father.

Mary spoke first. "David drove us up to where the Kenai and Moose Rivers join at the bridge at mile marker 82. Then we hiked along the Swanson River Canoe Trail."

David nodded his head. "Hope you didn't mind me taking the girls out and showing them some trails. We were careful and we saw a lot, didn't we girls? I think they had fun."

Eric patted David on the shoulder. "Thanks, David, for looking after them. You are a fine young man. Your dad should be very proud of you!"

"Yes, Sir," David answered. "He tells me that a lot. Eric, would you and Laura mind if Danny and I took the girls to the Sterling Days, this coming July? We would especially like to see the Moose River Raft Race, which is held then. They wouldn't be any trouble and I'm sure they'd enjoy it. I promise I'll be extra watchful of them."

"Why, David, that is real nice of you to invite the girls. What do you think, Laura? It is an opportune time for the girls to see the races. Since we can't take them, why not?"

"I'm sure it would be okay, if the girls want to go." She asked, "Do you want to go, girls?"

A resounding cheer went up from both the girls as they hugged their mom and dad.

"Good then. Danny and I will make plans and let you know the particulars soon." David continued on, "Thank you both; the girls are really no problem and we all have fun together. Well, I had better get going, now that you and Laura are home. See you later. Bye Mary, bye Patty."

"David is a very nice young man," said Laura. "Did you girls have fun and thank him for taking you?"

In chorus they answered, "Yes we did, Mom! And thank you both for giving permission to go to the raft races with David and Danny. We do have fun with them."

"Okay, now go clean your rooms," said Eric. "It'll be awhile before dinner."

The girls headed for their room and Eric said, "I do agree with you, Laura. David is nice, but then his dad is a super guy. I still don't see why in the world Connie ever left him. I hear she remarried a couple of years ago. Hope she's happy. I wonder why Sam hasn't remarried."

"Would you?" said Laura, "after your wife divorced you twice?"

Eric quickly answered her. "Any woman would be foolish not to accept a proposal of marriage from Sam. He would be a good catch for any woman. Speaking of good women, how about my good woman getting supper? I'm hungry, and I bet the girls are too, after hiking all afternoon."

Laura prepared supper and they all spent a quiet evening, with Eric thinking about his plans to start therapy in Seattle.

Chapter 18

❧

Fall came with the fireweed going to seed, and with Laura busy putting up the garden produce. Eric, of course, was quick to jokingly warn the 'Potato Lady' to begin thinking of harvesting the potato yield. September had come and gone with no thought or even a mention of being the seventh anniversary of Eric's accident. The only thought they had was that the time was approaching quickly when he and George would leave for Seattle. October came in with the first light snow and the girls were busy preparing for Trick or Treating. It was a normal routine for the family.

Laura was busy in the kitchen when she heard someone pull up to the house. "George, come in, sit down and eat with us," she invited him. "I'll put on the coffee and go wake Eric. He sleeps later during the fall and winter months, but he should be getting up anyway."

George came in, took off his boots and coat. "Where are the little Aleuts?"

Laura answered, "Oh, I got them off to school an hour or so ago. I usually take them, then come home and get Eric up and going for the day. Sit down and warm yourself, while I get Eric."

When the coffee was ready, George poured himself a cup. By then Eric came out to the table. "Hey, George, what's up, man? I thought you'd be working."

George sipped his coffee, poured Eric a cup. "No, I had some things to do, so I took the day off. Just wanted to stop by and tell you everything is all set for me to go with you to Seattle. I didn't want to leave you and Laura hanging on that plan. I checked again with Sam on watching my place. He said he was ready to, and that David could even stay there if I wanted him to. So we're all set. Is there anything I can do to help leave Laura and the girls in good shape?"

"No," said Eric. "Thanks to you and Sam, we're fine."

By this time, Laura set breakfast out for the three of them, "Come on and let's eat while it's still hot." As they sat down she continued, "While I think of it, we want you and Sam and the boys to come for Thanksgiving Dinner. After all, I have to keep all my helpers well-fed."

They chuckled and George accepted without blinking an eye. "Sure, it will beat a moose sandwich and bear stew at my place, and I thank you for the invite."

After breakfast, Laura asked George, "Will you be here for awhile? If you can stay, I'll go and do some errands. It will save me getting Eric out in the cold."

"Sure why not? I've done all I've planned on doing today. You go ahead; we'll be fine." George looked at Eric, "Won't we, pal?"

Laura cleaned up then headed for Soldotna. As she was driving into Soldotna, the old truck sputtered a few times, and she said out loud, "Oh, Baby, don't let me down now when it's twenty degrees outside. Guess that's why you're sputtering." Luck was with her; it kept running. She visited the post office, went to see Sue, invited her for Thanksgiving and then over to Sam's office to invite him and the boys.

Laura greeted Sam's secretary, and asked if he was in. He soon came out, and Laura greeted him, "Hi Sam, how are you? We haven't seen you for awhile. Is everything okay?"

"Sure just fine, and how are you and Eric? We've been pretty busy here, what with holiday deadlines on shipping and so forth." Laura was shivering. "Hey, you look cold. Come in and warm yourself. How about a cup of tea?"

"Oh, that would be nice, but what I really came for was to invite you and the boys for Thanksgiving dinner. George, Sue and Agnes will be there too. It's the least we can do, for all the help you've given us," she said as she followed him back to his office.

They had tea and Laura warmed up. "This tea tastes pretty good. It's very cold out today, thank you, but I should get back home. George is there with Eric now, so don't forget Thanksgiving... you and the boys."

"I won't," he replied as he helped her with her coat. "It'll be our pleasure. It'll give us something to be thankful for … your friendship. Let me walk you out." He walked her to the truck and helped her in. She turned the key to start the engine. No response.

"Oh no," she said. "This old truck was sputtering on the way here. Don't tell me she died!"

Sam opened the door. "Come on, I'll take you home. Give me the keys and I'll see to it that I get it home for you. I'll look at it later." Laura got out and followed him back into the office. As they entered, he said to the secretary, "Kay, Laura's truck died and I'm going to run her home. I'll be back soon, so just hold my calls."

He got his coat and they walked to his truck. He helped her in and then got in himself. He started the truck and asked her, "Do you need to stop anywhere before I take you home?"

"Well, I was going to stop at the grocery and pick up a few things."

"Done," he said, "and any other place you need to go?"

"No, just the groceries, then I usually pick up the girls, but they can take the bus."

"No, we'll pick them up. It's a very cold day, and we know that this truck is warm and will make it home. But first, we will go to the store."

Laura got out at the store, ran in to get what she needed, and was back in a few minutes. Sam took the groceries and put them in the backseat and helped her into the truck. "Now on to the school."

They were a little early arriving, so Laura went in to tell their teacher she was outside to pick them up, to please let the bus driver know she had them. When she got into the truck, she thanked Sam. "You're always there when I need you. You know Eric told me one time that should anything happen when he wasn't here, to call you. You would always be there for me. How right he was. You are always there when I need help or encouragement. How can I ever thank you for that?"

"Maybe someday, you'll find a way," he said. "But for now, a thank you is sufficient. You have been through a lot and still you smile and do for others. You're quite a woman!"

Just then Mary and Patty came running up to the truck. Sam helped them into the truck and they were off for home. Laura invited Sam in, but he declined. "Thanks anyway, but I must get back to the office. I'll get your truck back as soon as possible, but for now, should you need transportation, call me."

When Laura and the girls went into the house, Eric and George were full of questions as to what happened. Laura got the girls settled then told them the whole story.

George looked at Eric. "See, I told you Sam was a good choice to look after Laura and the girls while we're gone. He is a very steady, reliable person."

"Yes, I know," said Eric.

Thanksgiving Day was a busy day for Laura and the girls. Laura prepared the dinner with all the good aromas in the kitchen: the pies baking, the yeast smell of homemade hot bread, and the turkey with its inviting smell, filling the cabin. Their guests arrived and were greeted by all the tempting display. The girls had made paper turkeys to hold place cards on the table. The cinnamon candles were lit, making the setting more festive. Sam and the boys oohed and aahed over what a beautiful table they had set.

George agreed. "This is like heaven, all these good, luscious, smells. It beats my bear stew and moose burger all to pieces. I'm thankful for the invite."

They all gathered around the table and Eric offered a prayer of Thanksgiving. Everyone enjoyed the wonderful food. Over coffee and dessert, they talked of the many things that had to be done before George left with Eric for Seattle. George also briefed Sam on what he'd have to do to keep the plumbing from freezing in the cabin. It was then Sam offered an idea. "If you would trust my boys, they could stay there and see that the fires are kept burning in the stove. They could eat at our house and sleep there at night. During the day we could all keep an eye on it."

"Sounds like a super idea to me." George agreed. "I wouldn't trust anyone more than you or your boys. Besides, it's not fancy, just an old bachelor's cabin. And if people see smoke coming from the chimney and truck tracks in the snow, they know someone is there and they won't bother nosing around!"

"Done!" said Sam and then turned to Eric. "Is there plenty of firewood for Laura? We could cut some before you leave."

"No, we're pretty much set on wood, food and necessary items." Eric looked at him. "Just promise me you will look after her and the girls. I want you to protect and care for them, without fail, while we are gone.

Promise me! Promise me you will, no matter what happens."

Sam felt a real sense of urgency in his voice. It was as if Eric was giving him an order, rather than a request. Did he know something he wasn't telling him or Laura? "I promise I will, and you know that I never go back on a promise."

"Good," said Eric, "now I can relax, and enjoy this Thanksgiving Day with my friends and loved ones. All is well in my house and God is with us."

Chapter 19

It seemed as if 1991 would never end for Eric, now that he had made up his mind to go for intensive rehabilitation. Each day brought him closer to the time he and George would leave for the Veterans Hospital in Seattle. He kept thinking of his promise to God to go to Costa Rica and do His work. *Would he be able to give up Laura, Mary and Patty so they could start their lives anew, as he was going to do?* The long hours of darkness didn't seem to help much either, as he was unable to fight the famous *seasonal affective disorder, or SAD,* as it is better known, the condition forcing people inside by the weather, only to be driven crazy by *'cabin fever.'* He remembered how they used to do cross-country skiing, skating, skijoring, sledding, and even riding snowmobiles, to help ward it off. All of these things kept circling his mind. Finally, December 21 came and the daylight hours would lengthen again. Nineteen hours of darkness and five hours of daylight were wearing on Eric's nerves.

January brought a noticeable difference in the daylight hours, and Laura was able to keep him out on the porch to view the mountains for longer periods. As she pushed him out one day he commented, "Look at that beauty. How I love this country. I loved being out there in the wilds, hunting and fishing. Even working out in this weather wasn't so bad. You just had to learn how to dress and to respect the weather. But now, all I can do is to sit here in this chair and remember what it was like."

"Come on now Eric, we've taken you out with us on our cross-country skiing trips. They rigged you up with the ski sled to be pulled by the snow machine," Laura reminded him. "And in the summer, Jim and George put you in a canoe with them and traveled the lakes."

"Oh, Laura," Eric grumbled, "We both know very well that it's not the same. It'll never be the same. Even the cold is starting to bother my back now. I will just have to adjust." He went on, "We'll see what the trip to the Seattle will tell. When the results of my physical and therapy are in, we may all have to adjust to a new way of living."

"Now Eric," she hugged him from behind his chair, putting her arms around his neck, "we will just adjust, that's all. Let's not worry about things, until we know what we actually have to worry about. Are you cold? Want to go back inside?"

"Guess I better," he said, taking one long last look at that beautiful view of the mountains.

The time finally arrived when Eric and George were to fly from Anchorage to Seattle. They decided to have Sam drive his extended cab truck, taking Laura, the girls and David. George and Eric would go in George's truck and take the wheelchair and luggage. Then David could drive George's truck back to Sterling.

In this way, Laura and the girls could see them off at the Anchorage airport. The trip would take about two and a half to three hours. The plane was set to depart at one-thirty in the afternoon. The tickets were bought and all was ready.

They all met at Eric and Laura's after a good breakfast, and left for

Anchorage around eight o'clock. They wanted to get there in plenty of time. The girls and Laura had mixed emotions about Eric leaving, although Mary and Patty were excited about going to the big airport and seeing all the planes. While on the way to Anchorage, Mary asked, "Mom, why is Daddy going to fly to Seattle for therapy? Why can't we go along too? Why is George going with him and not you? How long will he be gone?"

"Whoa! Whoa!" said Laura, "that's an awful lot of questions for a twelve-year-old to be asking. Let's take one at a time. First, Daddy is going to the Veterans Hospital in Seattle to have a complete physical checkup. It's been eight years since his accident and it's time he had a good checkup. Don't you remember? We've talked of this before. You wouldn't want something to be wrong with him, would you? Both the girls chorused a big no from the back seat of Sam's truck.

Laura was glad to answer questions for the girls. She knew it would make the trip go faster for them. "Now in answer to your question as to why we can't go along, of course, you know how cold it is here, and you two are still in school and someone has to keep the fire going at home, so our plumbing won't freeze. So George said he would go and stay with Daddy, while we stay here and keep the home fires burning, and you two go to school."

"Oh yes, we forgot about school!" They giggled when they said that.

Even Sam chuckled as he was driving. "You mean you would like to forget about school!"

"No sir, Sam," said Patty, "we like school. Will you come get us if the old truck breaks down again?"

"Of course, all your mama has to do is call me, and I'll be there. There isn't anything I wouldn't do for you two girls or your mama! Besides, your daddy made me promise I would look after all of you when he isn't here!" Sam quickly glanced at Laura to see her reaction as he spoke.

"What did Eric make you promise?" she asked him.

"You heard what I said to the girls. That's what he made me promise." Sam glanced sideways at Laura. "Of course, I want you to know, promise or no promise, I will always be here for you and the girls. You know that."

Laura wondered why Eric would make Sam promise that. It rolled around in her mind. She began to think of a lot of things that Eric said to her lately. What did it all mean?

The rest of the trip to Anchorage was quiet, and they soon arrived at the airport. David jumped out and went to help George with the wheelchair and getting Eric out of the truck. Once out, Laura, the girls, and Sam took Eric to the ticket counter. He and George checked their bags through. David took George's truck to park while they waited for their plane to depart.

Once checked in, they had a little over an hour before they had to board. Sam, George and David suggested they grab a sandwich. They all went into the cafeteria and Laura, Eric, and the girls sat at one table, while David, Sam, and George sat at another. The guys wanted to give Eric, Laura, and the girls a chance to say their good-byes.

After they finished their food, Eric hugged and kissed the girls. "Now I want you to promise me you will be good for Mom. No trouble. I don't know how long I'll be gone. Depends on my physical and the type of therapy they do for me. So don't worry, I'll be fine. Remember, George will be with me. And you and Mom will be fine too."

"Yes, we will," Laura broke in, "so why would you make Sam promise to keep watch over us and take care of us if we need anything when you aren't around? You scare me when you talk like that!"

"Now honey, don't you worry. Didn't you make me promise to do something besides just sit in my chair? You said that I should use my intelligence and knowledge of things in general to do well and not just vegetate?"

"Yes, I did," she admitted.

"Well then, let me go and see what I can gain from this visit to the Rehab Center. But in the meantime, I wanted to be sure you and the girls would be cared for, as I would care for you!"

When the call came for them to board, they all hugged and kissed and said their good-byes.

Laura told George and Eric both, "Keep us posted on what's happening in Seattle." As George started to push Eric toward the plane, Mary pushed a bag onto her Daddy's lap. They all waved good-bye, as they boarded.

Chapter 20

The flight from Anchorage to Seattle would take about two hours, so George settled in to catch some extra sleep. It had been an early day for him and he was going to take advantage of the lull in activity. After he saw that Eric was settled he said, "Hey buddy, I'm going to catch a little shuteye. If you need help or anything just wake me."

"Yeah, sure," Eric responded, "but that's pretty doubtful. I'm sitting fine."

It wasn't long before Eric heard George's rhythmical breathing. Every so often, he would breathe out a puff of air, as if sighing deeply in his sleep. Eric wondered what he was dreaming about, and chuckled to himself. He shifted his arm and felt the bag Mary and Patty had placed in his lap as he rolled down the concourse to board the plane. He opened it and pulled out *Mr. Bear*, thinking, *Good old Mr. Bear, with me all the time I was in Anchorage Hospital, and Patty and Mary felt I should have him with me now.* Tears welled in his eyes as he thought, *I love my family so much, and when I think how much they love me, I just know that I have to do well at this rehabilitation center. I must! I don't want them to be giving up things for me anymore. They must have a normal life. It's now my time to be the one to give something up.*

"How cute that is!" A voice brought him out of his thoughts. "Is that for a child of yours?"

It was the stewardess. Eric blushed a little and said, "No, actually, he's mine. My little girls gave it to me to keep me company and to love while I'm in the hospital."

"Oh, I'm sorry," she said. "I didn't know! Is there anything I can get you? Are you comfortable?"

"I'm fine, thank you. I'm only going to the VA hospital in Seattle for a checkup and extended rehabilitation," he answered.

They had finished with their serving and routine duties, so she sat in an empty seat across the aisle. "I see your friend is sleeping. May I get you a pillow, or anything? How long will you be in Seattle?"

Eric answered vaguely, "I really don't know, but I hope not too long. Mr. Bear and I both get homesick for Alaska!" He chuckled. "Don't I look like the outdoors type? I used to be a good hunter and fisherman. But not anymore, as you can see!"

She rose. "I have to go now, but you do look like a determined man. I'm sure with the rehab, which the VA can give you in Seattle; you will be hunting and fishing again real soon. You ring if you need anything. Nice talking to you, and take care of *Mr. Bear.*"

Eric thought, *how nice of her to stop and talk to me; that usually doesn't happen. What was it she said? That I would soon be hunting and fishing again, real soon? Yes, I could be a fisherman of souls. Funny she should say what she did. Was that maybe a sign or a calling?* His thoughts were interrupted once again, this time by the captain saying they would soon be landing in Seattle. He woke George up.

It took them awhile to get the luggage and Eric's wheelchair. As soon as George found a map of the city, for his future reference, they hailed a cab.

The taxi transported them directly to the Veterans Hospital. George gathered the bags and took Eric into the registration area. The receptionist smiled and asked, "May I help you, please?"

Eric had his necessary papers from Mrs. Parker ready, along with the letter stating that he would have a traveling companion, who was to be lodged in the adjacent hotel at a special rate. He presented these to her, reading the name on her badge, and said, "Yes, Mrs. Kline, I think you will find all the information necessary for my admission to the hospital, and also, the papers for my escort, who will be staying next door at the hotel."

As she read the papers, she said, "Mr. Eric Adams and his escort, Mr. George Riley. Yes, your papers are all in order. I'll call someone to take you to your room. You'll be in room # 229 in the Rehab Wing. Meanwhile, Mr. Riley, you should take these papers next door, and ask for Mr. Cooper at the admission desk. He'll show you where you'll be lodging. There are direct phone lines from certain rooms in the hotel for escorts, such as you, to the hospital switchboard. All you have to do to speak to Mr. Adams, day or night, is to pick up the phone and dial his extension. The same goes for you Mr. Adams; all you need to do is to pick up the phone and dial 0 and then this number, Room #302, to speak to Mr. Riley.

"Those will be the only calls you can make direct. All other calls are to be put on phone credit cards. It's much simpler that way. You may purchase the phone cards in the PX, here in the hospital."

Eric nodded. "Sounds simple enough, all right; let's get this show on the road. When will I see my doctor, Mrs. Kline? I 'm anxious to know if I can be helped anymore."

"That's all I can tell you, Mr. Adams." She apologized and rang for an orderly.

"I'm afraid you will have to wait until they give you a complete physical, before even the doctor can tell you. The orderly will take you to your room now," Mrs. Kline continued, "and Mr. Riley can go get settled and come back to be with you by using this pass. Don't forget, Mr. Riley, he will be on the second floor, Room 229. This pass is good for you to use until Mr. Adams is discharged. So please don't misplace it."

"No worries, Mrs. Kline." George saluted her. "I'll see you when I get unpacked, Eric, I'll be back."

"No hurry," Eric said, "I'm sure I can get settled in. See you later, George. Let's go James," he said to the aide, "I'm ready!"

"Mr. Adams," the orderly corrected him, "My name is Alan, and I'll be glad to help you, sir. They say you live in Alaska. Is it colder there than here?"

"Well, Alan, and please call me Eric," he said to the young man and continued to answer his question, "I'm not really familiar with how cold it gets here, but in Alaska, where we live, just near Sterling, the winters actually seem milder than the ones in western New York. We don't get the damp cold or the wind blowing the snow into 'blizzard' conditions. It could be twenty degrees Fahrenheit outside and we could run out to the 'privy' with only a sweater on, because it is a still, dry, cold. We only have about five to six hours a day of daylight until about December 21, and then the daylight starts to get longer. Weird isn't it? Does that answer your question? "

"Yes Sir, Mr. Adams, oh ah, err, Eric." He said when he caught that look Eric gave him and blushed a little.

"Now you answer me a question," said Eric. "I know you aides pretty much know the scuttlebutt around here. When will I see a real doctor?"

"I'd guess, tomorrow. They will probably do a general physical exam. Then some spinal x-rays, blood work, blood pressure, all the usual stuff." Alan continued, "I'll be your aide except for my days off, and then I'm not sure who you'll have. But I assure you; you will have an A-1 doctor in Dr. Walker!" Alan stopped a minute, and then patted his own chest. "And you already have one of the best aides, if I do say so myself."

"Well, that's good," said Eric, "Guess I'll have to take all they give me like a man! I won't complain. I just want to know just how much I can do. That is vitally important to me. It will decide my future, for sure. Now, if you don't mind, I'm rather tired. Could you get me ready for bed? It's been a long, tiring, emotional day."

On the ride back to Sterling from Anchorage airport, Laura was quiet. She was thinking of Eric and some of the things he had been saying recently. *It has been a long, emotional day,* she thought. She sighed very heavily. The girls were asleep, stretched out in the back seat, as David was driving George's truck back. The quiet was deafening. She sighed again, not realizing she was doing so.

"Are you all right?" Sam asked, keeping a steady hand on the wheel as he glanced over at her.

"Yes, I'm just a wee bit tired. I've been running some things through my mind that Eric said to me before he boarded the plane." Laura quietly answered Sam. "I can't quite figure out why Eric made me promise to call on you should anything happen to him, or why he made you promise to watch out for the girls and me. I just wonder if he's not telling me everything I need to know."

"Laura, since you can't walk away if what I say bothers you, I'm going to level with you. Eric knows how I feel about you and the girls. He knows that I have been very fond of you ever since Connie left me. He knows there isn't anything I wouldn't do for you. That is why he made me promise to look after you and the girls. I know you love him and he loves you, and I would never tread upon that relationship, because you both mean a lot to me. That's why he made me promise what he did. I hope what I've just told you will not change our friendship. That would devastate me."

Laura reached over and touched his arm. "Oh Sam, nothing you could ever say or do would change the way either Eric or I feel about you. You know we love you and cherish your friendship." Then she leaned over and kissed Sam on the cheek. "Now if you are okay with driving and not the least bit sleepy, I would like to catch some rest. It's been a long, emotional and tiring day."

Chapter 21

Eric awoke to the sound of trays clanging. As he opened his eyes he saw George sleeping in the chair by his bed. He spoke to George, waking him. "Did you sleep here all night?

"Yep, when I came back you were tucked in and asleep, so I put myself in that chair, thinking you might wake up around supper. But you didn't so I went to the cafeteria to eat, came back and sat down again. You really must have been exhausted!"

"Yes, I was. I felt physically and emotionally drained. Have you seen any doctors come by? How about Alan? Where is he?"

George interrupted Eric, "He just shot by the door, in a hurry, and mumbled he would be right back!"

Alan popped in with a hospital wheelchair and said, "Well, you got your wish. Dr. Walker has lined up a bunch of x-rays and lab tests for you today. We'll go there first, and then down to an examination room for a thorough checkup. Are you ready?"

"You bet, let's get it done. George, you might as well go sightseeing for the day. Come back this evening and we'll swap stories. Okay?"

"Right on, Buddy," George got up to leave. "Can I send a message home for you?"

"Just tell Laura we're starting the complete physical and evaluation process. I'll call her later," Eric indicated. "Come on Alan, let's get to it."

Alan pushed Eric all over the hospital that day. First to the lab to get his blood work completed, then an EKG, and a check on all his vitals.

Next he pushed him to x-ray, where Dr. Walker came in for a few minutes to talk to him. "Eric, tell me how the accident happened, exactly. How long was it before Medivac transported you to Anchorage? I have both reports from Dr. Goodman and Dr. Miller. We want to x-ray your neck and hip area again. We want to see what is happening now. We also want x-rays of your entire spine. Then I want you to see a psychiatrist to give me an idea as to how you're emotionally handling your condition."

Dr. Walker then told him, that after all that was done they would start his intensified physical therapy. He explained to him, if all went well, as he thought it would, they'd be able to teach him how to drive a van with a joystick for control. They could teach him to swim, shave, wash his clothes, and do much more for himself.

We already know you cannot hold your hands or arms above your head, but you have advanced there, as you could not move your arms at all when you were first injured. We know you have use of your biceps now." He paused and asked Eric, "You do know that the biceps are the large front muscles that extend your arm upward, or the flexor? It's the lower muscle, the triceps, which works to straighten the arm; it is called the extensor, which you don't have use of at the present." He tapped a pen against Eric's chart. "We know after your September 1984 surgery, you were able to get your biceps to move enough so that you could feed yourself without excessive spillage."

Eric answered Dr. Walker, "In Anchorage, they gave me therapy to help me eat on my own."

"Well, Eric, after we work with you in extensive therapy, you should be able to put on your T-shirt. You can do it, but mind you, it'll be difficult. Are you up to all this?" Dr. Walker didn't even give him an opportunity to answer. "I know you need to be bathed every day and someone has to catheterize you. But you'll also learn to do that yourself, and I promise you, that you can manage it, if you absolutely have to do so, even though at first it'll be extremely difficult for you. Now I know you're wondering how you'll be able to do all this."

Eric jumped in, "I can handle all you can give me, Dr. Walker."

"We'll see. You must have someone to help you, twenty-four hours a day, seven days a week. Someone will have to assist you in and out of your wheelchair and bed every day… and bathe you."

"Do you have any questions? If not we'll begin your therapy. Alan has your schedule and will go over it with your escort. I'll be checking on you every day. Be of strong heart. You will see a difference. You won't be like you were before the accident, but we'll help you, so you can help yourself more. If nothing else, we can give you back your self-reliance. So be of good courage. I see by Dr. Goodman and Dr. Miller's reports you are a tenacious, strong-willed man. That's good. You'll do fine." Dr. Walker left Eric to continue his tests.

Most of the day was spent in physicals, lab and x-ray. By the end of the day, when Alan pushed Eric back to his room, he was exhausted.

"Boy, I can see I've let myself get soft," Eric said to Alan. "All this pushing, prodding and sticking has worn me out a little."

"Hey Eric," answered Alan, with admiration in his voice, "You have been through a lot for one day. I can tell you this: people with more mobility than you have, are bushed when they come through their first day under Dr. Walker's care and treatment. He is like a mad dog drill sergeant. Yes sir, Eric, you can be proud of yourself! You did fine. Dr. Walker is tough, but he is one of the best doctors you could ever have in your corner. He is admired and respected. His word is law!"

"That's good to hear," said Eric; "I don't want any favors. I want to be more independent. I need to be, for what I have to do. It's time I learned not to lean on my wife and two girls, not to mention all the help my friends have given us. It's time for a new life. I am determined that I will accomplish what I've planned. Now, just put me in bed and let me rest. Alan, you are the best! Thank you for your help. I'm grateful."

After getting Eric settled in bed, Alan left, and passed George coming in. "Hi, George, we put him through the ropes today. He's pretty tired. I just wanted to let you know."

"Hey, thanks, Alan. That's good to know, because he always puts on the macho act for me. But you know that I never baby him. He wants to do as much as he can alone. It's his pride, and I would never injure that. He has enough to contend with as it is, so thanks."

George patted Alan on the back, gave him a thumbs-up sign, and went on into Eric's room. "Hey man, what a day I had. How about you? Did they put you through your paces? I saw Alan in the hall, and he said you flashed through as easy as basic training."

"Yeah, I did!" chuckled Eric. He was too tired to talk, so he asked George, "So tell me about your day. What about Seattle? I've never been here, either. Tell me about it. You can leave out the part about the women you saw. That's your private stuff."

George pulled the easy chair closer to Eric's bed, settled down in it, and relaxed. Then he started, "Now let's see. I bet you think I didn't learn a thing about Seattle, except where the good hot spots were located! But I'm going to show you, I am a real historian when it comes to being in a new place. Are you ready to absorb all this?"

"Sure, go ahead," said Eric. "I want to hear it all."

George cleared his throat in a professor-like manner, smoothed his shirt, and began. "Seattle was settled in 1851 by a small group of pioneers from Illinois. It was named in honor of Chief Seathl, spelled S-E-A-T-H-L, pronounced as Seattle. He was Chief of the Suguamish and Duwamish tribes, who aided the settlers. You see, that's why they named the settlement after the chief."

"Yes, because the Indians helped the settlers. I see. Go on."

George continued, "Lumbering was the main activity. In 1853 a lumberman from the Midwest, Henry L.Yesler, built a steam-powered sawmill in Seattle, the first on Puget Sound. In the 1860s, Asa S. Mercer brought a number of women from the east to provide wives for the Seattle loggers."

Eric jumped in, "I knew you would get women in here someplace!" Then he laughed.

George laughed too. "Well, when you get down to it, I did meet a couple of hot numbers." Seeing that Eric was tiring more, George rushed and cut his talk short. "I'm meeting one tomorrow night."

Eric was lying with his eyes closed. George rose up to see if he was asleep. As he did so, Eric waved his hand. "Go on, I'm just resting my eyes."

"Hold on now," said George, "I'm about done. She's single and a redhead! There, how's that!"

"Great, very informative," said Eric sleepily. "Now will you please shut up and let me go to sleep?"

"Okay, pal," said George. "I'll see you later. I'm kind of tired myself. You call if you need me. I'm going back to my room."

By the time George finished talking, Eric was breathing soft and easy. Sleep had finally taken over. George stood looking at Eric for a while, thinking, "What a guy!" He patted his shoulder and quietly left.

Eric woke the next morning as Alan touched his shoulder and gave him a little shake. "Hey, are you going to sleep all day? We have a whole lot of work ahead of us again today. I know you were put through the paces yesterday, but Dr. Walker has a whale of a program for you, so how about some breakfast before we get you started on it?"

"Great! I was really beat when we got back here last night, but feed me and I'm willing to take anything Dr. Walker has in store for me today. I need to get independent and do for myself. So bring on breakfast and let's get to it!"

"All right!" answered Alan, "You're the man!" Alan sensed the urgency in Eric's voice and could not help but wonder what was in his mind. He seemed so driven. He set up Eric's breakfast tray after his bath, and got him ready for the day's program. "I'm going to show you how to make it easier to feed yourself, you do okay, but we want better, and I am sure you do, too." Alan continued explaining what they were to be working on. "After you eat, I'll show you how to shave. That won't be easy! All these tasks your caregiver will usually do for you, but you should know how to do them for yourself. Sometimes, it may be necessary for you to do them. That's the object of this program: to give you more independence, and the ability not to have to depend on someone else to do these things."

"Don't worry, Alan, I'll be the best student you have ever had, believe me!" Eric said, as he reached out for Alan's hand. "I know you'll do your best to show me, and I only hope that I can accomplish it all, because it's very important to me. So don't pull punches; be hard on me. I can take it. I want to do it all."

Alan knew he had a willing student, so he made a motion of rolling up his sleeves, looked Eric straight in the eye and he said, "Okay, so let's begin. Here's your breakfast tray.

Feed yourself, and I'll tell you what you can do to make it easier. I have to see what you can do by yourself, and how you're going to do it."

Eric paused for a moment, and then managed to get his eating utensils unwrapped, but with difficulty. All the months of therapy he had with Sue in Soldotna had improved his arm movement considerably, so he was able to manage.

Alan remarked to him, "You're doing well, but you're messy, so allow me to show you a few things. We have heavy handled utensils so it's going to be easier for you to grasp them. It'll take some time to feel comfortable with them. So, take your time. You don't have to rush; easy does it? Try to remember that. The more you do this, the easier it will become, but it's going to take a lot of practice. I'll give you some hand and smaller arm movements to practice, so when you're eating, it will be easier for you. Okay?

"You can do these exercises here in your room or even when you're in bed. The more you do them, the more movement of that type you will be able to do."

Eric looked at Alan with determination in his eyes. "You just wait and see how good I'm going to get at this. There'll be no more messes like today!"

"I have no doubts about it, Eric. I'm beginning to know you, and I know you and I are going to have the best therapy improvement record this hospital has ever seen."

Alan gave him a thumbs-up sign, "You're a man on a mission!"

For the next two hours they worked on the eating, shaving, and the personal hygiene part of the program. As Alan had said, Eric really was a man on a mission. He was persistent. Finally Alan said, "Okay, time for you to take a break. It's about time for George to pop in here, so you rest and visit with George. I'll be back in an hour. I want you to be sharp and rested. We are going to do some more therapy, and then I want you to read some books."

"What kind of books?" Eric asked.

"Manuals on driving; we're going to check you out on a simulator, to see if you could handle driving a vehicle if it was properly outfitted for you. There are no guarantees, but Dr. Walker is not going to leave any stone unturned in your case. He knows you can take whatever he has planned for you. You made a lasting impression on him, and that's good. He's one hell of a doctor." Alan paused a moment. "I thought if I got the manuals to you, you could study them in advance, and it would help considerably. Now, sit back and wait for George; he should be here soon. I've got to go. See you in an hour or so."

Just as Alan was cleaning up the shaving and food tray, George walked through the door. "Hey, how are two of the busiest guys in the hospital this morning? Did I come at a bad time? Do you want me to leave?"

"No, I was just leaving. How are you this morning, George?" asked Alan on his way out the door.

"Right as rain," replied George. "How's my buddy? Eric, what has Alan been doing to you now? Looks like a lot of stuff he's carrying out of here. What are all those little pieces of tissue stuck to your face?

"Oh, Alan was showing me how to shave myself and, as you can see, I didn't do so hot for the first time. Nicked myself a few times, but I'll heal."

"I thought you had an electric razor," said George.

"I do, but they want me to learn how to use a safety razor, should there be no electricity available." Eric replied. "Makes sense, I guess. They want me to be prepared. George, you can't believe the plans that Dr. Walker has set up for me to do here. Alan said they're even going to show me how to drive a vehicle with a joy stick, that is, if I pass all the preliminary tests to see if it's feasible for me. Alan is going to bring me some manuals on the schematics of it. He's one fine aide to have working with me. He's a good guy! By the way, did you get a call off to Laura last night? And did you buy the phone cards at the PX down stairs, so I could call her from here?"

"Hey, slow down; let me answer one question at a time. Yes, Alan is a great guy to have in your corner. We've talked out in the hall, and he admires you for your courage and intestinal fortitude. We all do. And yes, I called Laura last night. I filled her in on what they were doing for you, and she was really happy to hear it. She and the girls are fine, and they send you their love. Things are running smooth at home, and Sam is keeping an eye on them, as I called him too. I checked on my place and all is well there. So the home front is fine. I did get the phone cards, and I told Laura I'd have them today, so you could call her from here. Do you want me to get her on the line?"

"You know I do." Eric grinned. "There's a lot I need to tell her, and if you don't mind, after you get her on the phone would you step out of the room? I don't think a single man should hear what a husband has to say to his wife" He laughed as he said this.

George took the phone and dialed Laura's number. He knew how much Eric loved her, and he knew Eric so well, that he knew what he had in his mind for their future. He only hoped that Eric would not tell her about his plans on the phone. That would be cruel. He heard the phone ringing and Laura's voice answer on the other end of the line. "Laura, this is George. Eric's here and wants to speak with you. I'll jump off and step out of the room, so yell at him if you want for not calling sooner. Bye Love, now here's Eric." George handed the phone to Eric and left the room, saying on his way out, "Call me if you need help!"

Eric took the phone and quietly said, "Laura?" She answered back to him softly. He swallowed hard and continued. "Oh honey, how good it is to hear your voice. I'm sorry for not calling sooner, but as George probably told you, they are really putting me through my paces. You were so right to keep encouraging me to come here. They're helping me so much already."

Laura broke in, "Oh Eric, you have always been in control of things.

That's why I kept encouraging you to go to Seattle. I knew they could help you, more than we could here in Soldotna. They are so much better equipped to handle a case like yours. I couldn't stand to see you become depressed over the fact that you had to rely on so many people. That's not your style. I miss you, honey, and so do the girls. They keep asking about you every day. We're doing fine. Sam keeps a good eye on all of us. He's such a good man. Tell me more of what they're doing for you. George touched on a small bit of it, but didn't go into detail."

"Laura, it's so good to hear your voice. You've answered most of the questions I was going to ask you. I miss you too. George is a good pal, but he will never replace you. You are much prettier and softer too. Dr. Walker, my attending physician, is a number-one guy. He's tough, but that's what I need. I want more movement. They're going to teach me to drive a vehicle, with a joystick. Not that we could afford one. They are so expensive, but at least I'll have the knowledge of how to do it. I'm even learning to shave myself, with both an electric razor and a safety razor, in case I'm where there is no electricity. I'm not doing real well with the safety razor, cutting myself quite a bit, but I'll get better. Alan, my aide, is tops! Someone is really looking after me from up above, for I am getting all the best help here. You'd really like Dr. Walker. He is very thorough and likes things done right." Eric paused a bit. "Listen to me rattle on and on. But as you can tell, I'm trying to be a good patient and absorb all they have to throw at me. You and the girls really need a break."

"Eric, we love you very much and want to help you in any way we can. Sure, there are times when we get tired, but so do you. We're all in the same boat, honey. Don't you ever forget how much the girls and I love you. That is never ending. I wish I could be there with you now. Everything here is fine, so don't worry about anything but getting all the care and help you can while you're there. Do you have any idea how long you'll be gone?"

Eric answered her quickly, "Dr. Walker thought I might be here for about six weeks. It'll seem like an eternity, I know, but we can weather it. We've been through a lot, since we met, and we can handle this. You're a remarkable woman, Laura, and I'm so lucky to have you in my corner… the girls too. You and I, we're surely blessed. Some people would say differently, what with the accident and all, but we have to look beyond the negative and see the positive side of it all. I do love you. You are a strong person and can handle anything that comes your way. Never forget that. I'd best go now. I'm getting tired, but I'll call again when I have more to tell you. Kiss and hug the girls for me. Love you."

"I love you too, Eric," Laura replied, and swallowed hard, to hold back the tears. She didn't want him to hear her cry. "I'll kiss and hug the girls for you. I do every day when we say our prayers for you. God bless and keep you. Talk to you later." And she blew him a kiss.

Chapter 22

Laura hung up the phone and just sat staring out the window at the mountains Eric loved so much. The tears silently found their way down her cheeks. She was glad to have talked with Eric, but somehow even though he told her he loved her, she felt a sense of something he was holding back. It was like the eerie feeling of uneasiness she got before a severe thunderstorm. She knew something was coming, but it seemed like it took forever to get there. It was lucky that Eric had called while the girls were in school. She didn't want them to see her so worried. She did nothing the rest of the morning but sit and stare out the window at the mountains.

As soon as George heard Eric tell Laura good-bye, he came back into the room. "How did it go?" he asked, not wanting to pry too much. "Was she glad to finally hear from you? She wasn't angry you hadn't called before? You didn't mention anything about what you plan to do when we get out of here, did you? I'm sorry, so many questions; guess it just makes me nervous for you."

"No, it was just good to hear her on the phone. I do miss her, but you know it hurts me to see her and the girls work so hard." Eric seemed saddened by the phone call, but he continued. "I want them to have the kind of life they deserve. They should have a whole family, one where both parents can give. Not just them giving to me. I've been thinking for a long time now on this, and I definitely want to dedicate my life to spreading God's word. You know, I've been talking about Costa Rica for some time now, and that's where I want to do it. I know the Bible inside and out. You know how I was brought up. It's within me and I can do this. I've made up my mind, and I'm going to sacrifice my family to do it. I must let them have a full and happy life. Am I crazy?"

By now, tears were welling up in Eric's eyes, and he asked George to get him a tissue. George handed him one. "No man, you're not crazy. You are thinking unselfishly about your family. But it's such a sacrifice that you're thinking of making. Do you really think this is what you want to do?"

They both were silent as Eric wiped his eyes and blew his nose. George kept searching Eric's eyes. He could never keep his true feelings and intentions out of his eyes. They were a dead giveaway. He could see he had been thinking of this for some time. Now the question was… could he do it?

"When are you planning on telling her of your decision? I told you that you were welcome to come to my place and that I would go to Costa Rica with you, but I didn't realize just how serious you were about the whole thing. Have you thought of the impact it will have on Laura and the girls, to find out you're going to leave them? Have you thought beyond that?" George questioned him intensely. "What will you do after you leave home? I told you I'd stay with you and help you because I want to, as your friend. But I'd like to know what lies ahead for both of us. I can leave the slope for some time and still be able to come back to work when I want. After all, I've been there a very long time."

Eric looked at his friend intently. "I know this is an awful lot to ask of you. I wouldn't do it if I thought there was any other way. But George, look at me; I need to do something with **MY LIFE!** Laura can make a new life for herself and the girls, no matter how much it hurts to do it. We should be back in Sterling in April sometime. This will give me time to help her get the garden going and for me to pick a time to tell her. Are you sure you want to go to Costa Rica? I know I can't stand the cold in Alaska anymore. It gets to me too bad. I need to be where it's warmer."

"You know that Costa Rica is fine with me. I've never been there and I'm up to the challenge. If that is what you really want to do." George paced the floor. "I'll take advantage of the library and the computer here in the hospital and find out about the living situation and all things we need to be concerned about there. We have to know more information before we go. Are you sure you'll be up to going there?"

"I have to!" Eric responded. "By the time I get through all the therapy they can give me and instructions on how to make my life easier, I believe I can do it!"

"Very well then, I'll get myself armed at the library," said George.

Alan, coming in the door, interrupted their conversation. "Hey, big guy, are you ready to start your intense training period? We're going to give you all the stuff you can handle. Dr. Walker has even set you up to have a refresher course in communications. He felt that this might help you get some employment. He is really in your corner, Eric. He really likes you and your determination to do everything he hands you. So let's get at it. Are you ready?"

George said, "I'll leave you two to your duties. I have some very important studies to make too. So I'd best get at it. See you later, Eric."

"Alan, did you say that Dr. Walker is going to give me a refresher course in communications?" Eric said. "Does that mean if I do well, maybe the VA will help me to get a Ham radio outfit and license? If they would, that would be terrific!"

"Hey, I can't commit myself to saying they will, but it's a possibility," Alan replied. "But for now, let's get started on what you have on the program for today."

As Alan took Eric to therapy, George made his way to the hospital library. His mind was going over the conversations that he and Eric had about Costa Rica. He knew they had talked about going there many times, but he felt it was just something that Eric had wanted to do to occupy his mind while he was sitting alone, when Laura was working. He had spoken to Eric, about going with him, because he himself was curious about how it would be to live in a warmer climate. Now Eric had proposed actually going there. He never thought Eric would actually leave Laura and the girls. But after the phone conversation Eric had with her, and what he indicated about going home to Alaska to help her get the garden in for the year, before moving out of the house, he started to realize Eric was serious. He had been a friend with them both for many years, and he suddenly felt like he was aiding and abetting a breakup… one that he really could not see happening. Well, maybe when it comes right down to actually doing it, Eric will reconsider. When he reached the library he looked for the section where he could find information on Costa Rica. *Wonder why there? Oh well, he had promised Eric he would go with him, and a promise is a promise, so he set about his business.*

Back in Sterling, when Laura and the girls arose the next day, it was business as usual. Laura fixed the girls breakfast and took them to school. Only this time, instead of coming home and working, she went to the Therapy Center to see Sue. She greeted Laura. "Hey girl, how are things going? What's happening in Seattle?"

Laura laughed, "My, that's a lot to answer. Do you have time for me to tell you all that's happening?"

"Sure, I have a clear morning. What do you say we go out and get some coffee?" One look at Laura's face told Sue that she would like to speak to her alone, away from the office. They walked down the street to a small restaurant and found a secluded booth. They ordered and made small talk until the waitress left them with their coffee. "Now tell me what's up? I can tell by your face that you are upset. What's happening?" Sue reached out for Laura's hand.

"Oh Sue, maybe nothing, then again maybe there is something. I don't really know! That's why I wanted to talk to you. I have no one else who has insight on my giving Eric space, other than you. I spoke to him on the phone yesterday morning. That is the first I've talked to him since they left. I talked with George and he's been relaying all the information to me on what they're doing for Eric."

Laura gazed around the café but recognized no one. "George said they keep Eric busy all day with different types of therapy and instruction, and by the end of the day, he is so exhausted he just goes to sleep. How true that is, I don't really know." Again Laura paused and started to dig out a hankie. She wiped her eyes. "Eric told me last night that they were going to show him how to operate a vehicle with a joystick. He also said we would never be able to afford one, but it would be nice to know how to go about it. They are also showing him how to shave, even take care of his catheter, bathe, and everything. He said that all these things are a real effort to do, but Dr. Walker wants him to know how to do it. He sounded very determined to do everything they were handing him. He said we were lucky in a way, because we had been through a lot since we were married and came through it all. He told me I was a strong woman and could handle anything that may come my way, and to never forget that. Then he said, 'I love you,' and I told him I loved him and we hung up."

Sue squeezed her hand. "Well that sounds encouraging to me. It sounds like they are giving him both barrels and he is absorbing all he can. Why are you worried?"

"Sue, it is just a gnawing feeling I have in the pit of my stomach, that he has something in mind that he is not telling me, at least, not yet. He has been doing and saying some pretty weird things. He even made Sam promise to take care of the girls and me if and when he wasn't around. He made me promise to call on Sam if I ever needed anything when he wasn't around. It just gives me the willies." By now, Laura was wringing her handkerchief into a tight cord. "Do you remember when you talked to me some time ago about being tough on him and not catering to his every need? You also said to me not to pass by any opportunities should they come my way? Do you know something I don't know? You have to tell me, if you do."

"Laura, I only said that to you because I, too, had a premonition about Eric doing some strange things. He loves you very much—there is no doubt about that—but sometimes when we love something that much, we have to let it go free or it will die out and not be good for anyone. I sensed that from Eric." Sue looked at her directly. "Do you know something you are not telling me?"

Laura started to cry and Sue got up and slid into the booth beside her, putting her arms around her. Laura sobbed, "Eric spoke of dissolution of our marriage. Sue, I am afraid that when he comes home, he will eventually leave me for good. What will the girls and I do? I couldn't live without him."

"You will do fine! You have two wonderful girls and you have your home, garden and your friends. Do you think for a minute that your friends would leave you in a situation such as that? You could always go back to work at the hospital or the clinic or even a doctor's office. Good nurses are always needed in this country. No, Laura, I have faith in you; and if that happens, you will make it. You will find there will be opportunities around you that you have not even thought about. And if they come your way, don't let them get away from you." Sue reassured her. "You mark my words, Laura. I'll always be here for you and your many friends will too."

"Thanks, Sue," Laura hugged her. "You can't know what it has meant to me to be able to talk to you this way. I felt like I was going to burst. My heart was bigger than my chest and it hurt so much, I needed to let it out!"

"Of course you did." Sue said. "And I'll be here anytime you need to talk. And by the way, it will not go any further than here. No one will ever hear a word of what you said, from me."

"I know that, Sue. How can I ever repay you for your kindness to me and Eric?" Laura said as she picked up the check. "Let me get this; it's the least I can do. I know you have to get back to work. Thanks again. You are a true friend."

Laura felt better after talking with Sue, and felt she could go about what she had to do until Eric's return. She was hoping that what she believed was not true, and that things would be okay when he came home. She had to be positive in her thinking, or else it would eat her up. She had to be strong for everyone: the girls, Eric, and most of all, herself.

Chapter 23

❧

Eric and George knew it would take a while to gather up all the information they needed to go to Costa Rica. "George, I want you to go to the library every day to research the information I give you. While you are doing that, I'm absorbing all they can give me. I've finished the course in driving, and they set up a course on communications."

This he eagerly consumed, feeling that this would be beneficial to him later. He could reach people with his 'Ham Radio' station. It would be a great tool for him in doing his mission work. Eric was convinced this was his calling, to spread the word of God to others, from his wheelchair. He never felt stronger about anything in his lifetime.

But one thing was always in his mind: *The sacrifice he must make in order to go where he was needed to do this. How was he going to tell Laura? Would she fully understand? He knew he must leave her and the girls so he could go on with his life and she with hers. Laura is still young enough to find someone and make a life for herself. The girls are fast approaching the end of school and would need to further their education, and all that would cost money. He had to do this! He also knew that he must not let the idea of leaving her come into any of their conversations until he was home again. This was going to be the hardest thing he ever had to do, and he didn't want to do it over the phone.*

He would pray to do it correctly, without too much pain for either of them. It was going to end a life of love and happiness, but it must be done.

Their phone conversations were about everything he received at the hospital for therapy and instruction. He never failed to ask about the girls or if everything was going all right at home. They always ended the conversations with each saying I love you.

George was getting more information about Costa Rica, and about the money they would each need to fly to San Jose. He also searched for a reasonable place where they could stay and still have money to live on. There was much to plan. George could see that Eric was very serious about going. Then one day he said, "Are you absolutely sure this is what you want to do? How are you going to tell Laura and the girls? Man, I would never be able to do it! I'm not even married to her, but I think the world of her and the girls. It would be beyond my doing such a thing. I'm not that brave to make such a sacrifice."

"It'll be a shock. I'm sure of that, but when I explain everything to her, I'm sure that deep down, in a way, she'll understand. We've had the best of relationships. We not only have loved each other very much, but we've always been the very best of friends. There isn't anything that we wouldn't do for each other. We have always been straight-forward and honest with each other." Eric paused for a moment, cleared his throat, and sighed deeply. "I will give her my reasoning, why I want her to go and make a new life for herself and the girls, and for me to do the same. I think she may even be relieved."

Then he asked George, "What kind of married life do we have anyway? She needs to have a man who can love her as a woman should be loved. She needs the tenderness and loving that I can no longer provide for her.

She's my caregiver. I'm her patient! Don't you understand? You know the needs a man has, George. Well, women have them too. You of all people should know that." Eric dropped his head, holding back tears. Look at me; I have to be stronger than this when I tell her! I better brace up. It won't be too long before we'll be heading back to Sterling."

George took Eric by the shoulders. "You have more courage and fortitude than anyone I've ever known, and when you make up your mind to do something, there is no stopping you. Because of that strength and will, God must have something in mind for you, and no one could fault you for answering the call. I'm proud to say you are my friend. You're a rare person." George hugged him, stepped back. "And yes, the time is getting short. I spoke to Mrs. Kline at the admissions desk the other day about the arrangements for the airline tickets. As you know, we had to turn them in to her when we got here." George reminded Eric, "She said that she would check on them and make sure everything was in order for us."

Eric sat for a moment, cleared his throat as he wiped his eyes. "Good, Dr. Walker is scheduled to see me tomorrow. I should know if I get my walking papers soon. I also want to ask him about the VA helping me with a ham radio. He said he thought he could arrange for some help in purchasing one, if not totally outright, at least get some money toward it. That would be great. I want to ask him if I could just get a money voucher to put on one; then I could have it shipped to wherever I needed it."

"That sounds great. Now would you like me to get Laura on the phone for you, so you could tell her about the news? I mean… about us coming home soon."

"Why don't we wait until tomorrow night? By then, I will have talked to Dr. Walker to get his evaluation, and I can tell her about that too. Besides, I'm really tired and would like to get a good night's sleep and be fresh and sharp tomorrow when I see Dr. Walker."

"It's your call, buddy. I think I'll take a turn around the town tonight.

You know, blow the dust off my engine." George was grinning as he left Eric to rest.

"Go for it, but just try to stay out of trouble. I can't come and bail you out of jail."

The next morning Eric was awake when Alan came into the room. "Morning, Alan, what's up? Am I going to get to see *The Man* this morning?"

Alan answered, "Morning to you too. I think so. We better get your breakfast out of the way and get you polished up to see him. Is that a deal?"

"You bet. I have a lot of questions to ask him. I only get to see him occasionally and I want to thank him personally for being so tough on me." Eric laughed. "It was the best thing he could've ever done for me. He put me through a lot, but it did me a lot of good."

"Eric, if you don't mind my saying so, I want you to know that you have been an inspiration to me. I was content to work here as an aide, but now I've decided to go on with my education and become a doctor. I saw your determination, and I've no idea what you have in mind to do with your life after you leave here, but I do know that whatever it is, you will succeed because of your mindset. I learned from you we must always go forward in our lives and not be content with the mundane daily routine. There is a big old world out there, and somehow, we must be useful in it. I want to thank you for showing me that."

Eric took Alan's hand in his and gave it a hearty handshake. "Alan, good for you, I think you should definitely go for it! I'm really happy to hear that I inspired you. I guess I'm on my way to following my goal. Now let's get ready to see Dr. Walker."

After Alan had finished with Eric's morning routine and was cleaning up, Dr. Walker came into the room. "Well, Eric, are you ready for the world now? I put you through a lot while you were here, and you took it, as I expected you would. So tell me, what do you plan on doing with the 'new you' when you leave this hospital? I want to know before I turn you loose into the world again."

Eric looked him directly in the eye. "I know now what I must do with my life, other than let others care for me. I have some goals now, and I know that I can achieve them, thanks to what I've gained at this hospital, with your help and the help of my Lord. I am dedicating my life to doing the Lord's work among people less fortunate than we are. For some reason, it has been in my mind that I should go to Central America and do His work there."

Dr. Walker looked at him with surprise. "Aren't you married with a family? Will they go with you? Are you sure you want to take a family down to Central America? What about an education for your children?"

Eric replied very quickly, "Dr. Walker, I know this may sound very selfish to you or even a bit crazy, but believe me, I've thought about this for almost three years now. Before I came here, I applied for dissolution of our marriage. I talked it over with my wife, and she agreed to it. However, she thinks it is only for other reasons. I plan on telling her when I return to Alaska, that I am leaving our home and want her to be free to find another person to share her life. I know that sounds very bad, but we have a dear friend who has helped us both over the years, and I know he will not let her go downhill or want for anything. She must have a chance at a different kind of life, the girls too. They have been devoting most of their time to care for me. I love them too much for that. I know they will be hurt, but in time they will heal. They are all young enough to carry on with their lives. I have prayed about this, and this is what I must do. George has agreed to go to Costa Rica with me and we'll be fine."

"Well, you certainly seem to have it all planned out. I can't tell you what you should do with your life, only to be absolutely sure, before you open that door and go through it. Why pick Costa Rica?" Dr. Walker asked.

"I have read up on it extensively, and talked with a young man in therapy who was from there. He told me of the conditions there and how his people needed guidance, and how they hungered to know more about the Lord. So I've decided that it is a place to start. Besides, I can no longer take the cold weather that Alaska hands to me. It gets into my spine and I ache all the time. I have to be where it's warmer." Then Eric stopped for a minute, took a deep breath, and asked Dr. Walker. "Be honest with me, doctor. From all your tests, both physical and mental, do you think I would be foolish to try such an undertaking?"

Dr. Walker stroked his chin. "As I said, I can't tell you what to do with your life, but in answer to your last question, physically and mentally, there is no reason you couldn't do what you have in mind. You are a highly intelligent young man with definite goals on your side. Only you will have to deal with the emotional side of the question; I can't help you with that."

Remember, you will need a caregiver with you at all times. We have taught you how to do things, if it is absolutely necessary, but not as the normal daily routine. I whole-heartedly want you to understand that! We have armed you with the knowledge to help you get through most things, and I'm reasonably sure your faith in your Lord will bring you through the others."

Eric nodded his head. "Which brings me to another question; you put me through the refresher training for communications, as you knew that was what I did in the service. You had mentioned that possibly I could get some financial aid in obtaining a radio system. Is that at all possible? You see, I know that where I am going to do my life's work will be in remote areas. I'd like to have a radio to communicate both in the local area and with my daughters in Alaska. I don't know exactly where I'll be located for sure. Would it be possible, therefore, for you to give me a voucher to use when I do get settled, to order a unit and have it sent to me? It would be so much easier to do that, than have to carry it with me while I am trying to get situated."

"I can arrange that. You are truly a remarkable young man, and I say that without reservation." Dr. Walker took his hand. "I have explained all your limitations to you, and still you are going to go through with your plans. I wish you and your companion all the luck in the world. It has been a privilege to have worked with you, and helped you along the way to your goals. I'll have all the paper work for your release, as well as the vouchers, at the desk with Mrs. Kline. How does Tuesday sound for you to leave here? If you leave here on a Tuesday, the flights shouldn't be too full... easier for you to get back. Good luck to you, Eric. Here is my card. Should you ever need any help with a medical problem, just have your physician call me." He shook Eric's hand and patted him on the shoulder, started out the door, then stopped. "Keep me posted on how you're doing in your life. I will be curious to know. I would like you to come back here, once a year, for a routine check-up. Mrs. Kline will have all that information for you as well. Good luck!"

After Dr. Walker left, Eric just sat in his wheelchair and stared out the window, thinking. *This was Friday. In four days, he and George would be flying back to Sterling. His plans were falling into place, as he wanted them to do. The hardest part was still to come. He longed to see Laura and the girls, but he didn't relish the part of breaking the news to them. He prayed for the Lord to give him strength.*

He was still deep in thought when George came into the room. George touched him on the shoulder. "Are you all right, pal? You were sitting so still, it gave me a start."

"Oh no, I'm okay, just sitting here thinking on how things will be when the time comes for me to tell Laura of our plans. I certainly have to do this right... with no slip-ups. The last thing I want to do is to damage the love between us. I know she will be hurt over the ending of our marriage. I have the greatest respect and admiration for her outgoing personality and courageous attitude toward everything that has come her way. She is one fine woman, and any man would be proud to be associated with her. I know, I was and still am. Only... I have to let her go!"

George could see that he was upset, so he ventured to change the subject. "So tell me, what did Dr. Walker have to say? When is he releasing you to go home?"

"Tuesday, we will be out of here on Tuesday. He is making all the necessary paper work and Mrs. Kline will have it all at the admissions desk, when we are ready to go. Even our plane tickets will be in order, so all we have to do is check in and board the plane."

"Great! Now would you like me to find out what time we will arrive in Anchorage so we can call Laura to be at the airport to pick us up? Better yet, why don't you go down with me? We can even go to the PX store and maybe you would like to pick up something for the girls and Laura. How does that sound?" George asked, trying to lighten the moment.

"Good idea!" Eric said as he turned his wheelchair around. "Let's go!"

They found out the time their plane would arrive in Anchorage, visited the PX and found some gifts for Laura, Mary, and Patty, and returned to Eric's room after they had a bite to eat in the cafeteria.

Eric called Laura, and when she answered and found out it was Eric, she started to cry. "Oh, Eric honey, what is it? Are you all right? You caught me just in time, as I'm getting ready to pick up the girls from school. Can you call me back later when I get home with them?"

"It won't be necessary, Laura. George and I will be in Anchorage on Tuesday around noon. Can you pick us up then?"

"Yes! Yes! I'll get on it right away to make arrangements to be there when you get in. Can't wait to see you! The girls will be excited too!"

"You better get going to pick up the girls. You don't want to be late. I'll see you on Tuesday. I'll tell you all about what Dr. Walker said."

They both closed the conversation saying, I love you.

Chapter 24

Laura laid her hands in her lap after hanging up the phone; she should be the happiest person in Sterling. Eric had just phoned her and said that he and George would be in Anchorage around noon on Tuesday. That would be in four days! The only thoughts going through her mind now were why was she feeling this way? *I'm glad their trip was successful; I knew that it would help Eric. But there's an underlying feeling that something foreboding is going to happen. Why do I feel this way? There it is again. The same question I've been asking myself over and over, since Eric left for Seattle. Enough of doom and gloom, there's many things I've got to do, before going to pick up Eric and George, on Tuesday.*

Right now, she had to pick up the girls from school, so she thought that she would leave a little early and swing by Sam's office, to see if David would be available to take George's truck and go to Anchorage with her and the girls. As she pulled up in front of Sam's office, a light skiff of snow started to fall. She parked and ran inside, asking Sam's secretary, "Is Sam in? If so, could I speak with him for a minute?"

"Sure, Mrs. Adams, I'll buzz him. Have a seat."

In no longer than it took to buzz Sam, he appeared at the waiting room door. "Laura, come on in," he invited her. "What's up? Is anything wrong?"

"Oh no, Sam, I just got a call from Eric. He and George will be in Anchorage on Tuesday around noon. He's been released from the hospital in Seattle. Do you think it would be possible for David to drive George's truck up to Anchorage with me to pick them up?"

"No problem. In fact, I'll drive you and the girls up, in my truck. It's in much better shape than yours, and will be more comfortable for Eric. You are going to take the girls with you, aren't you?"

"Of course, I wouldn't be able to hold them back when they hear their dad and George are coming home. Oh, that would be great, if you and David could drive. I just hated to ask you, because you've been so good to us. Are you sure it will be all right for you to take off work?"

"Sure, it'll be all right. You'll probably be nervous, as it is, and you shouldn't have to do the driving. Looks like it's starting to snow, and I'd feel much better knowing you are with me, instead of going alone." Sam continued, "What time does their plane get into Anchorage? I'll see to it that George's truck, and mine, are all ready to go. Don't you worry! Let David and me take care of things!"

"Sam, you are such a great guy," she said, hugging him. "Now I have to get the girls from school. Why don't you and the boys come over for supper tonight and we can make more definite plans?"

"Great! The boys will enjoy a woman's cooking for a change. See you around seven p.m.?"

"Fine, we'll see you then."

Her next stop was the school to pick up the girls. She knew they would be ecstatic to hear of their father and George coming home. It had been a long six weeks, but they had managed to keep busy with school and planning the garden in May, and even the extracurricular activities at school. When Laura arrived at the school, she went in to explain to the principal that she would be taking the girls out of school on Tuesday, because their father would be coming home from Seattle. She gathered the girls and they headed for home. She wanted supper to be special; after all, Sam and the boys deserved a good home cooked meal, for a change. They could even gussie up the table a little bit with candles and the good china.

As they were driving towards the cabin she said to the girls, "I have two pieces of news to tell you. The first is something that you two have been waiting to hear for some time and I want you to contain your excitement. The roads are getting a little slippery and I need to keep my full attention on my driving. So I don't want you jumping around in the truck and yelling when you hear it."

"What? What is it Mom? We promise not to get wild in the truck." Mary coaxed, looking at Patty. "You won't jump around, will you Patty?"

"No, I promise to behave. Mom, tell us."

"I got a phone call this morning from your dad. He and George will be flying into Anchorage on Tuesday, so we must be sure to be there, to meet them!"

Both the girls let out exclamations of joy and hugged each other. Mary cried out, "All right, that's the best news yet! Can we go with you to pick them up?"

"Of course you can. I spoke with your principal before you got out of school today; Sam offered to drive us in his truck, so I asked him and the boys over for supper tonight, to plan the trip."

"Great, Mom, we haven't seen the boys for a while, and I like that idea," said Mary, "don't you, Patty?"

"I sure do. I really like being around David and Danny; they are so much fun. They can help us make welcome home signs for Daddy," Patty suggested.

"We'll have to figure out what special thing we're going to wear, so we can look good for Daddy," said Mary.

They soon arrived home and busied themselves with supper and getting ready for their visitors.

Around six, there was a knock at the door. "Well, look here boys," Sam said. "We're just in time to sit down to a beautiful meal with some very beautiful ladies." Sam looked at Laura and the girls dressed in their best clothes. "How did we ever get so lucky? We should've worn our best bib and tucker too."

"You all deserve to be treated in style," Laura said. "You're always *Johnny on the spot* when we need you. We can depend on you, for whatever needs to be done, without asking. This is the least we can do to show our gratitude. Besides, we had a lot of fun preparing the meal and getting dressed up. It's been a while since we have had such an occasion to do so."

David and Danny both chimed in, "We're happy to do it, Miss Laura. You're good to us too. It's only natural for us to be of help to you and the girls. You're all like family."

"We're so glad that you feel that way, aren't we girls?" said Laura, looking at Mary and Patty.

Mary quickly replied, "We sure are! David, we couldn't have gone a lot of places if you hadn't taken us. It was like having a big brother."

Sam quickly jumped into the conversation, "Let's eat before this lovely dinner gets cold."

They sat down, enjoyed the meal, and discussed the plans to travel to Anchorage on Tuesday. They set the time they would leave on Tuesday, and ended a very enjoyable evening, for everyone.

The next day, Laura decided to put all of Eric's bows and arrows, guns and snow gear out of sight. There was no sense in putting him into a depression as soon as he came home. He sounded so up and excited about what he had to tell her about the therapy and Dr. Walker. It was Saturday and the girls were home to help. They wrapped his hunting equipment in blankets and put it in the loft. Laura felt an overwhelming feeling of despair fall over her as she put Eric's things aside. She wondered if this was a sign of things to come. She could not shake the feeling that kept coming to her since he had gone to Seattle. She was hoping that the reunion at the airport would be a happy one and chase this foreboding away.

She freshened up the bedroom and the house. The girls put up their *welcome home* signs for their father. She hoped her feelings of despair would not affect the girls. They were so happy and looking forward to having their father home again. Tuesday would be here soon and then she would know, she could read Eric like a book. It was just the waiting that was getting to her.

Suddenly the phone rang and brought her back to reality. "Laura," Sam said, "would you and the girls like to go to church with the boys and me tomorrow? There are already signs of The *Spring Break-up,* and the side roads are not in good shape. We can come pick you and the girls up, and then we'll go out for lunch, and maybe to a movie. How does that sound?"

"Why, it sounds terrific, Sam. The girls would really like that. Sure, why not? It will help relieve a little of the anticipation we are all having about Eric coming home. The girls hardly know what to do with themselves, and neither do I."

"Good, we'll see you in the morning."

"Girls, guess what? Sam and the boys are coming to take us to church in the morning. Then we're going to go out for lunch, and then Sam said we would all go to a movie. How does that sound to you?" Laura asked them.

"Wow, Mom, this is really a great thing. Dad is coming home on Tuesday, and we get to eat out, and see a movie tomorrow." They were both talking at once. "Did you say yes?"

"Of course, sillies, I thought it would be good for us." She motioned toward the bathroom. "Let's wash and fix our hair and get our clothes ready, so we'll look nice tomorrow. Let's even do our nails!"

"Yeah, Mom," said Patty; "I'd like to have my nails painted, too."

"I don't see why it would hurt, but only clear nail polish."

They had a fun afternoon, fixing each other's nails and hair and picking out the clothes they were going to wear.

"While we're at it, let's pick out what we are going to wear on Tuesday, too." Mary spoke up. "Dad will want us all to look beautiful, too."

The next morning, as promised, Sam and the boys picked them up for church. They attended the services and then went to the local restaurant. It was nice to go as a family-type-group. It had been a long time since Laura and the girls were treated to a meal in town. After lunch, Sam paid the check and announced, "Heads up now, crew, we are heading for the movie theater to see the afternoon show. I don't know what's on, but I'm sure we'll enjoy it. There'll be popcorn for everybody. David, you get the corn. Danny, you pick up the sodas—the girls can help you. Laura and I will get the tickets. If we can't find seats together, we'll meet in the lobby after the movie. Understood?"

The answer was a chorus from all. They enjoyed the movie, met afterwards and went back to Laura's and played games. It was a wonderful afternoon and evening.

When Sam and the boys were ready to leave, Sam asked Laura, "Are you nervous about Tuesday? It's been a while since you've seen Eric. I'm sure that you have a lot to ask him about everything the doctors have told him about future plans. It'll be all right, so don't you worry. Just be yourself, I'm sure he'll be glad to see you and the girls. Let things come as they may. Let him set the pace. You'll be fine. I'll be there with you and Eric, should you need anything. Get some rest now. We'll be here on Tuesday morning to get an early start. See you then." Sam then put his arm around her shoulder and hugged her. "Be strong," He kissed her on the cheek, and left.

Chapter 25

Monday was a busy day for Eric and George; Eric was getting nervous waiting for Dr. Walker to speak to him. When he finally arrived, he told Eric that he had made arrangements for him to receive a check for a complete Ham radio outfit, and that he could order it whenever he felt he was ready to set it up for use. He also told him that he would receive a check to apply toward a vehicle conversion for his particular handicap, which would be available whenever he was ready to obtain and use a vehicle. He then told Eric that if he wanted to take some home study courses, he should write to the hospital and the arrangements would be made. After he finished, Dr. Walker took Eric by the hand. "You have been one fantastic patient. I don't know what drives you but it's working. You seem to know where your life is destined to go now and I have no doubt that you will achieve your goal. It's been my privilege to know you, Eric. May God bless you."

"Thank you for all you have done for me, Dr. Walker. It's much appreciated. We never know what life has in store for us, but it was my wife, Laura, who told me I could not give up. I guess I took her words to heart and finally put my energies where they belong."

"You married a smart woman! Don't let her down."

"I'll try not to hurt her, but sometimes we should not question what comes. Thanks again! You were sent to help me in my decision." He watched as Dr. Walker said good-bye to George and walked out the door.

"Okay Alan, let's get this show on the road," Eric was reaching for Alan's hand. "You, my man, have been help beyond belief, and I won't forget you, so take care. Now let's go check out of this place."

Alan was standing with moist eyes. "You don't have to, that's all been done. George and I went through all the paper work for you. All you have to do is to roll out of here and be on your way. But before you go, I want you to know what an inspiration you have been to me. I saw your determination to better yourself, so I've signed up to go to night school. They have given me an apprenticeship program here at the hospital to get my medical degree. So, good luck, in whatever you do."

"Here, George," he rolled Eric over to George, "I've got a new patient to show the ropes. Eric is all yours now." He shook both their hands and was off down the hall.

George pointed Eric's wheelchair toward the door. "Well, buddy, let's head for the airport. We'll have to hustle to catch our flight."

Eric took a deep breath. "Let's go!" They sat in silence all the way to the airport.

Sam had arrived early to pick up Laura and the girls. The girls had some little gifts for their dad and were beside themselves with anxiety. Being ten and twelve, they were worried if their hair and clothes looked all right. Laura hurried them and they soon were in the truck ready to head toward Anchorage. David was driving behind Sam and would follow all the way. This way the girls could look back, wave at him, and help by making sure he was back there. It would keep them busy and occupied.

Sam started out of the driveway, looked at Laura, and asked, "Can you handle this?"

"Of course, let's go!" she said, and then remained silent most of the way to the airport.

Many thoughts raced through her head as they drove along the highway. *Will Eric act the same toward me? Will he hug and kiss me? I know he will hug the girls. Did he file the dissolution of our marriage? No one knew of it but Sue, not even Sam. I wonder if George knows? I'm not even sure Eric filed it; no letter of verification has come. I'll just do as I normally do, be myself.*

She was hurt by it, but her love for Eric had not changed. She still loved him. She looked over at Sam and wondered about the feelings she had about him. She had depended on him for so much, and he was always there to help her and the girls. He had always done that, even when he and Connie were still married. He was more like a brother than anything else. She guessed there were different levels of love.

This long absence from Eric has opened my eyes. There was love for your parents, children, husband and wife, friends, things, and on and on. It almost was to the point not think about anything.

"Hey! Where are you?" Sam's voice brought her back to reality. "At first, I thought you must have been sleeping with your eyes open." He laughed. "When we get there, it will be pretty close to lunchtime so I thought maybe after the girls said their hellos to their dad, we could all go to the restaurant and have some lunch. If you would like, I could keep the girls. That way, you and Eric could have some time alone to talk."

Laura answered quickly. "Oh that would be good, but let's wait and see how Eric feels about it. Maybe he would rather wait until we get home. Maybe it would be best to just let the girls enjoy his company again, with all of us. But I thank you for being so thoughtful. You are a dear!"

"I know it!" said Sam. "I just can't help it when it comes to pretty and nice women, like you. We'll soon be there. Are you nervous?"

"Yeah, butterflies are winging their way around my insides, but I'll be fine. I'll handle it. I'm not only pretty and nice, I'm tough too." They both laughed and Laura felt better.

It wasn't long before they pulled into the parking lot at the airport. The girls were fidgety in the back seat, excited to see their dad after his long absence. "We have some time before Eric's plane comes in. How about David and Danny taking the girls up to the observation deck to watch the planes?" suggested Sam. "You and I can go check if the plane is on time. Then we can join them."

"Mom, can we?" pleaded Mary.

"Please, Mom!" begged Patty.

"Oh, all right, but you listen to David, you hear?"

Sam and Laura went to the ticket counter to see about the deplaning. The lady at the ticket counter told them the plane would be on time, and because of Eric's need for a wheelchair, he would be taken off last. Then she told them the gate number where the flight would arrive. They went up to the observation deck. Sam told the girls to watch Gate # 6, because that was where Eric and George's plane would come in. "We will watch the plane connect to the gangway, and then we'll go down to the gate. Your dad will be taken off last because he needs to have his wheelchair brought aboard to help him off. This will give us time to get where you can see him when he comes off the plane."

"Oh boy, we can hardly wait," the girls chimed in together.

"Don't forget your mom will want to greet him too! So don't be too long in saying your hellos."

"Oh, David, they'll have their mush and gush time when we get home," answered Patty.

"Hush, you two, and watch the planes!" Laura said, trying to change the subject. She looked at Sam. "They are full of hot air. They don't know what they are talking about."

Sam looked at her and chuckled, "I do believe you are blushing. Hey, girls, the first one to see the plane coming in gets extra ice cream at lunchtime."

The girls settled down and started watching the skies.

"Thank you, Sam." Laura whispered, relieved to change the subject.

The girls could hardly contain themselves as they walked up and down by the windows, searching the sky for a first glimpse of their daddy's plane on the horizon. Finally, Mary called out. "There it is! I see it! It's on the ground and it's headed for Gate #6."

An announcement caught their ears. "May I have your attention please? Flight #463 is now arriving from Seattle and will be unloading at Gate 6..."

"Mom!" Patty jumped around, and ran to Laura. "Did you hear that? Dad's plane is coming in."

"Yes, I heard," Laura tried to calm Patty. "I know you're anxious, but just be careful."

Slowly they made their way to the gate. Passengers were already beginning to make their hasty exits. Patty and Mary stepped in front of the people coming off the plane, anxiously peering around them, trying to catch a glimpse of their dad and George.

"Do you see them yet, Mary?" Patty was jumping up and down now, trying to see over everybody.

People were coming quicker now, bumping into the girls, as they pushed forward a little trying to see better. There was still no sign of their daddy. Soon there was a lull in the people. The girls stood in the center of the passage, looking intently. Finally, they saw George pushing their dad along the corridor. George caught sight of them first and speeded up his step. The girls rushed forward and got on each side of the wheelchair and put their arms around Eric. "Daddy, Daddy!" Eric encircled both the girls with his arms. Kisses and chatter were flowing like water. George steadied the wheelchair.

Laura walked over to Eric, knelt down by his side. "Hey, how about me?"

The girls ran over to George to hug him and Eric reached out for Laura. He took her face in his hands and kissed her. "Is it really you? I thought I was seeing things again. You look so good!" He kissed her again. "Let's get out of the passageway."

Laura rose, grabbed the wheelchair and started to push Eric toward the restaurant. "Eric, I know you have a lot to tell me, and I want to hear everything. I'm so happy to see you. It's been a long time to be apart. Let's all go into the restaurant where we can sit down and talk. I know we all want to say a lot of things before we head for home."

"Good idea!" George piped up. "I want to sit next to these two Aleuts." George picked up both the girls and continued, "My golly, they look to have grown a foot! Besides, I need to talk with David, Danny and Sam too, and find out about my place."

In the restaurant, Laura placed Eric at the table next to her. Sam, George, David, Danny and the girls filled in around the other end of the long table. The waitress immediately came over and the girls started, Mary first. "I'll have burger and fries and so will my sister, and we'll each have a chocolate milkshake."

George, Sam and the boys ordered the same, while Sam started filling George in on what was pertinent to his cabin. Mary and Patty were asking David and Danny about school and work and what they knew about Sterling Days this coming July. All this busy conversation gave Laura and Eric a chance to talk.

"Eric, tell me, how was the therapy? You're handling yourself a lot better than before you went. I'll just listen and you go ahead and fill me in." Laura took Eric's hand in hers.

"I really don't know where to begin. I guess when we arrived in Seattle is the best place to start, but that's going to take an awfully long time. For now, I will just say that I came to a lot of decisions while I was there. I do know that I'll no longer be so dependent on you and the girls. I worked very, very hard. Dr. Walker is an excellent doctor. He showed me an easier way to do things and to be more independent doing them. He put me through the training on how to drive a specially equipped car. Not that we can afford one, but at least I know what to do. He also told me the VA would help me get a Ham radio, a big help to me. He set it up for me to have a voucher to purchase one when I get ready for it. In that way, they can ship it direct, and George and I didn't have to mess with transporting it. You'd like Dr. Walker very much!" He paused and squeezed her hand.

"I'm really hungry," he remarked as the waitress served their food. "We hurried around this morning and I couldn't eat my breakfast, I was too excited about coming home."

"I bet you're tired too," Laura said. "Sam brought his new truck, instead of our old one, and the seats recline, so maybe you can get a little nap on the way home. The girls and I will sit in the back seat. They will probably sleep too; they were so excited they hardly slept at all last night. They have really missed you; so have I."

"Did Sam keep a good eye on you and the girls while I was gone?" he asked, knowing what the answer would be.

"Oh yes. He and the boys took real good care of us. I almost felt guilty. The girls and I had them over for supper to help pay back a little bit for what they did for us. They took us to church, out to eat and to the movies on Sunday. They are such a good family." Laura just beamed when she talked of them.

"I knew he wouldn't let me down. He's like a brother to me." Eric paused.

"Love, we can't go on the way we were before I went to Seattle."

Laura sat up in her chair and looked him in the eye. "What are you saying? We've been doing okay. Please Eric, what do you mean by saying something like that?"

Again the waitress interrupted, asking if they wanted dessert.

"We'll talk more about that when we get home," said Eric.

When everyone finished eating, they all went out to load up for the long trip home. It would be late when they got home, and Eric and the girls were soon out like a light. They had snuggled down in the truck and were fast asleep in no time at all. Sam was driving and Laura was in the back seat with the girls. "Are you okay to drive? You're not sleepy, are you, Sam?" she asked.

"I'm fine, but you can talk to me, to keep me awake, if you're not too tired. The girls are certainly excited about having their dad home."

"You've got that right, "said Laura. "It's good to see Eric with such a positive attitude. I haven't seen him this way for a very long time. He was that way when the accident first happened, but he seemed to lose it over time. I'm glad for the change back to positive. It will help a lot to have him want to be more independent."

"It sounds like this Dr. Walker was pretty tough on him from what George said. He said that the doctor was going to give Eric everything he could handle, because that's what Eric wanted. That sounds like the old Eric we knew, before the accident. Things should be a little different for you and the girls now." Sam's tone was soft.

"I think so too, Sam," replied Laura. "But I still want you and the boys to come over and spend time with us. I think it will be good for all of us. The girls have really enjoyed having the boys around to do things with them. And I've enjoyed the time we spent together as well."

"Yep, it was good. Now you know you only have to ask if you need anything or any help with Eric."

"I know." Laura reached forward and placed her hand on Sam's shoulder and gave it a squeeze. "I know you will always be there for us."

The rest of the way home, they rode in silence. Laura kept thinking about Eric's last comment before they ate lunch. Somehow it would not leave her mind.

Chapter 26

The next morning when Laura awoke, she quickly glanced over to see if Eric was still sleeping. He was very tired from the plane trip, and the drive from Anchorage, so she didn't want to wake him. She slipped out of bed quietly and got the girls up and ready for school. The days were getting longer and the spring thaw was showing more on the roads. She wanted to take the girls to school and get back home again before Eric awoke.

The girls understood what Laura wanted to do so they dressed quickly and ate their breakfast quietly. They tiptoed out of the house and into the truck.

On the way home, Laura couldn't get her mind off the statement that Eric had made in the airport restaurant. She had that queasy feeling again that had haunted her the entire time Eric was in Seattle. She decided that maybe, while they were alone this morning, they could get to the bottom of what he meant. She thought, *I coaxed him into going to Seattle, to get the necessary therapy that couldn't be given in Sterling or Soldotna. Now here he is making statements that don't seem like he's really glad to be home with me. Then there's what Sue said before Eric left for Seattle.*

There were so many thoughts racing through her mind, she felt like crying. She and Eric must get back to what they had before the accident: absolute honesty. She had taken on several extra jobs while Eric was gone and the girls were in school, and had managed to save up quite a bit of money. Maybe they could do something special to celebrate Eric's homecoming. Now, all of that would depend on their conversation this morning. She saw their house up ahead and slowed down to make the turn safely. Butterflies began to circle around in her stomach in anticipation of the two of them being alone together.

When she opened the door and went into the bedroom, there was Eric sitting up in bed.

"How did you manage to do that?" she asked.

"It was a struggle! I was afraid I would fall a couple of times during the process, but I did it!"

"So I see. I'm proud of you! Is this something you learned in Seattle?"

"Not really, I just thought I might try it on my own." Eric beamed. "But I didn't venture to get into the bathroom and start to clean myself up, because it really tired me to do what I did!"

Laura gave him a hug. "Do you want me to take you in there now? Or do you want to have some breakfast first?"

"If you don't mind, I'd like a cup of coffee first. I think I need to have a little 'go' power," he said, giving her hug back, as she lifted him into the wheelchair and pushed him into the kitchen. "I'm glad to be home. I missed you and the girls more than you will ever know. But, I'm glad that I finally relented to your wishes to go to Seattle. I've done a lot of thinking and soul searching. I learned a lot from Dr. Walker. I need to tell you all about it. We have some serious things to discuss."

The butterflies took a wide circle and dipped in Laura's stomach. *Here it comes,* she thought, and quickly said, "Let me get you a bite to eat and some coffee first. Then we can talk. You just sit there and relax; it'll be ready in a minute."

If the truth were known, she needed the coffee too, for what she felt was coming. She proceeded to get breakfast ready, thankful for the time to compose herself. "While I'm getting breakfast, tell me about Dr. Walker. What kind of person is he? What's his personality like? Did you like him? Listen to me rattling on. I'll be quiet, you talk."

In a way, Eric was relieved to just describe Dr. Walker and his procedures. It was a good segue into the more serious part of what he wanted to discuss this morning. He began to talk, "You would just love Dr. Walker. He's an excellent doctor and really knows his stuff. But he doesn't candy-coat things at all. I told him I wanted him to give me a rigorous therapy, and he did. He asked me many questions, some that I felt didn't even have anything to do with my injuries. But when all was said and done, I found out that they did have bearing on what he told me before coming home."

Eric continued after sipping the coffee Laura set in front of him. "He told me that I would never be able to move anything below mid-line on my chest, ever again. So he concentrated on therapy that would build up the strength in my arms and upper back. You will be surprised what I can do now, things I relied on you and the girls to do before I went to Seattle. He instructed his staff to teach me how to shave myself. I had to learn how to do it on my own, even if I never have to do it. I can feed myself now without making a mess, where I couldn't before. Just wait until you see how good I am. You only saw a small bit of my skill at the airport restaurant."

By this time, Laura had their breakfast prepared and set a plate in front of him. She sat, and they bowed their heads in thanks for his safe return and for the doctor who gave him such confidence. After their Amen,

Eric talked again about his therapy and treatment. He told her that Dr. Walker put him through a lot of paces and tests. "He wanted to know exactly what I could do and how much determination I had to learn to do more. He really tested my limits.

"By the way, Laura, this breakfast is wonderful. It sure is good to be eating home-cooked food again. That hospital food is all right, but nothing compares to home-cooking."

Laura beamed at him. "Why, of course, love; you married a gem, remember? My mom taught me all I know. I can do anything if I just put my mind to it."

"That you can, for sure, and you have proved that over the years. I've really put you to the test, haven't I? You've helped me do everything. Build this house; learn the ways of life, here in Alaska. You raised the girls, and have given me 24/7 care since the accident. But now I hope to change that last part. I had some good training in Seattle and I intend to use it. I don't want you and the girls to do what you have in the past. Dr. Walker has shown me that I can be a little more independent, more like the old me. You just wait and see; things are going to be different around here." Eric looked into his coffee cup. "Now how about some more coffee?"

"Sure, I do love you so, Eric Adams. You can have anything your heart desires. It's just so good to have you home again!" She poured him another cup of coffee; then she set the pot down, came over and gave him a big hug and a kiss. She lingered there with her arms around him, kissing his neck and ears, caressing his upper chest with her hands, hoping he would return the action, since they were alone.

Eric didn't react but went right on talking. "It's good to be home again, but you know, I've been thinking a lot about getting the garden in; you know it's almost May. It's just around the corner. Are you going to put in your potatoes this year?" He chuckled.

"You never will forget that, will you?" she replied, pinching him on the cheek and returning to her chair, "As a matter of fact, neither will I!" and they both laughed.

"Now tell me what's been happening here while George and I were gone. How is Sue? I don't think that I'll have to see her as often as I did before I went to Seattle. Dr. Walker seemed to think that once every two weeks would do it. He said to try it like that and if I needed more, to increase the amount of time as necessary. But I think I can do the exercises he showed me here at home. I may need your help on one or two, but it'll sure save you driving into Soldotna so much."

"I'm sure Sue would love to see you. Why don't we work on our garden plans, and just before it's time to get the girls, we can leave early and stop to see Sue first."

"Sounds like a good idea to me. I'd really like to thank her again, for all she did for me; it made my work in Seattle a little easier to do. She gave me a lot of pointers that really helped."

"Good, then, that's what we'll do."

They finished breakfast and Laura helped him with his morning routines. Then they settled down to plan the garden. Laura took stock of all the supplies they had left over in the pantry from the previous year and checked the amount of meat they had in the freezer. They decided what they would need to plant to get them through the next winter. It was good having Eric there to help her with the planning. But he seemed to be saying to her that she might not need as much as they did the year before, and this put that strange feeling whirling around in her mind again. *Why would he say that? He told me he would see Jim and George again about getting us a moose, and he knew that Sam's boys would be bringing salmon to be canned and frozen. He also said he could take care of getting someone in to prepare the garden spot for us, to plant for the coming season.* It was business as usual, and it made her feel a little better, except for that one statement.

Soon it was time to leave for Soldotna. Laura fixed Eric and herself a sandwich, telling Eric that they should eat something now, because as soon as the girls get home, they usually do their homework before supper, so sometimes supper is a little late.

"I don't want to interrupt the routine you and the girls have established while I was in Seattle," he answered her. "I want you to let me know if you do things differently, as well, because it's important to me that you don't build your lives around me, again. After all, that was one of the primary reasons I went to Seattle, to become more dependent on myself and less on all of you."

"Yes, I know," Laura answered with softness in her voice, "but we want you to be comfortable, and we know it's hard enough for you to sit in that chair and see others doing everyday activities. But then again, maybe you would be able to help me with some of the chores."

"That's the idea, Laura. It's very important to all of us to have me do as much as I can for myself. I know that I have to have care 24/7, but that doesn't mean you and the girls have to adjust your lives to mine. You must go on with your lives as if I had never had the accident. Well, to a certain extent anyway." He banged one fist into the other palm. "Do you understand?"

"Yes, I guess I do. Sue told me before you went to Seattle that I must let you do for yourself more than I do, that I was enabling you to become an invalid." Laura hugged him and continued, "But I just love you so much, and want to make life as normal for you as I can."

"But you aren't when you do everything for me. I have to do some of those things myself. Before the accident, I never would've let you do anything for me. I was a free spirit, doing pretty much what I wanted to do. I don't need you and the girls to deprive yourselves of a normal life to try to make mine more normal. I'll never have a normal life again, at least not like it was before the accident." He paused for a bit. "I know that now, since I've been to Seattle. I had a lot of time to think there, and I made the decision that my life had to change. I don't want people to treat me like an invalid. I'm still Eric! Do you understand? I need you and the girls to help me get back to the old Eric. The one who was not afraid to undertake anything, but to grab life with gusto! I can't sit here and 'vegetate,' as you told me once before. I have to meet the usual challenges of life!"

"Oh, Eric, I do understand. I know you better than anyone. I know how you always looked at life, and I never said anything about it, because that is what made me love you. There is no one else like you. When you make your mind up to do something, you get it done. It may take awhile, but you do get it done in the long run." She hugged him once more and wiped a tear from her eye. "And I promise that the girls and I will not smother you like nurses in training, but for now, we best get on the road if we want to see Sue. You know, she basically told me the same thing before you went to Seattle. She said I needed to treat you like one of my patients, instead of my husband; that I should be strict with you and make you do more for yourself. Guess she was right! Are you ready? Let's go!"

"Ready! And thanks for being you. You are my best friend as well as the love of my life. Hey, look at that beautiful sight," he said as she pushed him out on the deck to take him to the pickup. "Aren't the mountains gorgeous? I can feel the air getting warmer all the time. Summer will soon be here. We best get cracking on that garden come May."

The ride into Soldotna was filled with casual conversation. There was still a bit of a chill in the air, but you could tell that the *Spring Breakup* was beginning. As in years past, the road felt like Jell-O in places. Laura handled the truck like an old pro. They soon pulled up in front of the clinic.

Laura said, "Let me go in first to see if Sue is free. I bet she'll be surprised to see you!" Stepping into the building, Laura inquired at the appointment desk. "Is Sue with a patient? I have an old patient of hers with me, and I'm sure she'd like to speak to him."

The receptionist told her to wait one minute. She soon returned with Sue, grinning from ear to ear, "Where's that guy? I sure do want to see him. As luck would have it, I was just doing paper work, but that can wait. Let's all go and have coffee. It's my turn to buy this time!" Sue went to get her coat. Laura got Eric out of the truck, and they went down the street, into the restaurant.

"It's so good to see you, Eric. How was Seattle? What kind of therapy did they give you? You look great!" The words just poured out of Sue.

They took a table in the back, and before they ordered coffee, Laura said, "You know, I have a few errands to run before I pick up the girls. I'll do them, get the girls and come back. It will give you and Eric a chance to talk therapy. I'll be back soon. If you're not here, I'll come down to the office, just in case you have to return before I get back."

"Okay," said Sue, "but more than likely we'll still be here. I can be off the rest of the afternoon. I don't have any appointments, just that miserable paper work. We'll see you in a bit."

Laura was a little relieved to get away. She knew Sue would ask Eric some pertinent questions about his future plans. She also knew Sue would tell her everything that was said while she was gone. At the school she sat and waited for the girls to come out.

Back at the restaurant, Eric was filling Sue in on some of the therapy he had while in Seattle. "I think the one that helped me the most was when they taught me to eat without being so messy. Do you know what they did? They put my right arm in a sling—like a binder—and then had me swing my arm back and forth in front of me until I learned to control the area of the swing. In that way, I could use my fork or spoon and put it to my plate and use the sweeping motion to get my food on it. It took a lot of work, but I did master it to a point that I am not embarrassing myself or my dinner companions with my sloppiness."

Sue put her hand on his. "I knew you could do anything you made your mind up to do, at least within the realms of actual medical possibility. I'm proud to see you are so set on being more independent. This will be a big boost to Laura and the girls, I'm sure."

"I definitely have plans that will free them up to do what's important to them, and that is to live a normal life, and not wait on me 24/7." Eric was very emphatic when he said this. "There are times in our life when we have to be realistic, no matter what the outcome may be. Sometimes people can't see the forest for the trees. I believe that I have finally done that, and now I know what I have to do with my life. It is most important for Laura and the girls that I follow through with this. I needed that time in Seattle with Dr. Walker to show me what I can do, and can't do, to make my decision. It will be good for everyone. I'm sure of it."

Sue looked at him for a minute or two and thought, *what is this man saying?* "Eric, you really have been doing some serious thinking while you were in Seattle. I only hope you haven't bitten off more than you can chew. You aren't thinking of doing something foolish, are you?"

"Oh, no, Sue! What I have planned to do with my life, and how it affects the girls and Laura, is not anything foolish. It is a very definite move, and with God's and my friends' help, I can do it. Just you wait and see!" He patted her hand. "So don't you worry; I have things under control. You would like Dr. Walker. He's one fine man. He doesn't pussy foot with you, but tells it like it is. He's one direct-talking, tough doctor. He doesn't want to give anyone false hope. I found that out."

"Okay, Eric. I just don't want you to do anything that will hurt your family or yourself. I think too much of all of you to see that happen. Matter of fact, when I heard the news that you were coming home and had improved so much, I spoke with Agnes and we cooked up a surprise for you and Laura." Sue grinned, brightened up. "When Laura gets back with the girls, I want you and her to follow me out to Agnes' place. We have something we want you to see. Okay?"

"Fine with me, oh, here comes Laura now," he said, as Laura walked through the door. "Laura, Sue wants to know if we can follow her out to Agnes' place. They have something they want to show all of us. Can we do that?"

"Sure, let's go; the girls are waiting in the truck. They can ride with Sue. It will give you more room, Eric."

"Pull around in back of my office, Laura," Sue instructed. "I'll get the girls in my vehicle and we'll be off to Agnes', after I run in and call her to let her know we're coming."

It was only a few miles to Agnes' place, so it wasn't going to be out of the way for them. Sue pulled out first and led the way. They soon arrived, and Agnes, hearing the vehicles coming, came outside to meet them.

"Oh my goodness, I heard you were back. I'm so glad to see you are doing so well!" She opened the truck door to give Eric a hug. "You know, since my Hank died, you are the favorite man in my life!" She laughed. "Laura, before you get out of the truck pull it up to the barn by that big door there. I want Eric to see something in the barn."

As Laura pulled the truck up to the barn, everyone else ran out to open the big door. There, sitting in the barn, was a van, not new, but newer than the old truck that Eric and Laura had. Sue went over and started it up, then opened the side door and pulled a lever to reveal a ramp that came out and lowered itself to the ground. Agnes could hardly contain herself. "Now Eric, let's get you out of that truck and see how this thing works for you. It should be a lot easier than trying to lift you in and out of that old truck every time you want to go somewhere."

Laura and Eric were stunned. Finally Eric said, "I can't believe it! Where did you get this? How much will this van cost us? It certainly will be easier than the old truck. We were going to have to buy a different one soon anyway!"

Agnes said, "This is yours! You can keep the old truck to haul stuff in if you need to, but this is for you and Laura and the girls. You will all fit in it comfortably. Sue and I got together and decided you should have this."

Sue interrupted. "I was messing around on my computer one day, and an ad for this popped up, from an old bus company. They had used it to transport people from the hospital to their homes and nursing homes. It was reasonable, so Agnes and I and a few anonymous donors chipped in together and got it for you. I called Sam and he went to look it over to see if it was mechanically sound. It passed the physical, so here it is."

"We figured that you needed some sort of reward for working so hard in Seattle and not giving up on yourself, like a lot of people would," Agnes said as she wiped the tears from her eyes. "You've done so much for the people in this community; we just wanted to give something back."

Laura choked back tears. "How will we ever repay you for all your kindness? God bless you all. We have such good friends."

Mary popped up and said, "I know, let's name it 'Aggie Sue.' After all, we have always named our trucks!"

"By golly, we have," said Eric, "and we couldn't have come up with a better name than that. Thank you both. We can never repay you for this." He wiped the tears from his eyes.

"Hey, I've got a lot of bear stew in the refrigerator. Why don't you both come home with us for dinner? We'll call Sam and the boys to come too. Eric and I can drive the truck home. Sue, Agnes and the girls can come in the van, and then Sam can bring Sue and Agnes back home after dinner."

"Good idea, "said Agnes. "I've got fresh baked pies and homemade bread cooling in the kitchen. Let's do it!" Laura called Sam from Agnes' and he accepted the invitation. It was wonderful for everyone to be together once again.

Chapter 27

The rest of April seemed to slip by without incident. Eric, with Laura's help, did his therapy exercises at home except for every two weeks, when she took him into Soldotna. In this way, Sue could put him through his paces and keep a check on his progress. Dr. Walker called Sue and talked to her at length about Eric's therapy and his present condition. The first time Eric came in to see her, she told him that Dr. Walker had called.

"And what did the old drill sergeant have to say?" Eric asked.

"Only that you were, without a doubt, the best, and most dedicated, and unwavering patient he has ever treated, as far as meeting the goals that were set for you. He likes you a lot, and has only admiration for you, and hope for your future."

Eric was also wondering if Dr. Walker had said anything to her about his plans to serve God and leave Laura and the girls behind in Alaska. "And that's all he had to say? He didn't tell you how handsome and statuesque I am?" He chuckled.

"No, silly, all of us here in Soldotna already know that!" she joked back. "Are you and Laura having a planting party this year to get the garden in?"

"No not this year. George, Sam and all the kids are going to help Laura with it. I don't think we'll be putting out as much as we have in years past. The greenhouse has deteriorated so much that we are just going to take it down. Therefore, we won't have all the plant starts. Besides, Laura and I took stock on what was left from last year, and there's still quite a bit of food left."

"Yes, but you must remember that you were gone for a while during that time, and there was just Laura and the girls. They didn't use as much as if you were home, too. You often have company, who Laura insists on feeding. Did you consider that in your decision?"

Eric took her by the hand, looked her straight in the eye. "I have thought this through a lot, and Laura works too hard. Things are going to change around the house. She will not be doing all that extra work because of me. That's why I agreed to go to Seattle, to learn to become more independent of her and the girls. They have to have a life of their own. Do you understand, Sue? If you do, I want you to keep this conversation under your hat. I'm not ready to tell everybody of the changes I'm going to make, just yet. Can you do that?"

She looked at him with question in her face. "Why yes, if that is what you want, but I don't quite understand what you're saying."

"You will, when I am ready to explain my plans. Just continue to be the good friend that you are, and keep this to yourself. Especially don't say anything to Laura; you know how she is, whatever I have planned, she'll jump right into it and tell me that things are fine the way they are now. It's time I started to make more of the decisions in our household again. After all, I may be paralyzed, but my brain still works."

By this time, Laura had the girls and was back to pick up Eric.

"Remember what we just talked about." Eric said to Sue.

"You've got it!" Sue promised.

As they were getting into the van, Laura asked Eric, "What was that all about? What kind of an arrangement is up between you and Sue?"

Rolling himself into the van, Eric said, "Oh nothing. We had talked about Dr. Walker calling and telling her of my progress, and I told her that she hadn't seen anything yet! I was going to do a lot more! So we made a pact, to see that I do. After all, I want to take the responsibility off you and the girls. It's time these Aleuts had time for themselves, right, girls?" He looked at his daughters and winked; they were grinning from ear to ear. "How was school, girls? It won't be long before you will be out for the summer. Shall we celebrate tonight, and take in a movie? How about it, Mom? Since we have this nice van, we can go and celebrate the van, the girls getting out of school, and me being home and turning over a new leaf. Sound like a good idea?"

Mary and Patty thought it was a wonderful idea. "Please, Mom, let's do it," pleaded Mary. "We haven't seen a movie for awhile."

Laura answered as only a mother would. "But you two have school tomorrow. You need to get your rest."

Patty spoke up. "Mom, we promise to go right to bed when we get home, and not drag around in the morning, when it's time to go to school. Please!"

"Oh, all right, I give in. Let's go home, eat, clean up and then go to the movie."

Eric was glad. This would keep Laura from firing questions at him about his visit with Sue that afternoon. He didn't want to say any more about it… at least not yet.

They all enjoyed the movie, and were home in plenty of time for the girls to get to bed, to be rested for school the next day. Even Eric and Laura were relaxed enough that they too, went to bed and dropped off to sleep right away.

The next morning, Laura took the girls to school, without any dragging of their feet or indecisions about what they were going to wear, and she returned home promptly, wanting to talk to Eric about the planting of the garden. When she arrived at home, George was there, along with Jim. She went into the house, greeting them both.

"Hey guys, how about some breakfast and coffee? Eric hasn't had his yet. It will be no trouble to fix more," she said, as she put on a fresh pot of coffee.

"Thanks anyway, Laura, but we've both eaten already. We thought we'd come over and start turning the ground for the garden," George said. "I have the day off, ran into Jim and told him what I was going to do, so he said he'd help too. Coffee does sound good though."

"Well, at least you can have some blueberry muffins with your coffee. It'll be ready in a jiffy," she said as she put cups and a small plate of muffins on the table. "Do you think the ground is soft enough to dig for planting? I guess it should be. It's almost the end of May. The time has flown since Eric came home. It sure is good to have him here."

"That it is," said Jim. "I, for one, am so thankful that he is doing so well. Eric was saying how well the van is working out for all of you. I'm so glad that we could all help with that; it must make it a lot easier on you, I'm sure."

"It sure does," Laura said as she poured the coffee. "You will have some blueberry muffins, won't you?"

"You bet!" said George, "and then we must get busy on that garden. You can finish feeding Eric and get him ready to come out and boss us."

After some conversation, Jim and George went out to do the digging. Eric had his breakfast and Laura helped him out to where he could sit and call orders. As she situated him on the deck, she observed that the lupines were starting to bloom. They seemed to make a purple haze over the landscape, and soon there would be wild roses and then the fireweed. She told him to just sit there, enjoy the beauty, and supervise the planting of the garden. She needed to join in on the work. She grabbed a rake and started to smooth down the clods of dirt. It was hard work, but it needed to be done. She worked with the guys until it was time to pick up Mary and Patty from school. When she returned, she saw that David, Danny and Sam had joined them.

Laura instructed the girls, "Go change your clothes then grab a rake and pitch in to help break down the clods."

Laura got some fish out of the freezer and fixed fish and chips for everyone, as she knew they would all be hungry when they finished the job. She brewed more coffee and made some hot biscuits so they would all be tastefully rewarded.

Jim and George made it known they had to leave after supper; Jim's family was expecting him home, and George had other plans for the evening. Sam and the boys stayed for a while. The boys helped Laura and the girls clean up the supper dishes then played some games. Laura joined Sam and Eric, who were discussing the planting of the garden, and just how many potatoes they were going to limit Laura to planting. The potato planting was a tradition with Laura now.

"What's this you are talking about? Eric, did I hear you say that you were going to limit my potato planting this year? Well, maybe I should cut back a little on it; we have never run short on our potatoes." Then she giggled.

Sam asked Laura, as she pulled up a chair, "How do you like the van?"

"It's a lot easier than the truck to get Eric in and out of, and it's more comfortable for Eric, too… especially when the girls are with us."

"A lot of things are going to be easier around here," Eric added. "Sam, I especially want to thank you again for keeping such a watchful eye on Laura and the girls while I was in Seattle. It took a big load off my mind to know that you were here for them. You know that you and the boys are like family to us, don't you? I'm sure Laura feels the same way I do. The trip was good. I learned to have a different outlook on my life, and made some big decisions while I was there. Things will soon be a lot easier for Laura and the girls because of those decisions. I may be paralyzed, but my brain still works, and there is much that I can accomplish with my new attitude."

Laura, in her questioning way, looked at Eric. "We've been getting along just fine with things around here, so what are the big changes we're going to make?"

"I'm sure that Sam will agree with me on this," Eric jumped in to say. "One thing is that you will not have to work as hard as you have been. I want you to get back to a more normal routine, like we had when we were first married. Do you realize that come this August, you and I will have been married for nineteen years? And out of those nineteen, I have been incapacitated for eight years, come September?" He paused, took a deep breath and sat quiet, as if thinking. "All those years, I pretty much ran the show. I know that I was, and still am, a little strong willed and bull-headed at times, and we did pretty much everything my way. But that's going to change. I want you to take hold, and make some of the major decisions. I will be helping you in every way I can, so you'll do fine."

Laura started to protest and sputter when Sam spoke up. "Eric is right, Laura, and you're going to have to ease up a little on your workload. You'll soon be burned out, and then where will you be? I agree whole-heartedly with Eric. You deserve to take it easier. We can all help you do that. One way the boys and I can help is to thank you for the supper and conversation, and go home and get out of your hair, so you can relax and go to bed. Come on, boys; let's go home. See you folks soon."

After Sam and the boys left, Laura went over to hug Eric. "Well, love, since I am supposed to start making some of the major decisions, the girls are getting ready for bed, so why don't we do the same. I'm tired, and I'm sure you are too; it's been a long day. Getting the ground ready to plant is a big job, but it's done. All we have to do now is plant. Are you ready for bed?"

"Good decision, Mrs. Adams. See, I told you it wouldn't be hard to start making the decisions around here. I'm ready if you are, let's go. I'm going to say goodnight to the girls. I'll meet you in our bedroom," Eric said as he rolled his chair toward the bedrooms.

Laura tidied up the kitchen area and turned out the lights. She got Eric ready for bed, then got herself ready and crawled in next to him. He patted her and told her she did well today, working out there in the garden plot. All of a sudden she broke into laughter.

"What's so funny?" he asked.

Still laughing, Laura said, "Oh, Eric, working out there in the garden today, I was thinking how proud I've always been of our garden; it was always so beautiful, and had so much good food in it.

"Then I started to think about the very first garden we had, when we still lived in the basement. I remembered how one day when you and George were hunting up at Swanson River for our moose for the year. I looked out the window and saw a moose in our garden, eating the cabbage. Being from New York and living all my life on a dairy farm, when the cows got in our garden there, we would just go out and shoo them away. So I grabbed a dishtowel and ran out into the garden and flopped the towel around and yelled shoo to him. He reared up on his hind legs and was pawing the air with his front feet. The hair on the back of his neck stood up, and I thought, boy he's mad! I turned and ran back into the basement with the moose behind me. He chased me all the way to the house and stopped just at the porch. I could've been stomped to death. What did I know about moose? I know now, you don't shoo them off with a dishtowel. When I think of it now, it's funny!"

Laura sat up in bed. "The really funny part was, here you and George went all the way to Swanson River to get a moose, and I had one in the garden I was trying to scare away with a dishtowel. Are you sure you want me to start making major decisions around here?"

"Yes, I want you to; it'll be good for you. Now stop thinking about everything. Give me a kiss, and go to sleep." He chuckled too. "I'll always love you."

Laura kissed him, said the same, and turned out the light.

Chapter 28

The next morning, Eric awoke before Laura. He lay close to her, looking at her face, and thinking how she was so much a part of his life. But he knew that his decision to do the work of the Lord, and leave his family in order to do so, was the right thing to do. He had prayed about it so often. He knew she loved him, as much as he loved her, and it would be awfully hard for her to accept the news when he told her about his plans. He had to do it in the right way, and he was certain that God would help him through it. Somehow, she'd have to see where it would be right by the Lord. Eric too, had many moments of doubt, before he finally decided it was the right thing to do. It wasn't going to be an easy thing for him, either. He loved her and the girls more than anything. But he knew it was time for him to move toward his goals, and give them the opportunity to get back to reality. After all, the Lord would watch over them.

As he lay there looking at her, he thought of all the things he'd done since they'd been married nineteen years ago. How selfish he had been, thinking of only himself. He never once gave a thought as to how Laura might feel. When he told his mother and dad that he and Laura were moving to Alaska, his mom told him there's no way he could take Laura up there to live; she would never make it. She told him he'd have to live in New York or else go without Laura, which she knew he'd never do. He remembered how he just told her, *"Watch me!"* because he knew Laura would go anywhere with him. And she did, because of her infinite trust in him. That's why, he thought to himself, *she'll understand and accept my decision about leaving her and the girls.*

Laura started to stir, bringing him back to the present. She opened her eyes and seeing that Eric was awake asked, "What are you doing awake so early?"

"Oh, I was just lying here looking at you, and remembering the dumb things I put you through when we were first married." He reached for her hand. "Laura, I'm really sorry, I never thought about anybody but myself when we first got married. I didn't ask your ideas on whether you wanted to do the things I said we were going to do. I guess I was pretty bossy, although we did have fun; remember the hiking trip we took up into Canada? I never even thought to ask you if you had ever been camping before. You just went along with it."

"How can I forget it?" She rose up on one arm and leaned her cheek on her hand, looking at him. "You drove us up as far as we could go, and we caught a freight train, then we rode a flat car until the train came to a stop in the wilderness and you said, 'Come on, let's get off here.' We did and I had no idea where we were at all."

He jumped in. "Oh yeah, that was where the train stopped once a week for anyone who wanted to hitch a ride in or out. We were in the wilderness there. Then we back-packed in for a few miles and set up a camp. We had a small pup tent, just big enough for two, and two sleeping bags, along with our food supplies for a week. "

Laura hurried to finish the story. "You set up the tent, and we built a fire ring with rocks, zipped the sleeping bags together and put them inside the tent. Then we hiked around the area, just looking at our surroundings. It was beautiful! We were near a lake, and you said we should go skinny-dipping." Blushing, she giggled, and went on. "I'd never done such a thing in my life, and protested a little, but you said that we were out in the woods with no one around for miles, so I relented. We swam for awhile, and as we were getting out, an airplane flew low over the lake and dipped his wings at us."

Eric laughed. "You were so embarrassed, you immediately ducked back into the water, and I said 'Come on, he's gone now; he won't be back.' So you got out with me, and didn't he fly back over again? But that was the end of him. Then we dressed, ate supper and retired to the tent.

"We crawled into the sleeping bags and you told me to quit tickling you, and when I said I wasn't, it was then you screamed and jumped out of that bag like a jackrabbit. We looked into the bag and found that while we were eating, a chipmunk had crawled in the bag, looking for a snack bar you had put in there earlier. We got him out and settled down for the night, only to wake up to a rain in the morning, and it rained the whole week we were there."

"How well I remember," said Laura; "we even cut up the cardboard box we had the snack bars in and made a deck of cards to play with. We never left the tent, which wasn't all bad, until the day we broke camp, and hiked back to the place where we were to catch the train. I remember asking you if you were sure this was the right spot to catch it."

"Yes, 'it sure is,' was my answer," Eric laughed, "but you know I wasn't really sure. I was hoping it was, because we would have had to wait for another week, if we had missed the train. But soon we heard the whistle and when it stopped, we climbed aboard and headed for home. You were a good sport to go through all that!"

"Hey, it was fun. Besides, we were together, weren't we? I knew you would protect me." Laura kissed him on the cheek.

"I know, but don't you see what I mean? I was foolish to do that! What if something had happened to me? You were green as grass. It was a foolish thing to do, when you get right down to it. I put you in a possibly dangerous situation!" He kissed her back. "Let's get back to reality. I'm hungry and we really need to get onto planting that garden today. How about it, girl? Shall we get going?"

Laura threw back the covers and jumped out of bed. She helped Eric get up and get ready for the day. It was Saturday and the girls were still sleeping, so she took the time to get dressed herself. Then she went out to get breakfast, calling the girls to get up as she went to the kitchen.

After breakfast, they put on sweaters—there was still a spring chill in the air—and she and the girls went out to start the planting. Eric helped her to string the rows so they would be straight, and the girls planted and covered the seeds. Laura did the tomato plants and the potatoes as she always did. At noon, they took a break for peanut butter and jelly sandwiches. After lunch, David and Danny came to help, and it was back to work until they were all done with the planting. It didn't take as long to do this year, as they had a much smaller garden than in years past.

Once the garden was in, Laura kept busy with the daily routines of watering and weeding, and keeping the animals from eating the new sprouts coming up. School was out the first part of June, so the girls had the duty of keeping the plants watered. They did some weeding as well.

It was during this time that Eric asked George to come and take him over to his place so they could work on some repairs needed at George's cabin. That is what they told Laura, but really they were getting the last-minute plans laid out for their trip to Costa Rica. Eric told Laura that if he went to help George, it would give her some free time to do some things with the girls.

This seemed fine with all concerned until Eric said he was going to be over at George's all day. It was then Laura asked him, "Just what are you two doing over there that is taking you so long to finish? You could have planned a whole new cabin for him by now."

Eric passed her question off by telling her that it was just guy time together, so she could have free time, and not have to tend to him.

Eric felt it was time to tell Laura the truth. So he said to her, "Laura, when George comes to pick me up, would it be all right if instead, he took the girls out fishing with him today? I would rather stay here with you, without the girls around, because there is something we need to talk about, without interruption."

"Why yes, Eric, if it's that important; you know I trust George to take the girls anywhere. He's as responsible with them as you or I."

"Good, then that's what we'll do. I'll call George and tell him it's okay to take the girls for the day." He phoned while Laura told the girls they were going fishing with George. The girls hurried around to get ready, as they were excited to get away from the garden chores. It wasn't long before George came to pick them up and they ran out to meet him, said their good-byes, and were off. Laura took Eric back into the house and he asked her to sit down with him.

She was very puzzled by his actions. "What is it? What's all this mystery about, Eric? Has something happened I don't know about? Please tell me."

"Actually, I'm not sure where to start. I guess from the beginning. Just let me tell you what I have to say first and then we'll talk." He turned his wheelchair around so he was facing her and took her hands in his. He began to tell her. "You know, what we've both have been through since our marriage, nineteen years ago this coming August. How we struggled to fix up my grandma's house to live in, when we got married, in New York. And then, how I felt it was so all-important to keep my promise to

Carl that we moved here to Alaska. When we got here, the first years here were no picnic either. We struggled to get this home built and still have our family. Then on top of all that, I fell out of that tree almost eight years ago. It's been an uphill battle all the way. Oh sure, we had our good times too; I'm not saying that our marriage hasn't been a good thing. We have a love that doesn't come to just everyone. Ours is special. But I know my emotions have been on an up-and-down ride, and I'm sure yours have too. I put a lot on you and the girls, by you taking care of me around the clock, day in and day out. I know we made a promise to each other when we got married to be there for one another, in sickness and in health, and you have done that without a thought to yourself or the girls. And during that time, not even thinking of how it would make things harder on you, I thought of committing suicide. Had it not been for Jim coming by here one day and talking to me straight from the heart, I might have done just that."

He paused for a moment. "Would you mind getting me a drink of water and a handkerchief?"

Laura got up and got his drink, and the hankies. She grabbed one for herself too, wiping her eyes, and handed Eric the water and hankie.

Drinking some water, he wiped his eyes and went on. "All this time, during this whole period of nineteen years, I realized that it has all been about me. It was all about what I wanted, and you went along with it all. Had it not been for Jim saying the things he did, I'd still have the same mindset. But when we had that talk, I knew what I must do. I had to give back some of all the goodness that was given to me. I started thinking of what I should do with my life, not just to sit and let others do for me, but start doing for others. Ever since that day, I've been leaning toward what I must do with my life. We can't go on this way. You and the girls deserve better. So I've decided to give my life to God's work. There now, I've told you what's on my mind!"

"Oh Eric, that is a wonderful thing to do! How are you going to go about it?" Laura asked, wiping tears from her eyes again.

"Yes, it is a wonderful thing, but where I plan to do my work, I can't take you and the girls with me. That is why I wanted to get the dissolution when I did. I can't go on taking from you and the girls, and be able to give my life to save souls somewhere else. Can you understand that? I've thought and prayed about this for a very long time. I've heard the word of God."

Laura shrieked. "How can you plan to do good on the one hand and on the other, hurt your family so cruelly? I thought you loved me deeply. What about our promises to each other, to always love one another? Doesn't that mean anything to you at all?"

"Laura, wait a minute! You and I know that our intimate life changed drastically after the accident. You and I both enjoyed that intimacy, but now, there are needs that you have that I can't fulfill. You're a beautiful, vibrant woman, and should have a man who could take care of all of your needs, not just daily life, but intimate times too." Eric reached for her hand again. "I will always love you and the girls. Nothing will ever take the place of that love. I'll always be the girl's daddy and I'm glad we had them when we did. They're two of the best things that have come out of our marriage. This'll not change my feelings for any of you. But I must make this sacrifice; just as the Lord gave his only begotten son, that whosoever believeth in him, shall not perish, but have ever-lasting life! I must make this sacrifice so that I can do the Lord's work. In time, you and the girls will be fine. You will not perish, but you can and will make an ever-lasting life. You are young enough to do so, and you will be happy with your new life. Even though we will be going our separate ways, there will always be a bond between us. That feeling will never die. I will see the girls once a year and keep in touch with them forever. You and I will always be friends. It *will* all be fine."

Laura was sobbing by now. "But how can you just go away? Where are you going? How will you get along, alone? How will we manage alone, here in Alaska? You are our only family here! How could you do this to us?"

"In answer to your questions," he told her, "it's the hardest thing I'll ever do, but I know in my heart of hearts, that it must be done. It depresses me a lot, but I know that once I start spreading God's word, my heart will be filled with a sense of accomplishment in helping many people to understand God's word, and what lies ahead for them in their lives. As to where I'm going… George is going with me and we are going to Costa Rica, either at the end of August or the first part of September. How can I do this to you? It will probably be the best thing I have ever done for you and the girls. You will have a normal life again! You'll have money for the girls' education, not always for my health care. You'll see. You have many friends here. They'll be here for you. Things may be a little difficult at first; it will be for both of us. We don't have any assets to split up. We should just keep the house for the girls. I would like for you and me to have a stipulation that either of us could use it, until we die, if necessary. Believe me, Laura, I have prayed about this, and thought about whether or not this is the right thing to do, for a long, long, time. I mentioned it to George when we were in Seattle, and he's tried to get me to reconsider, but I just can't. I must do this! He asked me how we'd both live without each other. I told him I'd have my disability money to live on, and you can work at the hospital or the clinic and you'll be fine. You'll make a good income there, enough for you and the girls to live comfortably without all of my expenses. George is such a good friend he didn't want me to hurt you, but told me he could never do what I'm doing now. But by the same token, he said he could not let me go out on my own, that he would go with me. He has been with us both for a long time. He came here to Alaska with us; he and I were childhood friends. He's part of the family."

He stopped talking, looked her straight in the eyes. "Yes, I have thought this through, thoroughly."

Laura blew her nose and straightened up in her chair. "What are you going to say to the girls? You have to tell them of your plans. I want you to have to answer whatever questions they may have."

"I will do that, but not tonight. If it's all the same to you, I would like to go home with George. No sense prolonging the agony of leaving. I'd like to come back here tomorrow and tell the girls and pick up my things. Would that be all right with you?" he asked. "They should be back early this afternoon. That'll give me time to pack what I need. I'm not taking any of my hunting or fishing stuff; it can stay here. Maybe we could all eat supper together tonight, and I'll tell the girls that George needs me to help him with something, so I'll stay at his place tonight, and he'll bring me back tomorrow." Eric faltered a little, turned his head and looked out the window for a short time. "Maybe I'll tell the girls of my decision tomorrow and then tell them about Costa Rica, where we'll be going. I can tell them about the people who need my knowledge to help them in their lives. I think if they understand what I'm going to do, they'll be a little more forgiving of my leaving. I sure don't want to cause any more problems for you."

He rolled himself out onto the upper deck to sit and watch the mountains and the ever-changing sky.

Laura sat at the table, crying softly, still in shock. He was so matter of fact about it. She knew him well enough that nothing she would say to him would ever change his mind once he had it set. She had urged him to do something with his knowledge and abilities. But she had never imagined in her wildest dreams that this is what he would do. She could argue that she and the girls could go with him on his missions; after all, other families did that! But in her own practical mind, she couldn't think of uprooting the girls from the only home they had ever known.

Especially at the ages they were now. She had to pull herself together, and think about this some more, before she said anything more to Eric. She did not want the girls to see her in this condition. She wanted things to be normal when they came home. She wanted the news to come from their dad; this was his doing, and she felt he should be the one to tell them. She should be there too. It might make things easier for them to accept. She didn't know what to do and she needed time alone to think about it all. Maybe it was a good idea for Eric to go to George's tonight. Only time was going to tell. Right now, she must be strong and act as if nothing was wrong. She didn't want to upset the girls before Eric told them. She dried her eyes and started dinner. They'd be home soon.

Chapter 29

When Mary, Patty and George came home, the girls were excited to tell Laura and Eric about their day of fishing. They not only had wonderful fishing, but they had seen a beaver dam, and had to tell their parents about the beavers, and what they did.

"George also told us how the salmon make their run up the stream," said Patty excitedly.

"Yes, and he said there were different times for different kinds of salmon to be in season," reported Mary. "He said salmon season in general is from May through the end of August; for the King salmon it's May to end of July; Red salmon, third week in June to August tenth; and for the Silver salmon, mid July to the end of August. Then he told us how they make their run upstream to lay their eggs. It was so interesting to hear about it."

"Yeah," Patty added, "he also told us how the bears line the stream to eat those big fish too. Only I think it's so sad that after they make their runs upstream, and the moms lay their eggs, and the dads fertilize them, that they have to die."

Mary jumped in, "They are such pretty fish; it's awful that they have to die."

"But Mary," Patty said to her, "George said that is part of the cycle of life for them, and its nature's and God's way."

Eric saw a door of opportunity. "Yes, that's part of God's plan for life. Sometimes things happen that we have a hard time understanding, but there is a good reason for it. In this case, the parent fish must make a sacrifice of their lives so that their offspring may have a life of their own."

"What's offspring, Daddy?" asked Patty.

"Why, Patty," Eric said, "offspring would be their children, just like you and Mary are your Mom's and my offspring. We gave life to both of you. Only we didn't die after we did that, but sometimes we do have to make sacrifices to give you better lives."

Laura was worried that Eric was getting ready to tell the girls of his leaving now, but she wasn't ready to have him do it just yet, so she spoke up. "I'm sure you girls had a good time, but I think George deserves a reward. So, for him taking you fishing and giving you a guided tour as well, I have a super meal ready for us all."

George, sensing her discomfort, said, "So come on you Aleuts let's wash up for dinner. Your dad and I will clean the fish later!"

Over dinner, they laughed and talked about their day fishing, when George noticed Laura wasn't eating much, or being her usual self. Her happy smile wasn't evident at all. "Laura, you're so quiet. Is something wrong?"

"No, I don't think so; I just don't feel too well. Guess I must be extra tired from all the gardening and work I've been doing. Maybe I'm coming down with something."

Eric looked over at her. "Maybe the girls would clean up the table and dishes, and you could go to bed and rest. George can get me ready for bed."

George nodded. "Better than that, why don't I help the girls with the dishes? I'm sure they're tired out from the day, so they can go to bed early, too. And if Laura doesn't mind, Eric can come home with me. We'll clean the fish and fix my cabin door. There's something wrong with the hinges and I need help with it. I can bring him back in the morning."

Laura took advantage of the offer, as she needed to be alone to think. "Oh, would you do that for me, George? I'd really appreciate it. Besides, it will give you and Eric some *man time* together. I'm really tired, and the quiet time would be great." She motioned to the girls, "You two help George with dishes, then clean up and go to bed. Eric, I'll see you tomorrow." She kissed him goodnight, as well as the girls. "Thanks again, George. You're too kind."

George and the girls finished cleaning up, and then Eric instructed them to get ready for bed. When dressed in their pajamas, they came out and said their goodnights, along with kisses and hugs.

Mary hugged and kissed George. "Uncle George, thanks for the special day. See you tomorrow."

Patty followed with the same routine, adding, "Hope we can do it again soon; it was a lot of fun!" They disappeared into their bedroom, along with last-minute instructions from Eric to be quiet and not to disturb their mom.

There was no danger of that; she was already disturbed. As she got into bed, she knew that sleep was not to come. She had too many thoughts racing through her mind. By now, the initial shock had gone and the tears started to flow readily. She had barely been able to hold them back all through dinner. She knew if she had joined into the conversation, she would have broken down completely. She was glad George offered to take Eric home with him. She needed to have time alone to digest all Eric had said to her. She also wanted to figure out her reply. She had questions that needed to be addressed.

She also knew that she and Eric must both be calm, and be united in the decision to separate. They both needed to be willing to help Mary and Patty when they were told he was leaving. They were going to be confused, as they never saw any dissension or discord between her and Eric. They must plan how to tell them; the girls were the main concern now. They'd have to assure them of their love and answer any questions they might have. They mustn't feel they're responsible for Eric's decision to leave, and we're not divorcing them. We'll have to instill in them that we're still their mommy and daddy, and our family foundation will remain the same, even though Eric and I wouldn't be living together anymore.

It was at this point she had to break down and cry into her pillow. She didn't want the girls to hear her crying. As quickly as her tears started, she thought about what would happen to her and to Mary and Patty. It was here her mind went back to what Sue had told her at therapy. *Let Eric do his thing. He must be more independent. He has to feel like he is in control of himself. He doesn't want you and the girls to do for him. He wants you all to have your lives as they were before the accident. Treat him as you would one of your patients, not as your husband.*

Now here was Eric telling her he wanted to serve the Lord by spreading His word. *He had decided he could do that; with his background in church, and in communications, he could reach people in remote parts of the world through his radio. He was going to do what she had urged him to do: use his God-given talents. He was doing a positive thing, and to do all this he was willing to sacrifice being with his family, so that we could start to live anew too.* She couldn't think about it anymore. The answers were not to clear to her. She decided to take it to God and ask him to help her to understand.

After the girls had retired and things were put in order, George looked at Eric. "Okay pal, I guess it's guys' night out. I'll get the things you'll need for the night. I think Laura laid them out. I already have the fish on ice in the truck. Are you ready? Do you need anything else?"

"No, I think you have it all. I'm ready. We can lock up and head out. It's quiet now.

As soon as George started down the drive he asked Eric, "Did you tell Laura you were leaving them, this afternoon while I had the girls fishing?"

Eric cleared his throat and quietly answered. "Yes, I did. It was very hard to do, but I was very matter of fact and gave her all the reasons for my decision. I can no longer bear to have her and the girls going without things for themselves, to care for me. I told her I prayed about this for a long time, and she has wanted me to be constructive and use my knowledge and my ability to make things happen so I wouldn't just sit in this wheelchair the rest of my life."

"What did she say to that?"

"What could she say? She was quite shaken, and she loves me as much as I love her. I told her that would never change. We'd probably always love each other. There are many phases to that kind of love, and sometimes it is necessary to sacrifice it, for a higher cause. She said she understood that God moves in strange ways and that He has shown me new inroads for my life. Knowing how devout we all are in our faith, the three of us, it's natural to turn to it in this time of need. She just wanted to have some time alone, to talk it over with God. I'm sure she will come around to her senses. Right now, she is hurt deeply. Laura is an intelligent, sensible woman, and she will eventually sort it all out. She asked why she and the girls couldn't help me in my mission. I'm sure, given time, she'll see why that isn't possible. There would be no future for the girls. Their life, and all they've known of it, is here in Alaska. It'll be all right. It may seem harsh now, but this is the best way for everyone. There are many people who need to know more about the Lord, and I've decided to give my life to reaching them."

"And so, then what?" George questioned.

"I told her I would be the one to tell the girls, but we'll all be together when I do."

They were soon at George's cabin. "As strong as my faith is in the Lord, I never could have done it, Eric. You are truly going to do God's work! You're giving up a great thing to help spread His word. He has to have smiled on you, and helped with this decision. I have known you and Laura for a long time, and probably know the two of you, inside and out. For you to do this must give you unbearable pain in your heart. But still, you must know that it all is within the master plan of your lives. Your strength must be coming from above."

They both sat in silence for a long time. Then George opened his door. "Let's clean those fish and go inside."

Chapter 30

Somehow Laura managed to fall asleep and was able to get some rest, before Mary and Patty bounced out of bed the next morning. She slowly got herself up and dressed, after washing the previous night's tears from her face. Like a robot, she went into the kitchen, put on the coffee, and fixed hot cereal.

She told herself that she must keep her demeanor the same, as if Eric had not told her he was leaving them. It must be that way until they were all together and ready for the girls to be told. It needed to be done in the right way, so as not to scar them.

As the girls sat down to eat breakfast Mary asked, "Are you feeling better this morning, Momma?"

Laura managed a smile. "Why yes I am, and thank you for asking. I must have been overly tired, that's all. Did you girls sleep well? Patty, are you sure you're awake?" She hugged her as she walked by. "Finish up now and go make your beds. George will be bringing your father home soon. I'd like to go to town for a little bit, while George is still here with you.

We need some things from the store."

It wasn't long before George and Eric returned to the cabin. Laura greeted them, hugged Eric and said, "Did you get the door fixed? And where are the fish? The girls want them for supper tonight."

Eric replied, amazed at her composure, "Yes, we fixed the door and cleaned the fish. George, bring them in; they'll taste good for supper."

Laura took the fish from George and put them away. "George, would you mind staying until I return from town? There are some things I need to do."

"Sure, no problem, I'm sure the girls won't mind either. We have some games to get at, huh girls?" said George.

"Okay, then. I'll be on my way."

As she drove down the lane, her mind was racing. *I wanted to get out of there. I was about to erupt. I need to talk to Sue.* As she passed the post office on her way to the clinic, she stopped to pick up their mail. She opened their box and sifted through it. There was a letter from their attorney. She ran to the van to open it.

"Oh, my God!" It was a letter of notification that their divorce was final. Also, he had inserted papers stating, as neither had any money to give each other, it was a simple dissolution. *What a July this is turning out to be.* She stuffed the letter in her pouch and drove on to the clinic. *I have to see Sue for sure now!*

As luck would have it, Sue was there and didn't have anyone scheduled for the day.

"What's up?" greeted Sue.

"Sue, I need you to come with me, away from the office, please!" Laura pleaded.

"Sure, right away." Sue called the receptionist and told her, "I'm leaving for the day. Take messages, I'll call in later." She put her arm around Laura's shoulder. "Let's go out the back way. I'll drive."

"Now tell me, what's up? There is something wrong. I can tell by looking at you."

"Oh Sue, here, look at this!" Laura shoved the letter toward her.

Sue read the letter hurriedly. "Let's drive out to see Agnes. We need to have a private place to talk. You can trust her. I'll run into the office and call to let her know we're coming and to put on some coffee."

Neither spoke a word as they drove out to Agnes's place.

Agnes was standing on the porch to greet them. "My goodness, what is the matter? The way you drove in here was like the law was after you!"

"Let's go in," said Sue, pulling Laura by the arm. "Pour three cups of coffee, Agnes; we have some serious talking to do!" Sue pulled three chairs to the table and they all sat down. "Now, tell us, what's this all about?"

Laura handed the letter to Agnes. "Oh, my Lord!" gasped Agnes.

Laura burst into a barrage of words, telling how Eric had told her about his plans to do mission work, serving the Lord; how he said he felt it best to leave her and the girls, and how he couldn't take them with him where he was going to do his work. And the final blow today: the letter regarding the dissolution of their marriage, and that he was leaving for Costa Rica in September, with George.

Sue broke in, "Didn't you know he had filed before? Didn't you have to sign papers?"

"Yes, we had talked of it and signed papers before he went to Seattle, but when George said he would go, to cut down on expenses, I thought he had dropped the idea of dissolution, and I thought we were going to be all right. Then yesterday when he told me he was leaving and now today, the letter of notification confirming all he told me, I'm just numb!"

"How did you react yesterday when he said he was leaving; what did you say or do?" Sue asked. "What *are* you going to do?"

Laura wiped her tears, blew her nose, gulped and answered. "To tell you the truth, I really don't know what to do! When he told me of his plans, I felt so empty and alone. It seemed like all those years we had together just melted away to nothing. There was no meaning, no substance. We'd gone through so much together. The girls and I did so much with and for him, and now I don't know who I am, or even who he is, for that matter. We had been as one person over the years we were married, and now, half of me is leaving and what's the half that is left to do? What am I to do?"

As if in answer to her own question, Laura continued, "I do know we must be very careful how we tell the girls." She was soft spoken as she added, "It is very important how we handle this."

"By all means," agreed Agnes. "This you will definitely have to come together on and you must make a plan to tell them of the breakup."

Sue jumped in. "Yes, you have to know that your children are already aware of some stress in the family. They are pretty sharp with their observations. I've seen it in their eyes. I have seen and sensed it, so I know they're aware, especially with the way Eric has been putting you and them in contact with Sam and his boys so much here recently. Then, asking Sam to promise to watch over all of you when he wasn't around. Laura, remember when I told you to be aware of opportunities around you, not to pass up a good thing if it came your way?"

Laura nodded. "Yes, I do, but I thought you were talking about work opportunities!"

"No ma'am. Eric has said little things to me during therapy sessions, which I see now, were hints of what has happened here," Sue said. "But how to tell the children?" She paused a moment. "I know! Agnes and I will come over tonight and she can ask to bring them home with her to help with her new puppies. Would that be okay, Agnes? I know Sitka just had a litter about three weeks ago."

"Sure!" Agnes consented, "that is a grand idea!"

Sue went on, "In this way, you and Eric can discuss how you are going to tell the children. You did say George was there now, at your house; he could help you out, too. And I can stay, to be there for you. Then when Agnes brings the girls back tomorrow, we'll all be there with you, to help show them that we are all still their family, even if you and Eric won't be living together."

Laura was silent for a while, staring into her coffee cup. Silent tears trickled down her cheeks. "Yes, I think that would be best. I believe Mary and Patty know more than they ever talk about. I have a sneaking suspicion that they have spoken of it to David and Danny. The boys went through their parents' breaking up, and then too, Sam and the kids and I have been as close as a family while Eric was in Seattle. We have done a lot of things together, and you know how kids commiserate with each other. Yes, it will be good to do this. I'm so glad to have you two for friends. You make me feel so much better about how to handle this."

Laura looked at Sue. "I should be getting back home now, so it's best we go."

"Okay. Agnes, we'll see you later at Laura's tonight, around five. I'll be there, too. Let's go, Laura; I'll take you back to the van."

It was 4:30 p.m. when Laura pulled into their drive. When she went into the house, the smell of fish cooking greeted her. "Hey, you timed that right. Supper's ready," said George.

"How nice, George." Laura sniffed. "Smells good. What a pal you are! Did the girls help you?"

"You bet, so wash up and let's eat. It's not fancy, but filling."

They sat down to eat and were almost finished when Sue and then Agnes arrived. Laura answered their knocks and they came in and visited for a while, before Agnes asked if she could take Patty and Mary home with her, to see Sitka's new puppies. "I just stopped by to tell you Sitka had a litter of puppies three weeks ago, and I thought the girls would like to come over and see them. It's no fun to share such happiness alone, so I wanted Patty and Mary to share it with me. They can stay all night and I'll bring them home in the morning. Would that be all right?"

Eric looked at Laura, knowing she had set this up, and she nodded yes. "Okay," said Eric. "But you girls better be good, you hear?"

"They will be or I'll switch 'em," Agnes laughed. "Looks to me like with Sue and George here, you four can have some adult time to spend. Go get your pajamas and toothbrushes kids; we don't want to leave those puppies waiting too long." Whisking the girls to her truck, she called, "See you all tomorrow!"

After Sue and Laura cleaned up the kitchen, Laura said to Eric, "We need to sit down and talk over how you're going to tell the girls about this." She handed him the letter from the attorney. "George knows you are leaving me, because you both are leaving for Costa Rica in September. I told Sue this afternoon. I think she has suspected this for a longer period of time than I've been aware of it.

"We had once talked about it and signed the papers, but when George said he would go to Seattle with you, I thought you had given up the idea. Now I know that it is true. We have to tell the girls in the right way, and we should decide tonight, and tell them tomorrow. This letter is the deciding factor. So let's do it, while we have George and Sue as witnesses."

Chapter 31

Agnes and the girls enjoyed rolling and tumbling with Sitka and the puppies. Agnes pointed out how Sitka was gentle, but kept a watchful eye on them. She explained to Patty and Mary how much Sitka loved her offspring. "Because she knows you two, she is good about letting you touch and play with them. But if a stranger was to pick them up, she would get a little testy with them I'm afraid. There's nothing she wouldn't do to protect them. Sort of the way your momma is with the two of you."

The girls told Agnes that they understood what she was telling them. "We can sure learn a lot from animals, can't we, Agnes?" Mary said, as she stroked one little puppy. "See how Sitka licks my leg, as I'm petting this little guy? She is telling me she wants me to be careful because she loves me, as well as her puppy. She's a good mom, just like our mom."

Then Patty asked, "What about the puppies' daddy? Where is he? Doesn't he watch over them too?"

"Because I raise my puppies to be sled dogs, the daddy is not here. He is a champion lead sled dog and he's working all the time. He's only home with Sitka to breed her. But that doesn't mean that he wouldn't recognize one of his offspring. He's still their daddy. Animals are different from us in a lot of ways, but alike in many too. Moms and Dads always love their young and care for them. Understand?"

"Yes, we do, Ma'am," Patty said, "just like our Mommy and Daddy. They will always love us no matter where they are, or who they're with. Yep, they'll always love us."

"That's right, Patty. Even when Daddy was in Seattle with George, he told us that he loved us very much and that being away from us didn't make him love us less. In fact, I think it made him love us more." Mary gave a brisk nod to confirm her statement.

Agnes, wanting the girls to set those thoughts in their minds, quickly added, "I think you understand the love that parents have for their offspring, both animal and human. I don't think there's a thing that your mom or dad wouldn't give up, to show their love for the both of you. Now it's getting late. I'll let you play with the puppies a little bit longer, and then we'll put them to bed. You'll have to get ready for bed, too."

Agnes returned the girls home the next day after breakfast, and told them they could come over anytime to see the puppies. They entered the cabin and found their parents, Sue and George sitting around the table in the kitchen.

"Hey girls, Agnes!" called George; Sue greeted them also. George got up and got them all a chair so they could join the circle.

Eric called Mary and Patty over to give him a hug. "Girls, your mother and I have something we have to tell you. It is not going to be easy to understand, but we feel that you are going to handle this in a good way. We are proud of you, and we have shown you we always loved you, and still do. As you both know, I'm incapacitated to where you, Mom, and our friends have had to do for me twenty-four hours a day, seven days a week.

I have prayed about this, and the good Lord has shown me what I can do to help, not only myself, but others, as well. I can use the knowledge I have of the Bible and of communication to go forth and spread the word of the Lord to those who do not know of Him. I can become a useful human being again. But in order to do this, I will have to make a sacrifice, as will you and your mom. Just as God gave his Son to die on Calvary to save man from his sins, I am going to make a sacrifice of my family, to go and teach those who do not know the stories of our Lord, Jesus. I can't take you and Mommy with me where I must go. George is going with me, and I will be separating from your mom so she will be free to make a new life for herself and you two girls. I am willingly giving up all of you to teach God's word. Neither of you nor your mom is responsible for this divorce, or the difficulties we have had in the past. It is because of the injuries to my back. But God has shown me a way to come back and help in life."

Patty asked tearfully, "Does that mean Mary, Mom and I are going to die?"

"No, Patty, it just means that I'm giving up Mary, Mom, and you, by divorcing your mom. I won't be living in this house anymore."

Mary asked, "Aren't you going to be our daddy anymore?"

"I will always be your daddy wherever I am, and your mommy will always be your mommy. That will never change. Will it, Laura?"

Laura answered softly, "No, never, ever. We will always be Mom and Dad. Sue will be Sue. George will be Uncle George, Agnes will be Agnes, Sam will be Sam, David and Danny will be the same too; they'll always be the same. The only difference is your daddy, and the three of us, will not live together.

"Your daddy will be living in another place, giving his life to spreading the Word of God. When Daddy does come to see the two of you, or anyone else comes to visit, they will stay with us. You have grandparents in New York, and we'll go to visit them, within a week or so. I think it's time to go see them." Laura had her arms around the two girls and squeezed them tightly.

"When we get back in August, you can be with Daddy, before he leaves for Costa Rica in September." Mary and Patty had started to cry, and Laura held them closer as she looked them straight in the eyes. "Do you know how much you are loved by all of us? Your daddy and I will never stop loving you, no matter where we are or whom we are with; we will always love you! Now, you know how long your daddy has thought about this, and we mustn't make it harder for him, as he has made his decision. He feels deep pain, as we do, but he knows that God will help him to find a way to be strong and committed to His work. Let's not make this any harder for him to do."

The girls turned toward Eric and Mary asked, "But Daddy, why can't we all go with you and George? What is Costa Rica like? Will you tell Patty and me all about it? Will we be able to spend some time with you before you and Uncle George leave?"

Eric cleared his throat and answered her. "Mary, it's just not possible or financially practical for you girls and your mom to be with me. Of course, you will spend some time with me before I leave. I will tell you all about where I am going and what I'll be doing there. I'll always keep in touch with you and Mommy. God would not want me to turn away from you completely. All three of you must go forward too, and make something of your lives, just as I am going to do with mine. It will not be easy for any of us to do; we have been together for many years, but the time has come for me to let all three of you go. I hope you understand." He held out his arms to them and they rushed to him with hugs, kisses and tears.

Eric continued, as he hugged them, "Try to think of this as when I was in Seattle with Uncle George. I was away then, and you and your mom were on your own. You did fine. You are responsible girls and growing

229

every day. There will be many things that you will need to further your education, and it will help for your mom to save money that was being used to care for me. There's a lot to think about and someday you will understand fully why I'm doing what I am now. I know this is a lot for a ten- and twelve-year-old to digest right now, but your Uncle George, Sue, Agnes, and Sam and his boys—all your Alaskan family—will be here to help you, and your mom, and me, through this. Just remember, you are loved greatly, and none of this is your fault."

The rest of the day was filled with questions that the girls had for everyone. Sue and Agnes sat with Laura. They discussed many things, one of which was when Laura and the girls would be heading for New York to see her parents. Sue asked her, "Are you going to call your parents, and tell them, or are you going to wait until you get to New York?"

"I think I'll call them and tell them what has happened, and then ask if the girls and I might come to visit with them for awhile." Then Laura said that she would like to have Eric at George's when she did this, as she couldn't say what she'd have to say if he was here. She knew she couldn't do it without crying, and she didn't want to upset her parents anymore than necessary. As everyone knew, she had always been a strong person, and if she were to break down, then they would worry even more. Besides, she had to be strong for the girls; they must not see her crying.

Laura asked Sue, "Would you ask George if he would take Eric home with him tonight, so I can call my parents, and then call tomorrow and get a flight for us? I'll tell Dad tonight, that I'll call him when I book a flight. I want to be alone and think tonight. Is that selfish of me?"

"Most certainly not!" said Agnes.

"I think it is what you should do," advised Sue. "I'll suggest to George he take Eric and some of his things home with him this afternoon. The girls can help him gather them up. That way, it won't look so abrupt and cold. He and George can talk about the trip to Costa Rica, to the girls, while they pack. They might even keep them for the night."

"Good idea!" chimed in Agnes. "That will make it seem like the girls are helping him with the big move, as well as giving him the opportunity to explain about Cost Rica."

Sue went over to George and Eric and suggested the plan. They too, thought it would be a good thing. So George spoke up, "Hey, you Aleuts, how about you and me and your daddy getting some of his things and taking them over to my house. I have a lot of pictures and information on Costa Rica at my house, and we can explain to you where we'll be going. Besides, your dad needs some help getting his stuff together and your legs are younger and better than his or mine. You can carry some stuff to the truck. You might as well get your pajamas too. We'll just keep you all night, if that's okay with you, Eric?"

"Sounds like a winner to me!" he agreed, "and I couldn't ask for better help. Is that all right with you girls?"

"Of course, we want to help you, Daddy," they answered together. "Besides we want to hear about where you're going. What's the weather like there? What kind of clothes do you need to take? What will you be eating? How far away is it? Will you be close enough for us to see you, like we do now? There are just lots of things we want to know."

"Okay then," Eric replied, "let's get started. You don't mind us taking them, do you, Laura?"

"Of course not. You girls mind your manners now. Listen to Dad and George."

George, Eric, and the girls went about packing the things Eric needed, and carrying them to the truck. They also grabbed some nightclothes and a clean set of clothes for the girls, and were soon on their way to George's cabin. The girls were excited to hear about Costa Rica.

Agnes said she had better get home and take care of the puppies, and left.

Sue and Laura were finally alone and sat down to talk. "Let's have some coffee, Laura," said Sue. "I could sure use a cup. You sit still and I'll make it. I'm sure you have lots to think about. If you want me to, I will ask around, and see if there are or will be any openings for a nurse in the clinics or the hospital. You shouldn't have any trouble finding a job in your field. You are one good nurse, and everyone around here knows it. And besides, once the word gets out that you and Eric have split, you will be bombarded with questions, and probably more requests from guys than you can count on one hand."

"I sure don't care to have those kinds of offers. I want no part of anyone else in my life right now!" Laura said emphatically. "I don't think I could stand anymore heartache. Sue, do you realize just how much Eric has hurt me?"

"Has he really hurt you, Laura, or has he done you a big favor?" Sue looked straight at her. "You and I both know how much of a strain his condition has put on you. Not just physically, but mentally too. You know what you went through when he talked of suicide; anyone would have felt the same. Could you leave him alone? Was it safe to leave the girls with him? I know what you went through; I could read it in your face. You know you have shared a lot of things with me, and I have never said anything, to anyone. But you were not the only one who shared things with me. Eric did too. I gave my word not to say anything to anybody, about what he had confided in me, and I didn't. But now, since he has told you of his leaving, I can tell you."

Laura looked at her strangely, as Sue continued on with her conversation. "He told me of his plans to go to the mission field. He said he had prayed about it for a long time. He didn't want to hurt you by leaving, but he felt that he was hurting you more by staying and having you and the girls at his beck and call. He had laid out his plans very methodically. Why do you think he made everyone promise to do certain things for him? Why did you think he made Sam promise to watch over you and the girls when he wasn't here?"

"I just thought he was looking out for our welfare while he was gone! I did tell you that I had a funny feeling in the pit of my stomach about all the strange things he was doing. But I never really stopped to analyze all of it. So what is your take on why he did what he did?"

"Anyone with an ounce of sense could see that he had picked Sam for his replacement. It would be the natural thing to do; you all have been such close friends for a long time. And after Connie left Sam, I could see that he had only admiration for you, the way you were sticking by Eric. Laura, Sam was falling in love with you. Hasn't he ever given you an indication of that fact? You only have to sit and watch him when he is around you. You have completely mesmerized him. All you would have to do is say the word, and he would do anything for you. And it is not only Sam, but his boys too. You have been kinder, and paid more attention to them, than Connie ever did. Ask anyone!"

The coffee was ready, and Sue set two cups on the table for them. "I can't believe that you have not seen how Sam feels about you. You just haven't been looking, I guess."

"Maybe so," said Laura, sipping her coffee, "but there were a few instances when Sam made some strange replies to something I said to him."

"Like what?" said Sue, gulping the coffee she had in her mouth.

"Well, one time I said to him, 'how can we ever repay you for all the kindness you have shown to me and the girls while Eric is away?' He replied that maybe someday I would find a way. I thought that was a strange thing to say."

"See, I told you so!" Sue pulled her chair closer and looked Laura straight in the eye. "So, how do you feel about Sam?"

"Sue, you know that I have a deep love for Eric. It'll never go away! I've thought about all the different kinds of love: the love a mother has for her children, the love of your parents, and the love of your friends. I love Sam, but I am not in love with him. I'm in love with Eric. He is the one love that comes once in a lifetime, and I feel I was that love for him, also. We will always love each other. That kind of love you never forget. Sure, maybe in time, I will find someone to love again, but it will never be the same as that 'one and only love I've had in my lifetime.' Only time will tell."

"You may think this a strange thing to say to you, but how about the times Eric was downright mean to you, expecting you to be at his beck and call? Sam noticed it too. He told me that he once told Eric if he didn't start treating you better, that he was going to try and take you away from him."

Quickly, Laura came to Eric's defense, "Sue, you of all people should know how depressed a handicapped person can get. It alters their personality at times, and they say things they don't really mean."

"Laura, as your friend and confidant, let me say this to you. You have an opportunity for a love like Sam has for you, right now; think hard about it. I'm sure that you'll find it is almost as deep as the love you had or do have for Eric. Don't throw it away!" Sue grabbed her hands. "He not only has a deep love for you, but also for your girls. You will never, ever find anyone who could love you more than that man. He is a good man, and they do not come along every day, and you're not getting any younger, my dear. Eric knew that too. Why do you think he pushed Sam so hard to watch out for you? He handpicked Sam for you. Once the word is out, you'll have lots of offers for one-night stands, but you don't want that. Think about it. Think hard and long." Sue picked up her cup, finished her coffee and carried the cup to the sink. "I must go now, but remember what I've said to you today. I've heard it from Eric, and I've heard it from you. But think on this. Pray about it. I'll see you later. When you find out about your plane tickets, call me; I'll take you to the airport. Bye for now, get some rest. I love you." And she was gone.

Chapter 32
ༀ

Laura sat at the table holding her empty coffee cup, staring out the window at the mountains she and Eric loved so much. She began to mull over all that she and Sue just discussed. *Eric was willing to leave Alaska and the mountains he loved so well. He also was leaving Mary, Patty and me. How could that deep love he had for us change so quickly in a matter of time?* She thought of what he had said to her: I'll always love you and the girls and this place in Alaska, but I'll not think of it forever, like I will you and the girls. That's a love that will never die. Then he went on to say, we could learn to love again, although it may never be like that one love that comes along once in a lifetime. In essence, Sue had told her the same thing today. *Could this be true?* She thought not. She guessed that only time would tell.

She got up and walked out onto the deck, to breathe in the scent of the pines in the air, as she waited for the sunset. The sunset on the mountains was beautiful. She scanned the horizon and took in the view that she and Eric had looked at so many times together. *How could he leave that? How could he leave us?*

Suddenly, she heard the sound of a truck as it pulled into the drive. A familiar voice, one she knew so well, called to her. "Laura? Laura? Are you home?"

"Up here, out on the deck."

She heard Sam's hurried steps as he entered the house and came to her. "Laura, I just heard the news, is it true? Is this truth or just gossip? You know how these little towns spread the gossip! Are you here alone? Where's Eric? Where are the girls? Oh my God, tell me! I've been beside myself with worry. What's happened?"

"It's true," and she filled him in about Eric's plans. "Now, in answer to all your other questions, yes, I'm here alone; Eric and the girls are at George's cabin." She explained that the girls knew and took it pretty well. "And you needn't worry about me; I'll be fine, once I'm over the initial shock. I'll call my parents tonight, ask them if the girls and I can come and visit, and then tomorrow I'll get our plane tickets. Then we'll fly to New York for two or three weeks. I need to get away for awhile." Laura started to reel and grabbed onto the deck railing for support.

Sam reached out and put his arm around her. "Come, let's go inside and sit down. I think this has been more than you can take right now." He helped her to a chair at the table. "I smell coffee. Do you mind if I help myself to a cup? Do you want one?"

"No thanks, I have had enough for one day. Anymore and I won't sleep." She laughed, "Like I was going to be able to sleep anyway."

Sam poured his coffee and pulled his chair up next to Laura. Putting his hand on hers, he said, "Tell me all about it. What happened?"

Laura recounted the story to him. He listened intently to it all. Finally, when she finished, he drank down what was left of his coffee. Putting both hands on her shoulders, he turned her toward him. "I've listened to you; now I want you to listen to me. I don't want you to interrupt me, but listen until I've finished saying what I want to say to you. Can you do that for me?"

She wiped her eyes. "Yes."

"You have to promise, no interruptions," he instructed. "Promise?"

"I promise" was her soft reply.

"You and Eric, Connie and I have been friends for years. We were so close that it was more like we were brothers and sisters. When Connie left me, you and Eric were there for me. Then when Eric was going to be away, he asked me to look after you and the girls. I did, but how was I to know that the neighborly love I had for you and Eric would turn to a deeper love for you, more than I could ever imagine? Eric saw it happen, so that's why he made me promise to look after you and the girls. He wanted to further the love I had for you, and he did. I have the deepest and utmost respect for you, and Eric, so I never said or did anything out of line with you or the girls. But now that he has left you, I want you to know that I love you deeply, and if you would have me, I want you to marry me. Let me take care of you and the girls, for the rest of my life. And I don't need to make a promise to do that." Laura tried to break in, "Hey no talking yet, you promised to listen 'til I'm done. I know that you love Eric deeply; you had to or you wouldn't have stood by him the way you did. I was so envious of that love. I know you love me, but with a different kind of love, a friendship love, not the intimate type of love of need and desire. But I'm willing to settle for the friendship type of love. Maybe you'll grow into that intimate type of love for me someday. I'm willing to take that chance. I love you and the girls more than anything, and so do my boys. We've had lots of good times together, almost like a family unit. The boys have told me many times how they wish we could've had fun like that, with their mom. I hope you understand what I'm saying. I'll say it again and then you can answer me. I know you don't love me now deeply, but maybe in time you will. I'm willing to take that chance. Will you marry me, Laura?"

"Oh Sam," Laura's tears coursed down her cheeks. "I do love you, but not in that intimate desire type of love. I love you dearly, more than words can say, but there is just one big love in my life, and that was, and is, Eric. I can't be unfair to you and say yes, when I still have that deep love for him. Do you understand?" Laura reached out and touched his face, caressing his cheek and dragging her fingertips across his lips. "Maybe someday, but now isn't the time to say yes. I'm sorry."

Sam dropped his head and sat silent for a bit. He took a deep breath. "I do understand. But just let me do this much for you, right now. I want you to call your parents, see if you can visit for two or three weeks, as you planned. If they say to come, I want to go with you, Mary, and Patty. I don't want you to fly that far alone. I promise to be a good boy, although it'll be hard not to want to kiss or hold you, when you need it."

"You would do that for me, after I just said 'no' to your proposal? You must love me. Yes, I'd be honored to have you escort us to New York. I want my parents to meet a decent man; after all, your kind doesn't come along every day. Hand me the phone, I'll call now."

Sam handed her the phone, she dialed the number, her father answered and she told him of the divorce and some of the details. Naturally, he had lots of questions to ask her. "Dad, there's too much to tell over the phone, so could we come to New York, as soon as we can get tickets?"

Her father answered quickly, "Of course you can. Don't be silly."

"I'll call you and let you know when we'll be there, as soon as we get the tickets. Would it be all right if a good friend comes with us? My friend doesn't want me and the girls traveling alone all that way."

"That'll be fine. There's room here, so call us when you know what time you'll be coming in, and we'll pick you up."

Sam suggested, "I'll go to the office and get on the computer and make arrangements for the tickets. Then I'll call you when I have confirmation."

Laura reminded him, "The girls are with Eric and George until tomorrow, so make it for the day after tomorrow. I'll start packing some things for the girls and myself right away."

"Well, let me go and get those tickets," said Sam. "I'll call you when I know."

Laura rose to walk him to the door. "Thank you, Sam; you are a love." She reached out to kiss his cheek.

He gently put his arms around her, pulled her close, and gave her a good night kiss for her to remember until she saw him again. "Call me if you need me in the night. I'll come right away. You shouldn't be alone. I'd insist on staying, but I can't trust myself, since we'd be here alone," Sam whispered softly in her ear, kissed her again gently, and left.

As if this day didn't have enough things happen to keep her awake all night, the touch of Sam's lips on her lips, and the closeness of that embrace sent a feeling through her body she hadn't felt for a long, long, time. Had it not been for her deep love for Eric, she wouldn't have let Sam go.

Chapter 33

On the way to George's cabin Mary put her hand over the back seat and caressed her father, while Patty had her arms over the seat and around his neck. When George pulled up in front of his cabin, he finally broke the silence in the truck.

"Well crew, here we are!" He opened the back door for the girls. "You two 'Aleuts' have been awfully quiet back here. I thought you were asleep. Here, let me load you guys up, to take this stuff inside."

"OK, Uncle George," said Mary. "Come on, Patty. Help us."

They carried Eric's things in, and George helped Eric in, behind them.

"Dad, will we be able to see you whenever we want?" asked Mary. "How far away is Costa Rica? Can we come down there? How long will you stay?"

"Whoa, wait a minute. That's a lot of questions you have piled up there." Eric motioned her and Patty to him. "Let's sit down here and I'll try to answer any and all questions you have."

They both went to him and sat on the couch. George busied himself putting Eric's things away.

"There now, just settle yourselves and we'll talk. As to your first questions," Eric rolled himself so he was facing both of them, "you want to know if you can see me whenever you want."

He took their hands. "No; I'll be far away from here. Costa Rica is in a much warmer area, many miles from here. But I promise you both, I will see you every year, for I must report to the Rehab Center in Seattle once a year. When I go there, I'll come here and spend some time with you both. That is a promise I will keep forever."

They both started to cry, but finally Mary asked, "Dad, why do you want to leave us and go there? Weren't you happy here with us? Don't you love us anymore?"

Eric brushed their tears away. "Listen to me; I know you're only twelve and ten, and this is hard for you to understand now, but someday why I'm doing this will be clear to you. Please let me explain and don't interrupt. I want you to listen very close to this. There are many reasons, and I have thought a long time about all of them and prayed about them, and that's how I decided to do what I'm doing. So here they are. As you are aware, I can't move any part of my body from here down." He pointed to his chest. "I used to be an avid outdoorsman and could withstand anything: weather, pain, and anything that came my way. I could manage it and get by it. But now, the cold makes me incapable of doing that anymore. I don't have the mobility or the perseverance to fight it anymore. I have to depend on someone to do so many things for me now that I used to be able to do myself. A man has an inner pride, and a sense of being the head of the household, that sustains him. I don't have that anymore."

He paused, looked lovingly at his girls, patted their hands and continued. "I had to rely on your mom and you more than I wanted to, and it drained that feeling of manhood from me. Not only was it draining me, but also, it was robbing your mom and you two of your very existence.

You took care of me, every day, of every week. Not only you, but our friends and neighbors too, helped do the things that I used to do. I was no longer the breadwinner for our home. That depressed me."

Mary spoke up again, "But, Daddy, we love you and we want to help you, don't we, Patty?"

Patty agreed, "You bet. We can do a lot of things for you, Daddy; you don't have to go away. Mommy is sad and so are we!"

"I know this has saddened and hurt you. It has me too, but you will see in the long run, it is going to be better for all of us. It'll give us all back the lives that we've been pushing aside, because it was easier to do so. We have to think of the future."

Eric looked at Patty, "What do you want to be when you grow up, Patty?"

She answered quickly, "A nurse, like Mommy!"

"And what about you, Mary?"

"I want to be a therapist, like Sue."

Eric clapped his hands together. "There you go, and those are very admirable ambitions for your lives. But there is one thing that your youth hasn't grasped yet; it takes money to get an education, to do those things. Your momma is working very hard now to help meet the costs of my medical needs. She has given up her life completely, for you two and me. I love your mother too much for that to continue.

"While I was away in Seattle I learned a lot about myself. I took a good look at our lives and decided there had to be a change. I couldn't be selfish anymore. I had to do something with my life, using what I do know about, to make it happen." He paused. The girls were absolutely quiet. They were so mature for their ages. They had to grow up fast. Alaska did that to you; there was no room for foolish moves here.

Suddenly Mary asked, "Daddy, just what will you do to make a living? Does this work for the Lord pay well?"

Eric chuckled, "Mary, Mary, of course, I have much faith in my Lord now. He has brought me this far out of my conflict. I'll be fine. I'll have my disability from the VA, and living in Costa Rica is much cheaper than here.

"Your mother has a profession that she can work at, and support all of you. She is very stable. I have no doubts that the three of you will be fine. I tried to lay plans for your futures. I only hope and pray, it will come to pass, which I'm reasonably sure it will. I have prayed on it.

Patty jumped into the conversation. "But, Daddy, how do you know how to do the Lord's work?"

"Girls, when I was smaller than you two, my family taught me the Bible inside and out: I had great faith. Then, when I was in the Army, I lost my faith, somewhat, I guess. I didn't lose it; I just pushed it aside and forgot how to trust the Lord. But now I do, and I know, we will all be fine. He sent us all we have. Look, we all have George, right!"

"Right," said Mary, "we have Uncle George."

George appeared. "Did someone call?"

Eric smiled at his friend. "The girls and I did. How about showing them where we are going? I have already explained the rest to them, and I think they understand."

George said, "You do have a way with the words. I do believe everything will be all right. Supper's ready. Let's eat first."

The rest of the night was spent going over maps and discussing Costa Rica, and how the people live there. The girls seemed to be very calm now; only once did Mary and Patty wonder how Momma was doing at home alone.

Laura had almost worn a hole in the floor pacing after all the events of the day and evening. Besides all that, Laura, too, could not help but wonder what was happening with Eric and the girls.

Finally, when she felt she could not pace any longer, she crawled into bed, letting her mind wander over the day's events... *Mary and Patty seemed to take the news of their dad leaving pretty well. Of course, Eric had been away from home quite a bit, the six weeks in Seattle for the rehab, the three months in the hospital when the accident happened, and of course, the whole summer when he did logging work in 1983 on Quizinkie Island, off Kodiak Island. Then, there were all the times he was gone away from home, hunting and fishing. They were used to not having him around a whole lot.*

But the topper of all was the surprise of Sam proposing marriage to her! She had never even thought of Sam in that way. That was the last thing she had expected tonight. But what he said made some sense to her. She was alone a lot, with Eric gone so much of the time, before the accident. She did love Eric deeply; after all, he was her first love. But had her love blinded her to the fact that he was gone so much of the time? She couldn't think of that now, there was too much else to put into perspective.

Her head was spinning, and she thought sleep would never come. Her head was ringing.

Chapter 34

"Oh please, stop ringing, let me sleep!" Laura was thinking, when she realized the ringing was the telephone. She jumped out of bed and grabbed the phone, "Hello, Hello!"

"Hey, did I wake you? It's me, Sam. Remember me? I'm the guy who loves you and wants to marry you. But you said, No."

"Oh, Sam, let's not go there. I told you last night why I can't marry you." She whispered into the phone as if there was someone near to hear the conversation.

Quickly, Sam picked up on her whisper, and asked, "Is someone there?"

"No, just me. I had a very rough night. What's up? Were you able to schedule all of us a flight to New York?"

"Yes, I did. We can fly out of Anchorage on Tuesday and return the last Tuesday in August. That would make a total of four weeks we'd be gone. Would that be okay with you and the girls? How about Eric? When does he leave for Costa Rica?"

"Makes no difference; he didn't confer with me on filing for the divorce, so why should I have to ask him? I'm sure he'll have his time with the girls before he leaves. I'll tell him when we are leaving and returning and he can schedule around our return. Does that sound too bitter?" she asked. "How much will the tickets be? I have some money put away to pay for our trip."

"No matter," said Sam. "I took care of it. We'll settle up later. When will the girls and Eric be back from George's? Do you want me to come over when you tell him that you're leaving for New York, and that I'm going with you?"

"It isn't necessary, but I would like you to be here when they bring Patty and Mary home. You, Eric and I have always been so close, and I don't want to hide anything from him. I've always been honest with him. I want you here when I tell him. Please come."

"All right, I'll be over in a little while. Don't worry now." Sam reassured her. "It'll be fine. Eric will be relieved that I'm going with you and the girls. Just you wait and see. I know that is what he would expect me to do. See you in a bit."

Laura set about getting dressed and started to lay out the clothes they would need for the trip to New York. She also wanted to get things straight in her mind, about what she and Eric would have to get ironed out—about the girls, the house, and on and on. She needed to talk with her father about some things too; she needed her family right now.

As she finished gathering up the items they needed to take, she heard Mary and Patty calling to her. "Mom, we're home. Where are you? Are you up and dressed?"

"I'm in my closet. I'll be right out. Did you have a good time? Are you guys okay?"

"Yeah, Mom," said Patty as she ran into the bedroom. "We're fine. We know you both love us and will always be there for us, even though we are not going to be living together. You understand that too, don't you,

Mom?"

"Yes, honey, I do." Laura put her arms out to hug Patty. "I understand it completely, that you can still love and care for someone even though he doesn't live with you. I think I realized that fully last night. I'll always love you and your dad. There are many kinds of love, and it isn't always easy to see. The love you have for your dad and me, your love for your grandparents, Uncle George, Sue, Sam and the boys, all your friends, and on and on. That is what life is about. I know now that you and Mary fully understand that, as well as your dad and I."

"Yes, Laura, you are exactly right!" Eric was sitting in the doorway with Mary listening. "I am so glad we all understand!"

Surprised, Laura said, "Eric! I didn't know you were here. Is George here too? I thought just the girls had come in. I'll come out to the kitchen."

As she entered the kitchen area, she said, "Good morning, George!"

"Laura," he answered, "are you okay? Did you get any rest last night? I'm sorry."

"Thanks for asking George; it isn't your fault. I'm just glad that you're here to help. Did the Indians keep you awake all night? Want some coffee? I'll fix some."

Eric wheeled his chair toward her. "Laura, I want you to know how glad I am that you understand why I filed for the dissolution. I know you and the girls will be better off down the line."

"I do, Eric. Things are clear now, as to why you did things that didn't seem to make sense before. I do understand, and I hope you know why the girls and I are going back to New York for a month. I need to see my parents. That's not all; Sam is going to go along with us. He wouldn't hear of me flying back alone with the girls. We will be leaving on Tuesday and will return the last week of August. That'll give you time to get what you want, from here, and be ready to go to Costa Rica in September. I hope you schedule your departure at least two weeks after we return, as the girls will want to spend that time with you and George."

Eric was a little taken back. Here Laura was telling him what she was going to do, and what she wanted him to do. She was taking charge. "What are you going to do when you get back? Where will you be staying? You are going to stay here in the house, aren't you?"

Laura thought, *Sam where are you!* Then she answered Eric, "Of course, that's my plan. I'll get a nursing job somewhere; Sue is already putting out inquiries as to available job openings. We will be fine. No worry. I'll know much more when we return. I really do need to speak with my parents before I can tell you more. You don't mind that Sam is going to escort us to New York, do you?"

"No, no, I think that it's an excellent idea. Mary and Patty have never flown before, and for you to go alone with them would not be the best idea. You will need some assistance with baggage and all. Please try and make your parents understand that I'm doing this for a better future for you and my daughters." He hesitated, cleared his throat. "I only want you and the girls to be happy."

By this time, Sam was at the door. Eric turned toward Sam. "I suppose you've heard the news, Sam. What a bad person I must be, leaving a beautiful wife and family in the lurch as I am, and running away to Costa Rica."

Sam came over to Eric and gave him a hug. "No, not at all. I've heard you are leaving, but not for the reasons people are thinking. I think it takes a big man to walk away from someone you love. As you well know, I've envied you for a good many years, and you know that I'll watch over them, because I love them too."

"By the way, with your permission, George and I could watch over your place, and the boys, while you're gone."

"Sure, be glad to have you do that," said Sam. "Much obliged."

"Done!" said Eric. "Come on George, let's go home now, I'm tired." And they left.

"Now what was that all about?" said Laura as she set a cup of coffee in front of Sam. "What am I, a sled dog on the auction block?"

"He just gave me permission to care for you forever, my dear. Marry me and make me a happy man. I have wanted you for a long time now. I saw the handwriting on the wall. He knew that I knew he was planning on leaving you and the girls. He also knows that you love me, but you are not in love with me. You are still *in love* with him, but he thought that maybe in time, you could learn to love me. Please say yes!"

"Sam, I'm sorry. I told you why last night." Laura paused, thinking of his kiss from last night. "I just can't say yes at this time. My physical body says yes, but my heart still says no. Now let's change the subject. I need to call my parents and let them know our flight details."

Sam gave her the information and she let her parents know when they would arrive at Rochester airport. "The girls are looking forward to seeing you, Mom and Dad, and so am I. I need some good old kitchen table advice." She hung up the phone and sat very still for a long time.

"Hey," said Sam, "let's give Sue and Agnes a call, and all of us go out to eat; it would be good for everybody, and you can catch them up on our travel plans. I'll call Sue and Agnes, and you and the girls get ready. Does that sound like a plan?"

Laura nodded. "Girls, clean up. Sam is taking us out to eat, and we have to pick up our airplane tickets, to go see Grandpa and Grandma."

Chapter 35

"Look up there on the porch!" Sam pointed out as he drove up Agnes' driveway. Laura started to giggle. "Look, girls, there's Agnes, and the whole brood of puppies jumping around her. She's waving to us."

Mary and Patty started to wave frantically. As soon as Sam stopped the truck, the girls bailed out and started hugging Agnes and the puppies. Laura and Sam were right behind them.

"How are you doing, honey?" Agnes said, as she hugged Laura. "I've been on pins and needles waiting to hear how things went after I left the other day. Come on inside. Sue will be here soon."

As they stepped into the house, they were met with some mighty good aromas of a roast cooking and fresh baked bread. "My, but that does smell good!" Sam rubbed his stomach.

Agnes winked at Sam. "Well you know me. Sue and I decided we all could talk better here. I hate to spoil your plans, but I have our supper in the oven. We can all eat here, away from gawking people and nosy town folks. Besides, I cook better than any restaurant in town. Is that all right with all of you?"

"Agnes, you are the best," said Laura and hugged her again. "We are so fortunate to have you and Sue for our friends. We're going to pick up our plane tickets to New York, as I have decided to take Mary and Patty to meet their grandparents. You know they have never seen my mom and dad! Sam insisted that he go with me. He would not hear of me going alone. But we can always pick up the tickets when we get to the airport; Sam has already made the arrangements."

"Good, the girls can play with the puppies and we can all talk. I think I hear Sue's van coming in now. Let's go look!"

They all greeted Sue and exchanged hugs. Agnes and Laura went inside, but Sam and Sue stayed out on the porch to watch the girls play with the puppies.

Not being able to be quiet any longer, Agnes spoke. "Well, tell me what transpired yesterday. I'm busting my girdle to find out! Tell me what happened. Sue knows some of what happened, as she stayed with you until evening, and she told me what you and she talked about, and I whole-heartedly agree with what she told you. Keep it under advisement, girl. It was good advice. We know it's hard for you being up here, with your real family so far away. We only hope we can do as good a job for you as your parents would."

Laura responded, "Oh you two have, and I am thinking very hard on what Sue and I talked about."

"Agnes, Sue doesn't even know this yet, but Sam came over after she left. He heard the talk around town and he was concerned how I was taking the news. Agnes, he is so good and kind and Eric and I think the world of him. He told me that Eric knew how he admired me for sticking with him through thick and thin all these years. He said Eric so much as gave him permission to ask me to marry him, if and when he was no longer around. Well, he did! I told him no, that I was in love with Eric and would always love him. He said he knew that, but hoped I would grow to love him in an intimate personal way, not as I do now. Then he kissed me. Agnes, he stirred within me feelings I have put away ever since Eric's accident. It scared me." Laura paused, to gain composure. "He offered to go with us to New York next week. He didn't want us to go alone. I agreed to that. Am I wrong?"

"Heaven sakes no, girl!" Agnes took Laura's hands in hers, to keep her from wringing them. "You are human, you know. Time changes a lot of things, if you will just let it. Sue gave you good advice. Think on it hard. I applaud Sam. He is a good, decent man, and we all know how he feels about you. I think you are the only person around who couldn't see it. Go on to New York, and let things happen as they will. No one would fault you for doing so. Not even God!"

Laura kissed Agnes on the cheek and hugged her close. "Thank you; I will put my mind in motion again. I started to the other night, thinking back how much of the time I was alone, with Eric being away from us most of the time, doing his own thing. But when he wanted me, I was there for him. It was good, and we loved each other; but you are right, time has a way of eroding things away."

On the porch, Sue and Sam were in deep conversation while watching the girls play with the puppies. Sam told Sue he proposed to Laura and the outcome of it. Then he told her about going to New York next week for a month, to see her parents.

"Sam, don't you dare back off on your plan to marry Laura. It would be the best thing in the world for the both of you. I know the story of your divorce, remarriage, and divorce again, and of your friendship with Eric and Laura. I know all about it. Eric confided a lot in me, and I say you're right—he did give you permission to marry Laura, without coming right out and saying it."

"I did feel a little silly asking her so soon," Sam replied, "but I couldn't help myself. I love that woman so much. I hid it for a good many years. And the girls are like my own; they get along so well with my boys. We have done so much here lately, thanks to Eric pushing us together; we are like a family. I promised her I would be a good boy if she let me go with her to New York."

"Well then go—and do whatever you feel is right at the moment. You aren't hurting their marriage any now; after all, they are divorced. Go for it. Speaking of going for it, are you hungry? Let's go in and see about eating."

"Okay, let's do it! And I'll take your advice, Sue. What have I got to lose? Nothing and I have everything to gain." Sam reached for the door to hold it for Sue.

"Just one last piece of advice before we go inside: don't let Laura override you; she has been the head of the household too long. She needs a good strong, but at the same time, gentle hand. Understand?" Sue walked through the door as Sam shook his head yes.

Laura and Agnes had set the table and were putting on the last minute things for supper, when Sam called the girls in to eat. They ate and visited until it was time to leave for home. Sue asked if they wanted her to drive them to Anchorage. Sam said he had tickets arranged for the commuter plane from Sterling to Anchorage, but he thanked her anyway, for everything.

When Sam deposited Laura and the girls at their house, he asked if he could help with any packing or preparing the house to be left for a month. Laura told him Eric and George would be in and out getting his things, so not to worry. Sam escorted them in and Laura instructed the girls to go to bed. They said good night to Sam and vanished.

"Want some coffee, Sam?" Laura asked.

"No, I'm satisfied in the food and drink department. That was a beautiful supper Agnes put out."

"Agnes is quite the lady, she's good at everything. She made it alone after her husband passed on, and if she did it, so can I."

"There is only one difference between the two of you and your situations." Sam broke in. "Her husband left her well fixed, financially. Also, she didn't have children to worry about. She only had their sled dog kennel."

"Yes, but Sam, I'm a nurse and can make fairly good money here."

"And how much would you have to pay for someone to care for the young ones, while you are working? Then there are the deductions taken from your check. Did you think about that? I'd better go, it's getting late and I have to arrange some things before we leave Tuesday. Besides, it's not good that my truck be seen here too often, at night. You know how gossip grows." He pulled her to him, gently rubbed his hands up and down her back, while he gently placed a long, warm goodnight kiss on her lips.

"Sam?" Laura whispered, breathing a little harder than usual.

Sam turned back to her, waiting for what would come next.

"Yes, I guess you had better go. Good-night."

"See you Tuesday at five a.m. be ready. David will drive us." This time he left.

Chapter 36

❧

Laura was already awake when the alarm went off. She got the girls up
and dressed. As she finished combing her hair, she saw the truck
lights come into the driveway. They were ready. David and Sam came in;
David took the bags already stashed by the door, Sam got the girls into
the truck, and Laura locked up. When they got to the Sterling Airport,
Laura hugged David and told him to keep an eye on the cabin while they
were gone. She told him that Eric and George would be in and out, but
would he please go in and check things once in a while, and she gave
him the key. He agreed, she kissed him good-bye, his Dad hugged him,
and they were aboard for the first leg of their long trip.

They knew that once in the Anchorage airport, they would only have
time to get their tickets and clear inspection at the gate, before they were
to board their flight for Chicago. They would have lunch on the plane, but
since they would have a three-hour layover in Chicago, they would have
their evening meal at O'Hare airport. From there, they would catch a
two-hour flight to Rochester, and arrive around 9:30 or 10:00 at night.

Mary and Patty were very excited about the trip, having never flown before. As they left so early in the morning, Sam and Laura figured that the girls would sleep most of the way, but Laura had brought books for them to read, and cards for them to play with each other. Laura planned on calling her parents from Chicago to reconfirm their estimated time of arrival. Everyone was excited, as it had been a long time since Laura had been home, and the girls would be meeting their grandparents for the first time.

When they boarded the plane for Chicago, Laura and Sam gave the girls two seats together, across the aisle from them. Once in the air, Mary and Patty dropped off to sleep. Laura leaned closer to Sam and whispered to him, as he had his eyes closed too, "Are you asleep?"

Sam opened his eyes and moved closer to her, "No, I was just resting my eyes." He whispered, kissing her on the ear.

"Sam, you have to stop doing that." Laura fidgeted in her seat, leaning closer yet to him. "I don't want other people to hear what I have to say to you, so behave yourself. You have to watch what you are doing with the girls here. They love their daddy, as I do, and they may not understand. But I must say that you do stir me. I am human, and it has been a long time since I have felt feelings like this, and it's very hard for me to ignore them. Eric and I were very active sexually, before his accident, so please don't make it any harder for me. You know my feelings for Eric. I've loved him for a long time, all my life in fact. He was my first love and now, after the shock of the divorce, I have to examine my feelings very closely, and you're not making it any easier."

Sam reached over and held her hand. "Why do you think I keep doing this, kissing you whenever I feel the need to do so? You're divorced now, and Eric no longer has a right to harness your feelings, the way you are letting him. You have a right to a completely fulfilled life now. I'm human too, and my feelings are deep and honest for you. You don't know how long I have loved you from afar with feelings that have gnawed deep within me. I want to take care of you and the girls; and I want to love you in the most passionate way. You have to let me do this or I will surely die." He squeezed her hand, almost to the point of hurting her, and then he took it and laid it against his chest. "Please don't break this heart that is beating so passionately for you to say 'yes.'"

She caressed his face. "I promise you, I'll give it some very deep thought. You're right in what you say about Eric; he has released me to go on with my life. He has told me that very thing so many times within the last month or so. He pushed you and me together, and if you hadn't been such a perfect gentleman the whole time, and given me some hint of your feelings, I might not be so hesitant now. Eric hurt me deeply; he literally said he needed to go on with his life, in his own way, and there was no room for the girls and me where he had to go. Do you realize how much that hurt? We, the girls and I, had given our all to care for and love him. We built our lives around him and suddenly it all was shattered. Yes, I will give your proposal some very deep thought; I just wanted you to know that. But I need to speak with my parents before giving you a definite answer. Is that fair?"

"It's fair enough!" He moved her hand over his chest, placing his other hand over hers, holding it tightly over his heart, and closed his eyes. "Now lay your head on me and get some sleep. You'll be awake all night, once we get there and see your parents."

It seemed as if Laura had just closed her eyes when she felt the plane back off a little speed and the captain came on the speaker saying that they would be landing shortly in Chicago. She reached across the aisle, touching Mary. "Mary, Patty, we'll be landing soon, so gather your things and put them in your bag. We have a three-hour layover here, so we'll have a chance to eat, and look around a bit before our next flight."

They all went to the rest room and met to find a place to eat. They found where they were to catch the next plane and checked their carry-on bags in a locker before eating. They walked Mary and Patty around to see the airport and stretch their legs. Soon it was time to board the plane to Rochester. The girls watched the people for a while, read a little, and then fell asleep again. Laura was telling Sam about her parents and some of her background, growing up in Libertyville. The time passed quickly, until the announcement came about landing soon. Laura woke the girls, "As soon as we're in the terminal I need you to help look for Grandpa and Grandma. I know you have never met them in person, but you have seen their pictures. I know you have to be excited to meet them. So, wake up!"

The girls opened their eyes, stretched and gathered up their things, putting them in their small carry-on bag. Sam looked at Laura. "Trade me seats now, so I can step out into the aisle and keep people back, so you and the girls can exit without being separated. I'll be right behind you."

"Okay." She stepped into the aisle to let Sam out and then she slipped back into his seat. They would soon be on the ground. Her heart started to race. She wondered how her parents would take the news and all the details. *Would they wonder about Sam? Where should she start?* Her thoughts were still racing about her parents, when she decided, *I'll suggest that we wait until tomorrow, when the girls aren't around, and after they've had a good night's sleep. That way, I'll have time to compose myself.*

The seat belt sign flashed on, it wouldn't be long now. The wheels touched and the plane gave a little bounce. She finally spoke. "Here I am, back in New York State. It's been a long time."

The plane pulled up to the gate, the seat belt light turned off, everyone stood up, and even though they were at the gate, it was taking awhile for the passengers ahead of them to deplane. Sam stepped out into the aisle, and as Laura moved over to stand in front of him, he whispered, "Don't be nervous. Everything is going to be all right. You'll be fine. I'm here always, and don't you ever forget it."

Laura looked him square in the eye and smiled. He got the message.

The line started to move and Laura directed the girls to get in line behind the people in front of them. "Just follow those people. When we get out into the airport, stay by my side. Mary, you take my hand and Patty, you take Sam's. That way, we won't get separated. Hang onto your bags."

As they came off the ramp and into the airport, Sam told Laura to look to her right. There raised up in the air, high above all the people, someone was holding a sign with her name on it. They made their way to the sign. There under the sign were her parents. Laura dropped Mary's hand and the small bag she was carrying, and Sam took Mary's hand. She wrapped both arms around her parents in a great big group hug. Tears glistened in all their eyes, as they jabbered back and forth all the while they were hugging.

Finally Laura broke away. "Mom, Dad, these two young ladies here are your granddaughters, Mary and Patty. Give your grandparents a hug, girls." And hug they did. Laura let them hug and talk a little. "Now Mom, Dad, I want you to meet Sam Clark. Sam and his ex-wife lived about a quarter of a mile away from Eric and me for years, until Sam's wife left him. We've been close friends for years. All during Eric's disability, Sam pretty much kept our vehicles running, made sure we had wood cut and just generally watched over us for Eric, while he was away. He is one fine gentleman. He would not hear of me coming here, with the girls, alone. I'm sure glad he did, because I would've had my hands full, what with the luggage, on and off the plane and everything, not to mention, the moral support he's given all of us. Sam, may I present my parents, Mr. and Mrs. Morgan. You may just call them Joe and Mattie, which is short for Madeline."

Sam reached out his hand to Joe and shook it heartily and took Mattie's hand and kissed it. "So pleased to meet the both of you; you certainly do have one fine daughter. She is a tower of strength, and at the same time the most congenial person I've ever known. I'm here to tell you that she has faced every tough road that life has handed her. And yet, I've never seen anyone who is always smiling and looking for something good to do for someone. She is certainly a child of God."

"Well now, Sam that is quite a testimonial for anyone to give my daughter. I have always thought that she had a pretty level head on her shoulders, but I do have to admit that when she and Eric left to live in Alaska, I did have my doubts that she could stick it out."

"Well, she did, sir, a month shy of nineteen years. You and Mrs. Morgan—excuse me, Mattie—can both be proud of her." Sam grinned.

Mattie poked her husband in the ribs. "Hey Joe, these people have got to be tired and hungry; let's get out of here and get them home. I know these young ones will be happy to jump into Grandma's feather bed. I bet they'll be asleep before we're twenty miles down the road."

"Yep, you're right, Mattie. Let's go get their baggage and we'll be off. Good thing I put the luggage carrier on top of the car before we came."

"Yes, and you smarty, you even put a foam pad in the back of the wagon so the girls can lie down on the way home. I knew there was something I loved about you, you old coot." Mattie laughed as she said all this, and winked at Sam. "I guess being married to him for over sixty-five years has made me know a little something about him. Don't you think so, Sam?"

"I guess so, Mattie. Here, let me take that sign and put it in the waste can. We won't need it anymore. Let's go get the luggage; come on girls and hop to it."

After retrieving the luggage, Sam and Joe put it into the car top carrier, and put Mary and Patty in the back on the soft bedding. Then Sam opened the door for Mattie to get in front with Joe. As he held the door for her, she looked at him. "No, Sam, you sit up front with Joe. I'll sit in the back with Laura, so we can talk, and you and Joe can get acquainted."

"All right, Mattie," Sam said as he opened the back door for her and Laura. He then got in front with Joe.

"Anyone hungry? Do you want to stop and eat somewhere?" Joe asked as they started the drive toward home.

"Dad, it's pretty late to eat now and besides, we had a nice meal in Chicago. We had almost a three-hour layover there. Unless you and Mom want to stop?"

"No, honey, I'd just as soon get home. I'm tired. Sam, would you mind driving? It bothers me to drive at night, and we have precious cargo aboard. I'll stay awake and tell you where to turn."

"Sure thing, Joe, I don't mind. Pull over at the first safe place you can, and we'll switch."

The ride home consisted of getting reacquainted talk. No one asked any serious questions, and Laura asked if they could wait until tomorrow to get into what recently transpired, as she was too tired to get into it tonight.

When they arrived at the farm, Mattie went in and showed Sam where to deposit the sleeping children. Laura undressed them and covered them for the night. Mattie then said, "Laura, you sleep in your old room. Sam, come with me. I'll show you where my son Tom's old room is and you both can get some sleep. Joe and I will see you in the morning for breakfast. There are clean towels in the bathroom, all laid out for you. Make yourself at home. Goodnight."

She kissed Laura and said, "Good to have you home, honey. Sleep well. You too, Sam. If you need anything, just tell Laura. She can get it for you. I think she remembers where I keep things."

Sam and Laura both said goodnight and went into their respective rooms. As Laura crawled into her old bed and pulled the comforter up to her neck, she thought of the many years gone by since she last slept in this bed. *Much had happened in her life since then. She never dreamed she would be back here again, divorced, and left with two small girls to rear on her own. He was her first and only love, now she felt so empty. Thinking back over it all, Eric seemed to have feelings only for himself. Maybe she had lost some of her love for him, his being so distant with her. Sam and Sue were right. She did have needs. She was so confused, and tired.*

She pulled the comforter tighter around her neck and closed her eyes. Soon the only thing stirring in the room was the wispy thin curtain at the open window.

PROMISES TO KEEP

Chapter 37
꙳

Sam was awake very early, as that was his normal routine. He washed his face, shaved, dressed and ventured downstairs. Hearing someone moving about in the kitchen, Sam entered and found Joe sipping his morning coffee. He asked, "Did I wake you, Joe? I tried to be as quiet as possible. I'm an early riser and it just kills me to lie in bed once I'm awake."

"No, Sam, years of being a dairy farmer have taught me to rise early, too. I do have a hired hand now to do the milking for me, so I occasionally walk out to the barn and see if he is doing it right. I thought I might do that this morning, since he thought I might not be back from Rochester. Want to come along? I'll show you how a dairy farm works. Or maybe you know, do you?" Joe handed Sam a cup of coffee.

"Thanks, Joe." Sam reached for the coffee and added cream. "I don't know about dairy farming, but I'd like to know. My business has always been on the north slopes, working for an Oil Company. I started when I was fourteen; I lied about my age. But it was a good thing for me. I

263

learned a lot in thirty years."

"Sit and finish your coffee. Then we'll go out to the barn. Thirty years, huh? That's a long time to work in one place. Are you still working?

"Yes, sir! I had some time coming to me, so I took a month off so I could come with Laura and the girls on this trip. You see, sir, I think a lot of your daughter. In fact, I'm deeply in love with her. I have been for a long time. She, Eric, my ex-wife, and I have been friends for years, long before Eric had the accident and before my divorce. Then when Eric had the accident it was necessary for me to help them out. I was around their house quite a bit. I was a perfect gentleman though, as I was their friend. Then I saw how Eric was treating her and the girls, and it angered me somewhat, but I never said a word. I minded my own business. After my divorce, Eric started asking me to promise to take care of Laura and the girls, when he wasn't around. He more or less pushed us together, especially when he returned from Seattle and his rehab at the VA hospital."

"Did Laura know this? Did you let her know how you felt, when this was happening?"

"No, sir, I didn't. I kept my distance and never let her know how I felt. It was not my place to make advances to her; she and Eric were still married. I honored that fact." Sam sipped his coffee. "But that didn't change my feelings for her. I was always there for her, when she needed me to be, but she never knew how much I loved her."

"Does she know now, that you love her?"

"Yes, sir, she does. You see, when I found out that Eric was leaving her and the girls and that he had filed for dissolution of their marriage without her even knowing it, I came over to her house and asked her if it was true. She said it was, and was very upset about it. She was beside herself about what to do. I couldn't help myself. I held her to comfort her and I kissed her. Then I asked her to marry me. I told her I knew she still loved Eric, but maybe in time she could love me. After all, they were divorced. I want to take care of Mary, Patty, and her for the rest of my life."

"What did she say?"

"She told me that she loved me, but she was not in love with me. She still had feelings for Eric. She declined my offer. That's when I asked her if I might come along on the trip here, with them, just to be sure they were safe. But sir, I'm not going to give up. With your permission, I would like to ask her again to be my wife. I know this is quick, but she really has been alone for a long time, and has had to do everything."

"Sam, I would be proud to have you as my son-in-law, but it is not up to me or her mother, it is up to Laura to give you that answer. But you would have my blessings." Joe rose from the table. "Now let's go check on those cows in the barn. I hear Mattie getting up. She'll be out to fix breakfast soon."

Laura, hearing voices in the kitchen, got up, made her bed, went to the bathroom, and checked in on Sam. He was gone and his bed was made. *What a guy; he is sure a good guest;* she said to herself. *Eric would have never done that.* She hopped down the stairs after checking on the girls, who were still sleeping deeply, the trip having tired them out, not to mention the jet lag.

"Good morning, Mom! Where are Dad and Sam?"

"I think they're out at the barn. Dad said he wanted to check on the hired hand. He still worries about those cows. You know how he loves 'em. He worries about everything he loves. He said to me after we were in bed last night that he was very worried about you." Mattie looked at her with searching eyes for some sort of sign as to how she was really feeling. "Do you want to talk about things this morning? If not, that's okay, too. Maybe you would rather Dad and I be together when you talk about it?"

"Yes, Mom, that would be good, if you don't mind waiting?" She picked at the flowers on the table.

"Sam seems like a very nice man to me. Did you say you've been friends for years?"

"Yes, we have. You remember me writing about our neighbors, Sam and Connie, and the problems they had. Well, this is the same Sam. He is a good man. What do you want me to do to help with breakfast?"

"Set the table for the four of us. The girls can eat when they decide to get up, which I believe will be quite awhile, as tired as they were last night. Breakfast will be ready soon, and if the men aren't back inside yet, you can go out and get them."

Laura set the table and went out to the barn to call her Dad and Sam in for breakfast.

As they walked to the house, Laura put her arm around her dad. "Sure is good to be home here with you and mom. I'd like to talk with the both of you after breakfast. Sam, when the girls wake up, will you keep them busy until my folks and I have finished talking?"

"You know I will, Laura," replied Sam. "I think Mary and Patty have heard enough about what has happened. I'll bring them out to the barn to see the cows. They'll like that. You can turn on the back porch light when it's okay to bring them back into the house."

"Good idea, Sam." said Joe. "Now let's go eat breakfast. I'm starved!"

While they were eating, Laura began to tell all the details to her parents about what happened to create the divorce. She tried to be fair in telling both sides of the story. Sam helped out where she needed him to, and between the two of them, they presented a pretty true picture to Laura's parents. Joe and Mattie just sat at the table digesting all they had heard.

Laura cleared the breakfast dishes and poured them all another cup of coffee. Just as she sat down, Mary and Patty appeared at the kitchen door. "Morning, Momma, Sam, Grandma, and Grandpa," they chorused as they ran to hug everyone.

Mattie asked, "Did you sleep well? Are you hungry? I have some cereal cooked. How about a bowl and then you can get dressed, and Sam will take you out to the barn to see the cows and the rest of the farm animals. How does that sound?"

"Oh, goody," said Patty. "Come on, Mary, let's eat quickly."

"Now," said Joe as soon as Sam and the girls headed for the barn, "I want to talk with you, Laura, about Sam and his proposal of marriage."

Mattie looked surprised. "Proposal? What's this about a proposal? Laura you never said a word about that. Tell us about it!"

Laura told her parents about Sam's proposal and her answer. She also told them about her feelings when he asked her. Then she went on to reiterate on her thoughts while she was in bed last night. "Now, you both know all about it. What do you think I should do?"

Joe paused for a moment then sat back in his chair and looked straight at Laura. "Sam told me this morning about proposing to you, and he asked me for permission to marry you. I told him it was not up to your mother or me, but up to you to give him that answer. But I would like to say this to you before you decide. He does deserve a definite answer, you know. Last night while your mother and I were in bed we discussed what we thought you should do with yourself, now that Eric is gone. We know how lonely you have been for the past few years; we could tell it by your letters. We know you have many friends in Alaska, but there comes a time when you need an intimate relationship with someone to help you make decisions. Especially, when you have two daughters at the threshold of their teens. Your mother and I thought Sam was a wonderful friend last night when we met him. And after talking with him at length this morning, I whole heartedly agree with that. Just remember one thing. You are forty years old and have two children. What are your odds of finding a good man like Sam, especially up there in Alaska? Think about it. A good man doesn't come along every day. It's your decision to make. Your mother and I love you and will stand behind you in whatever you decide. Now, that is all I have to say. Do you agree, Momma?"

"Yes, my love, I do!" Mattie got up and hugged Laura. "I'm sure you will do the right thing. You know, you could stay here in New York with us. Mary and Patty could go to school here. It could be pretty tough for the three of you alone, in your home up there in Alaska. I know Eric was there and was incapacitated, but he was another adult in the house."

"I know we could, Mother, but the girls have only known Alaska since the day they were born. That is home to them and to me now, too." Laura wiped tears from her eyes. "I have the best parents anyone could ever want in the whole world." She walked over and turned the porch light on.

Sam returned from the barn with Mary and Patty in a flurry of excitement. They both seemed to be bursting to tell what they saw. Mary started, "Mom, did you know that all those cows were out there in the barn?"

Patty jumped in. "I can't believe how many cows Grandpa has! They were all lined up with their heads in what Sam called 'stanchions.'"

Mary said, "Yeah, and they had milking machines on them. Sam said that's what they were and he explained how they work. And golly, the cows didn't seem to mind."

Joe popped in and asked the girls, "Do you know why the cows don't mind the stanchions and the milking machines?"

Patty took this one, "No, why, Grandpa?"

"Because when the cows have grazed all day, they fill their udders with milk and when they get so full, it hurts the cows unless they are milked."

Patty answered, "Gee whiz! I didn't know that. That's amazing."

"Yes, Grandpa," said Mary, continuing their report. "Then Sam went on to explain how the milk was prepared for the big milk trucks that come here and take it to the dairy to be processed. It was so interesting!"

"And ah, and ah," stammered Patty, "then Sam told us how they separate the milk from the cream and make butter and have cream too. It was all so super. We don't have lots of cows in Alaska."

Mary then added, "Then Sam told us he learned a lot of that from you this morning. Is that true, Grandpa?"

"Yes, honey, Sam and I did have some conversation to that effect this morning, along with other things." Joe answered, and then added, "I also asked Andy, my hired hand, to save some milk so you gals can feed the barn cats later."

"Yippee!" squealed Patty, grinning from ear to ear, "we would like that!"

Mary went over to hug her mom and said, "Mom, I like it here. You must have had a lot of fun growing up here."

"I sure did, but I had chores to do, too. There is a lot of work on the farm. How do you suppose I learned how to garden, and can, and cook? From your grandma: she sews, and crochets too. Maybe she'll teach you two how to do that."

"Oh boy, this sure is terrific," Patty said.

"And it's sure different than Alaska!" Mary added. "I would like to have Grandma teach me to cook, sew, and crochet. But can she do it in three weeks or so?"

Grandma piped in. "Well, maybe we could talk your mother into moving back here, and then I would have lots of time to teach you those things."

"Oh no, we have to be in Alaska, so we can see our daddy when he comes back once a year, to go to the hospital in Seattle," Mary explained.

"And besides, we would miss Sam, and all our friends there, too," Patty added. "Sam and the boys take us a lot of places; we are like a family, and I'd sure miss them."

Mattie hugged the girls and whispered to them. "Well, maybe if you girls prayed hard enough, God would work things out for you."

Sam, overhearing what she whispered to the girls added, "I know I'm going to be praying for that, too!"

Mattie looked at Sam and suggested to her husband, "Joe, why don't you and I take the girls to see some of the countryside and some of the other farms around. Then we could take them to town, get some ice cream and do a little shopping for… anything they might see and want We need to spoil these girls a bit, you know."

"Sounds like a good idea; then Laura can take Sam around and show him some of her old haunts. I'm sure he would like to see where she grew up. Don't worry about us getting back too early; we'll probably take the girls to lunch in town and be home around suppertime. We need some bonding time with them. Is that all right with you, Laura?"

"Sure, Dad, have at it. Spoil them all you want. They deserve a little of that; they have been working hard lately around our house. You girls behave now, do you hear?"

"Yes, Mom," was their reply, and they went upstairs to get ready.

"Hurry it up, the car is leaving soon," joked their grandpa. "Now, Laura, you and Sam have a good time. Don't worry; we'll take good care of Mary and Patty"

The girls were downstairs in a flash. Mattie got her purse, and they were on their way.

Chapter 38

Sam and Laura watched as her parents pulled out of the barnyard and headed for town. Then turning to Sam, Laura asked, "Do you really want to go around and see some of my old hangouts, when I was a kid? They're not very exciting. I didn't date much; we always went in groups to do things. We used to have picnics at Moon Lake; there we could rent boats and explore all around the lake. We could swim, hike, whatever the moment moved us to do. We had fun, but it was nothing spectacular to do. What would you like to do, Sam?"

"Why don't we go down to the lake and rent a boat? You can show me the scenery and your secret spots."

"Okay, but don't say I didn't warn you. It might be boring."

"Never, not as long as I'm with you." Sam reached out to grab her.

She quickly side-stepped him, and as he missed her, she laughed and ran out the door, grabbing the truck keys off the key rack on the way out. "We'll take 'Nellie Belle. Come on, I'll race you to the shed."

They ran out, laughing all the way. When they reached the shed, Laura ran inside and jumped into the truck while Sam opened the overhead door. "Come on, slow poke! Jump in. I'll drive since you don't know the way. It'll be easier than telling you how to get there."

As she drove to the lake, they chatted about her parents and the farm. Then Sam asked her, "What did your parents have to say when you told them the rest of the story about Eric leaving for Costa Rica?"

"Not too much. They said they had felt that things were not just right from what I wrote to them in my letters, but they didn't know all of it. I also told them about your proposal of marriage to me." She looked at him to get a reaction; he just looked at her with love in his eyes.

"Well, then, that makes twice your dad heard it this morning. I told him while we were having coffee, before we went out to the barn. I asked him for permission to marry you and take care of you and the girls, for the rest of my life. I told him I loved you, and I do."

"I know you do, Sam, and I'm not surprised at your asking permission of my father to marry me, because that is so like you. You are so concise and prepared in everything you do, so down to earth honest and proper. Dad also told me I wasn't getting any younger, and maybe I wouldn't have many opportunities of marriage to come my way. He felt that I should think very hard on my decision. Oh, oh, here we are at the lake and the boat rental landing. We'll park here."

Sam helped her into the boat and sat in the middle seat to row. "Which way do I go? You'll have to direct me."

"Go to the left, over toward those rocks in the distance. We can beach the boat there and walk for awhile on the trails," instructed Laura and she started to chant for Sam, "Stroke! Stroke! Row harder!" They both began to laugh.

As Sam rowed the boat at an even pace, Laura trailed her hand down along the side in the water. Every once in a while she would flick water up at Sam's face. To retaliate he would splash her with a quick jerk on the oar.

Then they would laugh again. They soon came to the place Laura had indicated to beach the boat, and Sam pulled it up on the rocks. He then assisted Laura out onto the flat rock. "Let's sit down here and let ourselves dry off a bit in the sun. It's beautiful here and we might as well enjoy the scenery; we're in no rush."

Laura sat down on the rock and stretched out in the sun. "Oh my, but that sun feels good and this rock is so warm."

"It is beautiful here, and so are you, Laura," Sam said softly. "You're beautiful in every aspect of your life. You were so dedicated to Eric, even though there must have been times when you felt like running away. But you stood by your man and kept your wedding promises. I really admired you for that." Sam paused, picked up a rock and threw it into the water, watching the rings it made until they faded, then spoke again. "I only wish that Connie had done the same for me. It would have been so much easier for the boys to have a mom and a dad. They turned out pretty well, for what they've been through. It's hard on the kids, divorce is. They're pulled between two people that they love very much, and they don't want to take sides or hurt either parent. They hide a lot of feelings."

He sat down beside Laura and leaned nearer to her, "I know Patty and Mary are trying to be very grown-up. They have talked to David and Danny about it. The boys told me that they said they loved you and Eric very much, but they'll miss the family feeling they're used to having. My boys did, too. When we started doing things with you and the girls, while Eric was in Seattle, I saw a big change in my boys. They seemed to be more relaxed and at ease with themselves, as well as everyone around them. They told me more than once how much they love you, Mary, and Patty. And they aren't the only ones who feel that way. I do too, but of course you already know that to be true." He then reached down and picked her up and held her in his arms, closer to him. "I've felt this love for you for a long time. With Eric pushing me and making me promise to take care of you and the girls, it was like waving a red flag in front of a bull; I had to advance."

Sam leaned down and kissed her gently. Then he pulled her to him and laid her back on the rock and kissed her again, passionately. He held her close and kissed her neck and then again on the lips, whispering in between kisses, "Laura, I do love you and I want you so badly. Please marry me, so I can have your body next to mine, to satisfy my deepest desires."

He continued with the kisses, his hands caressing her body, pulling her closer to him with each kiss. She returned his kisses with fire in her lips, pressing her body closer to his, her breathing coming in short gasps for air. But she pushed him back away from her. "No, Sam, we can't do this now. As much as I want you to put out this fire I have deep within me, which I haven't felt for such a long, long time, we can't. Not now. But yes, yes, I will marry you, and then we can. I want it to be right. Sam, you can't know how much it hurts me to tell you to stop, I want you so badly."

Sam pulled back and looked her in the eye, "Did I hear you right? Did you just say 'yes' to my plea to marry me?"

"Yes I did!" She kissed him gently and caressed his face. "My love, my dear sweet man, yes, I will marry you. And let's do it here, so my parents can be our witnesses. I want them to know that Mary, Patty, and I will be safe and secure with someone who will love us forever and take care of us without question. I do love you, Sam Clark."

"Laura, I want to shout and scream and jump up and down, but I don't want to leave your arms right now. I want to lie here with you, holding each other like we are until this raging fire within me has subsided, and that may be quite awhile." He kissed her again. "Mrs. Laura Clark. Doesn't that sound good? And yes, let's get married as soon as possible, so your parents can see that we are going to be all right, married to each other. I know now you love me, and that our passions run high, but I know someday you will learn to say that you are *in love with me.* Then it will be complete. I'm a patient man and I can wait for that."

Laura whispered back to him, "Yes, the way Eric left me hurt a lot, Sam, but then the hurt turned to anger." She thought a bit, and told him she felt used. After all she and Eric had been through—building the house, scrimping and saving, going through the birth of both the girls, and her being alone with Mary and Patty most of the time, while he was off doing his thing. "Work was one thing, but we were left alone a lot while he went off to hunt and fish. I felt betrayed. Half of my life had walked away from me. For the half that was left, I didn't have a clue what I was going to do with it. And to be honest with you, having you around when Eric was gone did make me feel secure. I never worried about what was going to happen to us, if something happened to Eric. You were like a rock I could stand on, and not sink into the uncertainty of what was coming next." Then she reached up and kissed him, sealing the statements she just made.

They lay on the sun-warmed rock in each other's arms until the sun got high in the sky and became too warm for them. They decided to forgo the walk, return to the truck and head to town for blood tests, and then to find out where they could get a marriage license.

Sam thought, oh no, will I have to wait for another four days or so before I can have her? There was a lot to do to keep them busy though; they'd have to tell Mary and Patty, tell Laura's parents, which they were sure would be no surprise. Then they would have to decide where they were going to live when they returned to Alaska, and just how they would tell Eric when they got there.

Laura showed Sam the way into town and the doctor's office where she and her family had gone for years. As they pulled up in front of the office, Sam said to Laura, "Are you sure you want to come here to get the blood tests for the marriage license? What will these people think about you, just having Eric leave you, and the next week you're getting blood tests to marry someone else?"

Laura pinched his cheek. "Silly, the news of my divorce has not hit this area yet. I'm sure that mom and dad didn't tell anyone. For all the people here know, I've been divorced for quite some time. Besides, we're not staying around here. We'll be heading back to Alaska soon. The people I'm more concerned about will be in Sterling and Soldotna."

"Yes, I guess you're right about that. But most of the people up there have known for some time now the circumstances and what has gone on, so maybe it won't be so bad."

"Good afternoon," the girl at the reception desk spoke as they entered. "May I help you folks?"

"Yes, you can." Laura spoke first: "My fiancé and I are here from Alaska, visiting my parents, and we would like to be married while we're here. We'd like to have our blood tests, and then some information as to where we could go to obtain a marriage license. Before I left for Alaska nineteen years ago, Dr. Ward was our family physician. Is he still practicing here?" She chuckled. "Just listen to me blather on. I must be excited! My name is Laura Adams; back then it was Morgan. This gentleman is Samuel Clark; he has lived in Alaska since he was thirteen years of age. His hometown was in Minnesota. My parents, Mr. and Mrs. Joseph Morgan, know him and approve of our intentions to get married. I'm a licensed nurse in Alaska. Do we need to make an appointment for the blood test, or can we have the blood drawn and go from there?"

"Mrs. Adams and Mr. Clark, please have a seat while I check with the doctor, as to what we can do. It'll only be a few minutes."

As the waiting room was fairly empty, Laura and Sam had no trouble finding a seat next to each other. They sat down to await the news, whether or not they could get the blood test today. It wasn't very long before a man of about sixty-five, with a big warm smile and graying hair, appeared at the waiting room door and called, "Laura Morgan Adams and friend, would you come in please?"

Laura and Sam rose and headed for the door. Holding the door for them was Dr. Ward. "Laura Morgan, it has been nineteen years since I've seen you and you are just as pretty as you ever were. How are you anyway? Let's step here into my private office. I hear that marriage is on the horizon for you. Is this the lucky man?"

"Yes, sir," said Sam, extending his hand for a handshake. "Sam Clark… and I am one lucky guy, I can tell you that for sure. It's good to meet you, Dr. Ward; Laura told me all about you while we were in the waiting room. I'm very pleased to meet such a wonderful man."

"Sam, this is one special gal. I hear about her from her father and mother all the time. She's a strong person, but a very kind-hearted one at the same time. She is a gem. I knew her first husband only a short time. It was too bad about his accident, but I am sure he has found a way to keep himself in one piece and hurdle his handicap. But it's a pity it had to be at the expense of his family. So you two want to get married? Sounds like a very good idea to me." Dr. Ward was grinning. "You are looking at me with questions on your faces."

He told them he must confess. "I ran into Laura's mom and dad at lunch, met the children, and they are sweet as can be, and full of information." They girls told me non-stop about their daddy going to Costa Rica, to teach the word of God to people who didn't know our Lord. And that he made Sam promise to take care of them and their momma when he wasn't around. They like you, Sam, and your boys, and you all have fun when you are together. But that they would always love their daddy and that he promised to see them once a year in Alaska, when he came back to Seattle for his check up.

"Now I would say that they have been very well informed, in the right way, so that you two should have no problem whatsoever getting married so soon. By the way, your mom and dad filled me in on the rest and don't worry, I'm the only one who knows how long it's been since you were divorced. I even told Mary and Patty that they shouldn't tell anyone else around here, what they told me. I said they would find out in their own good time. I made them cross their hearts and hope to die, point their finger to the sky. I even went so far as to give them the zip the lip sign. And by the way, "Congratulations and good luck to you both."

"Well, Dr. Ward, you certainly did tell us a whole lot. Thank you!" said Laura, grinning from ear to ear. "I guess I was a pretty good mom after all. Either that or I have awfully smart kids. But tell us, can we get our blood tests and a marriage license? I've been away from here for a long time, as you know."

"I'll draw the blood now, while you're here, and take it to the hospital to get the results. I can have them back here the day after tomorrow. I'll call you, and then you can go to the court house and get your license." He reached for some syringes. "Who is going to be first?"

After the blood was drawn, they paid for the service, thanked Dr. Ward, and were off to the farm once again. When they pulled in, Mattie came out of the house and told them that they had run into Dr. Ward while they were having lunch and what the girls had said to him. "My land, child, they took to old 'DOC' Ward like ducks take to water. I think they just fell in love with him. He has a way about him, you know. He is one good old country doctor. This town will surely miss him when he's gone, not that he's going any place, just a figure of speech." And she chuckled.

"We know, Mom; we talked to him this afternoon, too."

Mattie had a surprised look on her face, "Where in the world did you see him? I thought he was going back to the office after lunch."

"He did!" Sam said, "And was there when we stopped in to get blood tests. I asked Laura to marry me again and this time she said 'yes'! Made me a happy man! Now all we have to do is tell the girls and Joe."

"Joe will be the easy part," said Mattie, "Mary and Patty may be a little more difficult."

"I know. That's why I wish you would let me tell them, Laura. May I have your permission to do that? I think I can do it easier than you could right now. Let me try."

"Sure, Sam, you do have a way with words; you talked me into marrying you, didn't you? Not that I put up much of a battle." Laura smiled and rubbed his face. "You are a love."

"I know it! I'm just one big sweet guy, because I have the best luck in the world to have you accept my proposal of marriage. Where are the girls, Mattie?" Sam asked, grinning and squeezing Laura.

"Oh, they're in the house telling Joe all about the wild life in Alaska. They have been chattering like magpies all day. They are sure wound up. They are all in the living room," indicated Mattie.

Joe looked up as they entered the living room and greeted them with a big smile. "I'm learning all about the wild life in Alaska. I certainly must say that these girls really know their stuff. They have been telling me what they've been told to watch out for, when they're outside by themselves. Someone has instructed them very carefully, I must say."

"You bet, Dad," Laura answered him. "Eric was very good at telling them how to read signs, know all the animals, their traits and just what they might do if cornered. It is very foolish not to know about those things, especially when you live there all the time."

Mary spoke up, "Yes, Momma, and not only has Daddy told us, but Uncle George, Sam, David and Danny too. David told us a lot when he took us on hikes and other places. He's almost like a big brother watching over us."

Sam took this opportunity to jump into the conversation, "What do you suppose those boys of mine are doing while I am here with you and your mom? I bet they really miss seeing the two of you. You've spent a lot of time together lately; what do you think?"

Patty jumped up and ran over to Sam and crawled on his lap. "Sam, you're so good to all of us and so are your boys. We have been together a lot, so I bet they do miss us, just as much as we miss them. We've had a lot of fun.

It's been a good summer!"

Mary interrupted her sister, "Yes, except for the news that Daddy will not be with us, that he is going away to Costa Rica. Sam, will you keep watching over us as Daddy made you promise to do?"

"Come over here, Mary," Sam motioned to her. "There is something that I want to discuss with the two of you. And I think that your mom and grandparents should hear it too. It concerns all of us. It's nothing bad, so don't get nervous."

Mary came over and sat on the couch beside Sam and Patty, and he put his arms around both of them. "You know that I love you two very much, as much as my own children, don't you?"

They both shook their heads yes.

"Well," continued Sam, "I did promise your daddy to look after you all when he wasn't around, and I kept that promise, as you well know. I knew that he was planning to go away, and that's why he wanted me to look after you. Well, I'd do that without even having to promise him, because you see, I love you and your momma very much. And now that your daddy will only be around once a year to visit you, I want to take care of all three of you. Not only because I promised your daddy, but also, because I do love you. You see, I'm in love with your mommy, and I asked her if she would be my wife so we could be a family; your mommy, you two, my boys and me. I hope that you both would agree. I'd never try to take your daddy's place in your heart, but I would be around for you to ask me anything or do anything for you, day and night. We'd be a real family. Maybe you could find a little love for me in your heart too, as I have a lot of love in mine for you. Your mommy said yes to all of this, and if it's okay with you girls, we'll get married while we are here at your grandparents."

Brightness started to come over their faces. Mary spoke, "Are you really serious about this? You aren't just joking with us?"

Patty jumped off her chair and clapped her hands. "I think it would be super! Momma wouldn't have to work so hard anymore, and David and Danny would be our brothers, for real."

"You don't have to call me daddy; I'll be Papa Sam if you like. You already have a daddy, who's very unselfish, in a way. Someday you'll understand why he is leaving." He went on to tell them, "He is doing that to regain his manhood and self respect, as well as giving you and your momma a chance to build new lives by not just taking care of him, day and night. He thought on this a very long time, and it took a whole lot of courage for him to do this. I don't want you to ever forget that. Your daddy is a very big man in that respect. He and I have been the best of friends for a very long time, and that will never change. When he comes to visit, he's to be with us as long as he chooses to stay. So what's the verdict? Will all three of you have me, for the rest of your lives, to have and to hold, in sickness and in health, 'til death do us part?"

Laura came over and joined the group, asking them all to stand up. She took the girls by the hands and huddled together with them for a bit. Then they made a ring around Sam and chorused, "We do, Papa Sam!" And they all laughed and hugged each other.

Mattie and Joe hugged too and wiped tears from their own eyes. "What a good thing this is going to be," said Mattie.

"Amen, to that," joined Joe. "Now let's all go out to a fancy place for dinner and celebrate. Dinner is on me." He walked over to Laura and held her tightly, giving her a kiss on the cheek and whispering in her ear, "You made a wise decision, both for you and the girls. It is time you got back to a normal life. Eric knew it. That's why he decided to leave. So have no regrets."

Then he took Sam's hand and patted him on the shoulder. "Son, you have taken a big worry off of Laura's mother and me, and I hope you know that! We would have worried ourselves to death about her up there in Alaska, so far away, alone, with Mary and Patty. Welcome to the family! Now let's go eat; we have wedding plans to make!"

Chapter 39

After dinner, they stopped and played some miniature golf until the girls started to wind down. Then they headed for home, to put the girls to bed and close out the day with a discussion of the wedding plans.

Laura started with her thoughts on the wedding. "Mom, I think that since it is so soon after my separation from Eric, we should just have a quiet ceremony in the church with just you and Dad, Mary, Patty, Sam and me. This is a second marriage for both Sam and me, and we don't need a big, elaborate affair."

"I agree with Laura on that," said Sam. "Actually, I've been married twice before, if you count being married to the same woman twice. I'm dead sure this one will last the rest of my life."

"I certainly hope so," said Mattie. "But I would like to have a small reception for some of our friends to help you celebrate the marriage, if that is all right with the two of you?"

"Sure, Mom, but you have to promise to keep it small, just your card-playing buddies and that is all. Maybe Doc Ward, too," said Laura. "Do you think Ruth and Tom might be able to come for the weekend? How about next Saturday afternoon at the church? We'll have just the family at the church. Tom and Ruth can stand up for us, and then we'll come back here for the reception. Small, just cake and ice cream, no more! Will that be all right with you, Sam? It's your wedding too, you know."

"That's fine with me. Will we be able to go away for a day or so after the reception? I'd like to rent a car and take you to Niagara Falls; that is the honeymoon place for a lot of people, isn't it? I'll make the arrangements early. Before we know it, the time for us to return to Alaska will be here."

"Good, then it's settled. A week from this coming Saturday is the date. I'll call Ruth and Tom," said Mattie, "and make the arrangements with the minister at the church. We'll go shopping and get you a new dress, Laura. And Joe can take Sam and buy him a new suit. That will be our wedding gift to you, or at least part of it."

Joe piped in, "Sounds like a winner to me! We can buy the girls each a new dress, too. We've all got to look good for this wedding."

"We should have the blood test back tomorrow, and then Sam and I can get the marriage license at the courthouse." Laura looked at her mom, "Just remember, you keep it simple and small! Now, I think we should all get some rest; we'll have a lot to do come tomorrow. Time is running short."

In the morning, Mattie was up early and in the kitchen starting breakfast. When Laura came downstairs, she kissed her on the neck. "Is Dad up yet? I bet he and Sam are out in the barn. Mary and Patty are still sleeping; they really like that old bed upstairs. What can I do to help?"

"Not a thing, just grab a cup of coffee and talk to me. We're going shopping right after breakfast or do you want to check on your blood tests, first?"

"I'll call Doc Ward after breakfast and find out if he has them back.

Then we'll know how to plan the shopping trip. I don't think a new dress and suit is in order for us to wear to get married in; just a good pair of dress pants and a sport coat for Sam and a plain dress for me will be fine. I want things simple and easy."

"All right, you're calling the shots. Breakfast is about ready; give a call to Joe and Sam."

After breakfast, Laura called Doc Ward and the tests were back. "Sam, we can go to the courthouse for our license today, the blood tests are back," said Laura as she wrapped her arms around Sam's neck and kissed him. "Are you sure you want to go through with this?"

"I wouldn't have it any other way. This is going to make me the happiest man in the world. I can't wait until we get home to tell David and Danny."

"Oh, yes, I bet they'll be surprised. I bet they won't be the only people who are surprised either, if you know what I mean."

Mattie poured another cup of coffee and motioned it toward the happy couple. "Why don't we all go with you to get your license and then we can do our shopping for clothes before we come home? Girls, how would you both like a new dress?"

"I'd love it! We hardly ever wear a dress in Alaska, only on special occasions," Mary replied excitedly. "Wouldn't you Patty?"

"Well this is a special occasion, so let's get ready and go!" Joe said. Mother did you call Tom and Ruth this morning? Are they coming?"

"Everything is set; I even called the Reverend Cain about the church and the service a week from Saturday. Let's move out. We've got lots of shopping to do!"

Sam set his empty cup in the sink. "While you gals are shopping, Joe and I'll go and make arrangements for Niagara Falls."

"Good idea, Sam, but don't forget, you and I are going to get you some new duds too! We can't let the women folk out-do us, can we?"

It was a big day for all and by the time they got home, it was quite late, so Grandma and Grandpa and the girls went to bed. Laura and Sam decided to stay up for a little while, to discuss some things.

"Want a cup of tea?" asked Laura. "I could sure use one; it has been a hectic day! I can't believe we've been here almost two weeks now and so much has happened. Are you sure we're doing the right thing?" She went into the kitchen and put on the kettle to boil, Sam followed her.

She was standing, looking out at the barn, when Sam said, "Does looking out there at the barn bring back memories of when you met Eric? Are you having some doubts? I truly believe, with my whole heart, that what we are to do, is to get married. There is no way you could make it alone in Alaska with Mary and Patty. You've had to work so hard these past eight years or so; now it's time someone took care of you. I know you had no choice. Eric was paralyzed. It was an accident. No one could have changed the outcome of that accident, no matter how much we all wanted him to recover fully. You did what you had to do." He walked over, put his arms around her waist and turned her around to him. He pulled her ever so close and kissed her with undying love. She returned his kiss and they remained locked in each other's arms kissing until the teakettle whistled them back to reality.

As she removed the teakettle from the fire, she whispered to Sam, "Oh Sam, I wish it was a week from Saturday right now. I have no doubts, whatsoever, about us getting married. I want you so badly! Did you make arrangements for our honeymoon trip today?"

"Yes, I did. But our first stop will be the first motel located outside of town. I have a feeling that you and I are going to be on one long honeymoon, probably for the rest of our lives."

Laura made the tea and they carried it out onto the front porch and sat on the swing. As Laura sat down she asked, "Sam, how do you think the people of Sterling are going to take the news of you and I getting married so soon after Eric leaving me?"

"Our true friends, Eric's friends, our close acquaintances, will not be surprised. By that I mean Sue, Agnes and George. They have known what Eric's plans were for some time now. He loved you so deeply that he couldn't see you wasting away and becoming something that you weren't.

"Even I could see you were changing toward the end of the time when he returned from Seattle. You'd been wondering about some of the things he said to you, and his making me promise to look out for you and the girls. He knew that I admired you for what you were, and that the admiration was turning to love. Sue and Agnes knew it too. And I am sure that George knew it, because he was with him in Seattle. George admired you too. He had to question Eric and ask him if this is really what he wanted to do.

"You were the only one who didn't want to see it. There will be those who will make something out of our marriage. They will say that we carried on an affair before Eric said he was leaving you. But we know different and we do not have to answer to anyone. Although, I must admit, there were times when I wanted to stay with you overnight and show you how much I love you. I'm sure it would have been easy enough for you to give in to me also. You've been alone for a long time. Eight years lying in bed with your husband, with no intimacy, had to be very hard on you. You were vulnerable to anyone who might show you love and affection. I think that is why Eric asked me to watch over you. He trusted me."

Sam kissed her again, rubbing his tongue lightly over her lips, saying, "I'm glad we're waiting until we're married. But you do , make it hard on a guy to wait."

She returned his kiss, "You best not do that. My bed is big enough for two and I'd hate to throw you out the door. We can wait one more week, can't we?"

Laura got up from the swing and walked to the porch railing, remaining quiet for a moment. "How are we going to tell Eric? Will we stay at my place or yours? I hate to change the girls so abruptly. Maybe we could let Eric and George stay at my place, with the girls, until they leave for Costa Rica, and I'll move into your house, with you and the boys. Do you think that will set well with Eric?"

"Laura!" Sam walked over to her, put his arms around her and looked into her eyes. "When we talk with Eric again, you will be Mrs. Sam Clark, not Laura Adams. Your place will be with me. That's all there is to it. I will share his daughters with him, but not you. You will be my wife, from now on, not Eric's. You'll have my last name to prove it, and I don't share."

"You're right," she whispered, "'Mrs. Sam Clark' does sound pretty nice. I don't want you to adopt the girls though. They will love you as they do Eric, I know, but I don't want to take his name from them. The only way that will happen is when they marry. I just can't take that away from him."

"No, you can't," said Sam as he put his arm around her shoulder, and they sat back down on the swing, drinking their tea and watching the moon come up over the trees along the barnyard fence.

"You know, Sam, Tom and Ruth will probably be here soon. Ruth can sleep with me; will you mind sharing your room with Tom? It's a good thing that mom has twin beds in there now. You won't mind, will you?"

"No, as long as he doesn't snore too loud and keep me awake. I'll need all the rest I can get before the wedding, because I don't intend on sleeping at all on our wedding night," he whispered, as he pulled her tight to him.

"Oh you, you sound just terrible. But I like the way you talk." She laughed. "Are you ready to turn in now? I mean, you go to your room and I go to mine."

"If that is the way it has to be, so be it." He got up and pulled her after him by her hand. He left her at her bedroom door with a kiss to think about all night.

Chapter 40

The next morning the sun began to peek into her window. Her eyes were barely open when the bedroom door flew open, and two bodies came hurtling through the air and jumped on her bed. "Hey! You! Get up. We drove all night to see you." Ruth was shouting.

Tom started to tickle her. "This'll wake her up. She never could take tickling."

They all tumbled around on the bed and hugged and kissed each other, laughing, "How long has it been?" asked Ruth.

"Too long," added Tom. "Get up, get dressed and come downstairs. Mom has coffee brewing, and she's making pancakes. I'm hungry, and I need coffee to keep me awake. I want to meet this really great guy that Mom says you have," and he raced downstairs.

Soon Mary and Patty were peeking into the bedroom and looking at Laura and Ruth with sleepy eyes. "What's going on, Momma?"

"Oh nothing, it's just your Aunt Ruth and Uncle Tom acting like gooney birds. Go get dressed now; Grandma is making her famous pancakes. Is Sam up yet? If he isn't, knock on his door, go in and wake him up."

Ruth poked Laura and said to her, as the girls left the room, "Tell me what's happened. Eric has left you, and you're getting married already? What gives? I know that you have spent a lot of time alone with the girls lately, but I thought it was because Eric was in Seattle for rehab. Come on and tell me. I'm sure that Tom will find out from Dad."

"Let me go wash my face and brush my teeth. I'll be right back. You make the bed, then I'll tell you all about it as I get dressed." Laura jumped out of bed and rushed into the bathroom. She was back in a jiffy and began to tell Ruth the story as short and sweet as she could. "That's it in a nutshell and Mom can tell you more when you two are alone."

As they started downstairs, the girls were coming out of the bathroom and heading for their room. Mary said, "Mom, Sam said we should get dressed, make our bed and go down for breakfast. He'll be down shortly. He said we should tell you that. Okay?"

"Okay." Laura answered, as she and Ruth continued to the kitchen.

Coffee was ready, and Tom was downing his first cup. Mattie was busy cooking pancakes and bacon. The kitchen smelled like old times, when Mattie used to cook for the family every morning.

"Gee, Mom," said Ruth, "I haven't smelled anything this good for a long time. It brings back old memories. Where's Dad? Out nosing around the barn, checking on the hired hand, I suppose. Tom, are you going out? Tell Dad breakfast is going to be ready soon."

Laura poured three cups of coffee for her Mom, Ruth and herself. "Maybe I best put on another pot; we'll need it." She poured the remainder of the coffee into the carafe, emptied the grounds and made a fresh pot. She knew Sam would be ready for a cup when he came down. He didn't function too well until he had his first cup of coffee in the morning. She no sooner got the pot on when he entered the kitchen.

"Morning you; here's your go power. Sam, I'd like you to meet my sister, Ruth. Ruth, this is Sam."

Sam took Ruth's hand, leaned down and kissed the back of it. "It's so nice to meet you. Laura has told me all about you and I feel like I know you already. I do see a family resemblance. Where's the masculine part of the family? Out in the barn, I presume? If you ladies will excuse me, I'll take my coffee and join them. Nice meeting you, Ruth. We'll get better acquainted later." He headed for the barn.

"Hey, what a nice man he is. You did good, girl. Oh, oh, Mom, I hear the patter of little feet, so get ready because the girls are coming. Have you got some pancakes ready to eat yet? We'll let them start. Here, let me help fix their plates, Laura," said Ruth. "This is the first time they have met their Auntie Ruth. My, but you girls sure are pretty. Better watch out for your Uncle Tom. He'll tease you terribly, but he means nothing by it. He'll love you, too."

Mary and Patty just finished their breakfast as the men returned from the barn. They were all holding out their coffee cups for refills. Laura told the girls to go wash up, and then they could go out and find the kittens. "Breakfast is ready, men, so wash and sit down to eat." They all seated themselves. Laura, looking at Tom, said, "I suppose Dad introduced you to Sam, so now will you say Grace?"

All enjoyed conversation and food and the morning seemed to fly by. Tom and Ruth were filled in with the plans for the wedding, and the men found things to do while the women stayed busy, talking in the kitchen. Mattie baked several kinds of goodies while Laura and Ruth caught up on years gone by.

"There is nothing better than a good old conversation between sisters. Letters are nice over the miles, but face-to-face is the best thing I know." Ruth patted Laura's hands. "I have missed you Laura. Alaska is a long way away, and the accident happening to Eric made it impossible for you to travel back here to visit, and conditions at home made it impossible for us to visit you. When you had your babies, school was still in session and I couldn't come to visit you then, and after that, I had summer school to keep me busy. I really regret not seeing the girls until now. I have planned to stay here with mom and dad while you and Sam go away for a few days. You are going to get away for a honeymoon, aren't you?"

"Ruth, I really hope I am not making a mistake by marrying Sam so soon after Eric let me know he was leaving us. I know mom told you that Sam proposed to me the day he found out that Eric was leaving me, and that I refused him, saying that I still loved Eric, even though the letter from the lawyer hurt me deeply. I had been unhappy with Eric's actions toward me for some time. I just considered his attitude was due to his condition. Who wouldn't feel depressed and grumpy facing what he did every day?"

"What did Sam say when you refused his marriage proposal the first time? I am sure he knew what was happening with you and Eric. Everyone else did."

Laura cleared her throat. "He said that he had admired me for a very long time, and he wanted to take care of me and the girls for the rest of his life. And maybe in time I would learn to love him too, as I loved Eric. I said I loved him then but I was not 'in love' with him. Then he kissed me and I felt feelings that I had put away a long time ago. It felt good. Then I wondered, was I confusing love with lust? Then he insisted on coming here with us. So I said all right, and I'm glad I did. It would have been a rough trip alone."

"Mom told me what Dad said to you when you asked his advice and I concurred with Dad." Then Ruth said, "After meeting Sam, I also think it's a wise thing to do. You two should get married. I'm all for it and Tom agrees with us, too. So go for it and have no regrets. Sam seems like a man of action and maybe with him you will come back home more often. Yes, ma'am, the rest of the Morgan family says, go for it! Isn't that right, Mom?"

"Amen to that! Here, let's celebrate with these fresh baked cookies and a cup of tea."

They all raised their teacups and cookies and made a toast. "Here's to having Sam in the family!"

The time just seemed to fly by for all concerned and before they knew it, the day of the wedding arrived. Laura, Sam and the girls had been in New York for three weeks. When everyone came down to breakfast that morning, there was a nervous feeling in the air. Mattie announced that all they were going to have was a continental breakfast: coffee, juice and rolls, and cereal for the girls.

She had the refrigerator full of sandwiches and salads for after the wedding. And of course, there was a wedding cake sitting on the dining room table. The house was decorated with bells and a few ribbons. After all, Laura wanted to keep the wedding simple. Mattie had called in a neighbor to help her with the serving of the food after the ceremony, and to be at the house to greet the guests coming for the reception.

Laura hugged the girls as they ate their breakfast then told them to take their baths, as she wanted the bathroom to be empty so everyone else could have a turn at getting ready. They had a schedule all made out. Things were in order. At the table, as they were all finishing their tea, she asked, "Is anyone nervous besides me? I thought this would be a simple thing to do. After all, I've been through it once."

Sam spoke up, "What about me? It was twice with the same woman!" He chuckled. "I know this time it is going to be for keeps. So let's get the ball rolling. The wedding is at one o'clock. We don't want to be late for our own ceremony."

Everyone got around in good time. They headed for the church, all spit and polish, dressed up fine. Sam whispered to Laura, "This is it love. We're starting a new chapter today in our lives. We're going to be the happiest family around. That is a promise." He hugged her and kissed her softly. "There will be more of that tonight when you will be Mrs. Sam Clark."

The ceremony went off well, and they all returned to the house to meet the friends of Mattie and Joe. They enjoyed the wedding cake and ice cream. Tom called Sam over to one side and inquired of him, "Do you have a rental car or are you using one of dad's for your honeymoon trip?"

Sam grinned, "Joe thinks we are going to use his car, but really, I have a car from a rental service being brought out at about five o'clock. I didn't want any funny business being pulled on us. We have a ways to go to Niagara Falls. So don't you say anything to anyone."

Tom chuckled. "No I won't; I just wondered, because Dad's car is all decorated with cans tied to the bumper and 'Just Married' written all over it. Will everyone be surprised? Believe me, I won't say a word; I know how important it is for you two to get out of here early. Don't worry about Mary and Patty. They are in good hands."

"I know that, and believe me, Laura and I appreciate all you have done for us. I promise to take care and love all three of them, for the rest of my life. They're as important to me, as they are to all of you. Thank God for this family." Sam shook Tom's hand and patted him on the back. "Now I want to look for Laura and see if she has everything ready to go. We're getting out of here!"

Sam found Laura and told her to get ready. "Kiss the girls good-bye, and let's thank everyone for all they've done. The car will be here shortly."

They raised a toast to everyone and thanked them all, and then Sam hugged and kissed the girls, and told them they would only be gone for a few days. "Remember, on Thursday we'll be flying back to Alaska. So you be sure and tell Grandma to have you all ready to go, okay? Your mom and I are counting on you."

A knock at the door announced the arrival of the rental car. Laura and Sam ran out to the car, got in, and started the engine.

"Hey, wait a minute," said Joe. "Aren't you taking any luggage? I thought you were taking my other car."

Sam grinned. "Sorry, Joe, Laura told me that you and your friends would probably have something up your sleeve and try to pull something on us. We beat you to the punch. I took our luggage up to the rental place and rented a car, and put the luggage in the trunk without you knowing about it. Sorry to spoil your fun! We'll see all of you on Tuesday, which is three days from now. Remember, we're leaving for Alaska on Thursday. See you soon."

Laura snuggled up against Sam as soon as they were on the road. "Well, Mr. Clark, we did it. Are you sorry? Do you have any regrets? I know I don't. I feel very happy to be Mrs. Sam Clark. I know you told me that, in time, I would learn to love you. I do now. I will always have a place in my heart for Eric, as he was my first love. That will never change. After all, we did have two daughters and have been through a lot together. But I know that he needs to go on with his life, and we need to go on with ours. So don't worry about me not loving you. I do; *I'm in love with you.*" She leaned over and kissed him on the cheek as he was driving. "There will be more when we get where we're going for the night, lots more. By the way, how much longer are we going to drive?"

"About another hour or so," Sam said as he squeezed her hand. "I hate to tell you this, but I didn't make arrangements for Niagara Falls. I found some nice little cabins on a lake that is off the main road. They are real nice, and there is a main lodge there too with a nice restaurant. I didn't want to wait to get to Niagara Falls. We'd never get out of the room anyway. I plan to love you like you haven't been loved in a long, long, time." He kissed her hand and moved up her arm. "That is only a start of where I'm going to kiss you. You will beg for mercy before morning."

"Oh hurry, Sam; it's been a long time! I hope I don't disappoint you. You know it's funny. Here my folks think we're going to Niagara Falls. Guess we pulled a trick on them. There'll be no tricks tonight, only treats." She reached over and ran her hand on his leg. "Look out world, here we come: Mr. and Mrs. Sam Clark! And he's all mine, now!"

In about an hour, Sam carried her across the threshold of the little cabin. Their perpetual honeymoon was about to begin.

Chapter 41

It was late Tuesday afternoon, and Ruth and Mattie were sitting on the front porch swing watching Patty and Mary play in the yard with the kittens. They were busy talking when Ruth poked her mom. "Look who's coming. Mary, Patty, look who's driving up the driveway. It's your mom and Sam. Put the kittens back in the box before you run out to see them. I figured they'd be pulling in here sometime this afternoon."

Ruth and Mattie got up and walked toward the driveway, Mattie cautioning the girls, "Don't get out onto the drive. Be careful now; wait until Sam stops the car." She waved a cheery hello. "Welcome home, you two!"

The girls were both chattering at once, "Mommy, Sam, where did you go? Did you have fun? We're ready to go back to Alaska. Grandma wants to keep us, but she did pack our bags. We do have tomorrow though, don't we? We've had so much fun while you were gone. Uncle Tom had to leave, but grandma said she and grandpa would take Aunt Ruth home when they take us back to the airport. Won't that be fun?"

"Sounds like you two have been giving Aunt Ruth and Grandma a run for their money. Did you have fun; did you miss Sam and me? We really had a nice trip," Laura said as she hugged and kissed Mary and Patty, and grinned at Sam.

Sam hugged them too. "Have you been helping your grandparents with the chores? You sure don't look any the worse for wear. Looks like they have taken pretty good care of the two of you, are you ready to go back to Alaska?"

Patty couldn't wait another second. "Could we take the kittens back with us? Pleeeeease?"

Mary poked her and said, "Of course not, silly, we would have to keep them in the house, and they are barn cats. At least that's what Grandpa said." Then she paused and lowered her voice. "I'm ready, because I'm afraid Daddy will be gone when we get home, and I want to see him before he leaves for Costa Rica. So does Patty, but she's too shy to say so."

Laura went to them, stooped down and hugged them both. "Don't you worry now; you will see your daddy before he leaves. Sam and I have talked it over and we're going to see if he and George want to stay with you, at our house, until they get ready to leave."

"We need to ask George if he wants us to look after his place, or what he is going to do with it," said Sam. "Maybe David and Danny could keep an eye on it for him. There's a lot we need to talk about before he leaves. So don't worry, we will be seeing him. But right now, I need to have someone follow me into town so I can return this rental car. Is Joe around?"

"I think he's in the house napping," said Mattie. "I'm sure he'd be happy to go with you. That'll give all of us women some time to talk. Besides, Laura should finish packing all your things, in order to leave early Thursday morning. We must get all your clothes washed up and ironed so they can be packed. I hate to see it, but I know you have to go. Sam,

297

I'm so glad that you will be with Laura and the girls to look after them; now Joe and I can rest easier."

"You're not half as glad as I am," Sam chuckled, "and it will be nice for the boys and me to have a family again. I know my boys have missed it; they really like being with Laura, Mary, and Patty. They have told me many times how much fun it is when we're together, like a family. And now they will have you, Joe, and your family too." He paused, looked over to Laura. "Laura go in and ask Joe if he will follow me to town to return the car, if you would please." Then he returned his conversation to Mattie. "You and Joe have been really nice to accept me so readily and I promise you, I'll love Laura and the girls with all my heart and I'll never leave them alone again. I have waited too long for the happiness I've had since Laura and I have been here. She and the girls shouldn't be alone in Alaska, or anyplace, for that matter. So let me assure you, that I will always be there for all of them."

Joe came out of the house with Laura. "So you need a ride back from town. I'm your man. Let's get going. I want to gas the car up and be ready to take you young folks to the airport Thursday. I sure don't want the old buggy to be running empty." He kissed Mattie. "We'll be home in time for supper, and you can count on that. Come on, son; let's get that car back."

Sam suddenly put his hands to his head. "Where is my brain? We could keep the rental car, and Laura, the girls, and I could drive back to the airport and leave it there. It would save you and Mattie a drive into Rochester."

"Nonsense. Do you think that Mattie and I would let you all go to the airport without taking you? It will give us that much more time together. We just couldn't say good-bye to all of you here. No, we'll take you to the airport," Joe insisted. "Besides, it will give me some time alone with you for a fatherly talk." He was chuckling to himself as he walked to his car.

The men headed for town and the ladies helped Laura get her clothes clean and packed to take home. Laura was helping the girls gather up their toilet articles from the bathroom when Mary said to her, "Momma, we've had the best time here with Grandma and Grandpa. Why haven't we come here before?"

"Well Mary, if you recall, you two youngsters were too small to travel with when you were first born, and we had a lot of work to take care of in Alaska. It kept your daddy and me both busy trying to keep our heads above all the expenses we had, and when your daddy had the accident in 1984, it was next to impossible for us to come after that."

Mary, being wise for her years, waited until Patty went to take some clothes to her grandma for the washer, and then said to Laura, "Momma, do you think that Daddy is leaving us because he wants us to be able to travel and visit? Not just to be home taking care of all the chores and him? I overheard him talking to George one night when he thought we were in bed asleep, and he said he wanted to give us a chance to have a life of our own. What did he mean, Momma? He told George that he loved all of us so much that to go away would be the best thing he could do now."

"I know, Mary, and you will understand it better when you get older. He does love us all very much. But this is something he has thought through for a long, long time and has decided it would not only be best for us, but for him as well, no matter how much we all hurt initially. He needs to go away and make a new life for himself, without us there to coddle and pamper him. He really is a strong-willed person and will do what he sets his mind to do and no one and nothing can change it for him." Laura hugged her as she talked. "I hope you understand and will never forget how much he loves you and Patty."

"Yes, we both know how much Sam loves you and both of us too. He has talked with us and said he'll never try to fill our lives with love like Daddy has for us, but we are to understand that he does love us and he wants to take care of us. We don't have to call him daddy, but we should call him Sam, if that's okay with you, Momma."

"Of course, you silly girl, and why wouldn't it be? There are many kinds of love, and we are fortunate to have had them all in our lives. We've had the love of your father—for both you and Patty, and me too. I am sure that will never change, for I know your father too well. Then we all have the love that Sam has for us, and because your father will never give in and change his mind about what he must do, it is wise for us to accept the love Sam has for us. We all have loved Sam for a long time, including your father. They have and always will be the best of friends. Sam has cared for us, watched out for us and now he is the head of our family. He is the one who will be making the decisions for us, of course, after talking it over with us first. But the final say-so will be his. Now let's get busy and get this packing done. Okay? Then you and Patty can go out to the barn and play with the new kittens. This will be the last day you will have with them. We leave in the morning for home."

After the packing was finished and the suitcases were stowed in the car, everyone took their baths before settling down in front of the fireplace. The girls snuggled between Grandpa and Grandma, soaking up the feeling of closeness to last them until they would see each other again. Once they fell asleep, Sam carried them to bed. Laura kissed her parents, saying she was turning in as well.

After climbing the stairs, taking in every part of the house she grew up in, she peeked in on the girls. Sam was tucking them in bed so gently that it brought tears to her eyes. As he finished kissing the girls, he turned and saw her brushing tears from her eyes. He came toward her, put his arms around her, kissed her gently and whispered, "It's going to be okay. I know the thoughts and feelings you have now, and I know, given time, you will love me as much as you have—and still do—Eric. We'll be just fine." He picked her up and carried her into their bedroom.

Chapter 42

The next morning, the alarm went off early and everyone dressed and went down to breakfast. No one spoke except for the hugs and the first "good morning" to each other. They attributed it to the fact that everyone was still sleepy, but no one wanted to talk, because they were afraid of breaking down and crying. Joe and Mattie hated to see Laura, Sam, and the girls leave, almost as badly as they hated to leave. After breakfast, they hurried to Rochester to catch the plane to start their long trip home to Alaska. There was not much time for talking at the airport, as they said their good-byes and rushed through security. They kept turning back to look at Joe and Mattie as they scurried down the corridor to their gate. They turned and gave one last wave and blew kisses before boarding the plane.

Sam secured their carry-on bags overhead, while Laura fastened the seat belts for the girls and gave them pillows, along with some books if they got bored. Then Sam and Laura took their seats across the aisle. Laura sat next to the window and took Sam's hand as the plane left the ground.

The first leg of their flight home to Alaska was without incident. It was only an hour and a half before they would be in Detroit, their first stop. The girls were content to sleep and read their books. Laura and Sam both had mixed emotions. Leaving Laura's family was not easy, as they didn't know how long it would be before they could return again. And too, Laura was deeply concerned about how people would take to her and Sam being married while in New York.

Sam sensed her uncertainty. "What's on your mind that has you so quiet? This is a first for you. Are you sure you feel okay? "

"I was just thinking about what I am going to say to Eric when we get home. I'm wondering how he will take the news of our marriage." As she spoke she wrapped her arms around Sam's arm.

Sam reached over and laid his left hand on her arms and rubbed them gently. "You have nothing to worry about. Eric practically shoved us two together the whole last year before he went to rehab in Seattle. I think he expected us to get married while you were home. He knew I was going with you and the girls, and yes, I'm sure he knew I was going to ask you to marry me. You do know that I told him one time if he did not start to treat you better, I was going to take you away from him."

"You didn't say that to him, Sam, did you?" She raised her head and looked him in the eye.

"I sure did. Many guys would have liked to get next to you. You are too nice to realize that they knew Eric's situation and how he could not perform, and they were ready and willing to help you out in that department. Why do you think Eric always asked me to look after you and the girls when he was to be away? You are just too innocent and good to even think about such things. You were devoted to Eric, so you didn't play games."

"Sam, it's strange you would say that to me. Eric said something almost like that when we first met. He told me he loved me because I was innocent and pure, and he liked the way I didn't play games. He told me he had been with lots of girls before me, and they all wanted to play games, but I was different. When I told him I loved him, I was sincere."

"You are! There is no one I've ever met in my life who is like you. You are one special woman! Any man would love to have you for his wife. I know I sure did, and now you are my wife. So don't worry yourself over how to tell Eric; he is expecting us to be married. You can count on that. After all, I think he planned it this way." He leaned over and kissed her. "So don't you worry yourself any; we'll still be as close to Eric as when you were married to him. After all, we've been friends for a very long time and that will never change."

"You know, Sam, I believe you're right in that respect. You, Eric, and I have always been close friends and looked out for each other. Yes, I do believe you are right!

"Sam, is David meeting us at the airport when we arrive in Anchorage?"

"Yes, that's our plan. I'll call him when we get into Detroit. We'll grab some fruit and water for the girls. Our next stop is Minneapolis/St. Paul, and we'll have a three-hour layover there. It might be best to wait to eat until then anyway. We can eat, and walk the girls around the airport, and then they'll be ready to rest on the flight to Anchorage. We'll get into Anchorage at 9:30 p.m., Alaska Time. By the time we get the luggage, and everything, it will be pretty late to start the three-hour drive home, so I'll ask David to get us some rooms at the hotel near the airport, and then we can start out for home the next day. Besides, we'll all be pretty tired and a good night's rest won't hurt any of us, even David."

"Oh Sam, you do think of everything! I'll be happy to be home again, and I promise I'll not worry about telling Eric about our marriage. It'll be fine, I'm sure." She then laid her head on Sam's shoulder and hugged his arm once again

It wasn't long until the plane landed in Detroit. They gathered the girls and their carry-on luggage and found their connection gate for the next leg of the trip. Laura and the girls went to the rest room, and Sam headed to a phone to make the call to David. Upon leaving the ladies room, Laura purchased some fruit and water for the girls, and a couple of packaged sandwiches to eat on the trip to Minneapolis/St. Paul. They went back to the gate to wait for Sam. He soon appeared.

"Well, everything is all set with David. Things are fine at home, and he said it would be good to have us back."

"Did you mention to him that you and I got married while we were in New York?"

"No, I thought that news blast would best wait until we see him. I didn't want the word to pass around until you had a chance to speak to Eric. I didn't think you would want him to hear it from the grapevine."

"You're right there! I think it best he hear it from the girls and me. Here, I picked up a sandwich for us to eat while we're waiting to board." It was good to end that conversation. She gave the girls their sandwiches, and they waited for the call to board the plane.

When they arrived in Minneapolis/St. Paul, Sam found a locker to check the carry-on bags, and then they looked for a place to have a leisurely dinner. By now, the girls were getting a little antsy. They walked around inside the terminal to keep themselves occupied and to stretch their legs.

When they found the restaurant, Sam asked the hostess for a window seat, so the girls could watch planes land and take off while they had their dinner. Once seated, he turned to them. "Once our next flight takes off it'll only be a little over six more hours until we'll be back in Anchorage. David is going to be at the airport to meet us. I bet you'll be glad to see him."

Mary spoke up first, "You bet, it was nice to go and visit Grandma and Grandpa, but I'll sure be glad to get home and sleep in my own bed."

"Me too," Patty chimed in. "Traveling is nice, but I miss all my things at home. And I miss Daddy, too; I hope he hasn't left for his trip yet. When is he going, Mom?"

"He and George will be leaving for Costa Rica soon. We'll be home in plenty of time for you two to see and visit with him and George, before they leave. Now eat your dinner and we'll soon be on our way again. We'll stay overnight in Anchorage and head for Sterling tomorrow morning. It'll be too late, and we'll be too tired to drive home tonight."

They finished dinner and boarded the plane for the last leg of their flight home.

David met his father, Laura, and the girls at the airport, as scheduled. After getting hugs and greetings out of the way, they went to pick up their luggage.

Sam asked David, "Did you make reservations for us at a hotel for the night?"

"Yes sir, I got two adjoining rooms. One with a King size bed for Laura and the girls, and one with two double beds, for you and me. I thought that it would be best to have adjoining rooms, so Laura and the girls would be close by."

"Good thinking, but Laura and I have some news for you. We got married while we were in New York State, and so the room with the King size bed she and I will use. You and the girls can use the one with the double beds. We'll put Patty and Mary in one bed, and you can sleep in the other; that way, you can keep an eye on them all night. Are you surprised?"

David grabbed his Dad and hugged him tightly. "That's wonderful news, Dad! But, do you think it's a little soon after Eric told Laura he was leaving? It didn't upset the girls, did it?"

"No, it didn't; they are tickled to have us as their family now. Laura and I explained everything to them. I can't begin to tell you how happy it made them to have a family again."

Then Sam explained to David all that happened in New York, and that Laura's parents felt good about it too. "As a matter of fact, her father said if she didn't accept my proposal, she was a foolish girl. So we had their blessings. The big thing now is that Laura has to break the news to Eric. I don't think it will come as a shock to him. I think he was hoping I would ask her to marry me, after he told her the divorce was final and he was going away. I would imagine that the whole town sort of expected us to get married."

Then he asked David, "Have you heard any rumblings about that sort of thing?"

"None at all. And I'm happy for all of us. It's fine with me to stay with the girls. You and Laura take the King size bed, for your first night together in Alaska as man and wife. Yes, sir, it makes me very happy!"

Laura gave David a hug. "How nice of you to do such a thing for us. Thank you!"

"Hey, I have to treat my new mom with care and dignity, as well as much love. You're a welcome addition to our family. You know, we all love you and the girls very much!"

"David said no one has any inkling of our marriage in Sterling, or it would've been all over town. Isn't that great? Now you will have a chance to talk to Eric, and can break the news to him yourself."

Looking at David, Sam asked, "Have you heard any more about Eric's plans to leave for Costa Rica?"

"No, no more than what we knew before you left for New York. George is still planning to go with him; as a matter of fact, he wanted to know if Danny and I would like to stay in his place while he was gone. He acted like he didn't think he would be away for too long."

"What did you say to his offer?" Sam was curious.

"I knew it would probably be okay with you if we stayed, since you'd be nearby and always did like to help out friends. I said, 'All right!'"

Sam nodded. "Good. That gives me an idea! But for now, let's get a bite to eat and settle in for the night. Laura and the girls are very tired, I'm sure of that."

Later, as Laura tucked the girls in bed and said goodnight to David, it flashed through her mind: here the girls and I are starting anew in Alaska. She could not help but think of how she and Eric had married long ago, and started their lives here in this beautiful country. It could be harsh, and yet it became a part of you, without your knowing it. It was good to be back here in Alaska. Now she needed to face Eric and tell him she was starting a new part of her life too, with Sam and his family. Sam and the boys loved her and the girls, so everything would be all right. After all, Eric had left them.

She closed the door softly between their rooms and walked to the bed where Sam was waiting. She paused before taking off her robe. Sam asked her, "Are you okay? You seem hesitant about something. What is it?"

Laura started to cry. "Oh Sam, have we done the right thing?"

Sam pulled her side of the covers back for her. "Of course we have, and I couldn't love you and the girls more. David told me he too was happy we got married. You are just nervous about seeing Eric and telling him tomorrow. Why do you have doubt? Don't you love me? Come on now, get in bed and show me that you do."

As Sam held the covers for her, Laura could see his strong, naked body waiting for her. She put her robe on the chair, dropped the straps of her gown off her shoulders and let it slip to the floor. She stood in full view, in the dim light, then turned it out and slipped into bed. Sam put his arms around her and she slid up close to him, flesh to flesh, whispering softly to him, "Sam, this feels wonderful, and I want more from you than just holding me, but that's what's bothering me right now. While we were in New York, a long distance from Eric, and not having consummated my relationship with him for so long, my body yearned for intimacy. I never thought about it before, until you started to kiss me and hold me so close that I could feel the hardness of your body next to mine. You awakened something in me, something I hadn't felt for a long time, and I wanted you to quench the fire within me. Oh sure, I felt it with Eric, but I kept it under control, because I knew it couldn't be satisfied, with Eric's condition. Sure, we had ways, but they weren't like the real thing. Can you understand what I feel now? We're back here where we're so close to Eric, and I wonder: should we have married on that basis? Is it possible to love two men at the same time? I am so confused!"

He pulled her closer to him, and as he did, her feelings of want and desire welled up and she wanted him desperately. She couldn't get close enough to him. "Oh, Sam, I do love you, and I want you to love me so badly! Am I crazy?"

Sam kissed her deeply. "Believe me when I say I love you more than life itself, and I know it was the right thing for us to do. I love you enough for both of us, and I'm willing to have the love you give me now. Maybe in time, it will be as pure and deep as mine is for you. Now put all those doubts out of your head, and let me have you, here and now. Let me quench that fire deep within you."

He kissed her gently then again with deeper kisses, prompting her to respond with a deep passion. She pulled in closer to him, begging him to love her more deeply. The night was not long enough for them.

The next morning, Laura woke at the crack of dawn, before Sam. She lay next to him, watching him sleep. He was breathing deeply in a slow and easy rhythm. With each breath, as she watched his chest rise and fall, she became more and more aroused. She knew now that she was *in love* with him, and started to caress him. She pressed her body to his until he awoke and made love to her again. When it was over, they lay breathless in each other's arms, and she whispered softly, "I do love you. All doubt has gone from my mind."

As they reposed, still entwined, Sam started to fondle her body, her hair, kissing where he caressed, until she responded to him, causing their passion to explode. Finally, she pulled away. "My darling, we must get up, even though I don't want too. We must shower and get dressed... then I'll wake the children, and we'll head for home."

Laura got out of bed to use the shower first. Sam watched her catlike moves as she crossed to the bathroom. He heard her open and close the shower door, and as she was soaping up, he followed, stepping into the shower with her... thrusting her up against the shower wall... kissing her passionately... caressing then entering her body. She wrapped her legs tightly around him, and they made love again. Laura's hot breath sank deeply into his ear, as her fingers gouged his skin as she pulled him tighter into her. "Oh yes! Oh yes... this is good... I did right by marrying you, Sam... I'm in love, deeply in love with you, and I love the way you make love to me. This is so right! We may never forget our first loves, but we can be in love again and it's wonderful! Don't stop now! I want more... much more!"

Later, when Laura finally left Sam in the shower, she did her hair and dressed. Then when he finished showering and dressing, she woke the girls and David so they could all go to breakfast and get on the road to Sterling.

Chapter 43

By the time everyone was packed up, had breakfast, checked out, and loaded in the truck to leave for Sterling, it was nine a.m. Sam headed the truck out onto the main highway toward home. The hum of the tires on the highway made Mary, Patty and David want to settle down in the back seat in the cab and nap, as they stayed up late the night before, talking. Turning around to check on them, Laura saw that they were all asleep. She reached over and touched Sam's leg with her hand. He looked at her, placed his hand over hers and gave it a squeeze. "What, my love? What is on your mind now?"

"I just wanted to say that I am *in love* with you, Sam Clark. I believe these past few days have made me the happiest woman alive. I have no doubts about my love for you, especially after last night and this morning. I want you even now. I want to touch you like you've never been touched before. You have turned me into a woman possessed. I have no qualms about telling Eric we got married in New York. I'm so glad you asked me to marry you the second time, after I refused the first. I guess I just needed time to think over everything that transpired over this past year. And talking with my parents helped, too."

Sam squeezed her hand again. "You're not the only one possessed. If the kids weren't with us, I'd put you in the back seat right now. But they are, and if we want to get home today, I'd better cool down. You know, I asked David if there was any talk of us going to New York together, around Sterling. He said he hadn't heard anything, if there was. So I don't see how Eric could possibly know until we tell him. I'll be with you when you do. I also asked David if he knew when Eric and George were leaving for Costa Rica. It seems like he said, the end of September or around the first of October."

"Yes, I believe that he did say early October, the first week or so, because he wanted to spend some time with the girls before they left."

"Good!" said Sam, "I have an idea. George asked David and Danny to watch his cabin for him while he was gone. He said he wanted someone to live there, so no one would bother it. So why don't you move into my house? After all, it is the Clark residence. Eric and George could stay in your place, and the girls can be there with them until they are ready to go. That would give us time to fix up rooms for them at my house."

"Good idea! I know the girls would like that. Also, it'll be easier to have the girls at my house, than for them to be with Eric and George, at George's place. We have food for them there, and George won't have to worry about anything when they do leave." Laura paused and rubbed Sam's leg in a sensual manner. "And besides, it will give us some time alone, too. I love being alone with you! Now, if you don't mind, I'm going to catch a nap; you wore me out last night and this morning."

"Be my guest, love. You wore me out a little too, but if you sleep, I can keep my mind on driving. We should be in Sterling around noon. We'll drop David off at my place, and tell Danny of our marriage. Then I'll take you and the girls to your house, and you can talk with Eric. I'll stay while you tell him of our marriage; then, if you want, I'll leave so you and Eric can have time to speak of other things. I can take George over to talk with the boys about staying at his cabin while he and Eric are gone. Okay?"

"That would be great, Sam. I'm sure Eric and I will have a lot to discuss. Now, I'm going to close my eyes." She sighed deeply as she propped a pillow against the door and settled down to nap.

The rest of the drive was quiet and uneventful, as everyone was sleeping. Sam said a prayer to God, thanking him for his marriage to Laura, and he prayed she would not have any problem telling Eric of it. Soon he began to see familiar sights that told him they were getting very close to Sterling. He called out to awaken his passengers. Mary and Patty became excited, as they knew they would soon see their daddy. Sam explained that he would drop David by their house first, and then they would go on to Laura's house.

When they arrived at Sam's to let David off, Sam grabbed David's suitcase and also his and Laura's. He left the girls' bags in the truck. They all went in, and Laura used the phone to call Eric, to make sure he and George were home and not somewhere else. "Hello, Eric? This is Laura. We're just here at Sam's to drop David off. He drove to Anchorage to pick us up, so I wanted to call and make sure you were there and not over to George's. The girls are very anxious to see you. We'll be there shortly. They have missed you so very much, and you and I need to talk about your trip, and more. See you in a little bit. Bye."

The second Sam pulled up in front of the cabin the girls were out of the truck, and into the house like a shot. Sam and Laura followed, and when they entered the house, the girls were hugging and kissing their daddy and jabbering away about Grandma, Grandpa, the farm, the cows, and the kittens. Their whole trip came rolling out of them.

Eric looked up and spoke to Laura and Sam as they came in. "I'm glad you took the girls to your parents; it sounds like they had a wonderful time. Sam, I'm also glad you went with Laura and the girls. It's a long trip, and for Laura to go it alone would have been stressful for her. She has had enough of that here lately. She didn't need any more. How are you anyway?"

Sam stepped over and shook his hand and patted him on the shoulder. "Fine. I couldn't be better. It was a pleasure to escort them to New York. I met Laura's parents and they're real fine folks. She comes from good stock."

Laura gave Eric a hug, and as she did, whispered in his ear, "When the girls finally wind down enough from telling you about our trip, we need to talk about some things too."

"Sure, George is outside somewhere and he'll be in soon, and I'm sure they'll swamp him the way they usually do. He can keep them busy while we talk. Is everything good with your parents? It isn't bad news, is it?" he asked.

"No, not in the least; it is just something that I want you to know before anyone else around here does. I think you will be pleased."

She held Eric's hand as she spoke to the girls. "When George comes in, you both can tell him about your trip, so I can speak to your daddy. Will you do that for Mommy?"

Starting toward the stove, she asked, "Have you any coffee to make? Would you like some? I know Sam and I would, after that trip from Anchorage."

"You bet; go ahead and make some. You know where everything is, and I could use a cup, too." He hugged the girls tightly, one on each side of him.

It wasn't long before George came in, "Is that coffee I smell? Is that Laura brewing it? Yeah! At last, I'll get a good cup of coffee!" He barely had the words out of his mouth when the girls ran to greet him. "Hey, you

Aleuts, how was the trip to Grandma and Grandpa's?" He picked them up and swung them around. They loved it! He put them down and said hello to Laura and Sam. But he then had to turn back to Mary and Patty, as they wouldn't leave him alone. He had to hear about their trip.

Laura gave everyone coffee. "It's a nice day, Eric; let's go out on the porch."

All three of them went out on the deck to enjoy the mountain view. Laura sat next to Eric, sipped her coffee then set it down. She began to tell him that not only was the trip to New York good for the girls, but her too, to think things over and clear her mind.

Then taking his hand, she said, "Eric, I finally saw that when you dissolved our marriage, it was because you needed to be your own man, and make your life useful again, and not be a burden on the girls and me. I knew that you prayed about this decision for a long time, and that I was part of that decision too, because I urged you to use your knowledge and experience to do something besides vegetate in this wheel chair. But, at the same time, I smothered you with care and enabled you not to go forward to your independence. Dr. Goodwin warned us that we should've gotten a caregiver. We thought I could do it all, but instead, I became your caregiver, not your wife, and because of that, and the fact we couldn't be physically intimate, you pushed me towards Sam, and further from you. Even though we still loved each other very much, you told me I should think about a new life too. We said all we needed to say and do about the house, about turning it over to the girls with the stipulation that either of us could stay here, when it was necessary. That was clear and there wasn't any problem with that or about you wanting to be your own man again. Now my mind was clear and I could finally see why you did what you did."

She stood up, gazed at the magnificent mountains, and then turned back to Eric. "There, I've said it. I just wanted you to know, I do understand."

"I'm glad you do, and I believe you've really been thinking a lot on this."

"I have, so when we went to New York, things made sense to me. You always wanted Sam to look after us when you had to be away, so I thought nothing of it when he went with us to my folks. He has always cared and watched out for all of us. You even made him promise and insisted he do so. I just thought it was because we were all so close, all these many years, and had love and admiration for each other.

"I guess what I want to tell you now, is… Sam and I got married while we were in New York. He first asked me when you told me you were going to Costa Rica. At first I said 'no,' but I would be at the mercy of Alaska, with two small girls, and even though I told him I still had love for you, he said that he was willing to wait until I learned to love him as much as he loved the girls and me. He's very good to us, and I needed to have the kind of love he can give me." Reaching for a handkerchief, she wiped her eyes.

Eric put his head down and sat quietly for some time. "Sam, what took you so long? If I can't have her, there's no one else I would rather see her with than you. You're a good man! Congratulations."

He reached over and touched Laura. "And I wish you all the happiness in the world, Laura. If anyone deserves it, it is you. Of course, you know I'll always love you; I just couldn't take you with me again to some out of the way place. I guess you might say I was balancing on the edge of being egotistical, maybe even closer to egoism. It was an emotional time, and I never wished for bad things to happen, but such is my make-up, and for you to tag along made for a bumpy, exciting ride at times. But this time, when the challenge was going to take me to places so far away with unknown endings, and my physical condition the way it is, I knew we both had to think of the girls and their future, too. I did what I had to do, and I prayed on it for a long time."

When he finished, Laura hugged and kissed him, and Sam shook his hand. "We're all one family now," Sam said. "We'll be there for each other, always. Now do you mind if I get George to go over what he wants the boys to do to watch his cabin when you two leave? Laura, if you two want to talk some more, I'll take the girls with us and we'll be back later."

Sam tilted her head and kissed her, then said to Eric, "I think Laura would like to talk to you some more."

"You bet! That would be fine with me, if it's good with Laura." Eric glanced at her to get her reaction. "Do George and I need to go back to his place tonight?"

"That's what I want to talk to you about," Laura said, "as well as when you plan on leaving for Costa Rica, and some other things. Would you and George like to stay here until you leave? There is plenty of food here in the pantry and the freezer. Then you won't have to worry about food in the cabin when you leave. Besides, wouldn't you like the girls to be here with you so you can spend these last few days with them? I'll check on them every day, and we're only a phone call away. Sam and I will be at his house. Is that good with you?"

"Yes, Laura, I would like to spend some time with the girls. That's very thoughtful of you. Is it good with you, Sam, having them here?" Eric asked.

"Of course it is!" Sam replied, as he called out to the girls and George. "Hey girls, bring George, and we'll all go to my place so David and Danny will know what to do at George's house, while he and your daddy are gone to Costa Rica!"

George answered for all of them. "Sounds good to me. Is Laura staying here with Eric?"

"Yes, we'll be back later to pick them up, and well all go out for supper," Sam suggested.

George agreed. "That sounds terrific to me; Eric and I are getting tired of my cooking." He laughed wholeheartedly. "Come on, gang, let's head 'em up and move 'em out!"

After Sam, George and the girls left, Laura and Eric finished their coffee and Laura carried the cups back into the kitchen. "Do you want some more coffee, Eric?" she asked, as Eric followed her into the house.

"No, but I would like to tell you some things I couldn't tell you when I turned in the form for dissolution of our marriage. All I had on my mind was trying to get me back into the life stream again, and getting more money to help me. Since then, I've had a lot of time to do some serious soul searching. When I had the accident, and was in the hospital in Anchorage, I had a positive attitude. But when Dr. Goodman told me I would be paralyzed from my upper chest down, with limited use of my arms, I began a slow process of depression. It was like being in a whirlpool slowly dragging me under, deeper and deeper. When I came home, it only progressed. You, in the meantime, stayed positive, urging me on... always. But Laura, the sight of all my hunting and fishing gear that were once part of my mainstay of life, even more than you or the girls, I guess depressed me even more. How was I ever to do that again?"

"But Eric, you adjusted some of your equipment so you could go with the guys, and they helped you," Laura said.

"Oh, Laura, you had no idea how that even made it worse for me. I was always going out on my own. I remember seeing a picture you had of me—standing on a mountaintop with my rifle on my shoulder—how that tore me up. I realized then, that it was over for me. I was only thinking of me, me, and me! I fell deeper and deeper into depression. You didn't even know me anymore. I was cold and bitter; I kept pushing you aside in bed. At one time, with great effort, I was able to get my pistol out of the drawer, load it and put it to my head. I didn't have any plan then to use it, but I knew I could do it if things got too bad. It was some relief. But that was short-lived, because when you got home you hid the gun. When you did that, I thought I could always throw myself down the basement stairs, but then that wasn't a sure thing.

"As the years went by, we had a lot of tough times. I was coming out of my depression, but you were not so lucky. You were overworked, had little sleep and little financial resources. You lost all hope of ever having a normal life. You were always a giver, and it became hard for you to change roles and be the recipient of donations people were giving us. And Sam was always there to help us out. This made me angry at first. It made me feel inadequate, and you were in the middle, getting torn apart. I didn't want to share, so something had to give. And this verse from Romans kept coming to me.

And we all know that all things work together for good to those who love God, to those who are called according to his purpose. Romans 8:28.

"So when I went to rehab in Seattle, it was then I made my decision to answer God's call. He came in and cleansed our house. You paid dearly for my actions; you put up with all my shenanigans. The world put you on a pedestal for staying with me, but no one can live up to all those expectations; the only way is down. People wanted to believe in us as the couple that beat the odds. So I made my decision. That is what I couldn't tell you, as the reason I did what I did."

"Oh, Eric, why didn't you tell me all this before? I had thoughts that took me up and down a roller coaster; I was unaware of a lot of this. Did George know all this?" she asked.

"Yes, and he wanted me to tell you, but I had already set my plan into motion. You know me well enough to realize that I set goals for myself that are obtainable, but complete rehabilitation was unobtainable. That's where my second life started. I chose life with Christ, not death."

Laura looked him straight in the eye. "Can you ever forgive me?"

"Why Laura? There is nothing for you to forgive me for, or me to forgive you at all. We both were confused, and God forgave us both. He has put us both on a way to starting life anew. We all must go forward now. We must stay friends, as we always have, and pray for success in each of our new beginnings. I'm sure we can still be as close as we have been in the past. Hey! I hear our crew coming back! Are you hungry? I know I am. Let's get ready to go eat, okay?"

Laura gave him a big hug and a long kiss. "Ready if you are! You do know I will always have love for you in my heart. You were my first love and the father of our children. Nothing will change that. But I love Sam too, and I am his wife now, and that will never change. It is God's will for us all to love one another."

Everyone came rushing into the house and expressed their readiness to go out to eat. Laura explained that she and Eric were ready, and had discussed everything they had to talk over. She told the girls that it was all right for them to stay with George and their daddy until they were ready to leave for Costa Rica.

This excited the girls very much. Mary ran to her father's side. "We're so glad to stay here with you, Daddy. There is much to tell you about New York and Grandma and Grandpa's place. Besides, we also want to hear what you and George will be doing on your trip."

Patty asked Laura, "Will you leave us our stuff from Grandma's too?"

"Yes," said Laura," But I'll check in on all of you, from time to time. Now, let's all go eat. Your dad and I are hungry!"

Chapter 44

The month of September seemed to fly by. Everyone was busy with things that needed to be attended to and they all helped each other in the completion of them. George and Eric were busy with last minute arrangements for their trip; Laura was busy getting the girls ready to return to school and fixing up their rooms at Sam's place for them to move into, and Sam and the boys were busy moving David and Danny over to George's house. The day that Eric and George were to leave for Costa Rica was fast approaching. Sam and David planned on taking them to Anchorage to catch their plane. Mary, Patty and Laura were to say their good-byes at home. Eric had gone over his plans with the girls, and what it would be like in Costa Rica, so they knew what he was going to be doing and how he planned on getting it done. They were content with that fact and said they would not worry about him, that they would always love him, and he would always be in their thoughts.

Finally the day came and they drove off to Anchorage to catch their plane. While driving, Sam asked Eric, "Are you absolutely sure this is what you want to do? Do you know what you are going to be up against? Can you and George handle living in a foreign country when you don't even speak the language? You know, it is not too late to change your mind."

Eric replied, "We've studied Spanish, and we feel with that under our belt, we can get along with the language. I've spoken with our minister in Sterling, and he has given me some names of people to look up, and maybe they can help me get established in the area. We'll be flying into San Jose. Nearly all Costa Ricans speak Spanish. There are many blacks that still speak a Jamaican dialect that's a local form of English. Ninety percent of the people belong to the Roman Catholic Church. San Jose is the capital and the largest city in Costa Rica."

Sam continued with questions. "So most of the people are Spanish and black?"

"No," said Eric, "many Spanish colonists who settled in Costa Rica in 1500 and 1600 have married native Indians. Their descendants are called Mestizos. Mestizos and whites of unmixed ancestry make up 97% of the population. There are about 70,000 blacks and 10,000 Indians. The blacks live on the Caribbean coast. They came to Costa Rica from Jamaica in the 1800s to work on banana plantations and build railroads. The Indians keep their tribes' traditional ways of life, and live in the highlands, and along the Caribbean and Pacific shores."

Sam was in awe at how informed Eric was. "You have really studied up on this move, haven't you?"

"Of course, I wanted to know all I could find out about what I had to face. It was the smart thing to do."

"But Eric, what about food and housing, have you thought about that?"

"Well, from what George and I have read, the farmers either live in brightly painted wooden houses or adobe cottages with thick white stucco walls and red or pink tiled roofs. The city people live in row houses.

They are alike and attached together in a row. They decorate their houses with plants and flowers. The wealthy have ranch style, or Spanish style homes surrounded by gardens. As far as food, I understand their diet includes beans, coffee, corn, eggs, rice, squash and tropical fruits, such as bananas, oranges, pineapples, guava, etc. They also eat beef, fish, poultry, and many kinds of soup. They often prepare tamales and tortillas."

Sam cleared his throat. "I'm sorry to be so inquisitive, but I know Laura was very concerned about you going so far away to an unknown country, especially in a wheelchair! So I want to be able to tell her just how much you do know about where you're going. You know how she is. She worries about everything."

"I know," said Eric, "I think we both know her pretty well. Tell her this: most of Costa Rica's people can read and write. Their law requires all children to complete elementary school. Then they can attend a secondary school, and then enter a University. There are several right in San Jose. I thought I might be able to tutor students in English.

"The people enjoy spending their leisure time outdoors. Many sports and festivals go on there. Tell her not to worry. The average temperature there is 75 to 80 degrees the year 'round. We'll be fine."

"I know you will," said Sam, "but she'll worry. She wanted to know how you would get around. What about transportation?"

"Tell her railroads connect port cities to San Jose. There is an average of one car to every twenty-seven people. Most families own a radio, and there is about one TV set for every six people. There are airlines to other cities, Mexico, and the U. S. What more do we need?" Eric wanted to reassure her. "We'll be okay, won't we, George?"

George spoke right up, "You bet! If we don't get along, we can always come back. Tell her, Sam, that I won't let anything happen to him. She knows she can trust me."

The rest of the trip was pretty routine conversation, and soon they were at the airport and boarding. Sam and David watched as the plane taxied down the runway and lifted into the air. Sam turned and said to David, "Let's go home, son. They are on their own now, and in God's hands."

George got Eric settled on the plane; the stewardess took the wheelchair and stowed it. They both settled back in their seats and waited for the other passengers to load. While they were waiting, George said to Eric, "Tell me something, I was listening to that entire question and answer period you and Sam had going on the drive to the airport. What was with some of your answers? We haven't learned to speak fluent Spanish, but you told him we did. I just sat and listened to it all, and only answered what I thought you wanted me to say, when I was asked something."

"I know, George, but we do know some Spanish; very little, I must say, but do you think I wanted Sam to go tell Laura that? I want them to have a normal life together, not constantly having Laura worry about us," Eric answered softly. "You know how she is; you probably know her as well as me. Laura and I had a heart-to-heart talk before we left, and she thinks I am going to do mission work for the Lord."

George replied with a question in his voice. "Isn't that the general idea of going in the first place?"

"Yes, George, but right now I have no interest in mission work. I only want to get away from the hurt. I didn't think Sam and Laura would get married so soon." Eric paused, reached for his handkerchief and blew his nose. There was a long pause as he looked at George, and then he spoke again. "You know the time I spent in the VA hospital was most likely the final straw in Laura's and my relationship, but it also gave me confidence again that I could still make it without her. I was just so co-dependent before that. The horror to be alone—almost nineteen years we were together—and ending up in a VA old folks home. You know, between Laura's and my problems, we left God out of the equation. Oh, there was a lot of praying going on, but it was about me, me, and me. Laura told me she had to wait and hope for such a change in my life for a long time. Well, now it has happened. I am a different person. She basically told me she didn't know me anymore. It was easier for her to continue life with Sam. You know the old saying, and I quote, "Those we love the most, can hurt us the most." I thank the Lord for the miracle that I don't have any bad feelings anymore. After all, I pushed them together constantly.

"I want to go to Costa Rica only as another adventure to get my feet on solid ground again. I have a big feeling, that I will like it, and it will be new and refreshing. Now, let's get some rest, I'm tired."

"Sure thing, Buddy," said George. "You rest, I'm going to listen to and study this Spanish language tape. We'll make it just fine. Dont worry; I've already booked us into a hotel in San Jose for a week, maybe more, until we can find cheaper lodging. At least we have a place to go when we land in San Josc."

When they landed and got everything settled into their hotel, they grabbed a bite to eat and both went directly to bed. George went right to sleep. Eric lay awake, going over what he and Laura had said to each other when they were alone at the home they had built together. He was wondering what Laura was feeling that night, as she retired. He felt that she too, was wondering if he and George were all right. Their lives together had been quite an adventurous and an emotional trip up to that point, and now, they were both starting a new life on their own.

Epilogue

For Eric and George, the next three months passed very quickly, Eric managed to get a few tutoring jobs, while George spent most of his time scouting for interesting people and things to see. They spent a lot of time traveling to the beaches.

They met a very engaging family, huddled under the hotel porch, trying to stay out of a sudden afternoon rain. The father's name was Mario Vasquez, who lived in Liberia, about a five-hour drive from San Jose. Mario showed them around San Jose and arranged to meet with them the next day with ideas of getting George for a son-in-law. The girl was only sixteen, which made George want to return to Alaska for apparent reasons.

When Eric had to report to Seattle Rehab Center the first of January, George went on to Sterling to re-establish himself in Alaska. He picked Eric up in Anchorage and Eric stayed with him until March of 1993.

Being able to see his girls only periodically because of school, seeing Laura and Sam so happy, and not being able to stand the cold made his desire to escape again strong. This time he decided to return to Costa Rica alone; hoping the folks he had met there would help him. On the flight down he felt he was alone but remembered his parents telling him he had Guardian Angels around him—for sure, the Holy Spirit. He was sad for leaving his daughters again. Everyone had concerns about his going by himself. He promised he would be fine; he had God's work to do.

Mario met him at the airport, so far so good, His Angels were with him. After a terrifying ride of five hours on a mountainous road, they arrived at Mario's home.

Mario found him a place to stay with a widow, her seven children, and her mother and father. Eric's Spanish was so limited it was hard to direct his care. The weather was near 100 degrees every day, and Eric contracted a severe kidney infection because they washed his catheter in the same water they used to wash their hands. Mario always came to check on him, but it was 3 or 4 days before he showed and Eric had a temperature of over 100 degrees. He was in bad shape and praying a lot. Once more his Guardian Angels came through.

Mario found Eric another place to stay in a small city called Philadelphia where there were twenty people living under one roof. Although conditions were unsavory, Eric stayed almost a year. He gave his testimony in his poor Spanish and brought in Bibles for the people, but he didn't engage in any real ministry. Eric finally rented a house in front of his church, where it was more convenient for him. He had many visitors; one man named Recco helped him build an antenna just before he traveled back for his yearly check-up and to go on to Alaska. Eric put his money under the cushion of his wheel chair, but when he awoke in the morning both Recco and the money was gone. Eric prayed about the missing money and Recco returned, saying he had gone to the mountains when a great hand come down on him and brought him back. He had only spent $7.00 of the money. Recco was an alcoholic as well as a drug addict. Once again, Eric's Guardian Angels were with him.

Another visitor was Bayardo, a Nicaraguan working in Philadelphia. He invited Eric to come and visit him in Posoltega, in western Nicaragua near Manuagua. He told him maybe when he returned from Alaska and Seattle.

When Eric returned, his caregiver was gone. The pastor from the church put Eric to bed at night and would get him up in the morning. Eric thought about visiting Bayardo, but didn't know where to go or how to get there. He and his pastor prayed together about it. A strange thing happened during their prayer, in walked Bayardo. Again, God sent his Guardian Angels. This led Eric to believe he was truly meant to start on this new venture in his life.

Because he just returned from Alaska and had no care-giver, he asked Bayardo to work for him, but he needed to continue his work here for at least another year. Bayardo agreed as he needed money to send to his sister in Nicaragua, who was supporting their mother on their farm.

Bayardo was a big help in Eric's mission work, as well as being an excellent care-giver, and he in turn dedicated his life to God. They were a good team. Two churches in Alaska helped by sending Bibles to give out and Eric even found a source for Bibles in Spanish.

Eric and Bayardo prayed about moving to Nicaragua, living expenses were much less there and the need of the people there was much greater than in Costa Rica. Once again, with God's guidance they moved to Nicaragua in 1996.

Many times Eric thanked God for his knowledge to use the Ham radio as a tool to reach the people in his work. He also used it to communicate with his daughters once a month. He linked to a telephone patch via computer. Many areas couldn't be reached by truck or auto.

Transportation in general was mules and ox carts. There was one vehicle for every 100 people. Mail delivery was very unreliable.

Eric married Bayardo's sister, he was worried she would be alone with no one to watch over her if something should happen to her brother or himself. Bayardo relinquished his job as caregiver to Ma'rietta, and he worked elsewhere, but still helped Eric with the mission work.

Eric believed God was at work, through him. A group called BFO— Blessing for Obedience—helped them. Also, a man from Texas, a Missionary from Calgary Chapel, helped Eric with the radio tower and station. God does move in strange ways.

Every year Eric returns to Seattle for his check-ups and on to Alaska to see his daughters, who are now married and each have two children. He sometimes runs into Laura and Sam when they are visiting Sam's family. They are still close friends and enjoy visiting Alaska, in the summer. Laura and Sam are doing well.

They've had a roller coaster life for sure, but by keeping the faith, they have all come through it to the present. Their lives are not over yet, and God has been good to them all.

They send you this message: "Through faith and fortitude, all things are possible." We all remain: Yours in Christ and may "God be with you until we all meet again."

CPSIA information can be obtained at www.ICGtesting.com
Printed in the USA
LVOW010031281011

252316LV00004B/4/P